**Pippa Roscoe** lives in Norfolk, near her family, and makes daily promises to herself that this is the day she'll leave the computer to take a long walk in the countryside. She can't remember a time when she wasn't dreaming about handsome heroes and innocent heroines. Totally her mother's fault, of course—she gave Pippa her first romance to read at the age of seven! She is inconceivably happy that she gets to share those daydreams with you. Follow her on Twitter @PippaRoscoe.

**Kim Lawrence** lives on a farm in Anglesey with her university lecturer husband, assorted pets who arrived as strays and never left, and sometimes one or both of her boomerang sons. When she's not writing she loves to be outdoors gardening, or walking on one of the beaches for which the island is famous—along with being the place where Prince William and Catherine made their first home!

# SNOWBOUND WITH HIS FORBIDDEN PRINCESS

## PIPPA ROSCOE

# INNOCENT IN THE SICILIAN'S PALAZZO

## KIM LAWRENCE

MILLS & BOON

First Published in Great Britain 2022
by Mills & Boon, an imprint of HarperCollins*Publishers* Ltd,
1 London Bridge Street, London, SE1 9GF

www.harpercollins.co.uk

HarperCollins*Publishers*
1st Floor, Watermarque Building,
Ringsend Road, Dublin 4, Ireland

Snowbound with His Forbidden Princess © 2022 Pippa Roscoe

Innocent in the Sicilian's Palazzo © 2022 Kim Lawrence

ISBN: 978-0-263-30076-5

03/22

MIX
Paper from
responsible sources
FSC® C007454

This book is produced from independently certified FSC™ paper
to ensure responsible forest management.
For more information visit www.harpercollins.co.uk/green.

Printed and Bound in Spain using 100% Renewable Electricity
at CPI Black Print, Barcelona

# SNOWBOUND WITH HIS FORBIDDEN PRINCESS

## PIPPA ROSCOE

**MILLS & BOON**

For my editor, Hannah, who lets me get away with
more than I probably should be allowed to,
and who always makes my books better.
My thanks are unending. (As is my penchant
for a trilogy!) xx

# CHAPTER ONE

'YOUR HIGHNESS? HIS MAJESTY will be with you in a few minutes.'

Princess Freya of Svardia nodded, resisting the urge to press her palm against the erratic pulse of her heart. She reminded herself that it was her brother who would take this meeting, not her father, who had—as Svardian tradition held—stepped down from the throne at the age of sixty-five, as his father had done and his father before him. The tradition ensured that whoever graced the throne was mentally and physically strong, whilst also reflective of the broadest generations of Svardia's subjects.

The reigning King—her brother Aleksander—would mark his first year while their father and mother left on a twelve-month sabbatical, away from the country and out of contact to ensure no risk of interference or influence while both the new King and the Svardian people got used to each other.

Three months ago, Aleksander had ascended the throne. And now, hands clasped firmly behind her back, she stood outside his office and prepared to go to battle with her King.

A bird soared past the window, catching Freya's eye and taking it over the spring green garden that extended all the way to the walls separating the palace from Svardia's capital city of Torfarn. It was a view she'd seen a million times but never given real thought to. Now, though, it had become uniquely precious to her.

The simple beauty of the ancient trees, the subtle delicacy of the hornbeam hedges used in the sixteenth-century maze, the neatly manicured lawns and the sprawling natural park just beyond, each was a piece of evidence left by the successive generations of one of the world's oldest royal families. Her heart pounded a single dull thud as she wondered what Aleksander, her brother, would leave behind for his future generations.

Perhaps after she stepped down from her royal title, she could get a job showing tourists around the palace. The laugh that should have followed the ironic thought got caught in her chest and she closed her eyes.

She loved doing what she did. Being who she was. The sense of history, the grandeur, the respect for tradition and the symbolism of it all. And most of all she loved having the ability to use her position and title to support the causes and people that needed it, ones that sometimes the people of Svardia and their politicians forgot. But she also knew that the responsibility of being royal was a duty that few could understand. And even now she felt a sharp sting at the cruel irony that meant she could only do her duty by *not* doing her duty.

The door behind her opened and two palace staff passed into the corridor, their conversation quietening and their heads bowing as they saw her. She waited, facing the door, able to see glimpses of the room her brother had taken as his office. It didn't matter how much modern technology Aleksander filled it with, his office—just like every other room in the palace—was inescapably *grand*. The preservation of the baroque style that filled the Rilderdal Palace had been a matter of pride for her father and a source of embarrassment for her brother.

'Freya? Get in here, I don't have much time.'

'You know,' she said, stepping into the room and closing the door behind her, 'you really should get a secretary. You can't just go about shouting at people from your office.'

'Didn't you hear? I'm King. I can do what I like.' Freya honestly couldn't tell whether the statement was pure arrogance or a dark notion from his new role, now that their parents were on their sabbatical. Not that it mattered. His statement hadn't required an answer.

Once, it might have been different. When they had been younger, *he'd* been different. But around his seventeenth birthday Aleksander had changed. The soft warmth that she'd shared with him gone in the blink of an eye with no explanation whatsoever. And in its place? A controlled and forbidding man who was closed even to her. Now she could rarely tell what he was thinking, let alone planning. In that moment, Freya wondered at the price they had both paid for the throne.

'Are you sure that this is what you want?' he asked as his gaze assessed her face for a reaction. She stared blankly into irises that were so dark they were almost black. Hers were the opposite—the palest amber—and their younger sister Marit's a perfect meld of the two, a startling hazel.

Freya could have laughed at his attempt to catch her out, so she might reveal that it was the last thing she wanted on this earth. But she'd been trained well—such a perfect princess that even in this she was the better diplomat than he.

'Yes. My mind is made up.'

Aleksander grunted an unintelligible reply and turned

to look out of the window, framed by the much-detested pink curtain. 'What do you think Father would say?' he asked, his tone surprisingly solicitous.

Her stomach turned. She knew what their father would say. That she was doing the right thing—the only thing that could be done. But saying that would make her brother more likely to dig his heels in, so instead she stalled. 'We won't know for another eight months until their return.'

'You could contact them. If you wish?'

Freya wondered why he believed that would make any difference at all. Their parents wouldn't thank her, instead seeing it as a concern only for the King of Svardia to handle. And if she expected emotional support, well... Freya, Aleksander and Marit each knew better than that.

'I don't think that he'd appreciate the break with protocol.'

'Even for this?' he pressed.

'This is *my* problem. I've always known how important the line of succession is.'

'If you give me time—'

'Aleksander,' she interrupted. 'If anything were to happen to you before you have children, or to your family in the future, the line of succession falls to me and...' She clenched her jaw, still struggling to vocalise it.

'Ifs,' Sander replied.

'Ifs that happened to our father!' Freya frantically tried to call back the emotion in her voice. Having had to take the throne after the shocking loss of his older brother, her father had always made sure she knew how important she was as the second child. And she had borne the weight and responsibility of that duty, and would have continued to do so until her dying breath.

Even after discovering that she could not fulfil the full extent of that duty.

'Marit is going to struggle.'

'Yes,' Freya agreed. 'But I will help her in any way I can.'

Her brother snorted out a frustrated breath. 'Of course you would help your replacement, no matter how much it costs you.'

'It is my duty. And she's our sister,' she replied simply.

'She's going to have to marry. And soon. And Freya—the same rules will now apply to her. She will have to marry a noble, just as you would have had to.'

Freya could only nod. She hated that Marit had been dragged into this. Hated not only the archaic legislation that determined the man she would marry, but also hated just how much her younger sister would struggle with the constraints of her new duties. Freya had been born knowing her duty, knowing the restrictions it placed on her life. But Marit had always been the wild one, and she and Aleksander had indulged her, enjoying her freedom even if they couldn't have it for themselves.

'I'm sorry,' she said, the words thick and heavy on her tongue.

'It's not your fault. And I'm still not convinced it's necessary.'

'Really? It's three months since your coronation. If the press find out about me when you are still unmarried and without—' Both her heart and mind stumbled over the word.

*Children.*

It whispered and screamed in the silence between her and Aleksander. Behind her back, she clenched her fists, warding off the visceral ache that swirled in spaces that would never be filled.

'Freya—'

She put up a hand to stop him. 'If the press find out, Aleksander, it would be carnage.' She could see it so clearly. The press would rip apart any dignity or privacy that she had. Across the globe, doctors, celebrities and everyday Svardians would be asked for their opinions on the failure of her body. 'But the backlash wouldn't just be on me, Aleksander. They would dig into your life, Marit's... And you are already under such incredible scrutiny—'

'Freya...' he warned.

'Aleksander, I believe in you. I believe in what you are trying to achieve for Svardia. But there are already whispers that you are too progressive, and too fast with your changes.'

'And that is my duty to bear, not yours.'

'And mine is to make sure that nothing disrupts what you are hoping to accomplish.'

'They will tear you apart, Freya.'

'Yes, they will,' she replied, not naïve about the backlash that would ensue. 'But not because of my failure as a woman. We will tell them that I have chosen to step down in order to spend time working on myself. We all know how much the press love to hate a self-involved royal. It should keep them busy for quite some time.'

And, that way, it would at least appear as if it were her choice. That way, she might be able to fool herself that she had managed to preserve her agency by controlling the narrative. That way, she might protect her dignity. Her *identity*.

Because to have her femininity questioned, her womanhood... Her heart shook, cowering from the threat of such a blow. She would lose *herself*. So, no. She couldn't face that. Better to let them think her selfish and uncar-

ing of the institution into which she had been born and
loved with her every breath.

'If I had children—'

'But you don't,' she said simply.

'But I *will*,' he bit out through clenched teeth, as if
it were something that would cost him greatly. But her
curiosity over it wasn't enough to distract her from the
argument they'd been having for the last month.

'Yes, but in how long? Two or three years' time? No
palace can keep a secret for that long. The news of my
infertility will get out in the next three months, maybe?
Six if we're lucky. If I step down, my fertility won't
even be a question and we have a much greater chance
of keeping it quiet for the length of time you need.' The
possibility that the media would never discover her infertility was only a distant hope for Freya.

'You have an answer for everything.'

'Because I have thought about it every which way.'
And Freya had. Her heart ached unbearably. She would
never have willingly stepped away from her family, from
her role. But if it meant securing the stability and future
of her family and country, then her decision was simple.

'Well, then I have one last duty for you to perform,
Your Highness,' he said, going to stand behind his desk,
no longer her brother but her King. 'I have a Medal of
Valour that needs to be delivered to its recipient.'

Freya frowned. 'I don't understand. Medals are received at the investitures.'

'The recipient refuses to attend the Investiture.'

The Medal of Valour was offered to military per-
sonnel who had demonstrated exceptional courage in
the face of extreme danger. But to refuse it from your
King—the Commander in Chief—was not only unheard
of but would reflect badly on Aleksander, especially at

his first Investiture. It would be seen as a vote of no confidence, no matter what reasons were behind the refusal, and that could be a devastating blow to Aleksander's rule.

'Why would they not want the medal?'

'That is for you to find out when you take it to him.'

*Him.* Her brother wasn't usually so coy with his words. She stared at him, just as able to play the royal waiting game as he.

Aleksander sighed. 'Kjell Bergqvist.'

Fire and ice swept in waves across her skin and her heart stuttered, forcing Freya to stifle the gasp of breath her lungs cried out for.

'No.' The word shot from her lips unbidden.

'This is not up for debate.' His voice was quiet but his eyes sparked gold and his tone was implacable. 'If you want to step down from your duties, your title and your family, then by God don't expect me to make it easy for you.'

'Sander—'

'The helicopter will be here in an hour. Be on it, or not.'

Her brother was no longer looking at her, peering down at a piece of paperwork in the same manner their father always had when he couldn't be bothered to utter a dismissal.

*No choice. No choice. No choice.*

'An hour?' she asked, hating the weakness in her voice.

'I believe there are weather constraints,' he replied, still not looking up.

Freya shot a glance to the window, frowning at clear blue skies.

The helicopter jerked suddenly, Freya's stomach lifting into her throat as she battled a swift wave of nausea, but no one in the small cabin would have known it. She had spent years perfecting serenity in the mirror and she wore it like a crown. The pilot righted the helicopter, apologising into the earpiece of her headphones, and she sent him a smile of reassurance.

Usually, she loved watching the ground roll out beneath her as the helicopter sped through the air, but all she could see was shifting shades of white as they crossed from Svardian airspace into Swedish.

'Who is this guy anyway?' she heard the young guardsman whisper to Gunnar, the head of her royal protection detail. Freya couldn't help it, she turned to find Gunnar's eyes locked onto her and she felt the burn of a blush rise to her cheeks. She turned back to the window and forced her gaze back to the shifting white shapes beyond.

'Lieutenant Colonel Bergqvist is a highly respected and valued member of the Svardia Armén,' Freya heard Gunnar explain behind her.

*Lieutenant Colonel?*

She tensed to prevent her body from betraying her reaction, trying to figure out how the tall, lean student she'd once known could have become such a powerful soldier. But then, she thought, turning back to the white static outside the small window, she hadn't actually known anything about him at all.

She gave into the hazy memory she hadn't revisited for eight years...

She'd been in a helicopter just like this one, shaking not from turbulence but from shock. What made it so awful was that it wasn't just a reaction to the terrifying news that her sister had been in an accident and was being treated urgently by Svardia's best doctors. No. It was the horror that had come from realising that her

boyfriend, the person who had made her laugh, made
her feel safe, wanted and desired, the man she had given
her kisses to, *herself* to, had been an undercover bodyguard, hired by her father.

*He sat opposite her in the helicopter that was returning
them from Switzerland to Svardia, staring at her as if she
were an unexploded bomb. She clenched her jaw as her
heart twisted, and turned away to look out of the window so that the three Close Protection Officers couldn't
see the tear that had rolled down her face.*

*Four. There were four CPOs with her in the heli-
copter.*

*Less than forty minutes earlier she and Kjell had been
in her dorm room, laughing. Freya couldn't remember
what about now. It had taken her months to make him
smile, and the first time he'd laughed she'd felt it deep
in her heart. They'd been laughing, but it had petered
out to a moment when happiness had settled and desire
had stirred and he'd been about to kiss her...just like he
had done a hundred or so times in the last few months.*

*She craved his kisses with a ferocity that over-
whelmed her.*

*His phone had rung and something had passed across
his eyes at the strange ringtone she'd not heard before.
Three seconds later her phone had rung too. It had been
her brother, telling her that Marit had been in an accident and they needed her to come home immediately.
Fear had slashed through her. Her heartbeat had raced
and concern had become a powerful white noise that
blocked out everything but the ringing in her ears.*

*Kjell had looked up and seen the horror on her face,
placed a hand on her arm to anchor her. And it had*

*worked. He'd calmed the storm and soothed her pulse enough to hear what Sander had said next.*

*'Marit's going to be okay, Freya. She is. But we need you here. We have a Close Protection Officer nearby who's going to come to you. We can argue about it later, but now he's going to bring you home. His name is Bergqvist. Kjell Bergqvist.'*

*Her stomach had roiled, filling her with nausea and horror.*

*She'd begged her father not to give her a protection detail. She'd wanted so much to prove to him that she could be trusted. That she would be a perfect dutiful princess during her time at the Swiss university. She'd meant every word of it.*

*Until she'd met Kjell.*

*Humiliation scoured her stomach. Not only had she proved herself to be anything but the perfect princess— she'd done it with the very man who had been sent to spy on her.*

*The man now sitting opposite her in the helicopter.*

*A tear rolled down her cheek. For the months of their secret relationship she'd fought it—the knowledge that it could never be. That neither her father nor the legislation that bound the royal family would allow her to marry a commoner. But in spite of that she'd wanted him. She'd taken a risk for him. She'd fallen for him because he'd made her feel loved for who she was, not what.*

*Freya battled the sob rising in her chest because the one thing that had become more precious to her than any other was based on a lie. And how could you love a lie?*

*She tensed her body to keep it from betraying the shivers that racked her heart. The betrayal she felt was like a bell being struck over and over again in the deepest part of her heart, vibrating outwards and causing her whole body to tremble.*

*'Freya.'*

*His voice made her clamp her eyes shut tighter.*

*'Bergqvist,' came the warning response from the senior CPO.*

*It was clear that while none of them knew anything specific, her reaction to the revelation of his identity had been extreme.*

*Humiliation painted her cheeks bright red. If they didn't know, they must suspect that something had happened between them.*

*'Freya,' he tried again.*

*When she ignored him, he ripped off the headset and released the belt holding him in place. He reached across the distance between them and took her face in his hands.*

*'Bergqvist!'*

*'We need to talk about this.'*

*'There's nothing to talk about,' she whispered harshly, trying to wrench herself from his hold.*

*Oh, God. It hurt so much.*

*'I wanted to tell you so many times.'*

*'Back in your seat, Bergqvist—that's an order!'*

*He stared at her, his eyes full of need and yearning, and all she saw was betrayal.*

*'It was real for me,' he said.*

*She tried to shake her head, but his warm hands held her firm.*

*'It was real for me,' he insisted.*

*She stared him deep in the eyes, the pain in her heart like nothing she'd ever felt before. She thought she heard it break.*

*'I never want to see you again.'*

*In shock, he released her, and she turned to look out of the window.*

*For the entire flight back to Svardia she didn't once take her gaze from the small plastic circle.*

*She waited for all the men to file out of the cabin before she moved, and when she did she kept her gaze on the floor until she could look ahead without even catching so much as a glimpse of him.*

*She cut him from her life and her heart that day, swearing never to think of him again.*

'Your Highness? We're coming in to land,' she was warned through the earpiece in the headphones, jolting her back from a memory that left a fresh bruise on her heart.

The pilot put them down much closer to the edge of the forest than Freya had thought possible. Yet it was still a good distance from the two dwellings she could barely make out, buried beneath what looked, worryingly, like several feet of snow.

She waited while green jump-suited men flipped buttons and muttered into their headsets, controlling her breathing by timing her pulse to the slowing blades above her.

'Okay, Your Highness. We're ready.'

She nodded to Gunnar and reached up to the handle just above the open door. The young member of the royal guard, eyes bright and cheeks flushed with excitement, held his hand out to her from the ground. This was probably his first assignment. Had she been Kjell's first assignment too?

'Your Highness?'

She turned back to look at Gunnar.

'We don't have much time. Conditions have worsened

unexpectedly. There's a storm coming in from the East and it's set to be a bad one.'

Freya didn't waste any more time. There was absolutely no way that she would risk getting stuck out here. None. She had one goal. Get in, have Kjell accept the medal and leave. He owed her that much at least.

She landed a little ungracefully, despite the support from the guard, the blanket of snow about three inches deeper than she had imagined. The action jarred, sending a hard jolt up through her body. She shook her head a little, righting herself and her sense of self at the same time.

This was what she wanted, she told herself firmly. This was what was needed.

Freya looked up at the large cabin closest to them, the red painted wooden boards barely visible through flakes of snow that were now falling thick and fast. But something drew her gaze to the cabin set further back, nearer the woods, and a sense of déjà vu struck her, even though she'd never set foot in this part of southern Sweden before.

She shivered as a snowflake snuck past the upturned collar of her coat and slid down her spine. The icy tendril clashed with the fast burn of ire, flaring to life at the mere thought of what could have been and what would never be, the past with Kjell and the future with children she'd never have all swirling out of her reach and making her heart ache.

Her head snapped up as she felt his eyes on her, burning her skin. She searched back and forth across the front of the properties and only on her second pass did she see him leaning lazily against the corner of the furthest building, watching them approach as if he had all the time in the world.

Pinpricks broke out across the back of her neck and

a shocking longing hit her hard and fast. It stuck in her throat and filled her lungs. Until the memory of his betrayal cut through the haze of need like a shard of ice.

Clearing her mind, Freya knew without a doubt that the only reason she had spotted him was because he'd allowed it. And now that she *had* seen him she refused to look away, half afraid that if she blinked he would disappear and all of this would have been for nothing. Her only chance at freedom gone, just like that.

The snow made it much harder to close the distance and consequently gave her more time to take him in. How was he standing there in the middle of a blizzard with a minus windchill factor in nothing but a dark long-sleeved top that clung to his torso like a second skin? The matching trousers looked military grade and even had she not overheard his army rank she still would have thought *dangerous*. He was twisting something in gloveless hands—a rag or piece of cloth? Her fingers stung at just the thought of how cold his hands must be.

Finer details began to emerge as she drew closer. His hair, still the colour of spun gold, had grown a little long at the top, was swept back by the wind but the close crop at the sides highlighted the fierce slash of his cheekbones. The dark material of his T-shirt pulled tightly over a chest that was bigger and broader and so much more defined than she remembered it made her palms itch. The narrow circumference of his hips was marked by a thick black canvas belt that looked utilitarian rather than affectation. And his height... She could have hurt herself looking up at the forbidding expression on his features.

Maybe it was the snow, maybe it was the isolated cabins, but she'd expected a beard. Full, thick, something a

Norse god could be proud of. But his jaw was clean, all hard angles and smooth skin, and still she wanted to—

Freya jerked her eyes up to his and bit her lip. The storm in his gaze was far worse than anything the elements could throw at her. He narrowed his eyes as if sensing her wayward thoughts, before he refocused on something behind her.

'Take her home, Gunnar,' he growled, his voice somehow carrying through the raging snowstorm, and without even a second glance at her he disappeared through the door with a slam that dislodged an unhealthy amount of snow from the sloped roof.

Panic shot through her. It had taken two months for Sander to even consider agreeing to her request to step down from her royal position. If Kjell didn't accept the medal, would her brother force her to endure the world's press poring over her failure as a royal? As a woman?

The thought of it gave her the fuel she needed. She clenched her jaw, turning back to the head of her security, sending her arm out to stop him. 'Don't even think about it,' she warned, barely seeing him raise his hands in surrender before she marched towards the cabin and the closed door.

'Fifteen minutes, Your Highness. Twenty at most,' she heard Gunnar call to her as she reached the cabin.

# CHAPTER TWO

*WHAT WAS SHE doing here?*

Kjell stood in the boot room, his hands on his hips and his eyes on the middle distance. It was only when his teeth started to hurt that he realised he'd been clenching his jaw. He tilted his head to one side; the wind was picking up even more speed outside and when it hit, the storm was going to hit hard, but it was the crunch of snow he was listening for.

He'd heard the helo above the *thunk* of his axe cleaving through the last pieces of firewood he was stockpiling ahead of the storm. The sweat he'd worked up instantly cooling on his skin, making the hairs stand up on the back of his neck.

He'd watched as the pilot navigated a decent proximity to the forest with the resigned determination of a military man who knew something grim was coming. But he hadn't expected *her*.

For a moment, his mind had blanked with a shock he didn't think he'd felt since he last saw her. His response to her twisting and morphing back to the present through layers of anger, shame, guilt and heat. Always heat.

He clenched his jaw. He couldn't afford to think like that. Her Royal Highness Princess Freya of Svardia was outside his cabin and, no matter what had happened, he was a Lieutenant Colonel in the Svardia Armén. She was his superior, as a citizen and as a serving member of the armed forces.

She always had been.

Kjell figured he had about twenty seconds before she reached the door, with a possible three-second margin given the worsening conditions. He knew that his order to Gunnar would have frustrated a royal who'd experienced years of people bowing and scraping. But even as that thought registered, he knew it was wrong. Freya had never been like that. At least she hadn't been eight years ago.

A thread of shame unspooled in his gut. Yes, he'd made a mistake back then. But she hadn't been fault-less—and the memory of that sparked anger and resentment through muscles already corded with tension. A tension that, in the last few months, had been far too close to the surface. Now it rose and rose, too much and too quickly.

A slice of light exploded like a flashbang across his thoughts and suddenly he was sweating, an infernal dry heat drawing moisture from his body as surely as it had done from the dry clay earth. He squinted, dazed, into the midday sun, surrounded by shouts and screams, a child crying, thick smoke in the air, and blood...

His heart missed a beat and he forced a deep inhalation of air into his body, holding it still for six seconds, and slowly exhaled. He did it again, until his heartbeat was back under control and the icy fingers of a cold sweat retreated from his skin.

The crunch of snow outside grounded him.

It didn't matter why she was here, he'd find that out soon enough. He just needed to be ready. Dragging his senses back under control just as he heard the creak of the wooden step outside the cabin, he turned to face the door, squaring his shoulders and steeling himself.

A moment later the door was pushed open and she was standing there, looking nothing like the girl he remembered.

*It was her laugh. That was what caught his attention, despite the fact that he was sitting at the back of the lecture theatre. Even without it, he would have known where she was. After all, he'd followed her that morning from her dorm all the way to the humanities building.*

*But the sound of her laugh as one of the other female students whispered something to her cut through the chatter of the other hundred and twenty-nine students, excluding the three who were missing that morning with Freshers' Week hangovers. He had helped compile reports on every single one of them and he knew more about these students than their own families.*

*Shaking off the strange sensation the sound had caused, he rubbed his chest, blew out a breath and bounced the rubber end of his pencil on his notepad. He shouldn't be here. He should be back in Svardia, completing his officer training assignments.*

*He'd wanted to be a soldier for about as long as he'd known his father had been in the army. Brynjar Bergqvist had been an Överste in the Swedish army, but had given it up when he moved to Svardia after marrying Kjell's mother.*

*While his typically quiet father had never said, Kjell understood how much he missed it and why, despite being offered a position in the Svardian Armén, his father had politely declined. Brynjar's heart might have*

*belonged to his Svardian wife, but his allegiance was to
Sweden and its King.*

*Kjell had hoped that his being in the army might
bring him closer to his stern, taciturn father, but he'd
never know. Because he was shadowing some princess
studying political science. He clenched his teeth, imagining his father's reprimand at the frustrated bent of
his thoughts.*

*She is not just some princess. She is the figurehead of
your country and she is owed your loyalty and your duty.*

*Kjell straightened in his seat and scanned the audience as the lecturer entered the hall. Two points of entry
and exit. The bank of narrow rectangular windows high
up across the back wall had no line of sight, and he was
four rows back and across from the Princess and could
get to her in under three seconds.*

*Of course, Kjell's job would be much easier if his
hands weren't tied by his having to be undercover. But
the King had decided that he would prefer to give her
the illusion of freedom—which required a CPO she had
not seen before. So he had been pulled out of the army,
having just passed basic with flying colours, and given
six months' intense training in close protection, then sent
off to university in Switzerland to guard a princess with
hair like molten chocolate and eyes that were hauntingly
pale, like clear amber.*

*He felt his jaw tense again and purposefully relaxed
it. During the prep for this position he'd watched every
single bit of footage he could find, explored every part
of her life on paper and online. In short, he'd done everything that someone looking to harm or leverage the
Princess's life would do.*

*What he'd gleaned was that Freya was an eighteen-
year-old who led a very structured life. Although she*

*had been heavily involved in royal duties from the age of fourteen, her school records indicated an excellence born of hard work as much as inherent intellect. Her extra-curricular activities were focused on helping others and she had absolutely no trace of scandal anywhere.*

*Unlike some of her European counterparts, Princess Freya seemed to have found genuine happiness in her title, as if she had been made to fit her role completely. Always perfect, always calm, and strangely open in a way that lessened people's natural inclination to cynicism. As such, Kjell had fully expected to be bored out of his mind.*

*But nothing had prepared him for the impact of her in real life. Because while he'd surveyed her from the corner of his eye, watched her openly, stayed within two feet of her in the corridors, hallways and walkways of the university, she'd never once looked at him. Until this moment in the lecture theatre, when she leaned her head back, frowning just slightly as if looking for someone, and her eyes rested on his and caught them.*

*In that exact moment a crack formed in the tight leash he kept on his control. A fine hairline fracture of his armour that was barely noticeable. Like a stress fracture. But if it was struck repeatedly the damage would be irrevocable.*

A cold blast of icy wind slapped him in the face, snapping him out of the memory and plunging him back into the present.

'Close the door,' he ordered, his voice harsh to his own ears, as he turned to toe off his damp boots. 'You're letting out warmth.'

He'd needed the excuse to look away, but it had been

too late. In a second he'd taken in everything about her, the after-image still bright against his closed eyes.

She was still utterly beautiful. Freya wasn't pale like some pampered European royalty. No, her skin was earthy, warm, and everything he'd ever wanted to sink into. Her eyes, hauntingly pale but bright and quick and...staring at him with hell fire.

A fur hat, the colour of espresso and dusted heavily with snowflakes, made her eyes look almost feline. They had always been utterly unique, a shade of brown so light it was haunting. The press, both local and international, had obsessively compared them to those of a fox.

Beneath the hat, long streams of rich mahogany-coloured hair would be swept up and bound against her head. It was a style she seemed to have adopted after the night of her sister's accident which, thankfully, hadn't been as serious as originally thought. Above a long elegant neck was a jawline that led to a chin you wanted to hold between your thumb and finger. Mainly to angle a face so beautiful it made you search it for flaws. But he'd looked for hours and never found a single one.

No, he thought. The flaws, the coldness that had shocked him had laid deep beneath the surface. As if that remembrance brought out the critic, he found her a little thinner, more angular, less...soft. The thought was so intense he'd almost sounded it on his tongue.

'Pardon?'

'What?' he asked, surprised by her question.

'You said something.'

'No,' he denied flatly, despite wondering if it were a lie. If he kept his words simple, she might leave sooner. He checked his watch. From the sound of the wind outside, they had maybe ten minutes before the storm struck. And no matter why she was here now, he was one hundred per cent sure that she wouldn't be in nine minutes' time. She couldn't be.

'Aren't you going to say anything?' she demanded, as if flustered by his silence.

'*You* came *here*, Princess,' he growled, unable to keep the animal in him at bay.

'Don't call me that.'

Her tone was defensive rather than angry and it wasn't what he'd expected. It piqued an interest he really didn't want to have *piqued*. So he shrugged off her complaint and focused on what was pertinent.

'Why are you here?'

'Can we go inside?' She looked around the small boot room separating the cabin's front and internal doors, not with superiority that might have been expected from a royal, but rather as if she were uncomfortable.

He nearly laughed, aware that he must be miles removed from the polite courtiers that surrounded her on a daily basis. No, he was far from civilised. He was a soldier, forged in some of the world's worst hellholes on his missions seconded to the UN. He wouldn't diminish himself for her comfort. Instead of replying to her question, he shook his head. He had no interest in letting her any further into his cabin.

A faint flush rose to her cheeks as she cast her eye around the space, the old butler's sink behind him and the bench that had become a shoe rack beneath the coats and layers hung up by the door. It looked more rough than rustic. Inside, the cabin was anything but, though he had no intention of her ever getting that far. Yet there was an irony to it, he supposed. After all, she'd been the one to teach him that looks could be deceiving.

'I need you to accept the medal.'

A burst of white noise exploded in his ears, levelling

out on a high-pitched ringing that left him a little disorientated. Then came a wave of outrage that washed away his patience. Fury tightened his chest. He'd told his commander he couldn't accept it. He'd even told the King directly. And he'd sent *her* here?

Kjell turned away and shut his mouth before he could curse, disguising his reaction by placing the rag in his hand on the shelf behind him. He breathed in and out through his nose, regaining composure, if not calm, before turning back to where she stood in front of the door.

'I informed command that I would not accept the medal.'

'I am not leaving here unless you do,' she warned, her tone making him combative. But it was there in her eyes, a flash that caught his attention. A desperation that didn't fit.

'Why is this so important to you?' he asked, following his gut.

'It will reflect badly on my brother if you do not.'

'No. It's not that,' he said, wanting to move, wanting to assess, to circle her like prey that had shown its weakness. Freya's words had been too smooth, too quick.

'It is all you need to know.'

The response cut him like a knife. Four months ago, it would have been enough. He would have stood to attention, saluted and done as ordered with a *Sir, yes, sir.* He would never in a million years have questioned a commanding officer, let alone his country's Princess or his King, no matter what had happened between them personally. Even now he wrestled with the need to obey, the legacy of his service and duty as one of the most respected and trusted soldiers of the Svardia Armén.

'That is no longer good enough for me, Your Highness,' he said through gritted teeth.

His tone, his words, they all said so much and so little. What had happened to him? Freya searched his face, his body, needing something, *anything*, to help her understand the change in him. This close up, she could see now, he was so very different. He stood with his arms crossed over his chest, emphasising the bulk of his biceps and the tense corded muscle along his forearm. Proud, determined, immovable. It was the kind of look that quelled rebellions and marshalled armies. She saw it then. The warrior that he'd become, the power that he wore like armour and hated that she found it magnificent.

She'd once told Kjell her fears, her hopes...her secrets. But to this man? No. This man was completely different. Maybe if she hadn't been so hurt, maybe if they'd spoken afterwards, maybe if they'd somehow made sense of the mess her father had caused when he'd sent Kjell to her undercover, she might have been able to tell him the true reason she was here. But she just couldn't trust him with that. Not any more.

He stared down at her, bright blue eyes shining with an intensity that threatened to strip away the layers of protection she had put in place. She had to get out of this cabin. And it had nothing to do with the fast-approaching storm and everything to do with him and what he made her think of. What he made her want. She hated it, the desperation she felt, the fear that had brought her here, to him. The tears that pressed against the backs of her eyes were hot and she blinked rapidly to try to keep them at bay.

'Kjell,' she said. His name so familiar on her tongue. Her body's instinctive softening around it like a muscle memory that hurt her heart. 'Please,' she said, hating the way that her voice nearly broke. 'I need this.'

But when she looked up at him the fierce anger in his eyes shocked her.

'You need this? *You*?' he demanded, his voice increasing in volume. 'You come here in a helicopter, demanding that I accept a medal like it's a favour to you after *eight* years during which I've not been able to go *home*?'

Freya stepped back instinctively to protect herself from the barrage of words flying at her. He'd not been able to go home?

'Kjell, I—'

He took a long stride towards her and she stepped back again. His eyes bored into hers as if she were the devil and he the righteous warrior. Another step forward, and one step back had her against the door of the cabin. She hated that he was using his body against her when that same body had brought her so much pleasure in the past. For a shocking moment she thought he wasn't going to stop. Wasn't sure she even wanted him to, and the blush that rose on her cheeks when he stopped as if reading her thoughts was one of pure humiliation.

That was the feeling he always made her circle back round to. Embarrassment. He had played her for a fool once. She knew it, *he* knew it. Thank God no one else did.

'I don't know what you're talking about,' she said, trying desperately not to raise her hands between them to ward him off or reach for him, she didn't know. Flustered, she tried to hold onto the thread of conversation. 'Why haven't you been able to come back home?' she asked, unable to mask the quiver in her voice.

His eyes were an arctic blaze, flaring and sparking, his jaw clenched, the powerful neck muscles bunched as if every single millimetre of his entire body was tensed and ready to fight, but completely and utterly restrained.

He would never strike her, never ever cause her physical harm. She knew that with a certainty that she had about very little in her life at that moment. But it didn't mean he wasn't a threat. The emotional vortex he was pulling her into was something she'd avoided for eight years.

Her pulse leapt at the heat of his breath on her lips and she pressed her thighs together, trying to relieve the intense pull she felt between her legs. No one had ever affected her like this, no one other than him. She'd not even been this close to a man in the time since she'd last seen him. The smell of him was tauntingly familiar and making her ache in ways that she'd thought she'd forgotten.

'You said you never wanted to see me again.'

Her throat ached, as if she had only just yelled the words at him. They had haunted her for months after that night.

'Yes. I did.'

'Those words were clear enough to my commanding officer.'

'Your what? I don't know—'

'Tell me, Freya, what made you think that they would all ignore such an order from their royal?'

She looked up at him, still without any idea what he was talking about. What order? Her heart had been breaking over his betrayal. The young student she had studied with, laughed with, danced with, drunk with and slowly and gently given her heart to, given *herself* to…why would she *ever* want to see him again when she found out that he'd been employed by her father as her bodyguard? She didn't understand what he was trying to—

'Exile, Freya. You exiled me.'

The beep of the satellite phone's ringtone cut through her shocked silence and he didn't know whether to laugh or rage. That she hadn't even realised what she'd been doing all those years ago was incomprehensibly cruel.

'Answer it,' he said, disgusted with her, with himself. He just wanted her gone. He turned his back on her and walked towards the internal door to the cabin. He nearly laughed at the irony that *he* now wanted out of the very space he'd enclosed them both in.

No matter how much he wanted to walk into his sanctuary, he would not do it while she was still here. But he was at the very end of his patience. Her brother had taken this too far in sending Freya to deliver the medal, but he'd overplayed his hand. This refusal would be his last. He would *never* accept that medal.

He heard Freya speak quietly into the phone, unable to resist glancing to the side where he could just make out her turning away from him in his peripheral vision. The words grew urgent and louder, until, 'No, wait! Gunnar!' she shouted, flinging open his front door and disappearing into a flurry of blinding snowflakes.

Kjell cursed loudly and violently, grabbing his coat before shoving the front door closed behind him as he ran after her. He threw an arm into a coat sleeve as he jogged in the direction of the helo and strained to hear Freya's angry shouts in the distance as he pushed into the other sleeve. His heart pounded even as his quick mind began to process the reality of this new situation.

The blades were already in motion and he hurried forward, knowing that in Freya's state of mind the danger they posed might not actually stop her. By the time he caught up with her the helicopter was already two feet off the ground and the downwash was fierce enough to have her shielding her eyes. Her hat had fallen off somewhere in the snow and her long dark hair was streaming out in waves, buffeted by the air from both the helicopter's blades and the storm that was now, for all intents and purposes, here.

He pulled her back from the downwash, their hunched forms blindly retreating until they were far out of reach from the pounding waves of air and snow. From a position of safety, they watched as the helicopter jerked up into the air, hovering momentarily as if offering its regret for leaving her behind, before gliding up and away from view.

Kjell watched her as she stared into the sky long after distance and visibility had made it impossible to see, as if she couldn't believe that it wouldn't come back. He peered at the cabin through bloated fluffy flakes of snow that looked harmless until they overloaded a helicopter's engine, making it too dangerous to fly, or too dangerous to wait for the very important person they had left behind.

'Give me the sat phone,' he ordered.

She held it out to him without looking, her fingers already red from the cold. She couldn't stay here. She wouldn't last five minutes. She was too soft for his world.

He pressed the button as he turned back and headed to the outbuilding. 'Gunnar,' he shouted into the phone past the howling wind, 'I can get her out to the other side of the lake.'

'It's too late.'

'Don't give me that. Your pilot has done far more in worse conditions,' he said, noticing that Freya had started to follow him more quickly as she realised that he was trying to get them to come back.

'Not with a royal on board, Kjell.'

'That's bull and you know it, Gunnar.' Freya reached for the phone but he lifted his elbow out of the way and turned so she couldn't reach it. 'What aren't you telling me?' Kjell demanded, trying to keep his question out of Freya's hearing.

'I have my orders, Kjell. We'll be back to pick her up when the storm clears.'

Gunnar disconnected the call his end, leaving Kjell standing halfway between his cabin and the outbuilding where he housed his snowmobile, seriously considering just jumping on and getting as far away from Her Royal Highness Princess Freya of Svardia as possible.

'Well?' she asked, the flush on her cheeks and hope in her eyes brighter than the north star.

He took one last longing look at the outbuilding.

'Sorry, Princess,' he said without the faintest trace of sympathy. Stalking back to the cabin, he threw his next words over his shoulder. 'Looks like you're stuck here.'

# CHAPTER THREE

FREYA STARED AT him as he disappeared into the white froth twisting and turning before her in gusts of wind that pulled at her hair and her clothes. Stuck? Here?

*No!*

For how long? What would she do? Where would she—

She shook her head, trying to lessen the cascade of questions falling on top of each other. She had meetings back at the palace. *Oh, God.* Fingers pressed against lips in shock. She was due to meet Stellan Stormare in three days' time. It was an appointment she could not miss. She looked back up to where she should have been able to see the cabins, but they were gone, hidden deep within the maelstrom of the storm.

The dull beat of fear joined her pulse as she hurried forward, her steps difficult and ungainly from where the snow hit her at her calves. Everything in her wanted to call to Kjell, but she wouldn't. She could just make out the punches his shoes had made in the snow and had enough sense to follow them to the cabin. She was panting by the time she reached the wooden steps up to the front door, sweat awkward and slick on her back, sticking her base layers to her skin. She pushed open the door, expecting to find the cabin empty, but Kjell was standing there with his back to her and—

'I can't stay here.'

She hadn't meant it to be the first thing she said. She knew how it sounded. Pampered and spoiled and demanding. But that wasn't why the words had rushed out of her mouth the moment she had caught sight of him.

He'd taken off his T-shirt for a reason Freya simply couldn't fathom and was standing there with his fingers on the top button of his trousers. He cast her a look over his shoulder, but she didn't catch it because she was too busy running her eyes over his back, the corded muscles and dips and…and scars.

'Don't look at me like that, unless you intend to do something about it.'

Distracted by the blatant sensual challenge, her head snapped up, her gaze clashing with the arctic fire in his. Anger, yes, a taunt, absolutely, but there was something else hidden beneath the boldness.

She looked away. She didn't have any more right to his secrets than he did hers. She doubted he would respect the retreat but she didn't know the rules with him. This wasn't the Kjell she had once known, who would tease her reasoning and thoughts out gently, with kindness and encouragement. This was a hard, unrelenting challenge and attack from a man with no reason for patience and she was owed no kindness.

He had been exiled? For eight years?

She opened her mouth to speak, but his words struck out like bullets.

'Boots off. Clothes off.'

She squeaked in shock. 'No.'

'Wet kills around here, Princess. If your clothing is wet, it's not coming into the cabin.'

'You can't be serious,' she exclaimed, looking for a joke, or the hint of one.

He simply levelled her with that glacial gaze. 'You might want to turn around.'

She felt distinctly as if the cold was affecting her brain function. Why would she want to—

The moment his hands went to his hips she spun on her heel, squeezing her eyes shut. Not that it stopped the images exploding to life on the backs of her eyelids. In her mind's eye she saw the full length of his naked body as she heard the slide of material against his skin and falling to the floor. Heat stung her cheeks as she imagined him plunging one leg and then the other into the dry pair of trousers she'd seen on the shelf unit by the door.

'You can look now, Princess.'

'Stop calling me that,' she said through clenched teeth. She waited an extra beat before turning around to find him looking at her with too much in his eyes.

'Boots off, clothes off,' he repeated tonelessly. He unhooked a white cord at the side of the room and lowered an old wooden slatted clothes pulley. He shook out his trousers and hung them up as she watched, eyes wide. He hadn't been joking. 'Hang your clothes here, there are dry ones there,' he said, pointing to the shelf. 'Boots go there.' He indicated the bench where shoes and boots were piled next to some strange spiked contraptions. Kjell cast one last look at her and disappeared through the connecting doorway.

Freya shivered despite the intense warmth of the boot room, clenching her jaw so that her teeth didn't chatter. Instinctively, she knew weakness wouldn't be tolerated by this man and she felt a wave of sympathy for anyone under his command. With red fingers that felt twice their normal size, she struggled with the laces on her boots. The sweat that had stuck her clothes to her skin now felt cold and clammy and she was beginning to see the benefit in shedding the layers.

He'd not been home in eight years, her conscience prodded. The thought of not seeing Marit or Aleksander for that long was inconceivable. But Kjell was an only child. No child should be cut off from their parents. Even if that child was a six-foot three-inch man with muscles that could have been sculpted by Michelangelo and a scowl that was, cruelly, more sensual than his charm.

She'd done that to him. She'd kept him from coming home.

*No*, she defended. She'd had every right to be angry, every right to be hurt when she'd found out the truth about him. Kjell had lied to her about who he was and had insinuated his way into her life... Her conscience yanked hard. Knowing that hurt was rewriting their history. In fact, he'd been reluctant to talk to her at the beginning.

*'Is this seat taken?' she asked, her heart in her mouth.*

*Freya had never before been so bold. She'd never really had the opportunity at the all-girls boarding school she'd attended in Svardia.*

*Ice-blue eyes stared up at her blankly. She was about to turn away, utterly devastated, when he said, 'No.' It was clipped and rough, as if he hadn't spoken in a while, and had a strange effect on her pulse.*

*She sat down with a sigh of relief. But now that she*

*was there, she didn't know what to do next. She opened
her mouth to speak, but stopped when he got up, gathered all his books and left the table.*

*She clenched her jaw until the blush of humilia-
tion had passed and promised never to speak to Kjell
Bergqvist again.*

Snapped out of the memory by a distant slam from
deep inside the cabin, she pulled the boots from her
feet and self-consciously stripped off her clothes. But
if he thought she was taking off her underwear, he was
sorely mistaken.

'Bra and knickers,' came the shout, as if he'd somehow divined her defiance.

'Absolutely not!' she yelled back.

'If I don't see them hanging up on that dryer, you're
not coming in.'

'You're a beast!'

'You're not the first woman to say so!' he shouted
back without missing a beat.

Cheeks flaming and an unwanted but completely
uncontrollable jealousy raging within her, she peeled
down her panties and unclipped her bra. She refused
to hang them up on the dryer though, like some trophy
for him. Turning to the shelf of clothes by the door, she
pulled out a pair of grey jogging bottoms, a white vest
and a petrol-blue jumper that was surprisingly soft. As
she put them on, the dry warmth that enveloped her
reminded her of what it had felt like to be surrounded
by Kjell, *protected* by him. What they'd shared eight
years ago had been too intense for peace, too frantic
for stillness, too risky to be safe. But she had found a
serenity with him that she'd never experienced before.

Which had made his betrayal so much worse. Freya used that hurt, that pain then, adding them to the layers of armour she would need. Because that was what being in his presence felt like. Going to war.

Kjell was prepared to admit he might have taken it too far, demanding Freya remove her underwear, but he'd needed to make a point. They were stuck here at the beginning of one of the worst storms he could remember in Dalarna, and if she didn't follow the rules there would be severe consequences for them both.

The cabin was state-of-the-art—not that she'd seen evidence of it yet—but it was still off-grid. The solar panels would be out of action from the snowfall in the next few hours, but the backup generator was ready to kick in. The ground source heat pump would be good for another day or two of ambient temperature but, even then, they'd have to rely on the wood-burner in the central part of the cabin. It was nothing he wasn't prepared for and there was enough food and water to last them both an entire month—not that it would come to that. The storm was bad, but would probably blow itself out within the week. Not that it made it any less dangerous.

To someone used to central heating, constant electricity and heat whenever and wherever they wanted it, the minus temperatures that this storm could reach would be shocking. All that kept them safe from the elements were the walls of this cabin, the ability to create heat and stay dry. If any of those were compromised, they would be in very real life-threatening trouble.

No matter what had passed between them, a threat to Freya was anathema to him. She was his to protect until the storm lifted. Something thick and heavy shifted in his chest. As if the thought was too much. Too close to what he'd once been.

*Freya wobbled on heels that she was clearly unaccustomed to and that made Kjell even angrier. Her so-called friend had stayed on at the half-term party, letting Freya walk back to her dorm alone, in the dark, inebriated.*

*Kjell was tempted to have the girl transferred.*

*In the past two weeks alone he'd redirected the interests of one student determined to 'bag a princess', and another who'd wanted to cash in on her fame.*

*Princess Freya had the self-preservation instincts of a duckling.*

*She leaned a little to the left and he caught up with her just in time to balance her.*

*'Are you drunk?' he demanded.*

*Freya shook her head. 'Absolute not.'*

*He cursed.*

*'Why do you swear in Swedish?'*

*'You know Swedish swearwords?' he asked, surprised.*

*She nodded. 'And Greek, English, German, Italian and several in Russian,' she said proudly.*

*'Svardian tax dollars at work, ladies and gentlemen.'*

*'No. That's for my degree. I learned swearing on my own time.'*

*He had to bite back a smile. Beneath the layers of royal etiquette she was funny.*

*'Okay, Princess, let's get you home.'*

*He pulled her against his side, but she twisted gracefully in his arms so that they were chest to chest. She craned her neck to look up at him.*

*'So small,' she whispered.*

*'I am* not *small,' he replied.*

*'No... But I am,' she said, shaking her head.*

*His lips curved and her gaze flickered between his mouth and his eyes, her own wide and full of glitter.*

*'What?' he asked.*

*'You smiled.'*

*'I didn't,' he said, scowling.*

*'You did. I saw it. You can smile, Kjell,' she accused him, as if it was something he kept from the world.*

The memory was a punch to the gut, more powerful for its sweetness. A possessiveness he'd never known before had filled him that day, one that had carried through until the very end. But even then it had just been an illusion. The Princess and the commoner? No. She could never have been truly his. He'd only borrowed her for a short time. And it had cost him greatly.

He had shamed himself and his parents by having a relationship with Freya, by lying to her and failing utterly in his duty. He'd accepted exile as his punishment, accepted that he deserved it. But that didn't mean it hadn't cost him, hadn't hurt him when he looked at his mother's teary eyes and met his father's distant gaze when he met them on the few hours each year he'd return to check in with Command. Didn't mean that he hadn't struggled to find his place in a different world.

The door to the cabin opened, the noise wrenching him back to the present, and he turned to find her face frozen in a look of surprise. Rosebud lips that had been ready to continue their shouting match dropped into the perfect 'O' as she took in the cabin that he'd poured years and savings into making perfect.

He'd just about calmed his breathing when he caught sight of her underwear in her loosened grip. Molten lava poured through his veins in a thick, slow crawl, lulling him into complete arousal that demanded appeasement. She'd been the only woman to ever have that effect on him. And he'd never tried to replicate it with another.

'It's beautiful,' she exclaimed, utterly unaware of the precarious position she was in. He tracked her progression through the cabin, jaw clenched and muscles tense. He wouldn't last an hour with her if he didn't get himself under control. *Now.*

Focusing his mind on the alterations he'd made to the cabin that had been in his father's family for generations, the mental exercise calmed him. Bare feet padded up to the window that wrapped around the entire length of the broad single-storey cabin. The feat of engineering had cost him four whole years' pay, but it was worth every single cent. As evidenced by the hypnotising effect it had on Freya. Unable to resist, he went to stand beside her, trying to see the panoramic view as she did for the first time.

'You did all this?' she asked, her hand reaching up to touch the triple-glazed reinforced glass created specifically to withstand the drastically cold temperatures that hit this central part of Sweden for nearly six months of the year, whilst simultaneously adjusting to the intense heat of the summer months.

He nodded. He felt her eyes on him but he locked his gaze on the most breathtaking view he'd ever seen. And he'd travelled the world. Even between the swirls of snow, the expanse of the view was startling. The large lake beyond was a smooth disc of grey ice, framed either side by the close press of trees that wrapped around to the front of the cabin, giving a sense of privacy, exclusivity, reinforced by the knowledge that no one else resided within twenty kilometres of these two cabins. The

spindly evergreens blanketed by thick fingers of snow
looked mystical and faintly threatening—black twisting into white, throwing off grey and disappearing into
haunting shadows.

But to be protected by the glass and witness the ferocity of the wind hurling huge banks of flakes back
and forth across the landscape, the sheer movement of
it, while standing in what felt like the eye of that raging
storm…that was the real pleasure, the real awe.

She turned to him, a smile on her lips and a spark in
her eyes as if she'd forgotten herself for a moment, and
that was when he saw her. The girl he'd once known. And
then *he* nearly forgot. All the reasons why he couldn't
just sweep her up in his arms to soothe the need that was
choking in its intensity. Her title, his lie and the gulf between them that would never be breached. He'd nearly
forgotten. But not quite.

As if reading those thoughts in his eyes, she turned
away to take in the rest of the living area. In the corner,
flames flickered in the wood burner warming the space
easily. A large caramel leather sofa ran the length of the
wall, covered in different types of fur throws, ones that
his grandfather and great-grandfather had made themselves from the animals that had died naturally on the
property. The Bergqvists had strong views towards living with and within their habitat. No animal was killed
needlessly and no resource was used mindlessly or completely. Every change Kjell had made to the cabin had
the highest environmental certifications and the latest
technological advances. The cabin was as ecologically
sustainable as humanly possible.

It was more than a cabin, though. It was his sanctuary.
But as Freya crossed the threshold to his bedroom it felt
like a cage. Having her here, invading his space, it made

him feel too much. Mentally he paced the room, feeling trapped by her presence. He had come here to face what had happened on secondment four months ago. Not the woman who had exiled him eight years ago.

Freya stared at one of the biggest beds she'd ever seen. It was less a bed and more a raised floor area. Low to the ground, the mattress took up two-thirds of the room. There were no side tables or lamps, but as the room had the same window as the living area she presumed that the natural light would be sufficient. She was drawn once again to the view that made the cabin feel part of the landscape in a fundamental way. It was simply incredible, and somehow so Kjell. As if it perfectly captured the duality of the man—raw wildness and controlled restraint.

She looked back at the bed and suddenly realised what had brought her to the room. Frowning, she peered through the door to where Kjell was moving about the kitchen. A kitchen that was on the other side of the cabin. A cabin with no second floor.

'Kjell?' She saw his shoulders tense. She ground her teeth together, realisation making her heart thud. 'Where's the other bedroom?'

He turned, glared at her over his shoulder and, having clearly decided that she could answer her own question, he went back to whatever he was doing on the stove.

*Oh, no. No, no, no, no.*

She ran to the table where she'd seen her sat phone and jabbed at the keypad with shaking fingers. *Answer... please answer*, she prayed. Maybe Henna, her lady-in-waiting, could do something to get her out of here.

'Freya?' an urgent voice demanded when the call connected.

'Henna!' she cried, so relieved to hear her friend's voice.

'Are you okay? I was told about them having to leave you…where… Okay?'

'Henna? Are you there?'

'Can't…you,' came the panicked response.

She sent a look to where Kjell was leaning back against the sideboard, holding his coffee mug to his chest and observing her distress with a passivity that bordered on cruel.

'Kjell?'

He scowled. 'It's a satellite phone, Freya. It needs to be visible to the satellite. And while I'm sure your model has indoor capabilities, there is deep cloud cover and snow has piled up on the roof.' He stalked to where she stood by the table and took the phone from her. 'Henna, if you can hear me, she's fine. Check in with Gunnar Sydow for her return ETA.' He disconnected the call and threw the phone onto the sofa, before disappearing into the bedroom and kicking the door shut behind him.

Freya was at her wits' end. Nothing about today had gone as planned, from the meeting with her brother to this moment. She was stuck here with a man she'd never wanted to see again. Not only that but he clearly blamed her for something that had happened as the result of one sentence; one heartbroken, devastated cry of a young woman who'd had the most wonderful love ripped away before her very eyes.

'I didn't ask for this, you know,' she shouted at him through the closed door, when what she really wanted to say was that she hadn't wanted him exiled. She'd just known that she'd never see him again. She'd known, even then, eight years ago, on that helicopter ride as he'd begged her to look at him, to let him explain… she couldn't allow him to. Because what she'd felt for him all those years ago had been too much. Too strong. She would never have been able to let him go, even though she'd known that she wouldn't have been allowed to keep him.

The door was yanked open and Kjell emerged, his arms full of bedding, his face a blank mask. He stalked to where the sofas were and threw the bedding down.

The, *'It's all yours, Your Highness,'* was a growl between his lips as he passed her, heading back to the kitchen, and it made her want to cry. She sucked in a shaking breath, keeping it as inaudible as possible and slipped into his bedroom, closing the door behind her. She sank down with her back against the door, pressing a fist to her mouth.

All she'd wanted was to stand down on her own terms, without the press finding out, so that she could lick her wounds in private. The moment the doctors had told her that she'd never be able to carry a child to term, that the lining of her uterus was too thin for implantation, she'd known how the press would react. They'd question her role—what use was a royal who couldn't produce heirs? And then they'd question Aleksander. Marit. And that was unbearable.

She was under no illusions, never had been. Her father had always ensured that the family did what was best for the country. It came first. Always. But he'd been especially hard on her. Perhaps because he saw himself in her. Before his brother's tragic death, her father had been second in line to the throne. Perhaps the shock, the weight of that responsibility, having to take that on while he should have been allowed to grieve had changed something fundamental in him. But it was as if he'd never seen her for *herself.* Only her ability to support Aleksander. Support the throne.

And she knew that when her father heard the news of her infertility his first thought would be that she wouldn't be able to do her duty. He would hurt for her, she knew that, but only after they'd protected the throne.

And it wouldn't matter what good she'd achieved as ambassador to her charities, as CEO to a women's science initiative, it wouldn't matter how skilled she was at smoothing ruffled diplomatic feathers. She would be known by absence for ever, by what she didn't have. A working womb. The chance for motherhood. Children.

She'd never, *never* thought there would be a problem. That there was something defective, broken inside her. And she hated that her infertility made her feel less. Less hopeful, less free, less of a woman. But it was more than that, she realised as she pressed her back against the bedroom door. She felt it deep within her, constant, unconditional, infinite: all the love she had to give, but no one to give it to. Absent parents, a distant brother and a self-involved sister. And, her heart shuddered, a man she couldn't share it with and the children she'd not be able to have.

Her hand shook. She saw them so clearly, the little boy and little girl, each with blond hair and arctic blue eyes. *Kjell's.* She was shocked to realise that she'd never given up that dream.

A tear rolled down her cheek and she pushed it away, only another came and then another as she stifled the sound of her cries. But she clenched her teeth, determination filling her. No matter what happened, she couldn't let Kjell know why she needed him to accept the medal. Because he had been and would be the only person who had ever seen her whole rather than broken.

Kjell paced the kitchen area, not liking how quiet Freya was. She'd always had a poise about her, regal, something contained and restrained. But she had closed the door behind her over three hours ago and not opened it since.

Dark had descended and she hadn't turned on the light in the room. He'd have been able to see it through the crack beneath the door. An hour and a half ago he'd knocked to tell her that there was dinner on the table if she wanted it, but there'd been no response.

The caged animal growled that it was her own fault. But his conscience jabbed him in the gut, his stomach twisting with guilt. He'd behaved like the beast she'd accused him of being. His tone, words, actions towards her harsh and unforgiving. He could admit to that. He'd make it up to her, he promised her deep in his soul. But not before he got to the bottom of why she needed him to accept the medal. Because there was one thing he knew for sure. It had nothing to do with him or her brother and absolutely everything to do with her.

# CHAPTER FOUR

FREYA WOKE FEELING absolutely awful. Her eyes were puffy and swollen and her throat sore, as if she'd swallowed sand.

Water. She needed water.

But that meant she'd have to leave the bedroom. And Kjell was outside. She closed her eyes. Kjell. There was just so much...*too* much. But she couldn't hide in here for the next however many days, no matter how much she wanted to. Last night, the hurt and pain had risen because she'd been shocked and exhausted. But she'd had her moment of weakness and now she needed to face reality.

Being stuck in Kjell's cabin gave her the opportunity to get exactly what she wanted. Him to accept the medal. And that wouldn't happen if she stayed hiding in his bedroom. Sitting up, she was struck by the stunning view from the windows. Unlike the sitting room, which was covered in pale blond wood, rich deep ochre-coloured leather and all the warm brown tones in between, Kjell's room matched the snowscape.

In the sitting room she'd felt cocooned and safe, protected from the outside world. Here, in his room, she was *part* of it. White linen, impossibly soft grey fur throws and wood flooring so dark it looked like charcoal. The wooden wall panels in here had been painted white but sanded back so that they blended with the wood's natural colouring. Even his clothes seemed to eschew colour as if he sought to camouflage himself in the winter wonderland.

As if thinking of him had worked some spell, her eyes snagged on movement out by the lake. Alert in an instant, she watched his figure move at speed across the edge of the frozen disc of water and into the woods. The misty breath streaming from his mouth spoke of a minus temperature that made Freya shiver. He was wearing a hat, gloves and layers enough to bulk out the torso she'd seen yesterday.

Heat, delicious, wicked and instantaneous, blanketed her at the sheer memory of him. Her woman's mind wondered how different it would be to make love to that man, but her younger self lashed out, still hurt and betrayed from years before, self-protection an almost violent need. Steeling herself, she threw back the covers and focused on showering before he could return. The temptation to raid the kitchen and grab everything she might need for the day was fierce, but she was done hiding. At least she would be clean, dressed and have her defences in place by the time they went for round two.

The freezing cold air burned his throat with every inhalation, but he forced himself on. He was no way near working off the intense need racking his body. All night long he'd had dreams of Freya, born from the past, tainted by the present. He was no stranger to frustration and was more than capable of handling it himself. But it was different now that she was in his cabin. Before, he'd been able to tell himself he'd imagined how perfect her skin was, how his skin felt on fire when she looked at him, that the heat of her body made his heart feel as if it were clawing out of his chest to get to her.

*'Please don't,' she begged him, turning away.*

*'Don't what?' he asked, pulling her back to him, needing to see what hurt she was trying to hide.*

*'Look at me like you want to kiss me when you clearly don't.'*

*Everything in him turned to stone. He couldn't move, because if he did it would be to give her the one thing she clearly wanted...and the one thing he had no right to give.*

*A blush rose to her cheeks under his gaze and, before he could react, she rose on her tiptoes and pressed her lips against his.*

*For all their softness, they struck him with the weight of an anvil. Shockwaves rippled out over his body, down his legs, to his toes and into the floor.*

*But when he still didn't move Freya pulled back and looked up at him with such hurt that it blasted the final brick in his determination to stay away from his charge.*

*She went to pull back, but instead he drew her to him, his lips found hers and his heart found home.*

That memory twisted in his chest and spurred him onwards faster and faster until his focus was solely survival—his body's needs reduced to breath, balance and determination. He added another circuit to an already punishing regimen before returning to the cabin, telling himself it was for his own good and not because she was there, waiting for him.

He took the steps, ignoring the twitches in his thigh muscles, and stripped off all layers, refusing to let his awareness go beyond the boot room. His skin was already on fire, the sweat pouring from his body from the exertion despite the minus temperature, cooling and raising the hairs on his arms. But in his mind's eye he saw Freya in the boot room yesterday, peeling off her clothes and, just like that, he was rock-hard and furious.

He threw on fresh clothes just to get to the bathroom and, taking a deep breath, pulled open the door to the cabin, scanning the space for signs of Freya. A coffee mug was missing and the dishes he'd washed up last night had been put away. She was awake but back in the room then. He frowned. When he finished with the shower they'd have to sit and talk. But first he needed hot water to soothe the muscles he felt already tensing up from the punishing morning run. Imagining the blessed relief of the powerful shower, he cut the distance to the bathroom in long strides.

He noticed that the shower had been used and a vague warning sounded in the back of his mind but, desperate to feel the heat of the pounding water on his skin, he ignored it. Turning on the shower, he stripped, stepped in and…leapt back from the frigid icy shards of water. Grabbing the rail to stop himself from slipping, his heart rate sky-rocketed and it had *nothing* to do with desire.

'Freya!' he howled before turning the air blue with more expletives than he'd uttered in the last two years.

She had used up all the hot water. Hot water that, without the solar panels in play to heat the large tank, was reliant on the much smaller wood burner. A supply really only enough for one shower a day. He cursed again. He heard bare feet skittering across the floor outside the bathroom and hoped she'd have enough sense to keep herself out of his line of sight until he'd calmed down—which would probably be just in time for Gunnar to return to pick her up.

Gritting his teeth, he rubbed himself viciously with the towel before getting dressed. He had what he needed in the boot room, and he had what he wanted in the garage. Warm clothes and a damn good distraction.

He prayed to whatever gods of old were listening to give him patience as he stalked towards the outbuilding, not realising that it had been the first time he'd not thought of Enzo or the mission in months.

Freya had returned to the room after the most amazing shower she'd ever had. The power and heat of the spray blasted away the fog from the night before and she'd emerged pink-skinned, refreshed and determined.

Until she'd sorted through the clothes she'd worn last night, finding her underwear scrunched into the pocket of the joggers, and clenched her teeth together. Having not hung it out as Kjell had ordered her to do, they still held the damp sweat from yesterday's exertion running back and forth between the cabin and helicopter in the snow. She'd thought he'd been punishing her, which was why she'd ignored him, but now she was very much regretting it. Contemplating confronting him without underwear—again—made her feel vulnerable but she would...

Kjell's yell shook the walls of the cabin.

Her head snapped round and she ran into the living area and stared at the bathroom door, her eyes growing rounder with each expletive. Only when she caught the Swedish word for cold did she realise what had happened and ran back to the room and just about resisted the urge to hide under the bed. She heard the bathroom door slam back into its frame and the stamp of heavy feet stalking towards the boot room.

'Freya—' his voice all growl '—keep the wood burner fuelled or there really will be trouble.'

The cabin door slammed, flinging another open in her mind.

*Trouble, Freya. I'm nothing but trouble.*

She walked out into the living area, desperately throwing up mental blocks against the memory pushing at her mind. Her heart trembled.

*I don't want to remember. I don't.*

She squeezed her eyes shut and clenched her fists as if the physicality of it would hold her in the present. But instead of the frigid dry cold, she inhaled the damp scent of wet leaves, pumpkin spice and autumn.

She pulled at the neck of the T-shirt, feeling the warmth of the knitted scarf she'd thrown about her neck before leaving her dorm room to find him. To find Kjell.

*Her heart pounded in her chest as she ran down the path she'd seen him on just seconds earlier. She swept around the corner and came to an abrupt stop at the sight of his back. The tension cording his neck and shoulders told her that he knew she was there.*

*'Kjell, please stop,' she begged, her breath frosting the night air and catching the light from the lamppost.*

*He did as she asked but refused to turn around.*

*'Kjell, that kiss—'*

*'I shouldn't have done that.' He threw the words over his shoulder, reluctant even then to look at her.*

*Her heart curled in on itself. 'Why not? Did you not—?' She broke off, hating the need in her voice. 'Did you not like it?'*

*'Freya...'*

*He turned and she could finally see the conflict in his gaze. Seeing the struggle in his eyes gave her courage.*

'Kjell, I've done everything right. I've been the perfect Princess. I've done everything that was ever asked of me. I've never been in a tabloid, never been a headline. I've never put a foot out of line and I've never ever asked for something I've wanted for myself. Until now. Until you.'

'Trouble. Freya. I'm nothing but trouble.'

'I don't care, Kjell,' she cried.

'But I do, Freya! I care so damn much. I care that I can't be with you. I care that I can't like that kiss, or look at you the way I want to. I care that I can't touch you, or hold you, or do the things you beg me to do every time you look at me. So yes, Freya, I do care. You're a princess and even I know that you can't be with me. Your parents would never allow it.'

His eyes shone in the dark, the conviction, the hurt, the need.

'I know it's selfish to want this,' she said, closing the distance between them, 'to want you. And yes, I know it can't last,' she said, feeling the sob in her chest like a physical ache. 'I know that this is all I'll ever have of you. But I'm asking you to give me this, knowing that it's selfish, that it's unbearably cruel to both of us, but knowing that I'd rather live the rest of my life with the memory of you than the regret of never having loved you.'

She *had* been selfish. It had been her. Her need that had driven it, driven them together. For two blissful months before it all came crashing down, she'd hoarded him like the most precious crown jewel. But she realised now that Kjell would never have laid a finger on her if she hadn't pushed at every turn. She'd been the one who had brought them together and he'd been the one who had paid the price.

An exile that had kept him from his family, his home, his country.

She rubbed at the chill that wrapped around her, arms rippling with goosebumps, her unseeing gaze slowly focusing on the snow falling beyond the window. He must have felt so alone. She frowned, the cold around her a little stronger now.

She looked at the wood burner and realised that it was running low. But scanning the room—she couldn't see any wood to fuel it. There was a box of kindling, but no logs. Frowning, she looked again, shaking her head and hating that she was missing something painfully obvious. It made her feel…inept, not being able to do something as simple as adding wood to a fire to keep herself—and this room—warm.

After another five minutes she was beginning to get angry with herself for not finding the secret stash of wood and frustrated that she'd have to go and ask him. But she'd rather that than risk the fire going out.

She hurried to the boot room and found her boots. There were plenty of coats and jumpers, scarves and hats, but she looked at her clothes up on the drying rack near the ceiling and remembered. Stifling her embarrassment, she quickly washed her underwear in the sink and hung them up to dry.

Zipped up, tied up, wrapped up five minutes later, she pulled open the door and nearly shut it again. The blast of sub-zero air slapped her hard and fast and she had to lean into the wind just to stay upright.

Where was Kjell and what was he doing out here?

With one hand, she shaded her eyes from the furious frigid little flakes peppering her with icy accuracy, not even able to see the other cabin in the distance. Even knowing it was the height of madness, she was about to step out into the maelstrom when she noticed—with great relief—a pile of wood just on the inside of the porch. Pulling armfuls of the wood inside the boot room, she left a pile by the connecting door and took the rest straight into the cabin and nearly dropped them when she saw the fire had gone out.

'No, no, no!'

She fell to her knees by the burner and went to pull the door handle, yanking it back when her palm burned. Finding a set of gloves, she thrust them on, ignoring the burn, and yanked open the door, terrified by the hiss of smoke and barely glowing embers. In a panic, she grabbed a fistful of the kindling, threw it onto the bottom of the stove and thrust one of the big logs on top. Seeing some tiny little pellet things that must be fire-lighters, she grabbed two, then two more—just in case. There was a box of long-stemmed matches and as she struck one her fingers shook.

'Please let this work...*please*,' she prayed.

She placed the match beneath the first firelighter and then the second, before she threw the match into the belly of the wood burner. But her sigh of relief choked in the moment that the wood started to hiss and flare. Tiny little sparks like furious fireflies exploded into being and, panicking, she hastily shut the door to the burner. The spitting white specks zoomed for a little longer but then went out. Smoke began to fill the chamber behind the glass door. Freya didn't know what to do.

Gingerly she opened the door and thick dark smoke billowed into the room. Terrified, she shoved another load of firelighters into the burner and, waving the smoke out of her eyes, tried to light the fire. But the smoke wouldn't stop coming and the wood was making a terrible hissing noise.

A thick black fog was seeping into the cabin and Freya began to choke. Her heart in her mouth, she scrabbled back towards the door to the boot room. She ran for her boots, not even bothering to tie them up, shoved her arms into the nearest coat and ran out into the snow.

'Kjell!' she cried, not even sure what direction he was. If he was even nearby. She screamed his name again and suddenly firm hands grabbed her by the arm.

'Are you hurt?' he demanded, pink slashes on his skin, no hat on his head and his jacket as open as hers.

She shook her head. 'I'm so sorry!'

'Are you hurt?' he asked again, shaking her ever so slightly to cut through her fear.

'No. I'm okay. The wood burner,' she cried, pointing to the cabin, where black smoke was coming out through the door she'd left open.

In three heartbeats he went from relief to fury to exasperated action. He realised exactly what had happened as he launched into the cabin, hating—absolutely hating—leaving the doors open, knowing how much invaluable heat was escaping.

Pulling his jumper up, he covered his nose. There was *so much* smoke.

She'd let the fire go out—that much was clear. He wanted to curse her, but really he was cursing himself. What would a princess know about keeping a wood-burning stove lit? He hadn't even shown her where the wood was kept. He eyed the storage box beneath his grandmother's knitted throw, which contained enough dry wood for two days, and just stopped himself from kicking the wet wood she'd brought in from outside. Fire out, damp wood? Just enough for a backdraught to knock out her attempts to relight the thing.

By the time he'd restarted the fire and ensured the dry wood was catching, he turned, expecting to find her beside him, but she wasn't. He exhaled a sigh of pure frustration. She was still outside.

*Stubborn little princess.*

They were going to have to clear the air—figuratively as much as literally—or things could get dangerous.

As commander of over six hundred soldiers, he knew how important communication was. And how deadly it could be when it was unclear. His stomach twisted and a cold sweat broke out on his neck. A sense of creeping panic rose as imaginary flashbangs exploded and screams sounded in his ears, but he willed it all away. Freya was the most clear and present danger at the moment. The ghosts could wait.

Gritting his teeth, he gathered himself for a confrontation that had been eight years in the making. He held back just for a second, watching her through the swirls and flurries of snow. Damn stubborn woman.

He could tell she was freezing from here. Making a quick assessment, he figured she'd need to be inside at least within the next five minutes or she'd be at risk of getting dangerously cold. Thankfully she'd grabbed his military jacket, thermal-lined for sharpshooting.

She was so beautiful, he thought as the snow raged and his conscience screamed at him to get her inside.

'Freya!' he yelled, beckoning her inside with a jerk of his hand.

She shook her head.

What was she playing at?

'Inside, Freya.'

'No!' she shouted.

This was not the time for her to be messing around.

Her body was shaking and her lips beginning to bleed into blue and still her eyes spat fire.

'Why not?'

'Because you're mad at me.'

'Yes.' He didn't deny it. He was mad as hell. But it had very little to do with her failed attempts to smoke out his cabin and everything to do with what he wanted to do to her when he got her back in the cabin. None of which involved clothes and every one of them involved using up all this pent-up frustration between the two of them until it burned out completely.

'I can't… I just…'

'Freya, you're freezing. Just come inside,' he said, taking a step towards her.

'I'm n-n-not. I'm f-fine.'

'Freya, don't be difficult,' he said, knowing the statement would rile her.

'Kjell Bergqvist, do not sp-sp-speak to me like I… I'm a child!'

'Then,' he said, reaching her in easy strides, 'stop *behaving* like one.'

She glared up at him—haunting pale amber eyes flashing like Goldschläger. He could almost feel the alcohol burn his throat. It was enough. He bent his knees, wrapped his arms around her waist and hauled her easily over his shoulder. Spinning in the snow, he marched back to the boot room and kicked the door closed behind him.

'Are you going to behave?' he asked, trying so very hard to keep the laughter out of his voice.

'How *dare* you?' came her muffled response as her little fists pummelled ineffectually against his back.

'I'm not letting you down until you agree to stop sulking.'

She froze. 'I am not sulking,' she hissed.

He was a Lieutenant Colonel and he'd dealt with more recalcitrant new recruits than could be imagined. Waiting out one little princess who'd always had the patience of a gnat was easy. Not that he wouldn't keep her on his shoulder until the morning if he had to.

'I'm sorry.'

The whispered words caught at his heart, the sadness in them as unexpected as his instant reaction to them. He frowned and bent his knees so that he could let her down, the delicious friction of her body against his lost momentarily in his concern for her.

'It's just smoke, Freya.'

'Not just about that,' she replied, her eyes locked onto the corner of the boot room, plucking at his heartstrings as if it were hers to play.

And finally he did what he'd been wanting to do since she'd turned up at his cabin. He took her chin with his thumb and forefinger and gently pulled her round to face him. He wanted to see her eyes as much as he wanted her to see his.

'Your exile, Kjell—'

'I deserved nothing less,' he replied honestly. It had hurt him—devastated him—not to be able to see his parents. To know that he'd lost his father's respect. That day had been matched only by losing Freya. Ever since that day he'd done what he'd needed to. He could do his job, and do it well. He could laugh with his military brotherhood and he could live in whatever country he was sent to next. But being cut from the very things that made him feel connected to his past, to his family, his people... Freya—it was a phantom pain that he'd only realised when he'd returned. The familiarity that always rolled over him like a tsunami for those hours had made him realise just how *un*familiar the rest of his life was. Just how much had been taken from him.

But he'd also known that he deserved punishment for what he'd done. He'd broken a moral code in lying to her about his true identity but, worse, by giving in to the temptation of her he'd put her safety at risk. And that was untenable.

'No one deserves that, Kjell. Certainly not for this long. We were kids, we didn't know better.'

Everything in him wanted to roar in denial. He might have been young, but he'd known exactly what he was doing. Yes, he knew that lying was wrong, but Christ, he'd… his mind snapped, his teeth biting together, cutting off the train of thought before he could finish it.

His free hand clenched and he watched her eyes flick down to it and back up to him. Forcing himself under control, he offered the apology she'd not wanted to hear all those years ago.

'I'm sorry too,' he said, unable to stop his hand rising or his thumb sweeping gently across her jawline. 'I should have told you.'

'Why didn't you?'

'Because I wanted you more than I could stand,' he said, before letting her go and walking away.

# CHAPTER FIVE

FREYA STOOD IN the boot room for long, long minutes after he'd left. Blinking slowly while replaying his words on a loop.

*I wanted you more than I could stand.*

Her pulse thundered in her chest as her mind assaulted her heart with images from their time together. Kisses, touches, laughter, love… The look in his eyes he would get sometimes when she caught him unawares. A kind of regretful longing. She'd not wondered at the time what had been on his mind, because she'd felt the same thing. Neither had been willing to admit that what they shared had an expiry date. Because even if he had told her the truth and even if they had spoken about it, the fact that she was a princess meant theirs was a future that could never have been.

In her hurt and anger, it had been easier for her to blame Kjell for the heartache than face the truth: that her status and her family would never have allowed him to become her consort. The thought of her father changing the legislation for her was as laughable as it was inconceivable.

And it was still in place, the decree that the consort for the first two legitimate heirs to the throne must have a title. It had been intended to protect the sanctity of the royal bloodline during a period when such things had to be unquestionable. None of her Svardian ancestors had needed or wanted to challenge the Royal Marriage Act since.

But if Freya was stepping down, then she would no longer be bound by that law.

Her heart raced as quickly as her mind.

*I wanted you more than I could stand.*

Blindly stripping off her coat and boots, she walked into the cabin, her insides trembling, unsure of what to expect.

Kjell was kneeling by the wood burner, feeding a log into the fire. He beckoned her over when he saw her, his gaze blank of the devastating emotional kick that he'd last looked at her with. She went to him, remembering this part of Kjell. His ability to shut down, switch tack, compartmentalise. It was probably what made him such a good soldier. She would get nothing further from him. Not now, anyway.

'So,' he said, his tone authoritative, 'if that happens again, you need to know how to start a fire.'

An hour later, and Freya was still watching the flames of the fire she'd help to build. Kjell was in the kitchen and the smells were making her stomach growl. She'd not eaten since the hastily grabbed bowl of cereal she'd had that morning, and she'd missed a meal last night. She could get a little like that. Henna always had snacks and protein bars in her bag, sneaking them to her in between appointments. Usually, every single minute of her day was planned out with precision, but here there was nothing to distract her thoughts from veering between the past and an unknown future.

But this was her second day here and she'd not thought

once about the 'next' meeting, or checking the daily schedule to ensure she knew everyone's names, faces and enough about their lives to make the connections that were so important to her and to the success of her charities.

She inhaled, low and slow. The kind of peace that was found here… She understood why Kjell had chosen this as his home. But it was a sad sort of peace as she recognised that while she might have this calm in her future, it hurt to know that she would be saying goodbye to all the good she could do as a royal.

And, rather than dwell on it, she allowed herself to be hypnotised into an aching sort of restfulness by the falling snow. The wind was beginning to slow—the eddies and currents in the flakes less frantic, more graceful and she couldn't help but wonder what the windows revealed in the summer. Where, instead of shades of grey, the landscape would be awash with greens and browns, blues and yellows. To be able to sit here and watch the seasons change…

She heard a pan drop onto the stovetop and another Swedish curse. Peering around to the kitchen area, she saw Kjell shake his hand, angrily staring down at the offending cooking equipment.

'Can I help?' she asked as he rolled his shoulders back, the muscles rippling beneath the fine thermal jumper that pressed as close to his skin as she wanted to.

'Could you set the table?'

It was such a domestic moment it struck right to her heart. For a second she was frozen in place, remembering how they'd once laughed in her dorm room at university the first time Freya had ever set a table. He'd always had her doing things that were unfamiliar to her, from the smallest to the greatest. He'd always encouraged her. Another clatter came from the kitchen, thrusting her into action. As she went to the shelves that held stacked plates, glasses, mugs and cutlery, she couldn't help but ask, 'You still swear in Swedish?'

When she looked up she caught his gaze and something passed across his eyes.

'My father is Swedish,' he said, turning back to the large pan on the stovetop.

Then she remembered. 'Oh, I thought that was...' She trailed off, wanting to bite out her own tongue.

'Not a lie, Princess,' he said, his tone brutally bland.

She hated the twist of shame that unfurled at her implied accusation. She wanted it gone. This tension, this awkwardness. She wanted the ease that they'd shared all those years ago.

'My father is Swedish but moved to Svardia to be with my mother when they married,' he said, as if presenting the information as a peace offering.

'He gave up everything to be with her?' she asked, surprised. 'Why?'

'He loved her. And her job is...important.'

'What does she do?' Freya asked, beginning to ease into the back and forth of the interaction.

There was a pause and when she looked up his back was to her, his hands pressed against the sideboard. 'She's the Principal Private Secretary of the Royal Household.'

Freya nearly dropped the plate she was holding. 'Anita Bergqvist? Your mother is—?'

'Yes.'

'Kjell!'

'What?'

'I see your mother almost on a daily basis!' she cried,

hating the feeling of pins and needles creeping across her skin, humiliation and guilt vying to win out.

'And?'

'And doesn't she blame me for separating her from her son?'

'I'd imagine she blames her son for making a monumental mistake and getting himself exiled,' he ground out, stalking towards the table with two bowls in his hand. 'The bread is on the side, there's butter in the cool box under the sink by the window.'

*A monumental mistake.*

If he only knew. Thinking of her diagnosis, thinking of the future she would now have, he'd had a lucky escape and just didn't know it. He'd always been interested in her siblings, not because of their titles but because of their relationship. The bond, as loving and frustrated and downright painful as it was sometimes. She'd told him how much her brother's retreat had hurt her, confessed that she had spoiled their sister sometimes but hadn't been able to help it. Kjell had relished every part of that because he'd relished *family.* By the time she returned to the table she thought she'd gathered herself, but the assessing gaze he sent her way made her think again. He'd always been able to do that. See the truth of her.

After placing the bread and butter on the table, she scooped up some papers and felt Kjell flinch as she placed them at the far end. Glancing down at the top of the pile, she saw an unfilled After Action Report with a due date of a week ago and felt her pulse leap.

Retreating behind a mask of innocence, she sat down and helped herself to dinner, while her mind tripped and turned over the report and Kjell's reaction. It *had* to be connected to the medal. But AARs were vital military assessments, to let one slide past the due date was...

*wrong.* It just didn't fit with the by-the-book excellence that would have been required for Kjell to reach Lieutenant Colonel in such a short time.

To cover her thoughts, she returned to Anita. 'Your mother is wonderful,' she said, her tone infused with genuine warmth.

Kjell's gaze hunted her features for any sign of a reaction to the AAR. The realisation that she might connect it to the medal had overridden the wave of anger and shame he'd felt when he caught sight of it; the report was a rope around his neck tying him to things he needed to be free of. But Freya had shown no sign of recognising the documents or their importance and when she'd returned the conversation to his mother the honesty in her tone was clear.

'She is,' he said truthfully. Anita Bergqvist was the best of them all. He knew it and his father knew it. She loved everyone unconditionally and there was not a malicious or mean bone in her body. How his taciturn father had ended up with a wife like that Kjell would never know. His mother was—as Freya had said—wonderful. She was also incredibly good at her job and even though Brynjar had been a military man when they'd met he'd understood in his own way that her role was hierarchically above his and his complete and utter respect for chain of command made the choice to leave his career and country behind for Svardia an easy one. That and the fact that his father loved his mother completely. Kjell just wasn't sure Brynjar felt the same way about his son.

'Please don't tell me your father works in the palace too.'

He shook his head, swallowing a mouthful of the

stew before replying, 'Mechanical engineer for an aero-space company.'

'How did Anita meet an aerospace engineer?' Her tone utterly mystified.

'They met before, when my father was still in Swe-den.'

'What did he do?' she asked as she buttered a thick slice of bread.

'He was an Överste in the Swedish Army.'

Her knife paused mid-swipe, and he felt her eyes on him. Assessing. Probing. Looking for more. Looking deeper.

'Following in his footsteps?'

Following the only thing his father had ever given him to cling onto. While his mother was all emotion, her love given freely with a kiss, a hug, an unconscious but ever-present touch, his father was the complete op-posite. Monosyllabic and contained to the point where every gesture was small, efficient and practical, he rarely displayed affection or emotion and often retreated to his workshop to tinker with broken bits of machinery at even the mere hint of it.

When he'd told his father that he wanted to join the army it had been the first time he'd seen something like pride in his eyes. His father had placed a hand on his shoulder and Kjell had felt as if his heart might burst. But the day he'd told his father what had happened with Freya, Kjell believed he'd felt that thin fragile thread be-tween them break and it had hurt him more than Kjell could ever have imagined.

'Something like that,' he said, finally answering Freya's question, wanting to shift and twist away from the memories her questions conjured. 'How was Marit? After the accident?' He knew that she was okay, he'd not been living under a rock for the last eight years. But he knew how trauma could change a person.

'Worse, if you can believe it.'

Kjell couldn't help but smile. Freya had always been worried about her younger sister's tearaway tendencies.

'There we all were, terrified that she might not actually survive, and the first thing she said when she opened her eyes? *Can I go again?*'

Kjell saw past the mock frustration in her tone, knowing the depths of her love for her sister. With essentially what had amounted to absentee parents, Freya had easily and willingly slipped into that nurturing role, given the age gap between the two sisters. It had been a precariously balanced relationship, but one utterly filled with love.

'She never seemed the type to buckle down to royal duties,' he said, instantly stilling the moment he saw her tense—as if what he'd just said had hurt her in some way.

It was as if they were playing a game. On the surface were innocent questions, two old friends just catching up. Beneath that, though, was a darker, more dangerous current: one that tested and pushed at old wounds and new hurts.

'No,' she replied. 'But what about you? You've been with the UN? All this time?'

The swift turn in direction Freya executed proved his point. Mentally he applauded, while almost feeling sorry for her. Because he wasn't going to leave this table without discovering what it was she was hiding, and what it had to do with that damn medal.

Somewhere deep down a part of his soul cried foul, cursed him for using her vulnerability to avoid Enzo. To avoid the AAR. To avoid why he'd come out to Dalarna four months ago and not returned to active duty like the good soldier he was. But he'd spent a long time stifling that voice and Kjell only felt it as a gentle nudge on his conscience now. One that was easily ignored.

'Yes,' he answered her question, while working out how to turn the conversation around.

'Where were you stationed?'

'All over.' He shrugged, his mind on—

'Kjell.'

He pulled up mentally. She'd always done that. No one else ever knew when he split his focus between two different things, but she had. Every time.

'The UN has peacekeeping missions across the world,' he answered, deciding to play along for the moment. 'I've been to the Philippines for disaster relief, ceasefire observations in India and Pakistan, Kosovo for human rights, I spent a secondment with UNTSO in the Middle East.'

'Truce Supervision?'

He nodded, not surprised that she knew the different units and their roles. She might have cut him from her life and never looked back, but he'd not done the same. Some might have called it self-flagellation. Enzo had called it stalking. His body tensed, braced against a sudden wave of shocking grief.

'Kjell—'

'It's nothing, he said, interrupting her before she could ask if he was okay. She saw too much. She always had done.

He got up from the table, reaching for her bowl before he'd even asked the question. 'You done?'

Freya wasn't stupid. She knew that something terrible had happened and that it was wrapped up in the AAR and the medal. She could have throttled Aleksander:

sending her here, knowing that she would do whatever it took to make Kjell accept the medal because she had no other choice was beyond cruel.

The ferocity of the silence Kjell pulled about him was, ironically, the most violent she'd ever seen him. The fight in him at that moment was real and vicious. And while knowing what had happened might make it easier for her to get him to take the medal, it was no longer self-interest that drove her. She couldn't see him hurt and not want to help. Her heart twisted to see him in such pain.

'Why won't you accept the medal?' The words were out of her mouth before she could stop them, but she would not call them back.

He turned from the sink and leaned back against it. 'Why is it so important to you?'

She stilled, trying not to betray herself. 'It's not.'

'Oh, Freya,' he said, all mock disappointment as he dried his hands on a towel. 'And there I was thinking that there were no more lies between us.' All that was missing was a tut-tut.

'I don't know what you mean,' she evaded, standing up from the bench, suddenly needing to get away from eyes that saw her too clearly, from a tone that needled her too much and a game she suddenly wasn't sure she wanted to play.

'You know *exactly* what I mean,' he said, stalking towards her, drawing close enough to trap her between the bench and the table, using his powerful shoulders to crowd her. He'd gone on the attack in the space of a heartbeat and she'd not been prepared. 'That little hint of desperation you get in your tone when you ask about the medal? The shadows shimmering behind your eyes…?'

She felt his gaze flick to the fluttering pulse beneath her jawline, its touch a physical thing. She knew the arrogant male smirk that pulled at his lips was a mask, even as her core muscles tightened. And lower. A pulse flared to life between her legs and she pressed her thighs together, trying to make it stop.

Not once had he moved his gaze from hers, but she knew he'd caught the movement, saw it in the flare of his irises, the heat that flushed his cheeks, matched only by that of her own. Flames licked up her spine and he'd not even touched her. Her breath caught and she was as unable to look away as she was to move. It was a sensual standoff, neither willing to back down or push them over the edge.

Skin humming and pulse throbbing, she hated that he'd done this to her. He was using her own body against her, to distract her from things he didn't want to answer, and somehow *she* was the one who couldn't escape.

Eight years ago, she had pursued him. Oh, she was under no illusions, it had been clumsy and even slightly awkward, but there had been a playfulness about it, a gentle innocence. Kjell's restraint then had required her to claim him for herself. But this? This power, this driving force Kjell had about him now...

Arousal built and built and built, flames pressing against the inside of her skin, wanting out, wanting Kjell. A fist was slowly tightening in her chest, squeezing her heart, her pulse flickering in its grasp. She couldn't not stare at his lips—the smirk having dropped ever so slightly from them, as if he too was caught in the vortex of their mutual desire. She bit her lip, hoping the sharp sting would cut through the sensual haze clouding her mind.

His gaze snapped to where her teeth pressed against the soft flesh and her breath shuddered in her chest. Fisting her hands, crescent imprints marred her palms as she fought not to reach for his shoulders, to mould them beneath her fingertips, to mark them with her nails...

She was shocked by the force of her want. Eight years had built fantasies and cravings she had never had the courage to consider all those years ago. Desires she was sure he could read in her eyes. Needs she felt pouring from her very soul.

They were barely an inch apart, his lips close enough to hers that if she moved even an inch... She closed her eyes in an act of surrender, of desperation, because she couldn't take it any more. The sensual tension pulling at her skin, her heart, her soul was too much to bear. He could have it. He could have it all.

But when the unspoken promise of his kiss never came, she only just managed to hold back the sob that racked her heart as much as her lungs. Shame, rejection, hurt, embarrassment swirled in a stomach already roiling from want. When she lifted her eyes to his, his cheeks were slashed with fury not need, his eyes spitting white sparks of indignation.

Kjell was trembling with rage. Seconds ago he'd felt a desire so intense, so powerful he'd never *ever* felt its like. But then she'd closed her eyes in submission and it had sliced through his arousal like the sharpest blade. She had sacrificed her agency in the one moment it would have meant the most, in the one moment they could have been *equals*.

He felt fury bleed into his gaze and prised his jaw loose enough to speak. 'I would never force a woman against her will.' His words were hoarse, as if he'd howled like the wolves that stalked the nearby woods.

'But I—'

He'd already seen the truth of it when she'd opened her eyes, and still she tried to evade him.

'What was that?' he demanded. 'Surrender?'

She turned away, shielding her eyes from his penetrating gaze, guilt written in red slashes on her cheeks. He shook his head in disgust. The tension and secrets between them were like an oil slick that turned his stomach.

Nothing felt solid any more. Ever since Enzo's death four months ago. As if he were still suffering from concussion, a dizziness that caused a slight delay, and Freya was only making it worse. More than just a friend, Enzo had been Kjell's tether. In a life that had so few constants, their friendship had been a bond that surpassed that of blood. To have that so cruelly taken from him had left him reeling in a way that he'd only ever felt once before. The night Freya had said she never wanted to see him again.

There was only one thing in that moment that would ground him, that he could grasp that would be real. He pressed forward, backing her up against the table without even having to touch her. 'Why do you need me to take the medal?' he said, the quietness of his words betraying the brutal demand in them.

'Aleksander needs—'

'Why do *you* need it?'

Freya paled and he wondered if she really thought he was so stupid not to have figured out that she had a stake in this. In the back of his mind a warning sounded. A dutiful soldier wouldn't push, wouldn't question. But maybe he was finally done being the dutiful soldier after all it had cost him over the years.

Enzo, home.

*Her.*

He drank in the sight of arousal shimmering beneath

the secrets in Freya's eyes like a man dying of thirst. Her fingers gripped the table behind her, holding on or holding back, he couldn't tell. Didn't want to any more. His body inhaled the scent of her, warm and sweet on the air compressed between them, just as her head rocked back, exposing the long length of her neck. Their breaths fast and furious with need and desire.

He'd never stopped wanting her. It had always been there, in the back of his mind like a second heartbeat, just a millisecond out of sync. A shadow beat, constant and living, deep within him.

That was why there had never been anyone else. Ever. It had only been her.

Rage and fury burned at the edges of his desire, inflaming his want and feeding his need and he hovered on the brink. But even if he gave into a temptation that could drive him beyond madness, even if they indulged in every whim he'd seen flash across her amber gaze— she was still a princess and he was just a soldier. She had always been out of his reach. As a young man he'd not realised what that meant, but the events of the last eight years had taught him well. So he marshalled his body with a ruthlessness that bordered on brutal and returned his gaze to hers.

As if sensing the shift in his focus, she averted her gaze, evidently more comfortable with her attraction to him than the secret she kept from him. And, like the trained hunter he was, he followed the trail of her deception.

'Why do you need me to take the medal, Freya?'

'I'm renouncing my royal title. And Aleksander will only let me go if you accept the medal.'

# CHAPTER SIX

*THWACK.*

Kjell spun, kicking out at the punchbag hanging from the ceiling of the outbuilding. Despite the sub-zero temperature and the howling wind pounding the insulated walls, sweat dripped from his body. Squaring off against the sand-filled heavy bag, he threw his fists in a punishing combination ending—again—with another rounded kick, before landing comfortably on his feet.

*I'm renouncing my royal title.*

'Why?' he'd demanded, truly shocked for the first time since she'd turned up on his doorstep. She loved being a royal. She always had. You didn't have to know her to see that every time she was caught by a photographer, interviewed or overseas on a diplomatic visit, public service made her *shine*. She did her duty with the kind of grace that was innate, natural and genuine. Everyone commented on it, internationally and at home, and of all the royals Svardia's people would choose her again and again.

'It's none of your business.'

*Thwack.*

Her tone had been as cold as the icicles forming on the solar panels on the roof—and just as deadly to his peace of mind.

'It is when it's conditional on me accepting a medal I don't want,' he'd growled. 'Don't bother asking me again until you're ready to tell me what's really going on.'

*Thwack. Thwack.*

She'd stood there and stared him down until he'd finally stepped back to let her leave or risk becoming the kind of monster he'd claimed not to be. She'd slipped past him and the last thing he'd heard from her was the door to the bedroom closing behind her.

His fists were a blur, his knuckles long since numb beneath the wrap he'd wound around his fingers, palm and wrist. Leaning in to add an elbow to the combination, he felt sweat flick from his skin as he stepped back and planted his non-load-bearing foot into the centre of the bag, sending it high into the air, before striking it again on the backswing.

Ignoring the unfamiliar tremble in his arms, he cycled through the routine, sweat shining his skin and his pulse tripping.

*She's not stupid,* he heard Enzo observe in his mind.

No, Kjell thought. She wasn't. The Italian soldier would have liked Freya. A lot. Or he would have liked who she'd been at university. The years in between had made her...sharper. Less soft. Less giving. But no less stubborn. Dropping to the floor into a plank, he counted down from sixty.

*'You have no sense when it comes to that woman,'* Enzo said through his laughter.

*Kjell smiled back as his team took some R&R in Bosnia. Eight of them, five men, three women, all of similar rank, sat round the table, drinking beer from ice-cold bottles under the umbrellas of the cobbled street café. War stories of the romantic kind were being shared be-*

*cause the real kind didn't really bear thinking about. Every single man and woman there had been shot at, near exploding IEDs, and had seen enough human misery to make even the hardest heart weep. And every single person at that table was staring at him as if he'd grown a second head.*

*'Really? Princess Freya of Svardia?' Suzu Kuroki asked.*

*Kjell considered it a feat to surprise the cool, calm intelligence officer from Japan.*

*Jean-Michel, a jarhead from France, slapped the table and laughed. 'No way, mon ami, no way!'*

*This was what he liked most about the UN secondments. It didn't matter whether a team had been together three days or three months, there was an understanding, a bond—a family. What was shared on downtime stayed on downtime, and Kjell never begrudged Enzo pulling out Freya to taunt him. He only ever did it when a team needed to let off steam, or just to laugh.*

*Sometimes Kjell would rip into Enzo about the beautiful Italian wife he'd left behind to bring up their two adorable children, dark-haired and dark-eyed, just like their father. Because there were times when they had to laugh or they'd go mad.*

*'You'll go to your grave with blue balls, my friend,' Enzo teased.*

Kjell had promised to kill him for that.

Only he'd not had to.

On another continent, six months later, someone else had got there first.

Snowflakes were hurled on the raging wind, as helpless as confetti, their jagged trajectory as chaotic as it was fleeting. Freya sat in a nest of throws on the sofa tracing flake after flake, heart bruised and mind numb.

*I'm renouncing my royal title.*

She'd told him. She'd said the words. And the world hadn't ended.

It should have been a relief—a release, the confession that set her free. But, instead, it was the moment she'd realised the horrifying truth of it all: that this wasn't even the hardest part.

Freya thought of the calm she'd consciously wrapped herself in throughout the invasive tests and check-ups, the different hormone medications to thicken the womb lining. She had borne the mood swings, sweats and the horrifying feeling that her body wasn't her own with a serenity that befitted the perfect princess. She had allowed them to test her as if she were a faulty machine.

And when she'd overheard the doctor giving his final diagnosis to her *brother,* not her, as if her womb was more important to the throne than her as a person, as a woman, as a little girl who had always dreamed of having her own family...she'd clenched her jaw and said nothing. Because she understood that a king needed to know anything that affected the lineage. Because she knew—had always known—that her duty was first and foremost to that throne. Just like the doctor, just like her brother. And all three had known that the best way for her to do her duty was to step down, even if Aleksander still fought her on it.

Throughout it all, she'd believed that the hardest point would be renouncing her title. The sacrifice she would make to ensure that Aleksander's rule wasn't questioned or tainted by the fallout. Yes, there would be questions, but between Henna and the palace's communications team they would come up with a reasonable out. An out that would have them focused on her, not the fertility of their King or their younger sister. An out that wouldn't jeopardise all the good that her siblings could do for Svardia. Freya would do *anything* to make that possible.

But last night, when she'd finally revealed her intention to Kjell, she'd truly realised that facing the press, stepping down, wouldn't be the hardest part. It was what would happen *after*. After the furore died down, after the practicalities had been dealt with. It would be in a year, maybe two, when there was nothing left to fight, when there was no one around and she had to finally face the fact that her body was broken and she'd never have what she'd always wanted to have.

The hurt in her heart made her selfishly want to reach out to Kjell for comfort. A comfort that, no matter the years of distance, the pains of the past, she still felt was possible between them. The familiarity of him, even in spite of the changes, of the man he had become, a hope in her soul. But the tension between them was a reality she couldn't ignore. And his demand one she couldn't deny.

*Don't bother asking me again until you're ready to tell me what's really going on.*

She knew him well enough to know that he was serious. He wouldn't settle for anything less than the truth now. She hated that she would have to tell him. And it was so much easier to hold onto that anger, the fury at the injustice of it all, after everything that she had sacrificed, all the good she had done, it raged in her heart.

A rage that demanded to be heard. It scratched along her skin and clawed at her chest. She wanted to howl at the moon, it was so unfair. It was so horribly unfair. A strange, determined fury fizzed in her veins, unpleasant but invigorating. It pushed away the numbness and made fissures in the serene mask she had made of her features. It broke and shattered the façade into a thousand pieces.

And now, staring at the fading shadows bleeding across the snow, she knew only that the seal on her anger had finally broken. And it was all coming out. The pain, the hurt, the shame, the anger, the fury.

*Don't bother asking me again until you're ready to tell me what's really going on.*

She flicked the tears away from her cheeks as she thrust herself into her own clothes, now dry in the boot room. Her shaking fingers were barely able to tie the laces of her boots, and she just remembered to grab a scarf as she launched from the cabin towards the outbuilding where she knew Kjell was.

Wind battered her, snow pelted her, but *she* was the wild one here. She felt the elements rise up within her to match the fury of the storm raging around her. Through the swirls and currents of the snow, she could make out the door to the outbuilding and was still too angry, too untethered to feel anything other than grim determination to confront the man behind the door.

Kjell spun round when the door flew open, his pulse still pounding in his ears from the brutal workout. Freya stormed into the outbuilding, slamming the door shut behind her, as angry as he'd ever seen her.

'You want to know why I need to step down?' she shouted at him. She looked incandescent and devastatingly gorgeous with it.

'Yes!' he yelled back, turning to face the fury coming towards him full-on. He welcomed it, the anger, the challenge—but if he'd thought it would cut through the desire he felt for her, he had been very wrong. Instead, it only inflamed his need. Too much had been kept locked away for too long. Something had to give.

She came to within kissing distance, their breaths clashing in an unsustainable rhythm. She looked at him, shaking her head as if he was wrong, as if she knew that he didn't really want to know.

It was the first inkling he had that something was very, very wrong. This was worse than the night of Marit's accident, but he honestly couldn't imagine what it could be. Freya was shaking with rage and he wanted it unleashed. He'd take every single blow, every strike she could give him if it meant release from whatever terrible hurt held her in its grasp.

'I can't have children.'

His mind flatlined. There was a high-pitched whine in his ears and no thoughts in his mind. It was the last thing he'd ever expected her to say.

A knife ripped through his heart for her. His eyes widened in shock, his mouth jammed shut in the next heartbeat, to prevent pointless words from refuting her statement. This woman—Freya—she had been made to be a mother. Everything in her nurtured, cherished, encouraged. She... He clenched his teeth together. Words of comfort streamed through his mind and he knew that none of them would help her in that moment.

'Okay,' he said.

'Didn't you hear me?' she demanded.

He nodded, the act ripping through the tension cording his neck muscles and shoulders. 'Okay,' he said again. There were so many words pressing against his heart and lips, but he wouldn't let them out. Couldn't. It wasn't about him, words that would make *him* feel better by appeasing *her* hurt.

'I said I can't have children, Kjell. I can't produce the

heirs to the throne. The family's future is uncertain until Aleksander has children. And Marit—'

'Stop it,' he ordered, hating the excuses and distractions she was covering her pain with. Her pretty mouth snapped shut and his heart broke a little more.

'Try again,' he growled, angry with her but most definitely angry with himself. He should never have pushed her. He didn't have that right. He should have known better.

'Try what, Kjell? You want me to parade my hurt-about for your amusement?'

'Freya, you know me. You know that's not what this is. You know *me*. So don't you dare give me the party line. Tell me where it hurts. Where it *really* hurts,' he said with a desperation in his eyes he knew she could see. He would never be able to take that pain away from her, but he would damn well die trying.

The confusion in her haunted amber eyes made him curse. Had no one asked her?

'Everywhere,' she whispered helplessly as tears brimmed in her eyes.

He couldn't protect her from this. It was a horrifying, stark realisation that gutted him to his core. He might have been a soldier for most of his life, but he never had and never would stop guarding her.

He reached up to cup her face, his thumb delicately sweeping to catch the tear that had tumbled over the edge. She leaned into his palm, her closing eyes sending more tears, too many for him to catch, down her cheeks.

He shut off the part of his mind that fixed, that planned, that created counter-moves and attacks. It wasn't time for thoughts of surrogacy, adoption, insisting that she didn't need to renounce her royal title or duties. If Kjell was right, then he'd imagine her brother would have tried that. No. This moment, right now, was about Freya.

He brought her to his chest, his hand gently tangling in her hair, his body absorbing shudder after shudder, but sending out heat to warm the chill of her skin, of her body—not from her clothes. It was a cold that went bone-deep. It was one he knew well. Shock. Mindless shock.

'Tell me,' he commanded, his voice barely a whisper. But he knew that she'd heard, that she'd understood.

'I fear that…that I'm not a woman any more.'

If he'd thought his heart had hurt before, it was decimated by the pain and devastation in that confession. A curse ripped through him and he drew her away from him gently, just so that he could see her eyes. Eyes that were full of evasion, shame and hurt. The torture he saw there would have broken even the strongest man and it had his soul raging.

Forcing his tone to gentle and his hold to soften, he pressed his forehead to hers. 'Yes, you are.' His words were low, soft and a promise he hoped she could feel the truth of.

'I don't know if I believe that any more.'

'What do you need to believe again?' he asked. 'What do you need?'

*I don't know.*

The unspoken answer ate at him, tearing him up. But as he searched her face for signs of what he could possibly give her, he saw the change in her eyes. Felt it like a primitive knowledge deep within him, an elemental reaction to her that had always been there.

As if for the first time, he realised how close they were. He could see the gold flecks in her amber eyes sparking and flashing, the blood began to rise through the paleness of her skin to slash her cheekbones in pink.

Just the sight of it ignited his arousal and he tried to leash it, forcing it back nearly broke him but now wasn't the time. Freya needed him to be more than the horny youth he was reverting to. His hands released their hold on her and he stepped back to try to get himself back under control. She deserved better.

Her amber eyes turned molten and he fisted his hands to stop himself from reaching for her.

'Ask me again.' Her words fell between them—his heart balanced on a knife-edge. He wasn't a fool. He knew her want as well as he knew his own.

*Don't do it.* She deserved better. So much better than him.

'Kjell?'

He couldn't deny her. He had never been able to and he never would.

'What do you need?' His voice ragged with a desire unquenched in eight years.

'You.'

He clenched his teeth, knowing that it was madness but more than willing to lose himself to such a delicious insanity.

'Then take what you need,' he growled. 'Take me.'

The temptation in her eyes inflamed his need, but still she held back.

'If this is about pity—'

'Pity?' he echoed, taking her hand and pressing it against the length of his arousal, so eager for her touch it jumped beneath the heat of her palm. 'Does that feel like pity to you?'

Freya shook her head, shocked to silence by the feel of him in her hand. Wicked heat crept up her spine, licking and laving its way across her skin. A desperate need built and stretched, filling her so completely there was no thought of anything else.

*Take what you need.*

Could she? Could she lose herself in him?

No. She could never use him like that, just as he hadn't been able to consider anything but willing participation the night before. But neither of those things were happening now. She might not want to name it, not be ready to acknowledge the ties weaving between and around them, but it was definitely more than a distraction.

He had offered her solace. A solace that required trust. And she knew in that moment that she trusted Kjell more than anyone else in the world, no matter what had happened in the past.

Her fingers flexed around the deliciously familiar shape in her hand. Because, no matter what she'd told herself during the waking hours, no matter how much she thought she'd removed Kjell from her life, her night-time fantasies had always betrayed the truth. She had never forgotten him. *Any* of him.

She felt him tense against the wave of need that rippled through his body. His thigh muscles braced against an instinctive desire to move towards her.

'Freya.' Her name on his lips was a prayer, a curse, a warning she paid absolutely no heed to. Instead, it was one she welcomed. He had offered himself to her but, like him, she wasn't interested in anything less than willing participation.

She gripped him through the soft material of his workout joggers, the heat of him flooding into her skin even through the material, her thighs clenching at the thought of him entering her, sliding deep into her welcoming heat, a thought made even more sensually torturous by the knowledge of the pleasure she knew he could bring.

His hands fisted, knuckles white, and she knew she was pushing him towards a line in the sand. He was only doing this for her. But she didn't want to be the pyre on which he threw himself. They had both sacrificed enough. And the only way she knew to bring him into this was to push. And push and push. If they were going to break, then it would be the most exquisite way to shatter.

She raised up on her tiptoes and pressed an open-mouthed kiss against his firm lips. Her chest pressed against his, the stiff peaks of her nipples indulging in the delicious friction of her jumper and his T-shirt. Her tongue laved against the thick, full bottom lip and nipped gently at it until his mouth opened for her. But, instead of sweeping into his mouth, just as she sensed his capitulation, she drew back, her body, her soul hating her for it.

'Why are you teasing me?' he whispered, her heart nearly crippled by the vulnerability of his question.

She took a breath, hoping to hell that her next words were rally rather than retreat.

'Because I want *you.* Not the dutiful soldier.'

Just like that the heat in his eyes flamed out and she thought she'd lost him. Until he pulsed in her palm and she gasped. He gave her one more second to luxuriate in the feel of him, the strength of his need *for her,* and then batted her hand away, stalking forward and forcing her to step back. Again and again until she was pressed up against the work bench that ran along the edge of the room.

This predatory male was so different from the younger Kjell she had known, but absolutely no less dangerous to her senses. This. *This* was what she'd wanted. What she'd seen glimpses of in the last few days. This was what made her feel like a woman.

Her heart pounded in her throat as if it wanted to leave her body and meld with Kjell's. He pinned her with a lethal focus that was nothing short of an adrenaline injection straight to her heart. Her skin was on fire from the layers and layers of outdoor clothing that felt constricting to the point of painful.

Their breaths comingling in the narrow space between them, he reached up to the scarf and slowly slid it from around her neck. She gripped the bench behind her, holding herself up, holding herself *back*.

He cocked his head to one side as if daring her to stop him.

She didn't. She couldn't.

His gaze dropped to her lips and she bit down instinctively, enthralled when she saw his swift inhalation. One final step brought his chest against hers, her breasts finding purchase against his body and delighting in the friction. Eyes still on her lips, his hands gripped the heavy-duty material of her borrowed jacket, as if torn between using it to pull her to him or pushing it from her body.

And then, finally, as if giving up the fight, his head bent to hers and he feasted on her lips. Her heart soared and her soul cried out for more as she opened to his possession, welcomed it, needed it. His lips demanded it all. This kiss was like nothing they'd ever shared before; it was a rending of the past, the present and the future all in one.

Pulling back from the kiss, he looked as shocked as she felt. Her breath shook in her lungs. 'I thought I was supposed to take what I needed,' she said, her voice trembling with desire, a shiver of want rippling down her spine and sheening her skin with need.

'You were taking too damn long—' his words short

and sharp '—I'm just going to have to give you what you need.'

Her breath whooshed from her lungs as he scooped her up as if she weighed nothing, spun and walked them back over to the opposite side of the room.

'I should take you back to the cabin and strip you bare before the fire and the wildness of the woods,' he said, claiming her lips with more punishing kisses. 'But I can't wait that long.'

'Wait for what?' she asked hazily, her gaze heavy-lidded with desire.

'A taste of you,' he said, laying her carefully on the soft workout matting as if completely lost in his need to satiate a craving he'd had for years. He pushed the jacket from her shoulders and, instead of coming back to kiss her, he reached for the band of her leggings. She instinctively lifted up, allowing him to sweep them over her backside and down, just as she realised his intention.

Her heart thundered in her chest as he pulled her panties halfway down her thighs, a self-consciousness building in her until...

Until she saw the way Kjell looked at her.

Stark desire had slashed his cheeks red, his arctic blue eyes on fire. He might not have moved a muscle, sitting back on his haunches, his eyes raking over every inch of exposed flesh, but there was nothing still about him. The energy, the need—for her—raging beneath his skin was electric. She had done that to him. And he let her see it. He'd opened himself up to her to show her the effect she had on him.

A whimper rose in her that had nothing to do with attraction and everything to do with a hurt beginning to heal. But the sound cut through whatever held Kjell back and, leaning back, he lifted her thighs apart, possessively positioning himself between them.

'Kjell,' she whispered.

'Changed your mind, Princess?' he taunted, wickedness in his gaze.

'Give me what I need,' she demanded hotly and the look in his eyes changed to something like pride.

'Yes, ma'am.'

# CHAPTER SEVEN

FREYA'S LEGS TREMBLED so much on the walk back to the cabin, Kjell needed to scoop her up and carry her to the boot room. At least that was what he told himself, as if he didn't know that he couldn't keep his hands off her, even for that short walk.

She'd orgasmed on his tongue, around his fingers, and he'd never felt anything more exquisite in his life. The sweet taste of her hadn't been enough. *More.* He wanted more.

*Insatiable*, she'd said—the laughter in her voice true music to his ears.

He couldn't disagree. But he'd not lied when he'd told her that he wanted her naked in front of the fire in the cabin. He refused to make love to her there in the outbuilding on his exercise mat. Wasn't ruling it out later on, but that wasn't how he intended their first time in eight years to be. Because there was no fighting it any more. The line had been obliterated and he had no intention of redrawing it.

But that didn't mean they didn't have to talk first.

He watched her unlace her boots, the flush of desire still bright on her cheeks, and when she looked up, grazing her gaze against his, the amber in her eyes glowed gold and he had to stop himself from reaching for her.

Roughly pulling at his outer layers, he watched her sweep into the cabin with a very feminine swish to her hips. It was only when he was alone that he allowed the sensual haze to dissipate enough to try to gather his thoughts.

In his mind he was back on the university campus green. Their studies had been interrupted by a frisbee that had scraped the top of Freya's head. The parent of the child had taken one look at her, eyes wide, offering profuse apologies.

It had taken Freya at least five minutes and a selfie to assure him that they weren't all going to end up in prison.

*'That was kind of you,'* he noted with a smile.

*'Not at all. I'm earning good karma.'*

*'What for?'* he asked on a laugh.

*'For my children. They're going to terrorise the palace. I'll make sure of it,'* she said with such glee he felt it in his heart.

*'Children?'* His heart thudded in his chest—painful, slow, heavy beats. Because they wouldn't be his. Couldn't be.

*'Three.'*

She almost shone...until clouds formed in her eyes.

*'And none of them will be a spare.'*

Back in the boot room, back in the present, Kjell clenched his jaw, his heart once again aching for the children that Freya felt she'd never now have. But he couldn't help but wonder if she was blinkered, as if those around her so focused on bloodlines and lineage had clouded what *could* be. And it was a conversation they needed to have before she went too far to take it back.

He pushed into the cabin to find her staring at the

stunning view. She was framed by falling snow, snow-covered trees—the natural wildness was stunning, but nothing compared to her innate beauty. And while his pulse picked up and desire flared anew, he forced it back.

'We need to talk.'

'I don't want to,' she said, her body instantly stiff with a tension that had nothing to do with desire or need.

He couldn't help but smile at the petulant tone he remembered well from eight years ago. He didn't want to cause her any more pain, but he knew her well enough to know that she'd probably not thought about her situation beyond the impact it would have on her family. He could have cursed them. Surely at least one of them had reassured her that she was more than just her worth to the throne.

'When did you find out?' he asked, coming to stand behind her, reaching out to snare her hips with his hands, delighting in the friction as she spun to face him.

She rose on her tiptoes, seeking his lips, but he leaned back from the reach of her kiss. Before, he'd been a willing distraction to take the edge off the raw pain in her heart. But now she needed something else, whether she wanted it or not. But that didn't mean he couldn't make it pleasurable. His hands held her in place and she scowled.

She turned her head away, purposely cutting him, but the smooth skin of her neck was exposed and he bent to press open-mouthed kisses, sucking gently, tempted to brand her as his but just managing to resist.

'I'll make a deal with you,' he offered. The stillness of her body told him he had her attention. 'For every answer you give me, I'll give you something in return.'

'Something?'

He smiled into the kiss he pressed to her collarbone. 'You'll have to answer a question to find out, Princess.'

He waited, withholding his touch to see if she would take the bait. He saw her pulse flicker delicately at her jaw.

'Confirmation happened a month ago,' she said and in return he drew his palms up to either side of her chest and swept his thumbs over her nipples, teasing them into stiff peaks. She pressed into the pressure gently and gasped.

'But you've suspected since...'

She flicked her gaze to him and back over his shoulder as if punishing him. 'I first went to the doctor a year ago.'

'Should you have gone sooner?'

The aching thought that she'd neglected herself as she had done even back then during university was a low throb in his heart.

She stared at him, an eyebrow raised, reminding him that he owed her and, smiling, he freed a hand to reach for her chin, thumb and forefinger angling her face to perfection. He teased her lips with brushing kisses, his tongue testing the seam of her mouth until she opened for him. His pulse raised to new heights as soft wet heat welcomed his tongue, until she nipped at his lower lip startling his eyes open to see mischief shining back at him.

'No. I had... Do you really want to hear this?' she asked, the wound audible beneath the cover of exasperation.

'Yes.'

She sighed, the sadness in it hurting him deeply. 'I've always had irregular periods. They were frustrating, but manageable, especially as I was on contraception. Two years ago I decided to come off it but the irregularities increased, rather than settling down.'

Freya forced herself to keep going. There was nothing wrong with talking about a natural body function.

If more people spoke about it freely, then maybe there wouldn't be such stigma. Such ignorance. Such awkwardness. Such *shame*.

'There was pain?'

'Yes.'

When he ran his hands over her body in payment for her answer it took some of the sting out of the conversation. As if he'd known that this was what she needed, known that this was the only way she could speak about it at all. His lips pressed down between her breasts, the heat of his breath warming her skin through the cotton of her long-sleeved top.

'Tests?'

'Yes. Invasive ones.'

His hand swept down to cup her backside, lifting her slightly in a way that pressed her against his erection, leaving her in no doubt of his desire for her, distracting her from thoughts of cold, sterile equipment and gloved hands.

She gasped as his hand swept between her legs, as if he were replacing bad memories with new ones, better ones.

'They revealed that the lining of my uterus was thin. It was the cause of the irregularities and—' she almost laughed at the cruel irony '—I was thankful that it was nothing more troubling. Until they told me that it would be impossible for an embryo to implant there. Impossible for me to carry a child to term. They tried increasing the hormones, but their effect on the lining was negligible.'

The press of his lips slowed and he pulled back to look at her. She read the next question in his eyes.

'They don't know why. There was no previous infection or scarring. It's most likely always been that way.'

She forced herself to meet his gaze as his fingers

played with the hem of her top, lifting it up and over her head and casting it to the side. Stripping back the layers of her hurt just like her clothing should have made her feel weak, vulnerable, but instead the way he looked at her, the pure desire glowing in his eyes made her feel bold, feminine, *strong*.

'Why do you have to renounce your title?' he asked.

She was about to answer when his hands stroked and moulded her breasts with possessive sweeps of his palm and her mind sought to lose itself in his touch rather than answer his question.

'Freya...' he nudged her.

And he tightened his hold as she clenched her jaw against the sudden tide of anger returning to wash against her heart. 'They will crucify me.'

A frown slashed across his brow, his eyes blazing with fury. 'Who will?'

'The press. The people. They will never let me forget,' she said, her soul shaking with her deepest fear. 'Not only that, it will taint my family. They'll question the fertility of my brother, my sister... They'll study the family tree, looking for signs and symptoms of this biological failure that I will come to represent.' She knew how bad it would be. She had been the perfect princess and still she'd felt the shocking lash of their censure if a camera had caught her in an unflattering angle. Heaven forbid anything worse.

'Freya—'

'Have you ever read what has been written about Princess Masako? The Duchess of York? Queen Letizia? Princess Diana? The Princesses of Monaco? The Duchess of Sussex? Princess Madeleine? The press can and often will be cruel, critical, snide, malicious...until they produced a child. Do you know that on any internet search, on any biography, info page or description, the first thing that is listed after a princess's official title is the number and names of their children? Every. Single. Time. As a princess, I have *one* job. And it's not one I will ever be able to fulfil.'

'You say that they'll never let you forget, that it will become your identity. But can't you reclaim that identity? Make it your own on your terms? Control the—'

'Narrative? I don't want to have to!' she cried. 'It's hard enough as it is. And you want me to be the poster child for infertility? The guiding light, leading by example, taking all the flack for future generations of royals?'

'Not just royals... There are people out there without the support that you have.'

'You don't get to make me feel guilty about this,' she warned, her stomach churning.

'I'm not trying to, Freya, honestly. But there are so many options available to you, I just don't want you to make a decision that you can't take back. What is the urgency? Can you not wait a little longer until you've made peace with how you feel about it?'

'No. There isn't time. Not for Aleksander. Or Marit. Svardia needs stability. Right now. And although it will be hard stepping down, much better for it to be seen as my selfishness than anything that would undermine the royal family.'

He pierced her with a penetrating gaze. 'Or are you just clinging to that so you can burn it all down?'

She hated it that he was even just a little right, and—worse—that he could see that about her. It might be brutal but turning her back on it all was so much easier than trying to grasp at what was left.

'You want me to expose my damage to the public, but what about you?'

Kjell became preternaturally still.

'No? Nothing to say to that?' she demanded, hurt and anger making her cruel. 'About why you won't accept the medal? About what happened to require an After Action Report?'

He didn't turn away but his eyes on hers had become fierce. Their gazes flaying lies like layers of skin to reveal the deepest, darkest truths and hurts. Until they both chose to burn on a different fire, an easier one but no less passionate.

They came together in a punishing kiss. Brutal, crushing and utterly delicious. Teeth clashed with tongues, pulses pounded and palms pressed desperately against hot fevered skin. Freya revelled in the power of their desire—the incendiary heat between them burning away the hurt, the sadness, the ache deep within her that she feared might never be healed, no matter what her future. But all thoughts fled when she felt Kjell's fingers dip beneath the vest top and slide it up and over her head. The arctic blue gaze burned white-hot when he saw what he'd revealed of her, his eyes devouring her and seeming to glory in every inch of her body.

He leaned over her, pressing feverish lips to her skin and she couldn't help but arch into his caress, gasp as his tongue toyed with her nipple and whimper when he palmed her other breast. Heat, intense, damp and urgent, built between her legs, shocking and already sensitised after the intensity of her earlier orgasm.

His hand around her back dropped to grasp her backside, moulding her to him and the evidence of his own arousal.

'Perfect,' he whispered against her lips. 'You're absolutely perfect.'

His words turned in her heart and she wanted to be

that. Perfect. For him. But before she could say so he gathered her up in his arms. Instinctively wrapping her legs around his hips, he lifted her, finally bringing them eye to eye, lip to lip, where the supremely arrogant male smirk made her smile.

'I wanted you like this,' he said. He must have seen the confusion in her eyes. 'From the first second I saw you, I wanted you naked, amongst the furs in front of the fire. I wanted it so badly.'

The confession felt precious, felt raw and honest—and she closed her mind to the part that warned that Kjell still hadn't trusted her with his hurt. But she needed this just as badly and she promised herself that it was enough. For now.

Kjell backed up to the sofa, holding her to him with one hand, drawing several of the furs onto the floor with the other, without breaking the kiss.

'Now you're just showing off,' she said against his lips, laughter in her voice and on the tongue that played with his when she'd finished taunting him and he thanked whatever deity was out there.

Her hurt, the fear that haunted her, had undone him. He couldn't stand to see her in so much pain. If he could have taken it from her, he would have. In a heartbeat. But he couldn't. So he'd do this instead. He'd distract her with pleasure and tease her with desire. And if a part of him called him a coward for hiding in that same plea-sure, then he'd own it. There was a time and a place for his story, but now wasn't it.

'You wound me. That is hardly showing off. I could bench press you,' he said in between kisses.

She pulled back to stare at him.

'Really, I could absolutely—'

She scrambled down his body before he could show her and he held back the laugh bubbling in his chest. How they could go from tearing strips off each other to tearing off clothes in just a matter of minutes was incredible to him.

But not as incredible as the sight of Freya standing there before him, unashamed of the body that had caused her so much hurt. He couldn't look at her enough, his eyes running over every inch of her, committing her to memory.

The finest merino wool clung to her legs, displaying the powerful curves of her thighs, and he wanted to turn her around so that he could see how it sculpted her backside. He cursed. He was getting hard just looking at her. A blush rose to her cheeks as if she could see.

'Take it off,' he said, his tone guttural even to his own ears.

She looked for a moment as if she might argue, but then those incredible amber eyes melted to lava and instead she hooked her thumbs into the waistband and slowly, *too* slowly, peeled it down from her hips, her thighs and to her ankles before stepping out of it and throwing it aside.

He was about to speak when she beat him to it, with a wryly raised eyebrow, her thumbs catching on the thin lace of her panties and lowering barely an inch before pausing in this new game that had sprung between them. His heart pounded in his chest, on the knife-edge of a pleasure just within reach. He'd never stopped wanting her. Not once.

'Your turn,' she said, nodding to the top he'd worn for training. She'd barely finished her sentence before he practically tore it from his body. She was doing a terrible job of hiding her amusement, but when her eyes refo-

cused on his chest the laughter died on her lips. Her gaze
scoured him. He wondered what changes she'd see in his
body after eight years apart. It hadn't taken him long in
the army to fill out to a breadth that was as impressive
as his height and without an ounce of pride he knew he
was very different to the boy she must remember.

'You want me?' she asked, as if afraid that he might
say no.

'I've never wanted anyone else.' The truth flying from
his lips as if it had always belonged to her.

'Yes, but there were others,' she stated, trying so hard
to hide the bite of jealousy that was easy for him to read.
She was so sure.

'No.'

Her eyes flew to his in shock. 'What? Never?'

'It has only been you,' he growled.

*It will only ever be you.* The words cried out silently
in his soul.

She took a step towards him, the finest tremor to her
legs as if she was as affected by his confession as he'd
been making it. He fisted his hands to stop himself from
reaching for her. This had to be for her. She had to take
what she needed and wanted.

She drew to a stop, barely an inch from his body, the
heat from her skin washing against him like a tide, pulling him towards her against his will.

Her hand raised and swept a lock of hair from his
forehead, her fingers shockingly cool against his face.
Her hand trailed downwards, across his jaw, his neck
and coming to a rest over his heart.

'Me too,' she said and, before he could process the
hint of sadness there, she kissed him so passionately he
couldn't hold back any more.

He swept her up into his embrace and knelt, plac-

ing her on the furs to satiate the incessant need that had
thrown images of her just like this into his mind again
and again and again. The fire blazed in the wood burner,
casting flickering shadows over her deliciously warm
skin. Outside, snowflakes were swirling and falling in
a moving curtain, letting through the dusk, and welcoming the oncoming dark of night. But the strange haunting white glow reflecting from the snow made it feel as
if they were in a magical land—one stolen from time, a
precious second chance that seemed as impossible and
fleeting as it was real.

Freya stared up at him from the furs, her earthy skin
perfect against the deep russet and browns surrounding her. She reached for him and he couldn't deny her.
He came over her in a kiss that stole his breath and his
heart, only to find himself smiling barely a second later
as she pushed impatiently at the waistband of his trousers. He was naked by his second breath and pure male
pride burst to life when he saw the glare of desire flare
in her whisky-coloured eyes at the sight of him.

Pulling him into yet another kiss, her body came to
life beneath his, her legs parting to welcome him between them, her thighs shifting beneath his hips, and he
couldn't help but run his hand between them to cup her
wet heat. Her head drifted back, exposing her neck to his
lips as he pressed open-mouthed kisses to her skin and
pressed his thumb to the delicate flesh that sent Freya
wild. He circled her clitoris before sweeping towards her
entrance, gently teasing the heated dampness until she
punished him with a bite to his bottom lip.

He smiled into her kiss as he gently drew himself
down her body, settling between her thighs, where he
could die a very happy man. Her hips twisted under his

focus, drawing his gaze to where Freya watched him, pink-cheeked and breathless.

As his tongue swept out and she shuddered from the sensual kiss, he knew he'd never seen anyone or anything more beautiful in his life than Freya. He would have spent every day of it worshipping her, if he'd been able. But a relationship between them would never be allowed. He wasn't stupid, even this was a stolen moment. The truth was, a Svardian soldier could never marry his princess.

*But she doesn't want to be a princess any more.*

She did, though. She loved doing what she did and he knew it. And she would realise that eventually. But until then...

Her legs shifted again and he turned to take a gentle bite from her thigh, smiling at the peal of giggles that sounded like music to him. Then he couldn't help himself. He pressed kisses to the inside of her legs, easing into the space she created as she spread them for him. Slowly he drew himself up, kiss by kiss, until he could feel her beneath the entire length of his body. She moulded herself against him, dips filling hollows, curves claiming arches, the feel of her skin like silk.

She reached up to frame his face with her hands as he positioned himself at her entrance. The trust, the need and the sheer honesty he could see in the warm whisky-coloured eyes humbled him. And they rode out the moment together before he slowly entered her, the wet heat welcoming him in a delicious sensuous glide that had Freya gasping on an inhalation.

She surrounded him in a slick grip that held him tight and urged him on, urged him deeper. His mind filled with stars and his heart hurt at the beauty of what he was feeling. Of what he might never feel again. His arms, braced either side of her, began to shake as he held himself while she adjusted around him. The air between them filled with little sighs and pants as she relaxed around him, making him even harder within her. She bucked her hips gently beneath him and he wanted to curse, he wanted to pray. And when they started to move together he was simply mindless.

Freya was drowning in pleasure, gasping through it for air, for something more, something indefinable. As Kjell moved within her she became incoherent with need. That need a physical thing in her chest, growing, expanding, building and desperate for more, for *him*. It wanted out. It wanted release. And she could see that same need in Kjell's eyes as he stared down at her in wonder. She knew. She felt it. That incredulity that something—*anything*—could be this…incredible. Until that need became so all-consuming that it pushed her right to the edge.

'Kjell—'

'I've got you,' he said as he nudged them closer and closer to the precipice. 'I've got you.'

It was the last thing she heard as they soared together over the edge and into the night sky.

# CHAPTER EIGHT

FREYA SIGHED AS she slowly woke. Kjell was watching her from the kitchen, holding a cup of coffee and willing her back to sleep just so he could watch her a little more.

*Stalker.*

Mm-hmm. He agreed with Enzo's observation. He turned the cup in his hands, missing the man who had been like a brother to him so much that morning it hurt.

*What now?*

He refused to answer the question that sounded like Enzo, him and even Freya. A Greek chorus commenting on his life. And it was too much, too soon after last night. Another sigh drew his attention back to Freya as she turned beneath the throw he'd had the sanity to cover them with before they'd drifted into sleep just as the sun began to peer through snowflakes that had started to gentle.

His heart thudded in his chest. That she'd never grow round in pregnancy, that she'd never feel the weight, the child growing within her... He could see how much it devastated her. And he wasn't obtuse. He did understand that she shouldn't have to parade her pain before the world's press and population if she didn't have to. It killed him that he couldn't protect her from that.

But he knew—as much as he wanted to fight it—he

instinctively knew that she shouldn't step down. She would lose too much. Her sense of identity was inextricably linked with her role and her place with her family. To lose that as well as the chance to carry a child to term... He shook his head, his heart breaking for her. She wouldn't make it. But he couldn't and wouldn't force that realisation on her. He could only hope to help her understand that for herself.

She stirred again, her body rippling with wakefulness, even though her eyes were still closed.

'Mmm... Coffee?' she asked, turning towards him with a smile. There was a hint of something there in her eyes. Nervousness? Not insecurity, but something... *uncertain*.

In an instant his thoughts and concerns were masked behind a smile, and he allowed some of the wicked heat she inspired in him to show so that doubt disappeared from her gaze.

She reached her arms out from beneath the throw and her body arched into a stretch that threatened to undo his plans. 'Shower.' She exhaled.

'Later. After coffee.'

She frowned.

'I have plans,' he said, answering her unspoken question.

'Plans,' she repeated, desire blooming behind those amber eyes.

He barked a laugh. 'Not *those* kinds of plans.' And he smirked as she pouted.

Freya put her coffee down on the table with a *thunk* as Kjell finished explaining what he had in mind, shock and no small amount of fear shimmering in her chest.

'No! Absolutely not. No. You're insane.'

'It's good for you.'

'There is *nothing* good about that. I'll die. Literally.'

'Don't be silly, you won't die. We do it all the time.'

'Who is this *we*? I don't see anyone else here, and I think you're lying. So, no. I won't do it.'

Kjell laughed again, the sound filling the cabin and warming her chest. It was a glorious sound. Even back at university, she'd not heard it that often and she delighted in hearing it now. Almost enough to give in to his plans. But not quite.

'You'll love it.'

'There is nothing to love about running through a blizzard to a hole in the ice and plunging into literally freezing water. It's dangerous.'

'It's not. I'll be there the whole time. I'll go first, if that makes you feel any better.'

'So what happens after?'

'We come back and shower.'

'There isn't even enough hot water for two of us, Kjell!'

'I've had the generator on and by the time we're back there'll be enough hot water for a whole platoon.'

'Well, good. You and the platoon can make use of it. Because I'm *never* going to do that.'

An hour later, adrenaline buzzed her body and hazed her eyes and for the first time in days it had nothing to do with arousal and everything to do with fear. She could *not* believe that he'd convinced her to do this. He'd left her while he'd found the best place to enter the freezing lake and bashed a hole through the thick icy surface.

'Kjell,' she said, shaking her head and backing away, 'I really can't do this.'

'Of course you can. But it's important that you do as

I do and what I tell you to do.' His tone was level, even and confident. And reasonable. So reasonable that it was *unreasonable*! Her heart was pounding in her chest and her palms kept closing instinctively, as if desperately trying to hold onto something that wasn't there.

She nodded, even though she had no intention of actually following him out to the lake at the bottom of the snow-covered slope and... Her mind stopped short as if trying to protect itself and she couldn't help but laugh at the bubble of hysteria building in her chest.

Dressed in her thermal layers, she was looking out at the lake, which she could now see properly for the first time since the snow had let up. Kjell had promised her the snow would return, the heavy winter storm not quite done with them yet, but here in the blessed calm of the eye of the storm they had a finite amount of time. Time to get to the lake, strip off their clothes while deepening their breathing and facing the cold before plunging into impossibly icy depths. Kjell had staked a rope ladder to the snow-covered bank and she knew it was for her comfort because he'd never need such a thing. The sudden shocking imagined vision of Kjell hauling himself naked from the freezing lake was nearly enough to tempt her into doing as he asked.

And it must have been in a daze of desire that Kjell took her hand and led her out of the cabin because, when she inhaled, the dramatically low temperature stung her lungs and shocked her back into the present, where Kjell was leading her down towards the frozen lake.

'Breathe, Freya,' he ordered, and she did as he asked, and he looked at her with a knowing smile that was as much a taunt as it was reassuring. 'Would I do anything to risk hurting you?' he asked.

Her answer was instantaneous. 'No.'

'And you trust me?'

'Yes.' The response was as instinctive as breathing.

'Move your legs and arms like a warm-up before exercise and deepen your breath.'

Self-consciously, she followed his directions and let her eyes take in the majesty of the surroundings. Rich forest green poked through the white snow, visible through the break in the storm. Deepening her breath, she tasted ice and pine and wildness. All things she would associate with Kjell for ever. Her heart began to slow, but not by much. Especially when Kjell pulled his thermal top over his head and she bit her lip, caging her tongue to stop it from sweeping her lips in delight.

'You scared of it?' he asked, as if unaware of the effect he was having on her right now.

She reluctantly shifted her gaze from the perfection of his chest to the dark, forbidding blackness stark against the snow-covered layer of ice above it. For a moment she wondered if he'd read her mind, asking if she was scared of the feelings building in her hard and fast for a man who, if she stepped down, she could actually have.

'Yes,' she answered, mentally referring to both her feelings and the ice. She didn't have to try to deepen her breath this time, but she slowed it before it could hitch and speed up.

'To face it you need to change the way you think about it. To not see it as a threat, but as an experience. An experience that won't be awful, but incredible.'

His breathing was louder than hers, his wide arms sweeping back and forth, his deep inhalations flaring his nose and just copying his actions was enough to cause adrenaline to rush around her body, for her head to feel light with excitement and challenge. With something that was earthy and elemental and animalistic. Nothing else mattered but them and the frigid water ready to test them, to push them. To see this terrifying blackness not as something to be feared but as something she could overcome was incredible.

Kjell's words were hypnotic, calling to something fierce within her, the sister of yesterday's rage and hurt, but this time more determined, exhilarating. Something that revelled at being on the brink of an act both terrifying and suddenly absolutely necessary to her. She needed to do this. She felt it in her soul and as strongly as she needed her next breath. And Kjell smiled as if sensing that change in her.

'Do you want to go first?'

She nodded, unable to open her jaw, it was clenched in fear and determination.

'Breathe. Relax into it. Be bold and brave and you will conquer it.'

She forced her body to submit to the world around her as she stripped off her layers, toeing off the boots he'd lent her and down to her underwear.

'You can take those off too,' he taunted, and she laughed out loud, the action cutting through some of the tension.

She stood there for a moment, breathing deep, her hopes and fears warring for mastery of her body.

'Remember. Go slowly and use the rope.'

He'd told her that the lake wasn't deep here, that she'd easily reach the bottom, but she clung to that rope with white knuckles as she stepped into the dark abyss, breathing through the impulse to cry her shock out loud.

It was so cold that at first she felt nothing. But her body had reacted even if her nerves were still playing catch-up. She gasped for breath, fighting the need to tense, but it was the adrenaline that shocked her the most.

She inhaled and wanted to laugh. Wanted to scream into the air around them. As sensation began to bleed into her skin, an inconceivable coldness drenched her. Her body was alive and bursting with something indescribable, her heart pounding, not from fear but from vitality, from life. From the utter shock that she was there, in the freezing cold, breathing through her body's reaction to the impossibly cold water.

Kjell joined her, his gaze locked on hers as if delighting in nothing more than simply her experience of this gift he'd given her. Because it was a gift. She'd spent so long feeling numb after her diagnosis. Numb to her body's failings and absence. *This* was something her body *could* do. The miraculous abilities that she still had within her.

She reached for him and drew him in to a kiss, powerful, demanding as their tongues clashed and tasted and tested and revelled. He slowed the kiss, as if reluctant, just as she began to feel her foot curl into what could soon be a cramp.

'That's probably enough for today,' he said, as if knowing her limits better than she. Freya would have protested, but actually her bones were beginning to ache from the cold. Kjell hauled himself out from the hole he'd dug in the ice and turned, his black trunks plastered to his skin, outlining every delicious inch of him and the powerful thighs that braced as he gave her his hand and pulled her from the ice water as if she weighed nothing. In an instant her teeth began to chatter and he wrapped a warm blanket around her, rubbing at her skin, less to dry and more to warm.

'You are incredible,' he said with a pride that stole her heart. And with that he lifted her in his arms, marched them back to the cabin and together they showered for a *very* long time.

Kjell placed a bottle of wine on the table, promising himself that, no matter how bad dinner might be, he would eat it. Freya had been a terrible cook at university, he doubted that she'd had much practice since.

There had been something seductively domestic about the afternoon. The snow had resumed almost immediately upon their return to the cabin—as if the pause in the weather had been just for them. The fire had blazed in the burner, Freya had teased a book from the shelves and curled up beside him before falling asleep on his shoulder. She'd been so deeply under that he'd turned lengthways on the sofa and pulled her gently up against him, cradling her with his body. And he'd done nothing but relish every second of it.

He'd felt a peace he'd not experienced for years and hoarded it within him for the years to come after she returned to her royal duties. Even if she couldn't see a way, Kjell would find one. Because it was in her blood, she'd been born to it. And he knew in his bones how damaging not doing the one thing you lived and breathed for could be.

'Ta-da!' Freya said, placing the pan on the table mat, tendrils of smoke escaping from the burnt edges of the pan.

'Smells...delightful,' he said, his voice high-pitched even to his own ears. She looked up at him, eyes wide but hopeful. He picked up a spoon from the table and plunged it into the mysteriously beige depths of the pan. 'What is it?' he asked hesitantly.

'You tell me.'

'Oka-ay,' he said, the word broken by his concern. He

put the spoon into his mouth and just barely managed to stop himself from spitting it back out. 'It's…um…' He looked at her and swallowed. 'You don't know what it is, do you?' he accused.

'Not really. Is it…*edible*?'

He barked out a laugh. 'You haven't even tried it?'

'God, no. It smells awful.'

He'd forgotten this side of her. The playful, fun, teasing side to her. He wondered if she had too, from the way that the light sparkled in her eyes.

'You could teach me, you know,' she said, removing the pan as he entered the kitchen space to pull together a half decent meal. Thankfully, the bread was still fresh and would certainly work with smoked fish, pâtés, pickles, cheeses and smoked meat.

'Teach you what?' he asked, distracted, setting the rye bread to toast.

'To cook.'

His actions slowed as he caught the tone of her voice. 'That could take a while,' he replied cautiously.

'It will take *years*, Kjell.'

He clamped his jaw shut, turning back to the table to pour them some wine, his fingers white-knuckled around the green glass bottle. He knew what she was doing. Building a dream around a future that wasn't possible. He'd done it himself and had been devastated when that dream disintegrated. So devastated that he'd agreed to every single UN overseas mission possible. He'd stayed away from his family, from his country and anything that had reminded him of her.

And, despite that pain, he still wanted to give in to the picture she was painting, to get even just a glimpse of a future in which there was no throne, no active service, just them. The ache of knowing how perfect it would be was worth the agony of it being taken away. Because in that moment, for just a heartbeat, they'd been together, imagining the same future. But he'd stopped lying the day he'd last seen her eight years ago. To others. To himself.

'Freya,' he said, turning towards her.

'And I was thinking,' she pressed on, ignoring him, ignoring the warning in his tone. 'Perhaps I could come here? You know. After I step down from my title. It's just so peaceful here. And I'd *love* to see it in the summer. I imagine that it's stunning. Is it? Stunning?'

She was rambling, clinging to this fantasy with desperate fingers. It was there in her eyes.

*Please. Please let me have this.*

He heard it as clear as if she'd said it. His heart turned over. There was time. The storm still raged and there was *still* time, he promised himself. He looked up at her, knowing that he'd never be able to deny her anything.

'It's absolutely breathtaking,' he said. 'The sun's rays filter through the trees and in the early morning, as the earth warms, before the rest of the world wakes, it's like heaven on earth.'

'I want to see that one day.'

'Then you shall.'

He placed the meal he'd cobbled together on two large chopping boards on the table. Cool white wine filled large old glasses, the condensation forming against the warmth of the room from the wood burner.

'Forget what I said about learning to cook. I'm never cooking. Dinner will be on you every night,' she said, her eyes large and hungry looking at the food and he smiled in spite of himself.

'So what will you do?' he asked, hypothetically playing along for the moment.

'Probably something in the charity sector. It's what I love doing most.'

'What are you currently working on?' he asked, subtly leading her back to her current role. Her eyes were bright and her cheeks pink, this time there was no rambling. Just pure confidence and joy in her work, at what she helped achieve.

'I'm trying to get Stellan Stormare in front of parliament, but they're still resistant to it.'

'The man whose daughter died?'

Freya nodded. 'Lena Stormare was on a train filled with hundreds of people and not one of them knew sign language, not one of them was able to help her in time.' Freya's fury was simmering bright in her eyes but, rather than overwhelming her like it had yesterday, it empowered her, gave her something that few others were capable of. 'She died from an allergic reaction and couldn't tell anyone.' She shook her head, the loss clearly a burden on her heart. 'I don't understand why we're not teaching it in our schools.'

'You could argue that funding should go where there is the greatest need.'

'And what greater need is there than to be able to communicate?'

He raised his hands. 'I'm playing devil's advocate.'

'Yes, I know the arguments—there are fewer children with hearing difficulties, there are more worthy or urgent causes. But why do people think that it only benefits the young? What about the elderly with hearing loss? If sign language was learned by the many, used regularly, then I *know* it would be beneficial there too. In this day and age shouldn't we be doing everything we can to ensure we can *all* speak and we can *all* be heard?' Her passion made her fierce—worthy and admirable. He wished she could see what he saw. Someone ready, willing, able and more than capable to fight for those who could not fight for themselves. But why couldn't she fight for *herself* with that same passion?

'What about Aleksander? Surely your brother can help?'

'He's got enough on his plate at the moment.'

'It can't be easy,' he said truthfully. As Lieutenant Colonel, he knew what it was like to lead hundreds, if not thousands of people. He also knew what it was like to be tied to a course of action he knew in his gut was wrong but was helpless to change. Whether Aleksander's hands were tied by royal statutes or political gambles, it was hard to make changes when all were against it.

'Will you be able to help Stellan before you step down?' he asked, knowing instantly that he'd found a weak spot in her plan. If he was on the attack, if he truly wanted to hit home, this would be the way to do it. It was a low blow, but it was for her. Always for her.

'I will do everything in my power before then and after if need be.'

Of course—they were both ignoring Aleksander's stipulation. That in order for Freya to step down, he would need to accept the medal. His gut clenched with the suspicion that Aleksander had done this on purpose. It would have been a win/win for Aleksander; either he expected Kjell to convince her not to step down, or Freya to convince him to take the medal.

The crisp bread dried on his tongue, leaching moisture from his mouth, parching his lips and throat and he reached for his wine. Everything in him roared in denial. The food turned sour in his stomach. How could he accept a medal for the mission that had put Enzo in the ground? No. It wasn't the mission that had put him in the ground. It had been Kjell.

Freya noticed the change in him almost immediately. It was a stillness. A retreat. He filled her glass and peppered her with questions about what kind of help Stellan's cause might need in the long-term, but it was as if Kjell wasn't really there. For a man who had been so truly focused on her since the moment she'd arrived it was a stark absence—and one that she knew was deeply enmeshed with the AAR and the medal.

A medal he would have to accept if she were to actually be allowed to step down.

She hated that her freedom would come at such a cost to him. It silenced the question every time it lay on her tongue. Kjell was the most dedicated, determined man she knew. Time hadn't changed that—in fact, it seemed to have only made him more so. It was one of the things that she had admired about him, that connected them on a fundamental level: a sense of duty. That he had respected hers, understood it rather than questioning or resenting it had made him even more precious to her. And it was also why she knew that something truly awful must have happened to affect him so. But it was hidden behind a wall of silence, a wall that could damage as well as protect.

Freya looked out of the window. The interior light picked out a few flakes as they twisted and fell across a nightscape dark and forbidding. The wood burner was glowing with heat and she should have felt cosy, but the chill from Kjell was as brutal as the shocking cold water she'd plunged into today.

'Coffee?' Kjell's question interrupted her thoughts. She looked down at her plate and found it empty and nodded as he picked it up and took the rest of the things to the kitchen.

'Yes please,' she answered, wondering how to even begin to approach such a difficult subject. He had teased a confession from her with sensual delight and pleasure—but that wouldn't work for him. The soldier in him wouldn't appreciate anything less than a direct confrontation, but she felt deep in her bones that it wasn't the soldier she needed to reach.

She heard him fill the percolator and couldn't sit still. Standing up, she went to him, unable to resist the need to reach out to him, to forge the connection his retreat complicated. Freya wrapped her arms around him from behind and placed her cheek against his back, comforted by the steady pulse of his heart and warmed by his body. He tensed, as if caught by surprise, his muscles rigid before he gave in, his body relaxing within hers as he placed his hand on top of hers, holding them there in that moment.

'Please don't.' His voice was quiet but raw, knowing the question on her tongue.

She closed her eyes, hating that she couldn't let this go. But it was no longer about whether he took the medal or not, this was about so much more. He needed to face whatever it was that was ravaging his soul.

'Will you tell me what happened?'

# CHAPTER NINE

Kjell gripped the handle of the percolator with white knuckles, thankful that Freya was tucked behind him and not witnessing his reaction to her question. He considered it. Refusing her. For the first time in his life, he actually *wanted* to deny her.

Anger and fear were bitter on his tongue. 'I can't help you, Princess,' he said, taking the bubbling, spitting percolator from the stove. 'I'd take the medal in a heartbeat if I thought it was the right thing for you, but I don't,' he said honestly. 'So I won't.'

She held onto him, despite his small movements and his harsh words. Her arms were loose but strong. Determined but with a softness that somehow reminded him of a comfort he hadn't known in years. His heart pulsed beneath the touch.

'I won't be distracted, Kjell.' Her tone patient, calm, *kind*.

'It doesn't mean it's not true.'

'Neither does it make it an answer to my question.' Again, her gentleness. If she'd come at him with commands and orders, he'd have been able to fight her. But she hadn't. Whether she knew it or not, it was this, her natural empathetic will to understand that made her the perfect princess. He inhaled, the scent of rich coffee invading his senses, but in his mind he could smell cheap instant granules, thick as syrup and foul as earth.

*It's the only way to drink it, mio amico.*

Enzo's laugh melded with the piercing rumble of the IED explosion and his heart thumped, a cold sweat threatening to break out at the back of his neck. He clenched his teeth, trying to ground himself in the present.

But that wasn't what brought him back. He looked down to find Freya's fingers slipping through the spaces between his own, her palm over his hand, light, warm but more of an anchor than any he'd ever felt.

*You trust me?*

*Yes.*

The gift of her trust, after their past but also because of it, meant she deserved nothing less than the same in return. He'd not spoken of it once in the last four months. He'd not been able to. But now, with Freya, the words, the thoughts, they were clamouring to get out. As if they'd been waiting only for her. He turned to find her looking up at him, warm whisky-coloured eyes patient and open.

'Go sit down,' she said, nodding back towards the large sofa, clearly having sensed his decision. 'I'll bring the coffee.'

He picked up their joined hands and pressed a kiss to her knuckles before releasing their hold and heading to the sofa on feet that left imprints in sand. Already his mind was back there, straddling the past and the present. He could feel the sweat dripping down his spine, soaking his T-shirt and chest, and was half convinced that if he wiped at his forehead his wrist would come back slick and salty.

He swallowed around an arid heat that sucked any and all moisture from his body. Over the sounds of coffee being poured, he heard the sound of children's laughter. A beautiful chatter clashing with the tinkle of a spoon against ceramic.

And Enzo, laughing like the biggest kid in the playground, kicking the football into the square in the sand that marked the goal.

Freya pressed a hot mug into his hands before pulling up the foot stool so she could sit opposite him. Within touching distance—if he wanted—but also giving him space.

'Where were you stationed?'

He shook his head gently. 'It doesn't really matter. We're stationed wherever violence meets the shift of power. It could have been anywhere around the world,' he said with a finality he felt to the bottom of his heart. That man's ability to cause great acts of violence in the name of both justice and injustice didn't surprise him any more should have been warning enough.

'We were there to facilitate the transition of political power, but also for DDR.'

'Disarmament, demobilisation and reintegration?'

Kjell nodded. 'Some of these guys, they've been fighting since they were just kids. It's all they know. And when the peace process begins there's no job to walk into, there's no place in society for them, because they've been on the outside with no way back. It's as important to bring them back into their community as it is to disarm. Training, education options, ways for them to contribute to society—if peace isn't people-centred, then it has no hope.'

Kjell had seen it time and time again in the last eight years. The need to work *with* a community, to support, facilitate, enable rather than lead, dominate, overpower.

That was peacekeeping at its best. That, to him, was a duty with the highest of callings.

'I was responsible for nearly six hundred soldiers.'

'How many are deployed?'

'In that region? About eleven thousand.'

She seemed surprised. 'Do the units stay the same?' she asked.

'People circulate. Most do their secondments and return home. Others…' He shrugged. Even now, as he looked back he could recognise that he'd had a choice. He could have challenged the exile. In fact, his commanding officer in the Svardian Armén had been trying to get him back on home soil for at least two years now. 'We come from all around the world—each member state contributing certain numbers if and where they can,' he explained.

'Some of you stay?'

'When we can.'

'Do you want to go back?' she asked hesitantly.

He didn't know if he could. Not now. Not after. And that thought alone cost him greatly. He looked across the room to the stack of paperwork Freya had pushed to the side and saw the AAR on the top. The report, nearly two weeks overdue now. A year ago such a thing would have been inconceivable.

'I'd known Enzo for about five years. We'd crossed over on a number of missions in a number of different locations. He was all Italian charm. Quick with a joke, a leer and a laugh. But he loved his wife,' Kjell said with the first sincere smile she'd seen lift his lips since dinner. 'At least once a day we'd be subjected to rhapsodies about her beauty and her kindness. He gloried in his love for her,' he said, Kjell's tone full of amusement. 'The sonnets he could have written about her hair alone...' He half laughed, and Freya felt her lips curve into a smile.

Kjell leaned his head on his hand, elbow rested on knee and eyes locked on somewhere Freya would never likely see, remembering someone she would never meet. Her heart ached, instinctively knowing the end to this story and wishing there could be another way for Kjell to face his demons.

'We were at the end of our patrol. We should have been heading back to base, but we were rerouted.'

There was something about the way he said that last bit, a shift in tone that didn't sit right.

'You disagreed with the command?'

'I would never disobey a direct order.' Grim-lipped and pale, Kjell's eyes were locked on a distant horizon.

Freya frowned, trying to find the right words. 'Did you question it?'

His jaw flexed, the muscle tight and his skin flushed with anger. 'No.'

Oh. Her heart ached for him. She could see it now. He had disagreed with the order but, as a dutiful and conscientious soldier, couldn't, *wouldn't*, question it.

'Chain of command is just as important on the ground for UN missions as it is with any other deployed army,' he ground out through teeth clenched so hard she feared something might break.

She placed her hand on his forearm, but he didn't seem to notice.

'But I could feel it,' he said, his unseeing gaze finally clearing enough to lock onto hers. 'In my gut. We both did. We both knew it was wrong. We were to help safeguard a group of foreign nationals who had gone off-itinerary to visit a local community centre. The intention was good enough, but the security plan wasn't in place to cover it and they clearly didn't realise how unstable the region was. Absolutely they needed the support, but there were two other patrols who were fresher and just as close.'

'So why were you sent?'

Kjell's eyes shifted from dusk to midnight in a heartbeat. 'They were showing off. They wanted to send *me*,' he said, jerking a thumb back into his chest, 'a high-ranking senior officer.'

Freya felt her eyes grow wide and round. The agony in his tone, the bitterness and hurt, was awful for her to hear.

'We all knew it. Showboating for the oil execs. The squad shared eye-rolls and friendly banter, but I didn't like it. It was *wrong*.'

'Kjell—' She wanted to tell him he could stop, wanted to protect him from reliving such great pain, but it was as if he couldn't hear her.

'When we got there, the visit from the oil execs had drawn a lot of unwanted attention and a crowd was beginning to form. Some of the young teenagers at the community centre had been part of the reintegration programme, having turned their backs on the local militia. Most of these boys, Freya—they'd been taken when they were five or six…and at sixteen they were still fighting for their freedom.'

Her heart ached for children she would never meet, their struggle as impossible and inconceivable to her as it was an anathema.

'Foreign execs and ex-child soldiers. It was exactly the kind of target that the militia liked best. We were on the radio before the convoy could pull to a stop, calling for reinforcements.'

Freya wondered what he saw in his mind—his gaze fixed over her shoulder.

'They were probably already there—the rogue militia, indistinguishable from the people in the crowd who had gathered to support the centre or had been drawn there by curiosity about the visitors.'

The weight of eyes on the back of his neck lifted the hairs on his arms. They'd all felt it, each member of his team, the way that the crowd's energy changed like a discordant note rippling through a piece of music, changing the tone irrevocably.

'The glass bottle, thrown near the steps of the centre, was just a test.'

The glass had shattered suddenly on the dry ground, but a community ravaged by decades of violence and tension needed barely a spark. They knew what was coming. Screams echoed in his ears as hundreds of people scattered into chaos, making it impossible to identify where the threat was. The unit spread out, each soldier knowing their individual role. Four of his team took up defensive positions around the execs and students in the community centre, while Enzo and six others spread out into the seething mass of the crowd.

One shot. Then two, then three, the tattoo sounding his ears. The dry wood of the community centre shattered and splintered around the bullets.

'There were at least two enemy combatants in the crowd, but a third holed-up in one of the buildings off the square was pinning down a small section of the civilians Enzo and the others had managed to corral behind some of the market stalls.'

He'd caught Enzo's eye across the chaos, gesturing sharply with his hand, the communication clear, but not to the other man's liking. They never went off alone, but there wasn't time to debate. He repositioned himself and when Enzo lay down covering fire, Kjell slipped out from behind the vehicle and covered the space between him and the corner building in a heartbeat and a prayer. Training kicked in—clearing the entrance, the first room, the second and into the stairwell he knew would lead up to the third man.

Enzo and the rest of his team would handle the two rogue militia that had lodged themselves into positions in the marketplace, of that he had no doubt. But the civilians in the square had no chance with this man in the equation. Backup was far enough away for him to pick them off one by one. On silent feet, Kjell timed his steps with the gunshots coming from the room one floor above to his right.

'You killed him,' Freya said, a statement rather than a question.

'It took me seven of his bullets to traverse two floors and get him in my sights. Seven bullets that wounded two women, three teenage boys, and killed one child and one man. A man who had used his body to shield six young children who had been on a day trip with their class to the community centre.'

From the corner of his eye he saw Freya press a shaking hand to her lips, but in his heart he saw dust and blood.

'Enzo died instantly, protecting children who survived with nothing more than cuts and bruises.' Backup had arrived, the oil execs were rushed into waiting vehicles, while he and his team… It had been a terrible thing to be united in. A shared moment of horror. And then training and duty had kicked in, the area split into quadrants and searched for any sign of the rebel militia.

His team had stayed in the market square, guarding the injured until the medics arrived.

Guarding the dead.

Freya's breath hitched, drawing his gaze to hers, the haunting pale amber of her eyes filled with a sorrow so pure he was humbled by it. She anchored him back in the present, picking up his hand and placing it over a heart that beat for him, the rhythm stuttering, hurt and somehow matching his own. He closed his eyes, savouring the moment, the feeling. The comfort she gave allowed grief to fill the spaces in his heart that had been consumed with such *anger*.

He fisted his hand, remembering his return to base. 'I was called in to discuss the fallout,' he said bitterly. 'It was just me and the top brass.' He shook his head, biting down, hearing again the way the situation had been presented to him. 'Everything that was reported ...the order, it was all perfectly correct. But...' He steeled himself, his body flexing, his shoulders squaring and his back straightening. 'I am a *good* soldier. Dutiful. I *believe* in the mission. I believe in the chain of command. I understand it. But I'm not sure that I...trust it any more. And if I can't do that...'

He shook his head, unwilling and unable to follow that thought to its logical conclusion. It wasn't just a job for him. It was an identity; his units, his placements, they'd become his family, his home.

'I haven't questioned a command since—' He snapped his teeth together.

'Since me?' she asked, her eyes glowing in the dim lighting of the cabin. His answer was in his eyes. She seemed not to need more than that. 'What is stopping you from writing the AAR?' she asked gently.

'I can't see the situation dispassionately. I can't outline the events without bias, without anger, without the clarity to know whether what happened could have had a different outcome, because every time I think about it, it makes me question everything I know. Everything I've given up for this job, this life.' It was the first time he'd finally said it out loud. Finally put his fear into words that explained, that made coherence from the chaos of his feelings. 'I don't know whether command made the right call. I don't know whether they should have sent another unit, I don't know whether I should have waited... I just... Enzo was...'

He hated that the words he needed to say were getting caught in his throat. That he couldn't speak for his friend, for himself.

'Enzo was a hero.' Freya's reverent voice slipped around his soul.

'Yes, he was,' he said, refusing to acknowledge the dampness pressing against his eyes. 'But,' he said, turning to Freya, '*I* am not. So your brother can keep his damn medal.'

He stood up before he could betray himself any more and went to step away when he felt Freya's hand sneak around his thigh, gently holding him in place better than any restraint could have ever done.

'What would have happened if you hadn't gone after the third man?'

'What?'

'If you'd not been there to do what you did?'

He looked down at her, unable to lie. It would have been a massacre. He didn't need to say it to know that she heard his silent response.

Freya let him leave. She knew he needed time and space, but was worried when she heard the door to the outside open and close. Looking through the window, she was surprised to see that the snow had stopped again. Clouds still blanketed the sky, airbrushing the finer details from the view.

Her inhalation was shaky from the way her heart still trembled for him. Kjell's pain and grief for his friend was beyond anything she knew or had experienced. She could only hope that talking about it had drawn the poisonous pain from his soul.

But even if she had helped him somehow, she knew that the damage had been done. In his exile, Kjell had found a family and found a place he could lay his head. But Enzo's death had changed that for him. Once again, his family, his support, had been stolen from him.

She had believed him when he said he'd had cause to question his decisions, his job, himself. And she knew how that could be—how painful, disruptive...how damaging. But, oh, she wished he could see what she saw when she looked at him.

A conscientious soldier who thought about the impact of his actions. Who cared about the people under his protection in the present as much as in the future. A man whose moral compass was so strong he had punished himself for the lie of a boy bound in duty to a king, long into his adulthood.

A man who she had never stopped loving. In all those years, it had been there. Him. In her heart.

And a man who she could absolutely have for herself if she walked away from the throne. She didn't need Aleksander's permission. Not really. It had been a lie that she'd told herself, because it gave the power to someone else to decide her fate. Because she couldn't trust herself to choose correctly. She knew that walking away from her title would be best for her brother, her sister, the royal family. But would it be best for Svardia?

Her heart in turmoil, she finally heard what Kjell had been trying to tell her. That yes, she could walk away, she could find true happiness with the man she loved. Or she could return to Svardia and stay, do something real and good with her life and her time for the people of her country, for women all across the world. She could give them a voice, just as she'd wished for Lena Stormare.

But it would cost her Kjell.

Earlier, over dinner, she'd woven a fantasy that was so pure it hurt too much to want it. Behind her closed eyes, Kjell chopped wood in the sunshine. Bees buzzed and butterflies zigzagged across the meadow outside. The windows were thrown open to let warm summer air into the cabin and the sounds of children's laughter danced on the breeze.

And she opened her eyes to release tears that stung as they fell. Loss. Grief. For what could never be. This. This was more of a loss than a crown or a title. And it was a loss and a grief that she refused to tie Kjell to. He deserved a home. And children of his own. A whole platoon of them to order around, to teach...to love. She couldn't bind him to anything less than that. He would— she knew—sacrifice anything for her and she could not, would not, do that to him again.

Kjell watched the night sky as the thick bank of clouds began to shift beneath strong winds. He wondered if they were working their magic on him too, or whether that was Freya. She had always hit him like a tornado. A storm, swirling him up in its eye, as if she were the centre of everything, grounding him, focusing him.

His muscles hurt as if he'd just finished a particularly brutal workout—the tension becoming acidic the moment he gave up the fight of holding everything in. His heart ached for Enzo and guilt at not being able to save him stabbed his conscience. But for the first time since that awful day he felt that he could breathe a little easier, that his anger was just a little less.

Fury and grief had been so huge in his mind and his heart, he'd not known whether he'd still be standing when the tide of words washed through those feelings. But Freya had been there to anchor him. Not to hold him in place, but to come back to. A tether he'd needed in order to face those fears, to survive them.

He'd come out here, not because he needed to be alone but because if he'd stayed he would have said the words carved into his heart so many years ago. And if he spoke them he knew that it would make it harder for her to leave. And no matter how much he loved her, how much he desperately wanted the future she'd painted over dinner, he knew that it was not *her* future.

She had been born to be Svardia's Princess. More so than any other member of her family. The faith and love she had in and for her people, *all* her people, was the true jewel of the crown. And he couldn't let her sacrifice that. Not from fear. Not when he knew, he *knew*, she had the strength and determination to face down anything that was thrown at her. That she would be integral to turn the tide in attitudes, to ensure a greater understanding and, even more, that she could be an advocate for that change.

Deep within him was a conviction so sure, so strong, that she would achieve truly great things. Pride, fierce and powerful, rippled through him at the thought. She was already magnificent in his eyes. He just couldn't wait for the world to see it too. Even if it meant he could never be by her side. Even if it meant that he'd never get to tease her about her cooking, or argue with her views, kiss away her anger or soothe her hurts. Even if it meant that he could never tell her that he loved her.

He heard the crunch of her boots in the snow behind him and he turned, not wanting to miss a single second of the little time they had left together. Shapeless in the thick outdoor jacket, hat, boots and scarf, Freya had never looked more beautiful to him. Her eyes gleamed as the last of the clouds passed from the sky to reveal the scattering of diamonds against velvet above them and still the majesty of the natural world wasn't enough to draw his gaze from her.

She looked as if she were about to say something when her eyes locked on something over his shoulder and widened in awe as a gasp fell from her lips and even then he couldn't look away from her. He imagined what she was seeing. Invisible until the thick heavy clouds passed from the sky, the northern lights bathed the stars in colours that seemed unnatural. Her eyes danced across the twists and turns of a kaleidoscope, focusing in and out on a whole palette of incandescent greens, purples, pinks and more.

'It's incredible,' she said, the words dropping from her lips in whispered awe.

'It is,' he agreed, thinking only of her, his heart stuttering over a beat when she moved her gaze from the sky to his.

'How long do you think we have?' she asked, and he was unable and unwilling to pretend not to know what she meant.

'They'll probably arrive a few hours after dawn.'

She nodded, something passing across her gaze before she blinked it away.

'I'll take the medal.' The words rushed out of him

but he wouldn't take them back. It was the only thing he could give her. She smiled then. It was sad but strong, hurt but alive, and then it was his turn to smile.

It killed him, tore his heart in two, but he wouldn't have it any other way. 'You're going to keep your title. You're going to stay a princess.'

He lifted his hand to cup her jaw and she nodded into his palm, turning her lips to press sad kisses that mixed with the single tear that escaped across her cheek.

'I can't say goodbye. Not yet. Please don't make me say it.' She spoke into his hand, her eyes pressed closed as if in denial of what was happening.

'Then we won't,' he said simply as if his heart hadn't fractured a thousand times over.

# CHAPTER TEN

FLAMES FLICKERED FROM the wood burner in the dark cabin; the light left off from when she had gone to find Kjell by the lake. She went to the switch but he stopped her, taking her hand in his and leading her to the window, where the entire landscape was a glowing display of vibrant colours that burned her heart.

She would never see this again. Not from this cabin, not from beside this man. He stood behind her and she felt so safe. So protected. But she knew that she couldn't have him. She loved him but, for the first time in her life, she thought that it wasn't enough.

'Make me forget. Just for tonight?' she whispered into the room. From behind her, he placed a kiss on her shoulder, then her neck, then that secret place that sent shivers down her spine and across her stomach. She spun in his arms to face him, to see him for as long as possible, even if they only had hours left. Her hands reached for his face, drawing him towards her, and she curved into him as his lips took hers. Tongues thrust and parried, teeth nipped and teased, hearts pounded and pulses tripped.

She couldn't get enough, touch enough, taste enough. She wanted to consume a lifetime's worth of him and still it wouldn't be enough. His skin was hot and smooth beneath her palms, her fingers inching beneath the jumper, sweeping up over muscles that rippled beneath her hands, and she wanted it against her own.

She tugged at his jumper impatiently, pulling and pushing, but not managing either, until his hands swept hers aside and he drew the jumper over his head, cast it aside and returned to a kiss that had her toes curling. It should have been funny, but it wasn't. It was sad and she wanted to cry and the kisses weren't enough and the need she felt would never be sated. The hurt she felt would never be healed. She gasped into his kiss, grief a hitch in her breath, the feeling of loss too soon and too much.

His kiss gentled and became soothing and reassuring as if trying to calm the ferocious hurt that swept over her. His palm was hot against her back, his fingers toying with the hem of her top, but it wasn't enough, not nearly. She pulled the top over her head and, like he had, cast it aside. She'd not worn a bra that morning and his eyes feasted on her, roaming her flame-licked skin as if imprinting it on his mind for years to come.

He reached up, palming her breasts at the same time, the warmth, the possessiveness of his touch, the way his thumbs toyed with her nipples bringing fissures of pleasure to a shell she'd not realised she'd worn ever since the night they'd parted eight years ago. It shattered beneath his touch, exposing the vulnerable untouched heart of her. She wanted to give him this. He deserved that much at least. If this night—this stolen night—was all they were to have then they would make enough memories for them both to last a lifetime.

Her determination made her bold. She pulled him back to her, this time *her* lips, her touch possessive and needy. She had been consumed by him once. Now she wanted to consume. Her tongue thrust deep into his mouth, his eyes flaring at the invasion, the primal claim she laid against him. Her fingers rifling through the thick golden strands and framing his head as she pressed herself up against his chest, delighting in the friction of his skin against her already taut nipples. His hand swept down and around her backside, squeezing her against him and pressing the length of his arousal against her core. Through the layers of clothing she felt him, felt his heat, his need for her and she wanted it, she wanted it all.

He drew her thigh upwards, hooking her leg over his hip, the angle a heavenly pressure on the sensitive bundle of nerves at the heart of her need and she cried out into his mouth. Shivering, her fingers flew to his trousers, freeing the button and pulling at the tab of the zip, but before she could draw it down he hoisted her up into his arms and she was forced to wrap her other leg around him for stability.

'You're rushing me,' he growled against her mouth.

She held back a smile. 'I am not. I'm rushing *me*.'

'There's no need. I'm going to take my time with you.'

'Actually,' she replied archly, 'I had planned to take my time with—'

He dropped down to the sofa, cradling her in his lap, but shocking the breath from her lungs and hauling her up against his chest. His hand palmed her backside, long fingers inching further beneath her, sensual anticipation driving her wild. She lifted to give him more room, arching into him, her breasts pressing against his chest, her breath expanding in her lungs, wanting, needing. But an arched brow above a knowing gaze pressed her back down and Freya knew she was being toyed with. Perhaps, Freya thought wryly, he had forgotten who he was playing with.

Having Freya hot and wanting in his lap was a lifetime of fantasies rolled into one. She twisted and turned like flames in his grasp, but if this was the last night they would share together he wanted to savour every minute of it. And he wasn't above teasing her to get what he wanted. He pulled gently on her shoulders, pressing her into his lap and sending her head backwards, the pleasure she found there shivering across her skin, but by the time she raised her head to look at him, wickedness sparked in her gaze and he stilled for long enough to wonder what she had planned. That second was, apparently, all she needed.

Placing her hands on his thighs, she lifted herself off his lap and slid between his legs. It was so quick he'd not been able to catch her and, before he could move, she'd undone the zip of his trousers and his heart was pounding so hard in his chest he thought he'd be able to see it.

'Freya...' It was supposed to have been an admonishment, but instead it came out half plea, half prayer and all curse. He wouldn't last. Not like this. Not even in his wildest fantasies had he seen his princess on her knees before him and just the sight of it was enough to undo him.

And he didn't doubt for one second that she knew it too. He reached for where her hands sat at the top of his thighs and she batted him away. Clenching his jaw, he pressed his fists down on the sofa cushion beside his legs and watched her like a hawk. The curve to her lip was victorious and he wouldn't do anything to take that away from her. It made his heart soar. Until it stopped altogether as her eyes widened to the size of saucers when she realised he wasn't wearing anything beneath his trousers.

Pressing apart the trouser opening, she reached for him and he flinched, his erection jerking against her palm in arousal and need. His fist tightened on itself, pressing deeper and harder into the cushion as he held himself back.

Her fingers wrapped around him, flexing against his hardened length, drawing her caress upwards, slowly, *so* slowly, before gliding down and, before he could think to stop her, she took him into her mouth and he turned the air blue with curses that would have shocked even his soldiers.

He pressed his fisted hand against his mouth to prevent anything further escaping—like the groan that was building in the back of his throat and the pleas that were threatening to undo any semblance of manhood he'd ever had. Begging was not an option.

At least not until she swirled her tongue around the delicate head of his penis and he knew he was going to hell.

The thrill of holding him in her mouth was something Freya could never have imagined. The power and trust of it humbled her. But it was the pleasure she took from it for herself that was the surprise. Skin like smooth velvet wrapped around steel that she couldn't get enough of. She took him in further and deeper until he filled her mouth completely and she didn't think she could take any more. But the sound of the growl Kjell made, primal and desperate, and all the things he made her feel… it made her wet with want. Her eyes flickered up to his and she froze.

The sheer ferocity of need in his eyes had her heart tripping over itself. The low pulse that had throbbed incessantly now stung with the intensity of arousal flickering over her skin and in the hollow of her body that wanted nothing more than him to fill it. She thought she'd felt empty before, when she'd received her diagnosis. But the *force* she wanted him with…she would never feel complete without him.

In that moment before she could properly understand her own thoughts he claimed back control, gently pulling her up, both of them slick with want and need. He wasted no time in peeling the thermal layers away from her waist, down her hips and from her legs, one at a time. And just like that she was naked in his lap, the rough feel of his trouser zip on the underside of her sensitive thighs sending shivers through her body.

She shifted in his lap, teasing herself against the hardened length of him, and when she saw him watching her she blushed.

'Don't stop.' The rough words sounding ripped from him.

'What?' she asked, avoiding the fierce heat of his gaze.

'Never stop taking your pleasure,' he commanded, his eyes dark with desire and something that looked almost like desperation. 'There is *nothing* more beautiful to see than you taking your pleasure from me.'

She speared her bottom lip with her teeth, as both an anchor and a bloom of infinitesimal hurt to keep the need coursing through her veins in check. She was breathless with want—the look in his eyes a challenge, a *dare*.

*What do you need to believe again?*

He was showing her how much of a woman she was— whether she could have children or not. Whether they had a future together or not—he was giving her this. He was showing her how to take her power.

She rolled her hips, sliding against the hard length of him, the sweep across her clitoris sensual, slick and violently arousing. It came on fast—the waves of desire washing through her body, building and building, sighs and groans hitching her breath higher and higher. Before her mind could process the incredible sensation, Kjell gripped her hips, adding his hold to the pressure and her back bowed as she came, her eyes saw stars as Kjell worshipped her breasts, his hold on her safe and protective.

Freya returned to the feel of Kjell's arms around her, holding her upright in his lap, pressing delicate kisses to her collarbone that threatened to reignite a fire only just tempered.

'Stay with me,' he said between kisses. 'Don't return to Svardia.' Her heart twisted at his words, her soul aching to say yes. Open-mouthed, he kissed down to her shoulder and back, his tongue teasing and teeth gently marking. 'We can spend the rest of our days making love in front of the fire, watching the seasons change, the sun rise and set before the northern lights, and eat absolutely none of your cooking,' he said and she could feel the smile on his lips against her skin. 'Stay with me,' he whispered.

It was a call she felt to the depth of her soul. She wanted it so much it hurt to breathe.

'Kjell…'

'I know. I know I shouldn't ask, and I know even more that you shouldn't stay here. You need to be the Princess you were born to be. I would never take that away from you. I just… I need a minute to be selfish before I let you go.'

It was those things, but it was also more. More than he could see at that moment. Deep down, she couldn't put words to the fear that she'd never be able to give him enough. As a princess, her focus and her time would always be split between him and her people. As a woman, she could never carry the children he deserved. And no matter how much healing had happened here, between them and for each of them, that shamed her still. Hurt her deeply. And she would never bind them together in that hurt. She would never damage the love that they had for each other in that way. She thought of a thousand things she could say, all full of love, regret, sorrow and even some of joy. But instead she chose the words that had given her so much.

'Take what you need.'

The flash of fire in his eyes was all the notice she had before her world turned into one of pure sensual sensation. He rolled her in his arms so that she lay on the soft buttery leather of the sofa. His forearms were braced either side of her head, the flex of his powerful shoulders, so broad they made her feel crowded in the most delicious of ways. Completely surrounded by his body, but free to move as she wished, she arched into him, desperate for the touch of his skin.

His hands swept over her body, leaving trails of burning embers in their wake, heating her body, igniting an arousal that built touch by touch, kiss by kiss, until she was damp with need and panting with desire. His worship of her felt endless and she allowed herself to indulge purely in him and what he was giving them both.

He removed his jeans before gently pressing her thighs apart. They fell to his touch with shocking ease. She felt exposed but not vulnerable, on display but not for him: for *them*. She'd never felt such a sense of power, of confidence. Her heart beat just for him.

'Can you see what I see?'

She nodded, unable to look away from his face. She couldn't find the words to answer his question as his gaze covered every inch of her with exquisite intimacy. She wanted to reach for him, but she couldn't move. Wouldn't move. Everything she'd ever wanted was right there in that moment. And it was a moment that would have to last her a lifetime.

For a second she thought she saw him tremble as he came over her, but he covered her body with his, peppered her skin with kisses and touches and everything fell from her mind when she felt him at her entrance.

She felt the stillness come over him, demanding she look up at him. Demanding that she was with him in this exact moment.

'There will never be anyone else, do you understand that?'

She wanted to tell him the same. She wanted to tell him how much she loved him, but the words stuck in her throat a second too long and he seized that moment to slide into her with a thrust that felt endless and utterly complete.

Kjell's eyes drifted shut against his will as the feel of her encompassed him wholly. To be encased within her was a pleasure that was indescribable. Blood pounded in his veins, his heart lurched dramatically and the world as he knew it shifted for ever. He was marked by her. Branded.

And he wished to stay there for ever, his body reacting to the tightening of hers, the way she gripped him, as if taking him even further into her, until he couldn't tell where he ended and she began.

Her back arched, bringing her chest upwards against his, and he snaked an arm behind her, holding her to him as he began to move, as the need in him became fierce and demanding, pushing them both towards an impossible conclusion. Sweat beaded the base of his spine as he thrust into her, her legs spreading for him, welcoming him deeper, her cries urging him on, hands pulling him harder against her, pleas demanding *more, faster, harder*.

Anything. He'd give her anything she wanted.

Sweat-slicked skin slid together, the heady erotic sounds driving their passion to maddening heights and depths. The cries of her pleasure a symphony he'd never tire of hearing, inflaming his need to wildness.

His orgasm pressed at the edges of his consciousness, but he thrust it back fiercely. He would fight to make this last, to make this something that Freya would never forget. Her head rolled back against the cushion as he drove into her. But he wanted to see her. To watch pleasure fill her gaze.

'Look at me,' he commanded selfishly as he encased himself to the hilt in her, relishing the gasp of pleasure that fell from lips above closed eyes. He withdrew so slowly it was a punishment for them both. 'Look at me,' he said, nearly leaving the warmth of her body completely. 'Please,' he begged, almost willingly losing his pride.

Her eyes burst open, a skyscape of clouds, stars and golden lights. The sight of it was the only thing that calmed the raging of his heart and loosened the leash needed on his restraint. He thrust into her, hard and fast, again and again, shamelessly driving them towards an orgasm so powerful that, when it broke, it shattered them both completely.

Kjell should have been in a sleep so deep that only Freya could reach him. But he wasn't. Sleep remained as elusive as the future. Soft, gentle sighs came from Freya's slumber and although he didn't want to leave her for even a minute of the time they had left, he knew what he had to do.

Slipping from beneath the fur throw that was warm from Freya's body, he pulled on his trousers and went to the stove, trying hard not to think too much about his actions. He put on a pot of coffee and turned to where he had last seen the AAR.

He retrieved the pages and placed them on the table, barely able to look at them. He found a pen and flicked it between his fingers as he waited for the coffee to filter through. He hated that he was away from Freya. That he was wasting even a single second, but he needed to do this. Because he might not be able to do it after she left. He poured steaming, thick black coffee into his cup and, with determination steeling every single inch of his being, he sat down at the table and put pen to paper.

*At sixteen hundred hours on the seventeenth of November...*

The smell of coffee woke her. It wasn't the full hit of recently brewed coffee, more of a scent left in the air, long after consumption. Warm not hot, sweet not bitter. She felt the addictive heat of Kjell's body beside her and turned, taking in the look of serenity across features that were hardly ever so still. He seemed so much younger in that moment and she resisted the urge to trace the angles of his face for fear of waking him. One long arm was stretched out, his cheek resting on it, as if taking up as little of the deep sofa as possible. Even in sleep he was conscious of her and giving for her. Her heart curled in on itself as she realised that this was how she wanted to remember him.

Gently, she slid from the sofa and, wrapping herself in one of the throws, she went to the kitchen—pausing at the beautiful hand-made wooden table to see the AAR. Kjell's tight, neat handwriting filled page after page and she sighed, thankful that in this, at least, he had found his peace.

She pressed a finger against the cup half filled with coffee. It was cold. He must have worked through the last hours of darkness to complete the report. She cast a look back to where he slept, the sight filling her with a sense of warmth that took her by surprise.

She must have stayed like that for a while because it took her a moment to register the sound of the beep. Frowning, she had to hear it a few more times until she realised that it was her sat phone. She followed the next beep quickly, hoping to get to it before it woke Kjell. She took the phone with her into the boot room and risked the frigid icy cold as she opened the door and leaned out to get enough signal.

'Your Highness?'

'I'm here, Gunnar.'

'We will be with you in about thirty minutes.'

'I'll be ready,' she lied, her words frosting the cold air. The shiver that racked her body had nothing to do with the temperature and everything to do with the thought of leaving Kjell behind. She knew she should wake him, but she'd meant what she'd said the night before. She couldn't say goodbye. He might have given her the strength to embrace herself and face the public fallout, but no one could ask her to be strong enough to say goodbye to the man who had her heart.

Kjell heard the door to the cabin click shut and his heart lurched. Instantly he was awake, shock severing his connection to sleep. She was gone. He felt it more surely than he'd ever known anything before. Rage roared from his heart as he threw himself into last night's clothes. The sound of a helo nearby raced his pulse and rode him urgently forward. He had to see her, he had to stop her before she could leave.

*He hadn't told her.*

With an arm half in his jacket, his feet thrust into untied boots, he flung open the cabin door and hurled himself out into the snow. Clear blue skies taunted him and he could see Freya up ahead, getting into the helicopter.

His heart yelled her name and, as if she'd heard it, Freya turned at that exact moment and the hurt and sorrow in her gaze nearly felled him where he was. He stopped in his tracks, knowing that to go any further would only hurt them both.

But the damage was done. She'd left without saying goodbye. Without letting him tell her how much he loved her. His body was stuck, torn between the urge to pull her back to him and push her from him. She deserved to be the Princess she could be. To help others—as she always had. She could not do that and be with him. He knew that. He understood that duty and hated that it was a sacrifice they both would make over and over again.

*There will never be anyone else.*

His words from last night were whispered back to him on the wind as the helicopter lifted from the ground, the downwash throwing snow into the air, and he took them to the deepest parts of his soul.

# CHAPTER ELEVEN

FREYA STARED AT the leafy green palace garden and in-stead saw snow. Cold tendrils snapped out at her and even in the spring sunshine of Svardia she couldn't get warm. Ever since she had left Dalarna two days ago, she had felt a fine shiver across her heart and it spread a chill through her body. This was what it felt like when a heart broke, she realised. She would have to take it deep within her, because she would live with it for the rest of her life.

Just then it was too raw to think of Kjell. To imagine what he was doing, what he was thinking, to wonder what he'd felt when he'd seen her disappear into the sky without having said goodbye.

*Coward.*

She cursed herself. He had deserved more than that and she hadn't been strong enough. She forced her hands to unfurl, not needing to look to know that her nails had imprinted crescents onto her palms. She should have told him. He should have heard the words.

But she *had* done the right thing by returning to Svardia. She could do so much good here and he could be so much more without her. A father. A good and lov-ing husband.

*There will never be anyone else.*

His promise taunted the future she saw for him but she

knew, *they* knew, it had been the right decision. Even if it left a scar on her heart that would never heal.

'Come.'

The command cut into her thoughts and Freya entered her brother's office, struck hard by the garish baroque design after the stunning simplicity of Kjell's cabin. She felt Aleksander's eyes assessing her. And suddenly that ice-cold thread winding around her heart turned to white-hot fury.

'How did it go?' Aleksander asked, his tone unusually gentle. But she wasn't ready to be gentled. No. She was ready to show a little of the less than perfect Princess she had learned that it was okay to be.

'You bastard.'

Anyone else would have flinched, but her brother simply stared back at her, waiting for an answer.

'You knew what you were doing when you sent me there. You knew what had happened to Kjell.'

'Yes.'

'So, either you set me up to fail because you knew he would refuse the medal, or you set him up to face the most painful experience of his life and take the medal so that I would be free. Because you *knew* he would do that for me.'

'Yes.'

'That isn't an answer.' Her voice was harsh with accusation. She hated this cryptic, cold man her brother had become. Oh, she had absolutely no doubt that he'd be the perfect King, a good ruler for Svardia...but at what cost? 'When did you become so cruel?'

'When I realised just how much damage had been done to my little sisters by our parents' overzealous focus on monarchy.'

Freya reared back as if she'd been struck. They'd

never really spoken of their parents' behaviour or treatment of them. It had been a sort of mute acceptance. Duty to the crown first and always. 'I don't…' She trailed off, unsure what to say.

'You are staying, yes? Maintaining your title and role?'

'Yes,' she said, a little unsure as to the swift turn of the conversation.

'And Bergqvist is refusing the medal?'

'Yes.'

There was a beat while her brother took this in. To the world, he might look as if he were deciding his next step, but Freya knew the speed with which his quick intelligence worked. Knew the way he considered people and decisions like pieces on a chessboard, weighing up all possible consequences of each move before it was made.

'Okay. The investiture is set for two weeks' time, but the Vårboll is on Friday. If you are staying, I shall expect you to be in attendance.'

Freya had forgotten about the Spring Ball held at the palace every year. She was nodding her agreement. 'I'm meeting with Stellan in—' she checked her watch '—about ten minutes. I still want to get the matter in front of parliament before the May recess.'

'Okay,' Aleksander replied. 'And you have a plan to address the press?'

And, just like that, Princess Freya of Svardia returned. Only this was a new Princess, and she couldn't help but see a little more assessment, a little more respect from her brother as they parried back and forth over the next seven minutes on the plan she had developed with Henna to reveal her infertility to the press. Aleksander insisted that they wait as long as possible before going public. But 'as long as possible' really only covered a few months.

And the royal household's PR department would need to get going on it immediately.

And even in that short time Freya felt emotionally drained by the conversation. She would have to stretch these muscles, learn how to build up the emotional strength to become an advocate, not a victim. And Freya promised herself she would make the time to do so. She couldn't, wouldn't, go back to being half a princess—part fantasy image and only part herself. Svardia—and she—deserved nothing but her truth.

'When are you going to tell Marit?' Freya finally asked.

Aleksander looked up at her and Freya couldn't shake the feeling that there was something at play. Concern twisted in her heart for her sister. 'Aleksander. What have you done?'

'I'd rather wait just a little longer before informing her of your decision.' It didn't escape her notice that her brother had refused to answer her question.

'Sander,' she said, using his childhood name, calling on the long-ago bond between them.

'It's important.'

'Will you explain why?'

'Soon.'

A knock sounded on the office door.

'Yes?' Aleksander called.

Freya turned to see Henna in the doorway, looking apologetic for interrupting. 'I've put Stellan in your office,' she said to Freya.

Freya nodded and, looking to her brother, was surprised by the fierce look in the gaze Aleksander cast at Henna. Frowning, she turned back to Henna but she was already gone.

Freya opened her mouth to speak, but her brother spoke before she could even form the thought.

'Good luck with Stellan.'

'I'm going to need it,' she replied.

'Yes, you are,' she heard, as she left the King of Svardia's office.

Adrenaline flooded Kjell's body, his heart pounded so hard it should have given up long ago, sweat poured down across his skin. An hour-long punishing run and it still wasn't enough to rid him of the memory of watching Freya disappear into the sky in that helicopter.

He yanked open the door to the boot room, stripped himself naked and blindly made his way to the shower, refusing to even look at the sofa. It didn't work. He clenched his jaw against the cascade of erotic images that poured through his mind like the sigh that Freya made just after she came. He was going to have to burn that sofa unless he wanted to lose his goddamned mind.

He ignored the way the bathroom door slammed against the wall, ignored the shiver of disapproval he felt from his ancestors, ignored the instinctive reminder to feed the wood burner in case it went out.

He stepped into the shower, spun the dial to cold and braced himself against the tiles as the frigid spray poured down on his overheated skin. He was breathing hard and he couldn't honestly say that it was just down to the run. But arousal was so much better than the unappeased ache that he'd been left with the moment Freya had gone.

Her back arched in his mind, her head lost against the pillow, her breasts in his hands and her taste on his tongue, a long slow sweep of her clitoris and the cry of her pleasure in his ears. He took himself in hand, his grip like steel sliding slowly down to the hilt of his erection, and all he wanted was her hands. Her mouth. Her touch. The mockery of imitation sad and pathetic, enough to cut through his arousal.

He slammed the fleshy side of a fist against the wall. Once. Then twice. It wasn't right. Something deep inside was itching and scratching as if to get out and he hated it.

*To face it you need to change the way you think about it. To not see it as a threat, but as an experience.*

His own words came back to haunt him. He flicked off the shower and grabbed a towel, drying himself with ruthless strokes that grazed his skin. He pulled fresh clean clothes on and poured a cup of coffee, turning to lean back against the sideboard.

He looked over to find the note Freya had left him.

*You should go home now, Kjell.*

His gut clenched. He saw his father—the disappointment that would be waiting for him. He'd failed again. As a soldier. As a son. He clenched his jaw. But he wouldn't fail as a friend. Before he could change his mind, he picked up his phone and keyed in a number he knew by heart. The international dialling tone sounded harsh, impatient, and for a second he thought the call would ring out.

'*Sì?*' Distracted—irritated, even—the tone wasn't what he'd expected. '*Pronto?*'

'Marella?'

'*Cristo*, Kjell? Is that you?' Enzo's wife asked in English.

'Yes.'

Static shifted in his ear as if she had covered the speaker. Faint Italian words sounded in the background and the static shifted again, making way for a deep sigh.

'Are you okay?' she asked him.

He barked out a sad laugh. 'That was my question to ask you,' he chided. He could imagine her smiling a little, but he knew she was waiting for him to answer. 'Yes. No. Maybe?'

'That would be my answer to the question you wanted to ask,' she said quietly.

There was a moment of silent grief shared across skies and countries.

'I'm sorry I didn't—'

'No. No, there's no apologies here,' she interrupted him before he could even finish. 'None, Kjell. Enzo was a soldier. It was more than a uniform, for him as much as you. I knew that before I married him and I knew it when I…when I buried him. He was and always will be the love of my life. And I wouldn't have changed him for the world.' The strength of her words, the fierceness of her love—he felt it in his heart.

'He saved them, Marella. The children he protected. He saved every single one of them.' He couldn't give her much, but he could give her that. He heard the tears that Enzo's wife cried in that moment, felt them as if they were his own.

'*Grazie*, Kjell. Thank you.'

'I should go—'

'Wait,' she said, cutting off his attempt to end the call. 'He would have wanted…' Her breath hitched and she tried again. 'He would have wanted you to take the medal.'

'What?' He felt the blood drain from his face.

'The guys were talking about it at the wake. The medal you were refusing. Enzo wouldn't have wanted that, Kjell,' she said, the rebuke in her tone gentle but clear. 'He always said that you deserved more than one for what you'd done over the years.'

Tears thickened her voice as she thanked him for calling and he felt his own rise up, not feeling an ounce of shame for the evidence of his own grief. They spoke for a few more minutes, made promises to visit each other as soon as possible, and Kjell ended the call feeling bruised but not beaten.

Once again, his gaze drifted to the crumpled note Freya had left him.

*You should go home now, Kjell.*

Freya had left him without saying goodbye. Without hearing the words she deserved to hear. Screwing up the note she'd left him, he threw it on the flames of the wood burner.

Kjell was done with unfinished business.

Freya took one last look at the selfie her sister had just sent her. Marit was pressed up next to a man handsome in all the ways that Kjell was not: dark, lean, silver-eyed, with just enough of a glint of danger to match her wayward younger sister. But it was the smile on Marit's face that had caught Freya's notice. The purity of it, the unconscious joy of it, warmed the ache in Freya's heart. She wasn't sure what games her brother had been playing, but for her sister it had turned out happily at least. There would be time to catch up with all the dramatic events, but now was not it. All Freya needed to know was that her beloved sister had found a man who loved her as she deserved to be loved.

Putting down the phone, Freya looked at herself in her bedroom mirror, turning from to one side to the other. Hundreds of thousands of crystals sewn into champagne-coloured silk sparkled in the light, sending a shimmer

rippling across the exquisite art deco pattern made with
the hand-sewn beads. Thin straps caressed her shoulders,
connecting to a deep V neck that stopped a little below
demure and just above risqué. The corset that hugged her
torso stopped at a belt around the waist before dropping
into layers of tulle mixed with silk, making the beads
look like rivulets of water falling to the floor and into a
train that trailed behind her.

With her hair plaited and pinned back into a neat nest
above her neck, she looked exactly like the royal she was.
Henna had left the Prussian blue velvet box her brother
had sent her on the dressing table. Freya knew what it
was. She had worn it at the Officers' Ball in Vienna,
which had counted—for the most part—as her coming
out or debutante ball.

Wearing the tiara now, Freya felt as if she was reaf-
firming her promise to her family, her country even: the
promise of her duty. And that her brother had thought
of it made her heart soften towards him, hoping that the
boy she'd once known was still in there somewhere. She
lifted the lid on the box containing the family heirloom,
knowing the diamond-encrusted gold tiara matched her
dress perfectly.

This was her brother's first Vårboll and it would be
nothing short of exquisite. Champagne had been brought
in from the choicest vintners, caviar from sustainably
sourced fisheries, and the music was being performed
by the finest of Svardia's musicians.

International royalty, global dignitaries, billion-
aires, tech magnates and titans of industry. They had
all been invited to help Aleksander bring Svardia into
the twenty-first century as a powerful player on the
world's stage. And until he found a wife, Freya would
be there to help him.

She cast a last look at herself in the mirror, her pale gaze haunted by the memory of snow and heat and the man who had her heart, before turning away. Flexing her hands in the hope of shaking off some of the cold that nipped at her fingers, Freya caught the unrestrained sorrow in Henna's gaze.

'Henna,' Freya gently admonished. 'Please don't. It's fine. *I'm* fine. Really.'

Henna gave her one long considering look and nodded reluctantly. Freya had told her only the bare bones of what had happened in Dalarna, half afraid that if she spoke any more the words would open the fissure in her heart and she would break completely.

'Let's go,' Freya said, marshalling her courage to become the Princess she wanted to be. She would never be perfect. She had learned that, not because Kjell had made her feel anything less, but precisely because he'd made her feel perfect in her imperfections. Now, Freya wanted to be *herself.* Only by accepting that would she be able to survive the fallout of her infertility. For her family to survive it.

They approached the staircase that led down into the Rilderdal Palace ballroom from the first-floor balcony that wrapped around the grand chamber, and Freya paused for a moment to take in the majesty of the sight.

Chandeliers of glass cut a thousand times over a hundred years ago hung from the domed ceiling high above them, scattering light onto the gold filagree and inlay on the mouldings and cornices and shining down on the floor below. Waiters in red fine wool jackets served flutes of champagne and canapés on silver trays, candelabras provided atmosphere beside exquisite flower displays trailing ivy and eucalyptus from fountains of white peonies.

*Opulence.* It was the only word that came to mind. Her gaze grazed emeralds in earlobes, diamonds on fingers, rubies on wrists and sapphires nestled in bosoms of the female guests. Gold, silver and just as many jewels graced the cufflinks of the men, enough to fill the greatest of war chests.

A war chest the like of which she could hopefully one day put to use for causes that affected not just Svardian people but *all* people. Determination schooled features that she would once have hidden behind a picture-perfect mask. She would hide herself no more.

'Freya—'

'It's time for me to make my *grand* entrance,' Freya interrupted, her tone strong, and feeling it too. She had faced freezing cold water, she had faced the loss of every single thing she had ever wanted, and she was still here.

She arrived at the top of the staircase and the music faded into the background. Slowly descending into the Spring Ball, she used the confidence Kjell had helped her to find in her own strength to be the Princess that Svardia deserved—that *she* deserved.

Her brother waited for her at the bottom of the staircase with his arm out to hers in welcome. Despite their tense exchange earlier in the week, they'd quickly and easily forgiven each other and focused their attempts to ensure Svardia thrived under Aleksander's rule.

As she was introduced and reintroduced to the most important of people, she found a rhythm that was familiar but also new. It held traces of who she had once been, but also who she would become. And while it didn't chase away the cold that nipped at her heart, it did appease it a little.

She was just about to greet the Minister for Agriculture when she felt her brother's arm tense beneath her hand. Looking up and finding his gaze locked over her shoulder, she turned to find the source of his agitation... and her heart stopped.

Making his way towards her in the full dress uniform of the Svardian Armén, clean-shaven, tall, powerful and determined, Kjell looked utterly magnificent. Not only did he not look out of place—he outshone every man there. Her starved gaze took him in, the crisp cream coat with gold brocade and Prussian blue sash would have been eye-catching on anyone, but Kjell wore it to devastating effect. The display of medals across his chest made her hand clench in memory of the honour he and his friend deserved. The dark trousers in fine wool showed off the powerful muscles of his thighs, their forward march towards her seemingly unending and impossible to stop.

Female heads turned in his wake, lascivious gazes on every face. Men watched with eyes full of jealousy, envy, some just as lustful. But every single person parted for him without question or direction, they simply moved for him.

Freya's heart leapt painfully in her chest, and for the first time since leaving Dalarna her body was warmed by a flush that crested over her like a wave. For the space of a single breath her heart soared, believing that he had come to claim her so that they could be together finally. But then her brother shifted beside her and she remembered. Remembered that it couldn't be. That, without a title, he would never be allowed to marry her. And on an exhalation a heartache so acute filled her lungs she feared she would never recover.

Intense arctic blue eyes held hers with a thousand

promises and apologies, as if he'd known that this would hurt her but that he'd not been able to stay away. Her hand dropped from Aleksander's arm and she took one step towards Kjell, then another, even though everything in her wanted to *run* to him.

They met in the middle of the ballroom floor, bound in silence by a spell only love could weave. He bowed to her, low and deep. Ignoring the barely hushed, curious whispers of the guests around them, Freya curtsied to him so deeply that there was no doubt to anyone watching that she saw him as her equal. No matter what rank or title he did or did not have, she would always meet him as such.

Kjell straightened to see Freya curtsy deep into the silk of her skirts. Her head bent in deference to him was a sight so humbling he felt red slashes form across his cheeks. The gentle slope of her breast encased by the jewelled corset offered him the most vulnerable part of her—and he felt as if she had known it, had offered it to him on purpose; the soldier in him roared against the fragility of her heart, but the man in him growled contentedly in appeasement.

He held his hand out to hers and when she placed her palm against his, his heart ached to realise that this was the *true* home he'd been exiled from. Eight years he'd been without her and there would be so many more years to come. But this, *this* he was selfish enough to take.

The tap of the conductor's baton called the musicians to attention and Kjell brought Freya into a hold, his palm pressing against her back, the heat of her body calming him like nothing else had ever done in all the years since he'd first met her.

Freya looked up at him, her amber eyes trusting and

utterly uncaring of the surroundings. With one hand in his, she bent to pick up the skirt of her dress with the other, and his heart pounded just to see how incredible she looked, the beads on her dress not even close to the sparkling beauty of her eyes.

The music started the moment he took them into the first step of a waltz and the rest of the world disappeared. She was alive in his hands, her movements lithe and graceful, her natural poise so profoundly balancing to his erratic heart, he feared he genuinely might not survive without her. But it was her trust in him that moved him the most. Her trust so complete that he could lead her anywhere and she would follow. Her trust that even then he would never lead her away from the duty they had both sacrificed so much for. A sacrifice he would continue to make. But only if he was finally able to speak the words in his heart.

'You left without saying goodbye.' His voice was low, audible only to her.

Her eyes flared, but still she didn't look away. 'I... I couldn't. I couldn't say it,' she confessed, pain breaking through the words. 'I'm sorry.'

'Don't be.' He looked away only briefly, catching Freya's brother's glare. 'I wouldn't have been able to let you go,' he admitted, the truth of his statement evident in the raw edge of his voice.

'But you can now?' she asked. He pulled her just a little closer into his hold, his legs sweeping through the layers of tulle and silk and beading, desperate to feel the warmth of her body.

'You were born for this, Freya, not *into* it. The title, the role...these things were meant for you.'

*I was meant for you*, a part of him cried, but he thrust it aside. For her.

'But you need to know—'

Her hand tightened in his hold, stalling his words, as if half wanting to stop him and half wanting him to never stop. He blew out a breath, steeling himself against the inevitable pain that would follow his words. But he stood by them. And she deserved more than anything to hear them.

'I love you.' His voice was a whisper but the power of those words struck like a bell's toll that changed their worlds. Her eyes filled, but not a single tear fell. Amber shimmering into gold. 'I will always stand by your decision to remain royal. But I will always love you.'

Her lips trembled until she speared her bottom lip with her teeth and he wished for all the world to reach for it, set it free with the pad of his thumb, but he felt every single set of eyes in the entire room on his back, watching intently, trying to fathom what was happening.

'Eight years ago, we didn't get the chance to do things properly. And when you left Dalarna...' His heart shattered all over again at the memory of her getting in the helicopter and disappearing into the snow-filled sky. 'We need to say goodbye.'

For the first time since he'd appeared, Freya dropped her gaze from his face and whispered, 'What if I can't?'

The waltz was reaching a crescendo, she could hear it and feel it in her breast.

'You can. Because you're the strongest person I know.'

Breath shuddered in Freya's chest and everything hurt. Her body, her skin, her heart... But instead of feeling the icy frigid grasp that had held her heart since leaving Kjell in Dalarna, a pulse of warmth beat within her. His words, his love, igniting a single ember into an inferno that bloomed and twirled and twisted until she felt the truth of it feed her, forge her strength anew. She looked up to find his head angled over her shoulder, the stark line of his jaw, the powerful and proud man she loved whole-heartedly. A man she would never touch again after that night.

She felt a single tear escape down her cheek. 'I love you,' she whispered, even though it broke her. It hurt and wrecked her, but he deserved to hear it too. 'I will never stop loving you.'

His jaw clenched, the muscle flaring, and when he turned his gaze to her, the raw pain in his eyes was only matched by her own. The music came to a crashing climactic conclusion and he drew them to a stop in the centre of the ballroom, watched by a hundred pairs of eyes.

He released her from his hold, stepped back, bowed low and deep, and this time the perfect Princess forgot all about etiquette, forgot to curtsy at all. Struck completely still, Freya watched as Kjell turned on his heel and left the ballroom.

On the far side of the ballroom Aleksander watched Bergqvist walk away from his sister, his jaw clenched and fury pounding in his veins. He was about to go to Freya when Henna appeared by his side. His sister's lady-in-waiting looked as angry as he felt.

'Fix it,' she commanded. Two little words in a tone that no one ever dared speak to him in.

He raised an imperious eyebrow that had quelled heads of state and countless politicians.

'I don't care what you have to do, just fix it.'

And she stalked off, leaving him just as confused as he always was whenever she was around. He looked up to see Kjell disappear through the large doors of the palace ballroom and decided that the time for subtlety was over.

# CHAPTER TWELVE

KJELL LEFT THE palace in a daze that no self-respecting soldier would tolerate. His heart pounded in his ears and his eyes were full of the last look Freya had given him, leaving him half blind and deaf and utterly vulnerable to attack.

It had been the right thing, but it had left him devastated in a way he would never recover from. Even Enzo's voice in his mind was quiet. Kjell made his way down cobbled streets in the old part of Torfarn, gently illuminated by streetlights wrapped in wrought iron filigree. He stumbled, feeling drunk without having touched a drop of alcohol and cursed, desperate to get himself under control before he arrived at his destination. Everything in him made him want to leave, to return to Sweden. But Freya had been right. He had to go home. Even if he wasn't sure that Svardia was it, he needed to see his parents. Needed to face his father.

His mother and father had moved out of the palace a few years ago as Brynjar had needed space for a workshop, which had been impossible in the palace staff housing. Kjell wondered if his mother missed it, having spent her life surrounded by the hundreds of live-in staff, the constant buzz he remembered from his childhood that had made integration into the army seamless.

After three hours of walking, he came to the front door of a modest house on a quiet suburban street. At two in the morning, he was surprised to find a gentle light glowing from the back of the house where his father's workshop was. He made his way through to the garden with the silent steps instinctive to a soldier, but still his father was waiting for him. The wide wooden door of the garage was open, revealing the workbench where Brynjar Bergqvist sat, polishing a small piece of metal.

His father peered at him over wire-framed glasses and, although he didn't smile or seem surprised, Kjell was half convinced he heard love in his father's voice when he said, 'Welcome home.'

Kjell nodded, unable to speak past the lump in his throat. He wished he could be stronger, wished he didn't have this need crawling beneath his skin, desperately reaching for something he could never have. But he knew that he needed to face this.

'It's good to be back,' Kjell replied.

'Is it?' his father asked, seeing more than he would ever say.

'No. Not really,' Kjell said, not having the will to mask the hurt with a laugh.

His father kicked out a stool for Kjell to sit on as he carried on tinkering with the piece of equipment half dismantled on the bench. Kjell sat on the stool and leaned back against the side of the workshop, letting the sounds of the night seep deep into his soul.

'Start at the beginning,' his father commanded, as if knowing that he needed to talk but wasn't quite sure how to.

With a voice rusty and raw, Kjell told his father about his first deployment with Enzo, what it had been like working with the UN. Kjell admitted how hard it had been coming back to Svardia, knowing that he couldn't stay but also feeling guilt for not wanting to stay.

Brynjar poured a couple of inches of the *akvavit* he kept in the drawer of his old workbench and passed a glass to Kjell. They drank their first mouthful to the woman they both loved, the second to absent friends and the third to the old Norse god of war, Odin, for allowing Kjell to return alive. The alcohol burned Kjell's throat and stung his eyes like a young boy taking his first sip. But his father never said a word.

'I'm not sure I can be a solider any more,' Kjell admitted, the words scraping his throat raw and unable to meet his father's eye. He held his breath until his father's next words, surprised by the question.

'Why did you want to be a soldier?'

*Because of you.*

But they didn't have the kind of relationship that would welcome such raw honesty in that deep visceral way.

'Because I wanted to serve my country. Because I wanted to give myself to a greater cause. But... I'm not sure it's enough any more.'

'Do you know why I left the *Försvarsmakten*?'

'Because Mum needed to be here?'

When there wasn't a reply, Kjell looked up at his father, realising for the first time that they'd never actually spoken of it. He had always assumed that his father had sacrificed his career for his wife and that resentment had been thrust so deep that it had kept Brynjar Bergqvist short worded and silent. He realised in that moment that he'd done his father a great disservice in thinking so.

Brynjar nodded sadly into the silence, as if divining his son's thoughts. He grabbed a stool and brought it beside Kjell and sat, finally putting aside the piece of metal that had consumed his attention.

His father took a deep breath. 'No. I left because I found that my heart had a new duty. A new purpose that would always come before King and country. And I didn't feel that I could honestly give Sweden my whole allegiance when it would always be elsewhere.'

'Mum was that purpose,' Kjell said, beginning to see his father in a different light.

'Yes,' his father admitted. 'And you.'

Kjell felt the sting of wetness press against his eyes. 'I'm not sure I'm worthy of it.'

'The fact that you even doubt that makes it clear that *I* am the one not worthy.'

Shock marred Kjell's features and heart.

Brynjar frowned into the distance. 'Your mother, she is the one who is good with words. I find them…difficult. My father? Now, he was truly terrible. At least you are better than I. It will bode well for your children.'

His heart lurched. 'I'm not sure that…' He bit off the words that cut his heart in two. There would and could never be anyone other than Freya. But even if they had come together, her infertility meant that was an impossibility. But something in his heart turned over. The memory of the children Enzo had saved, the savage destruction of communities he'd witnessed, the thousands of orphans he'd encountered over the years. There were so many children who needed and deserved the kind of unconditional love Freya was capable of. That *he* was capable of. The thought vanquished what he'd been about to tell his father and planted a seed in his heart that would one day grow into something more beautiful than he could ever have imagined.

'I think you have found a new duty,' his father said, nodding sagely. 'Well, she is definitely worthy of it.'

Kjell looked over at his father in shock, and not only because of the wry humour in his father's tone. 'You know?'

'About Freya? Yes,' Brynjar concluded.

'How?' Surely he hadn't caused that much of a scene at the palace.

'Because I told him.' The strong, authoritarian voice came from the other side of the garden and Kjell's head snapped up to see the King of Svardia. Pinpricks of shock and self-recrimination covered his skin. No one should have been able to sneak up on him like that. But he was beginning to suspect that Aleksander wasn't quite what everyone seemed to think he was.

In his peripheral vision Kjell saw his father pick up the piece of machinery and resume his focus on the object as if the King of Svardia wasn't there in his garden at three o'clock in the morning.

As Aleksander approached, his lazy gait might have fooled many but, now that Kjell was aware, he saw right through Freya's brother's assumed ease. Tension thrummed on the air as Kjell stood to meet his King, the informality of the setting making any display of courtesy awkward. Not to mention anger at what Aleksander had put Freya through by sending her to him in Dalarna.

'You sent her to me in the middle of a storm,' he growled, uncaring of hierarchy or power. The man in front of him had put the woman he loved in jeopardy.

'She was never in any danger,' dismissed the King of Svardia.

'Threat isn't always physical,' he replied, knowing how significant the emotional damage could have been.

'Which is why I sent her to you.'

Kjell scoffed, and purposely gave the man his back in a display of such disrespect even his usually stoic father frowned.

'Frankly, Kjell, I couldn't care less if you spend the rest of your life with your back to me. But is that what you would do to my sister?'

'I have given her the only thing I can,' he said bitterly. 'Her freedom. If I kept her she would never be fulfilled. She would never reach the potential she has within her. She would never do all that she could do for Svardia.'

'But you would if you could? Keep her? Love her?' The soft word sounded awkward and unusual in the harsh tone Aleksander had used, but that barely scraped Kjell's notice.

'With every single ounce of my being. Unquestionably and unendingly,' he said, the truth of his words shining bright, and he felt the unfurling of an impossible hope fill his breast.

'It will require the sacrifice of everything you know. Your freedom, your independence. Your allegiance would be to her and your privacy would never be your own again.' This time there was an undertone that Kjell couldn't ignore. It spoke quietly but deeply of secrets and hurt, and all but demanded to be heard, listened to and seriously considered. Kjell did Aleksander the courtesy of doing so. But when he met his King's gaze and spoke, his voice was level, powerful and sure.

'She has my heart. Everything else is immaterial.'

Aleksander nodded once. 'Good. Then let's get to work.'

Freya's cheeks hurt, her heart ached, her stomach twisted, but she smiled as the group of people around her all cheered. She accepted the congratulations of her team, Stellan's teary-eyed thanks and the begrudging acceptance of the minister she'd persuaded to help bring Stellan's worthy fight to parliament. Freya might have strong-armed him into it, but she knew that the minister wouldn't have agreed if he hadn't believed in the cause himself, or thought that there was hope of getting it through.

*This* was why she had returned. Why she had made the choice she had. And if she was given that same choice again, she'd make the same decision, even knowing how much it hurt to leave Kjell behind. To leave her heart behind.

With him she could achieve small steps, but here she could make giant leaps. And the same could be said of Kjell. With her, he would only take small steps towards the life he deserved. And he deserved so much more.

Henna stood at her shoulder with a smile so beautiful it eased some of Freya's hurt. 'I knew you could do it.'

'Of course I could.' Freya shrugged. 'It only took us four years,' she replied, thinking of how much she had invested in Stellan's cause, of the sacrifices the people in this room had also made.

'Do you know what you will turn your attention to next?' Henna asked, her gaze careful but watching.

Freya started nodding before she answered. 'Yes,' she replied, feeling the solemnity of it rise within her to fill spaces that would never be filled by a child. 'Yes, I do.'

Kjell had been right. Lending an empathetic ear, giving an understanding voice to women who might not have the ability to speak for themselves had become an all-consuming need. Freya felt it; all around the world people were experiencing this incredible moment where, instead of being scared and fearful, they had the opportunity to question, consider, explore what it meant to be who they were. To be *curious* about how they identified, who they wanted to be with. To be flexible rather than rigid in their feelings about it. The question of what it was to be female, feminine, womanly, *woman* was so bound up in the body and what it could do, that when it couldn't or *wouldn't* do what it was supposed to do it rocked the deepest foundations of identity. And without support or understanding that could be a devastatingly terrifying place to be. She never wanted anyone to feel that way and if she could bring even the slightest attention or support to ease people into that place of curiosity rather than fear then...*then* she would find peace.

She would never have her own children. She knew that. Surrogacy was a possibility, but emotionally Freya knew that wasn't for her. But on the other side of infertility, she thought of all the children who needed homes and families and all the love that she was capable of feeling. She knew that, just as surrogacy wasn't an option for her, adoption wouldn't be an option for others. But she marvelled at this wonderful world where those choices were even possible. Understanding might just have to catch up a little. It wouldn't be for everyone, but that was okay. At least it was there for some.

In the blink of an eye, she imagined herself with two little children and wondered at the audacity of the once perfect Princess daring to be a single mother to two adopted children.

*It would be perfect*, she heard Kjell whisper in her mind and this time it warmed her rather than hurt.

'I hate to draw you away, but the Investiture is due to begin in ninety minutes, and you might want to change.'

Freya's heart thumped at the reminder. She knew that she'd been pushing the event that would have seen Kjell awarded the medal of Valour to the back of her mind, had perhaps even been hoping to miss it. But Henna seemed unusually determined to ensure that she was not only ready but also presentable.

She looked down at her clothes. 'What is wrong with what I'm wearing?'

Eighty-seven minutes later, a prettily dressed Freya was half laughing as Henna pushed her up to the side entrance on the lower level of the ballroom. The space had been transformed for the Investiture with a red velvet stage fitting the baroque style, and the ballroom was half full of guests. Unlike the other night, there was an excited hum. Freya had always preferred investitures to balls, where the people of Svardia came to be honoured for both everyday heroism and extraordinary acts of valour equally.

She caught her brother's gaze from the far end of the stage, standing in the frame of the side entrance opposite. For a moment his eyes were warm, smiling—and they shared a moment of real joy at being part of the royal family—before the shutters came down and the boy she remembered from their youth disappeared behind the mask of the man he had become. She felt the loss but had long given up hope of trying to reach deep enough to know what had happened to the smiling, laughing teenager she barely remembered.

The gentle music in the background changed and increased in volume and the commencement music played as brother and sister came onto the stage to meet in the middle.

The genuine joy at the attendees' pride and awe in the day soothed some of the hurt that had taken up residence in Freya's heart. And she was watching a little girl reach up for her daddy to take her in his arms when she heard a name that cut through her thoughts immediately.

She forced her attention onto the crowd of smiling faces until a figure approached the stage so familiar, so handsome, so heartbreaking that she had to blink several times just to refocus. She fisted her hands to hide the fine tremors tumbling through her body and clasped them together, hoping that no one had seen.

Her heart thudded and she wasn't sure she dared risk a glance at him, but couldn't hold out against the desperate need to see him. To take him in. Her eyes flickered between him and the audience and she realised that Kjell's incredible focus was on her brother and only him. It hurt just a little until she realised it gave her the opportunity to stare as long and openly as she wanted to.

Unlike the last time she had seen him in the ballroom, Kjell was dressed in the mess dress uniform, the deep blue-black wool of the rolled collar jacket and waistcoat contrasted with the ivory white shirt, reminding her of the view of the snow-covered forest from the windows of the cabin. Somehow the more civilian style of suit made him look less civilised. She could feel the raw power of him vibrating beneath his skin. It called to something deep within her, something that raged at being ignored or denied as Kjell continued to focus solely on her brother.

*He was taking the medal.*

A part of her wanted to stop the ceremony, feared that he was only doing this for her, not because he'd finally made peace with the traumatic events that had caused the death of his closest friend. But when Kjell finally stood before her brother, rather than bowing his head to receive the award, he did something else entirely.

Her brother swept his arm in invitation and Kjell lowered to his knees. Confusion twisted through Freya like a tornado. Medals were awarded at a bow, not a kneel. Only…only titles were bestowed at a kneel.

Goosebumps rose over her skin, her arms, her neck, her breasts. She stared at her brother, his back now to her as he reached for the ceremonial sword, and Freya felt tears press against her eyes before her mind caught up fully with what was happening in front of her. The consort for the first two legitimate heirs to the throne had to have a title; it was a lesson she'd learned over and over and over again.

*Could this be really happening?*

On the opposite side of the stage, hidden in the shadows just beyond her brother's shoulder, she caught a glimpse of Henna, her eyes bright, shining and a smile so beautiful, so encouraging. Her oldest friend, her lady-in-waiting, nodded as if divining her thoughts from across the room.

Freya's heart beat so loudly in her ears she couldn't hear the words said by her brother, but she knew them in her heart as her brother took the sword that had been in their family for five generations and, in reward for his honour, loyalty and valour, touched the sword to one shoulder then the next.

In that moment Freya realised what he'd done. What he'd sacrificed. Kjell would never be a soldier, he would never return to duty. After all she'd tried to do, all she'd tried to protect him from…

'Rise, Viscount Fjalir,' her brother said.

Freya was torn, agony roaring through her at his sacrifice, but that selfish need burning in her chest wanted to run to him. And then, as Kjell stood, his eyes turned to her and, as if reading her fear, her fury, he stalked towards her—absolutely nothing civilised in his gaze.

Uncaring of her surroundings and utterly in thrall to this man, she took a step backwards and another as he kept advancing—the sheer force of his determination pushing her and crowding her into the shadows of the curtained section of the stage. Distantly she was aware of the music resuming and the low hum of the crowd as her brother led the participants off to the reception further into the interior of the palace. But her mind was only on the terrible sacrifice Kjell had just made.

'What have you done?' she asked him in a trembling voice as she stared up at the man she wanted to pull to her as much as push away. Arctic eyes flared at the sound of her voice, his legs only finally coming to a halt as her back pressed up against the wall. The breadth of his shoulders surrounded her, protected her, warmed her. She leaned towards him against her will, desperate to feel the heat of him. 'You stopped being a soldier?' she asked, the quiver in her voice betraying the emotion she felt for him.

'Yes.' His response was swift and sure.

'Kjell—' She tried to take control of the situation, but he wouldn't let her.

'Congratulations on getting Stellan to parliament,' he whispered as he raised a hand to cup her cheek with the gentlest of touches, as if he wasn't completely sure that she was real.

She'd been about to turn away from his touch in shame, but surprise stole through her instead. 'How did you...?' Ignoring her question, Kjell's eyes searched the depths of hers, as if hoping to divine a truth she'd desperately tried to keep a secret.

'I think you've been trying to protect me,' he said, his tone solemn, stalling any attempt to hide from the man she loved with all of her being. She bit her lip, not in the least surprised that he knew her well enough to realise exactly what she'd been doing. 'I think,' he said, 'that you pushed me away because you think I deserve something you believe you're not capable of giving me.'

Freya tried to hold his gaze as he stared down at her, a stare that displayed the magnitude of hurt she had left him with.

'I think you've done this because you felt you didn't have a choice. But now you do.'

'Kjell...' Her heart broke for him, but he shook his head, his eyes not leaving hers.

'I couldn't have stayed a soldier. I didn't believe in it any more. It wasn't who I wanted to be any more.' He leaned back a little, giving her enough space to take his next words seriously. 'My duty, my allegiance? All yours. My heart? You've had it since I was twenty. My hand you can have now and for ever.'

He could see the emotions warring in her eyes, the guilt traversing across them. 'I know that you thought my exile prevented me from coming home. But all it did was make me realise that my home isn't a place, it's not Svardia or even my parents. It is—and has been ever since the moment I first laid eyes on you—with you.'

'But, Kjell...' she said, her heart breaking for the children she would never be able to give him. He cupped her jaw, his thumb sweeping away a tear she hadn't realised had fallen. She trembled in his arms, the force of emotion hitting her like a train. 'I love you so much,' she said. 'I love you so much that I want to say yes, I want to keep you with me for ever. You make me all the things that are truly me and more. I have laughed with you, cried with you, learned with you...

You complete me,' she said simply and truthfully. 'But you deserve more, and I would hate to tie you to what we will never have.'

Kjell felt the agony in her heart, knew how much it cost her to even say it. 'My only thought is to all we *can* have,' he said, pressing kisses across her cheeks, her nose, her forehead. 'We will adopt a hundred children if you want, or instead we will be happy pouring all our love into each other and the people of Svardia. The future is nothing to fear, Freya, it is to be shared and relished. It was my job to protect you. And, facing the future ahead of us, I will continue to do that with my heart, my body and my life.'

She looked up at him with those hypnotic whisky-coloured eyes—wide and, yes, full of trust—and nodded, shifting the foundations beneath the wall of anxiety around his heart. Fear by fear, block by block, those walls began to tumble, until nothing was left but a love so sure, so strong and pure that it would never dim—no matter the years that came and went. It would never tarnish, no matter the struggles that were overcome, and would never be less for anything that was taken from them. Their love was abundant, in that moment and all the moments to come.

'Princess Freya of Svardia,' he said, pressing his forehead to hers, covering her body with his, 'will you marry me?'

Freya's heart pounded in her chest, joy a sparkle that started at the floor and rose up to surround them both in light and love and hope for the future.

'Viscount Fjalir, it would be my honour.'

And then, as if he refused to miss a single second

now that he knew they could be together for ever, he pulled her into a kiss that promised so much joy and so much wickedness her heart didn't know whether to roar with need or love and Freya finally settled on feeling them both at the same time, as befitting the way her solider, her love, her protector made her feel, then, now and always.

# EPILOGUE

*Five years later...*

THE SOUND OF children's laughter danced on the warm summer breeze flowing into the cabin through the open windows. Freya was talking on the phone, finalising the details of a meeting following her return to Svardia at the end of the month. And while her mind quickly provided the necessary information, her heart was calling her down to the lake, to where her husband was teaching their three children to swim.

'Your Highness?'

'Just make sure that the delegate's husband is invited on the tour too.'

'Yes, ma'am.'

'Are we done?' Freya asked, unable to keep the childlike impatience from her tone. A gentle laugh and an assurance that they were indeed was enough to have Freya hanging up and grabbing the sunscreen she had come to find when the phone had rung. As she followed the steps down from the deck wrapping around their cabin and through the well-trodden path of trampled grass bisecting the large wildflower meadow towards the lake, Freya paused.

She could just make out the sounds of Kjell's voice,

the tone he used for their children so full of love that she almost couldn't contain her reaction to it. She could just about see their eldest, Alarik, who they had adopted at the age of six, standing knee deep in the water, all skinny limbs and sharp angles. His thick dark hair, soaked from the lake, swept back from his forehead as he laughed when Kjell was attacked by the much smaller, blonder forms of Mikael from one side and Malin from the other.

Freya inhaled slow and deep, relishing this moment. Years ago, she had promised herself that she would take the time to process her emotions, the reality of her diagnosis and her feelings about it and herself. And—she nodded to herself—she had done. It had become part habit now that when she felt the need sweep over her she would take that pause and recognise all the good that had come into her life with a sense of welcome that was joyous.

So much had happened since her first visit to Dalarna and she wouldn't change a single thing. All the assessments and meetings needed to ensure that the adoption process for Alarik first, and then later Malin and Mikael, who had come together as siblings, was successful had been worth it. At first Freya had feared that, given her position, the public nature of her life and role and what that would mean for her children, it might have been an outright 'no' from the agency they had approached. But the amazing team of people there had given Freya, Kjell and their children all the help and support they'd needed in the transition into a family.

In the early years, a lot of effort had been put into working with the press rather than against them and without it Freya genuinely believed it would have been a much harder road. But it had been Marit's suggestion to see them as collaborators rather than adversaries. And now the Svardian press, and increasingly the international press, were ferociously protective of their children and what was written about them.

Freya smiled in anticipation of Marit's arrival in a few hours with her husband and their children and felt her heart expand with happiness. The love she had for her sister had developed in the last few years from one that bordered on maternal to one that was now balanced and firmly based in sisterhood. It felt right and good, and Freya knew without a doubt much of that was due to Marit's husband, who had given her sister the space and love she needed to be confident in who she was and it was one of the things that Freya was eternally grateful for.

Excitement swirled in her chest as she thought of Aleksander and his family, also joining them the following day. With their parents in Svardia, prepared to handle any royal duties, the siblings would soon all be together. Although it had been difficult for their parents to adapt to the changes that Aleksander had made during his rule, they had come to see the benefits of his decisions. And although it was highly unlikely that the love between their parents and her and her siblings would ever be relaxed and free, it was beginning to get easier.

'Daddy!' screamed Malin as he picked her up, cradled her in his arms and dropped down into the water, splashing Mikael and Alarik in the process.

Freya's breath hitched, as it sometimes did when she realised just how close she had come to not having all of this. If she'd let fear overpower her love for Kjell, if she'd given into the darker side of her grief, she would have built barriers that kept the world out and walked her path alone, never knowing the true contentment and peace that came with loving and being loved.

Kjell looked up at that exact moment, his gaze locking onto hers as if he'd sensed the direction of her thoughts. As if to tell her that he never would have let that happen. He had promised to protect her, and had for her whole adult life. He was the soldier of her heart, the warrior of her soul.

He had once told her that he couldn't have stayed a soldier, that he hadn't believed in it any more, and at the time she hadn't been so sure. But Freya had watched as he had negotiated the most appropriate roles for him to assume as consort, with her brother, who clearly had respect for her husband. Over the years they had spent hours in discussions, long into the night sometimes, and Kjell had become a confidant to her brother. Just as Marit's husband had. The three men had formed bonds nearly as close as their wives. Each couple had gone through their own journeys, deep, painful sometimes, but ultimately it was that which formed the glue that held them all together.

Kjell's bear-like growl bellowing out across the lake to the delighted squeals of their children, drew Freya's eyes back to her family and her feet onward. Kjell hadn't lied when he'd said that the view of the lake was breath-taking in the summer. It was a deep sapphire-blue that sparkled as the sun glinted off the ripples of water like the facets of a jewel. The rich emerald-green forest that framed the lake was full of wildlife that the children both loved and respected. Although their life was in Svardia, Freya's role and duty to her country's people a fierce beat in her heart, her true home was here, in the months they were able to gather with family and friends.

A car's horn beeped and the sudden cry of, 'Far! Far!' from a chorus of children's voices announced Brynjar's arrival with his wife Anita. The first time Freya had met

Kjell's father she had been struck by the contrast between the joyous and freely affectionate Anita and the conservatively spoken Brynjar. But she would have to have been blind not to see the love contained in that restraint, as if the ferocity of it was so great he needed to hold it back. She had worried that their children might see it as reticence, but they instinctively responded to his quiet, fierce kind of love. It seemed to balance out the effervescent affection from his wife, to an evenness that filled everyone with a sense of calm and love that was utterly unshakeable.

Brynjar and Kjell had used the last five years to transform the building that Kjell had used as a gym into a cabin with accommodation enough for two families. Using as many traditional methods as possible, what had started as a practical necessity had become a labour of love for the two men as they'd provided home and hearth for their families and future generations to come. Throughout, Freya had watched in wonder as the bond between her husband and his father became stronger and stronger with each passing day and year and, although some wounds were deep and would always be there, the healing was powerful enough to soothe that historic hurt.

Freya was still standing in the wildflower meadow when her children ran past her, focused solely on greeting their grandparents—and whatever treats Anita might have brought with her. She couldn't help but laugh as they raced each other to the cabin, Alarik showing all the restraint of an older brother. Looking back to the lake, her breath caught in her lungs to find Kjell, thigh-deep in the water, his hair slicked back, rivulets of water trickling down his firm muscled torso glinting in the sun, and a gleam in his eyes that was pure heat.

He crooked his finger at her, beckoning her to him,

and her cheeks blushed under the weight of his gaze. She shook her head, teasing them both, but his raised eyebrow was a taunt and a promise. He would chase her, she knew, to the ends of the earth if needed, and she would never tire of being caught by this man—her husband, her consort, her one true love.

It was as if she were tied to him by an invisible thread that connected their hearts so, no matter how far apart, they always came back to each other. Now he tugged on it, pulling her to him, and she walked straight into the lake and into his arms, uncaring of the summer dress that was plastered to her skin by the water, and marvelled as he pressed kisses to her lips, her neck and her shoulder, that the once always perfect Princess had finally got her forbidden love.

* * * * *

# INNOCENT IN
# THE SICILIAN'S
# PALAZZO

KIM LAWRENCE

**MILLS & BOON**

# CHAPTER ONE

THERE WAS NO one at Reception. It was totally silent but for the sound of her own feet on the parquet floor.

Anna dumped her carefully packed box on the big desk that took centre stage and peered over it, careful to avoid the vase of fragrant garden roses and lavender, and stood back with a sigh of relief before she twisted the leather-bound ledger around to face her.

Pen in hand, she bent over, pinning the curtain of thick dark chestnut waves from her eyes with her forearm as she signed the visitors' book, her swirling signature a replica of many before it. You had to go back a lot of pages and many weeks to see any other signature next to the column beside her grandpa's name.

One by one his visitors had fallen away and she couldn't really blame them. Some days she approached her own visits with a sick feeling of dread in the pit of her stomach—she never knew what would await her... would he even know who she was?

Not that it would ever occur to her to not come. She owed her grandfather everything. Without him her life could have been very different—before he had stepped up to become her legal guardian, social services had been taking a lot of interest in her.

She huffed out a tiny preparatory breath before she

picked up the box, her aching muscles complaining. As luck, or rather lack of it, would have it, there had been no room in the car park conveniently adjacent to the Edwardian building thanks to the shiny monster designer car that was taking up three spaces and attracting an audience of admirers.

So, courtesy of the *ridiculous* flashy car, Anna was forced to park at the main entrance the other side of the Merlin's park-like grounds, and the box that had seemed comfortably light when she had begun the trek had felt as if it weighed a ton by the time she reached the clinic.

Taking the now familiar route up to the first floor, she reached her grandfather's suite without dislodging the carefully stacked pile, and she was relieved to see the door to his private sitting room was ajar. Wedging her chin on the photo album on top and shifting the box a little higher, she turned to back cautiously into the room, bumping the door with her bottom as she did so.

'Hello, Grandpa, sorry I'm late,' she called out, wondering with a little ache of her heart if Grandpa Henry would even know who she was today. 'But wait until you see what I've got, some more photos, a lovely one of Dad and—' Tongue now caught between her teeth as she concentrated on not bumping into anything, she placed the box carefully on the bureau that had once lived in her grandpa's study at home. 'And some more of your vinyl collection—'

'You are not allowed to touch my collection. That was a very rare recording you scratched. Did you use gloves, Anna?'

'Yes, Grandpa.' The record-scratching incident had happened when she was ten.

Soren, who was standing with one hand on the headrest of the chair that held the man he had been searching for over the past twelve years, had turned at the sound of the door being opened. He had watched the entrance of the new arrival, who was totally unaware of his presence, and had seen no reason to alert her.

When Tor responded to her words, his attention shifted back to the man.

They were the first words that Tor had spoken.

He caught the flicker of intelligence in the faded blue eyes for a split second before it was replaced by a cloudy belligerence.

But it had been there, and it only confirmed Soren's belief that this was an act; it *had* to be an act. He would not contemplate another option. For the past twelve years he had never lost the belief that one day he would look into the eyes of the man responsible for the destruction of his family and see fear, see the despair that must have been in his own father's eyes before he took his own life.

After years of trails growing cold and with the help of a small select team, he had finally tracked down his quarry and reached him before he pulled one of his vanishing acts. This time there would be no new identity, or new continent.

And just when you thought you had seen everything this man was capable of, that he could not get any more slippery and devious, he pulled this one out of the hat— dementia!

But when you thought about it, it made a perfect twisted sort of sense. What did a man like Tor do when he guessed the net was closing in around him and there was no place left to run? He picked out a nice place in the country with a sympathetic staff and waitress service and played his unfit-to-stand-trial card.

Soren was willing to acquit the clinic of collusion— they and the medical professionals were pawns in this latest scam. They might be unwitting accomplices but my God they had laughable security.

Soren had walked in without once being asked who he was, and his arrival had hardly been inconspicuous. Security—at least, that was what he assumed the uniformed pair had been—were more interested in his car than him.

Locating the suite of rooms occupied by Henry Randall had been straightforward too—there were names beside the numbered keys hanging on the wall. It was only when he'd entered the small sitting room that he had encountered any problem.

An unforeseen one.

Tor, ever the artiste, was deep in character.

Soren had been here ten minutes and tried everything he could think of to break through the facade. It was like coming up against a brick wall. By this point he was feeling a degree of sympathy for the professionals Tor had taken in. If Soren hadn't known what Tor was, he would have fallen for the act himself.

Totally in character, the con artist had wholly occupied the role he had chosen to play, that of a fragile, innocent, broken old man.

Struggling against the frustration banging away like a hammer against his temples, he silently berated himself for being overconfident as he dealt with a very different scenario from the one he had envisaged—which had been Tor, shocked by his unannounced appearance, betraying himself.

His initial 'Hello, Tor. It's been a while…' had drawn no response at all.

In fact Soren had seen nothing in those watery blue eyes except blankness illuminated briefly by a seemingly genuine confusion, until the disturbance in the doorway accompanied by the soft, husky voice.

Soren, whose mindset would never allow for the possibility that what he was seeing was not some sort of performance, watched with clinical interest as the figure in the upright chair raised a shaky blue-veined, waxy hand towards the figure with her back turned.

All part of the act, a *good* act, he conceded. But following this man over the years had taught Soren that it was a mistake to underestimate the cunning, twisted mind of Tor Rasmusson, who possessed the ability to run several scams simultaneously and *always* had an escape route. Over the years the man had displayed an uncanny ability to vanish like smoke, leaving carnage in his wake.

'I predict that Anna will come top in her exams...' the shrunken figure said suddenly, looking directly at Soren. 'All that girl lacks is confidence.'

The figure with her back to him, and still oblivious to Soren's presence, sighed. 'It's lovely you think I'm brilliant, Grandpa, but you're the only one.'

Soren watched as the other man glanced down at an invisible watch on his wrist.

'I have a meeting, Anna.'

*Yes, with the fraud squad. Save it, Tor,* Soren thought grimly as he waited for the woman to notice him.

'I hate tardiness, Anna.'

The petite figure turned and froze.

'I'm here now, Grandpa. Did you have a good night?'

The voice, pitched low and soft, held none of the wary suspicion that was now being levelled at him from a pair of eyes set in a face that on a screen just thirty-six hours ago he had casually dismissed as *almost* pretty... The below-the-belt kick that for one split second had nailed him quite literally to the spot when she had turned brought home the truth that real life, and in this case *real women*, were sometimes poorly served by pixels.

This was a *real* woman and Soren was experiencing a very real reaction to her. The flash of heat that settled in his groin was proof that his famed control had limitations.

The image had accurately recorded the proportions of her face, a face that *ought* to have been overpowered by a generous, carnally curved mouth and thick dark brows that framed wide-spaced kitten-big green eyes.

All strong features that should in theory have fought with one another, but instead they melded into a vivid, breathtakingly sensual whole.

The difference lay in part in the creamy texture of her skin, the forest green of her eyes—the lack of symmetry actually *added* to the sensual impact.

He'd have liked to see her in snug jeans, but her wide-legged linen trousers suggested legs that were proportionally long for her height, and the plaited leather belt emphasised the narrowness of her waist. The boxy baggy white shirt she wore was not meant to emphasise her sleek, slim curves but it didn't hide them.

A sound of self-disgust locked in his throat. This was not a moment to be distracted by a woman, especially if the woman in question was the granddaughter of his enemy and was probably up to her pretty neck—Soren lifted his gaze from the smooth slender column of her throat, ruthlessly leashing his hormones, before he produced a smile as he stepped forward, hand extended.

Soren had a wide repertoire of smiles; very few had anything to do with sincerity. Some instilled fear in the recipient, others melted hostility like ice cream in the sun and opened doors, frequently bedroom doors.

A faint widening of her eyes was the only indication that Anna Randall had even noticed his effort. If anything the wariness she wore like a force field seemed on the verge of tipping over into guard-dog open hostility.

Anna looked at his hand, took in the length of the long, tapering fingers.

The brief war of attrition between the deeply embedded instinct of good manners, and the shockingly shameful heat unfurling low in her pelvis that made the idea of feeling her hand in his far too attractive, ended in a draw.

Her hand stayed firmly at her side.

The faintest quirk of his lips and the hint of an ironic gleam in his eyes could have been her imagination as his hand fell away. Relieved she'd had the decision taken out of her hands, she surreptitiously rubbed her sweaty palms against her trousers and kept up the paper-thin pretence that she was immune to the stranger's cynically confident killer smile.

The muscles along Soren's angular jaw quivered, though the truth was he was more intrigued than offended by her ego-bashing attitude.

His ego was pretty robust.

There might be more to Anna Randall than her rotten gene pool and the face. He allowed his glance to skim the fascinatingly unsymmetrical, stunningly sexy features for an indulgent split second too long: the stubborn chin, the wide-spaced intelligent eyes, the smooth high cheeks, the generous carnal mouth that made him aware all over again of a hunger inside him.

Soren was not a man who avoided the truth, especially when it was staring him in the face, and the simple fact was he was attracted to the granddaughter of his enemy. The acknowledgment did not improve his mood.

'Good morning...?' She paused a split second, adding in a colder voice. 'Can I help you?'

The frigid words were polite, the suggestion underneath was anything but, but, God, she had the most *incredible* voice... Even when it was cold it had an earthy, seductive quality. Having just got his hormones in check, he didn't want to think about what it would sound like warm.

'You must be Henry's granddaughter...?' Although he allowed his voice to rise on a questioning inflection, he knew exactly who she was. The only thing about her his investigations had not revealed was just how deeply she was involved in her grandfather's latest profit-making charity fraud. That she was not involved did not even cross his mind.

Now that he had met her, he could see how useful a woman who managed to combine innocence and earthy sexiness would be to Tor. Despite the sketchy evidence, his working theory was that, as Tor's only blood relative, she was being trained to take control of the family business.

*Or she might be as innocent as she appears?*

He dismissed the possibility out of hand. No one related to Tor could be totally innocent. It wasn't *if* she was involved, it was how deeply.

'Yes, I'm Anna...?'

Instead of picking up on her strong verbal cue, to her frustration he ignored the silent question mark and just smiled. She fought the urge to melt and decided that he rarely had to do anything beyond smile to sidestep any question.

'I had imagined you being older,' he responded truthfully, and saw the questioning flicker in her eyes again, though actually he *had* imagined her looking older. He knew her age was... The exact number had not stayed with him, but she barely looked twenty, let alone mid-twenties. 'I understand that you have inherited... Henry's love of books? Librarian, that must be interesting...?'

She didn't react to the question but she had dialled down her antagonism a notch or two; he was making the effort but Soren still wasn't feeling the love.

'Are you another journalist?'

Nothing in his face showed he had noted the *another*. 'Do I look like a journalist?'

'What do journalists look like?' Few, she conceded, could have worn the sort of exclusive-looking suit he was wearing. 'So if you're *not*, just who are you exactly?' Beyond quite obviously the most sinfully good-looking man she had ever seen or even dreamt existed.

It had initially taken her a couple of startled blinks to take in the superficial details, namely his height, several inches over six feet, the immaculate tailoring, steel-grey suit and a tie a few shades paler lying against a snowy white shirt, which gave an air of steely exclusivity and did not disguise the fact his broad-shouldered frame was lean and athletically powerful.

Now she was taking in details beyond the way his hair hugged his shapely skull but was long enough to curl against his collar and was worn swept back casually from a broad brow. It framed symmetrical features that were set in a square-jawed face that was all hollows and angles, slanted cheekbones sharp enough to cut, an aquiline nose and a carved mouth that required a blink in its own right, a firm lower lip and a full, overtly sensual upper. But it was his eyes that were the real showstopper—bluer than any blue she had ever seen, not warm sky blue but arctic-ice blue, and were set beneath the dark ebony bars of his brows and framed by crazily long sooty dark lashes.

Now she was taking in the intelligence in the eyes, the ruthlessness suggested by the firm lower lip and his armour-plated aura of raw masculinity.

Not that this set her apart from any other woman with a heartbeat; this was a man who no doubt took female admiration as a given.

Annoyed that she was fulfilling his smug expectations, and determined not to give him the satisfaction of knowing her stomach was quivering violently, she kept her expression still and filed this disturbing fact away for later consideration, swallowing a couple of times to lubricate her dry throat and ignoring how her legs still felt disconnected from her body.

Luckily they carried her without incident to her grandfather's side. She smiled down as the claw-like hand caught her own before he reached out awkwardly for the glass of water just out of reach.

'So how do you know my grandfather, Mr...?'

'Sorry, I thought I had said,' he lied smoothly. 'Soren, Soren Vitale, your grandfather was my late father's... *mentor* way back when.'

Aware in the periphery of her vision of the hand extended once more towards her, Anna listened to the inner voice that told her it would be a bad idea to feel those long brown fingers close over her own...mainly because the idea was so attractive.

Eye contact had just about shredded her nervous system so skin contact was definitely something to avoid, she decided as she carefully pushed the glass towards her grandfather, dragging out the process until hiding behind her hair was no longer an option without looking a little deranged.

She lifted her head, experienced the grab of those blue eyes, the jolt finally reaching her toes, and she could breathe.

'I'm sorry...'

'It was a long time ago.'

*'Mentor?'* Unable to ignore the hand any longer, she allowed her fingers to touch his. By this point she would have been surprised if there *hadn't* been the tingle of an electric shock, she decided as she surreptitiously rubbed her hand against her thigh.

'When your grandfather had...' He paused and the blue focus shifted a little to her left. Free of the full beam, she compressed her lips against a sigh of relief. 'When he had business interests in Iceland. They shared offices outside Reykjavik.'

*'Iceland...?'* She shook her head, the absurd suggestion tugging her lips into a condescending smile. 'I think you're mistaken. You *are* mistaken. My grandfather has never been to Iceland,' she told him firmly.

The dark brows lifted as his hooded eyes watched her. 'He never spoke of his time there?'

His intense scrutiny made her shift uncomfortably. 'I think,' she began crossly, 'I would have known if my grandfather...' She paused, remembering the long unexplained absences, though in truth it was the gifts that always accompanied his return that had stuck in her mind as a child. 'I suppose it's possible...' she conceded reluctantly.

'What reason would I have to lie about such a thing?'

Anna shrugged but didn't acknowledge he had a point.

'How about we go back to the moment you walked in? I can supply character references if you like?'

His sarcasm and the gentle mocking smile that played across his carved lips made her skin heat. 'I was surprised. I didn't know my grandfather had visitors. There were no names in the book when I signed in.'

An unconvincing look of dismay spread across his face and his smile came with attractive crinkles that fanned out from his spectacular eyes, eyes that held no humour or warmth, just a soul-dissecting intensity.

'Oh, dear, have I broken the rules?'

*Oh, yeah, and you're really going to lose sleep over that, aren't you?* she thought, allowing her gaze to travel upwards from his feet to the top of his attractively ruffled dark head.

'They are quite strict here at the Merlin,' she retorted primly. 'People staying here are very vulnerable.'

Soren watched as she planted a protective hand on the back of her grandfather's chair and thought, *Sure, vulnerable like a wolf.*

'And yet your journalist slipped in...?'

Unable to contradict this observation—she had sent an email to the management that said as much—she kept her lips clamped tight.

'Odd name that for a...place.' He looked around the room that, despite the half-panelled walls and the antique furniture, still held the clinical paraphernalia of a hospital, including a mobile oxygen tank. He had to admit the window dressing was convincing.

'Place?'

His mobile eyebrows twitched into a straight line above his hawkish nose. 'Like this.'

'Merlin was the original owner's stage name. Back in the Edwardian era he was a magician, quite famous, he owned several hundred acres, although now there is just the house and gardens.' She had reached the point where she knew she sounded like a guidebook when she felt her grandfather's hand go limp in her own.

She glanced down and saw that he had fallen asleep, his head to one side.

Her throat ached with emotion and sadness as she pulled her hand free. He looked so vulnerable it was hard to imagine he had until recently been a person with the sort of presence that could fill an auditorium—she had seen it happen and been proud when the people sitting there had been inspired by one of his lectures. She lifted a hand to her mouth to hide the quiver she had no control over.

'So how long has he been here?'

Her head lifted and she found he was watching her with a disturbing intensity. 'Six months. Sorry if I sounded, as if... The staff caught a journalist in here last week.' Her anger sparked green flame in her eyes at the memory. 'People are... He'd hate anyone to see him like this and, actually, no one does,' she said, unable to keep the bitterness from creeping into her voice.

'Your grandfather is not allowed visitors?'

'He's allowed but...he had visitors before his condition deteriorated...'

He watched as she lifted a hand and, under the cover of brushing strands of hair from her brow, took the moments it required to steady her voice, which was flat and expressionless as she delivered the bleak addition.

'He doesn't recognise people nowadays.'

If this was an act on her part, it was good, Soren admitted, watching the muscles in her slender throat contract as she blinked to clear her tear-misted eyes and lifted her chin, unwilling to own the emotional vulnerability she was vibrating.

Soren weighed the possibilities. It *could* be that she was not privy to her grandfather's act...? That would, he mused, watching as the emotions she was struggling to suppress played across the surface of her face, explain her seemingly genuine reaction.

It would require an utterly heartless bastard to put his only blood relative through that sort of hell, but that was not an issue for a man like Tor.

'I imagine that dementia scares people, embarrasses them…maybe it makes them conscious of how fragile life is?' Soren knew all about the fragility of life.

He stood, head tilted a little to one side, his stance relaxed as, with hands thrust deep into the pockets of his tailored trousers, he watched his words flash shocked recognition in her eyes before she slowly nodded.

Her wariness remained but she no longer looked likely to clobber him with the nearest blunt object as she turned her gaze to the chair and its occupant.

There was a gentle snore and Tor had slumped lower in the armchair… It was a sight that would have wrenched the hardest of hearts, but Soren had no doubt that this was part of the act—the authenticity helped by a physical frailness. But then everyone got older.

Including him. He doubted he bore any resemblance to the seventeen-year-old who had walked into the barn that day and seen… He had no idea how long he had stood guard over his father's lifeless body before a neighbour had found him.

'It does scare them… People who last year worked closely with my grandfather…' Something about his presence and his vague explanation for it still seemed not right to her.

The silence lasted for several heartbeats, as did the unblinking regard of those ice-chip-blue eyes. Anna wanted to look away but couldn't have if her life had depended on it; the mesmerising stare had grabbed her in a vice-like grip.

'Iceland is small, population wise, everyone knows one another and for some time your grandfather was almost like one of the family.'

They had invited the enemy into their home. There had been warm cosy family dinners. Tor had been sympathetic to Soren's teenage problems, listening when he moaned about his parents. He had always seemed interested and genuine, Soren remembered, making unfavourable comparisons with his own father.

It turned out that Tor's only interest had been in emptying his father's company's pension fund.

*'It's all gone, Soren, there's nothing left.'*

His father's words, the sound of utter bleakness, had stayed with him. They would never leave him; they were branded into his memory along with the images.

His mesmeric blue stare had moved away and she felt her shoulders sag, could breathe again. 'Vitale? I don't actually recall...'

'Not Vitale... Steinsson.' The ice-flecked blue eyes were back on full soul-stripping beam as they landed on her face. 'When I moved to Sicily after my father's death, I added my mother's family name.' Not out of choice—it was part of the deal that made his mother's future safe.

Biagio Vitale did not give anything for nothing, and Soren had not been in a strong negotiating position.

Feeling like a bug under a microscope, Anna shook her head. 'Sorry, he might have...' Her brow wrinkled. 'Vitale sounds a little familiar,' she conceded.

Probably because she had to have at least one gleaming luxury kitchen appliance that carried the logo. Most people did. Though of course the arms of the Vitale empire were not all so visible to the general public, except in their individual fields. The engineering arm, the financial services, both had a global reputation, but the jewel in the multibillion-pound crown was claimed by the green initiatives that had been Soren's first act as CEO. His diversion of funds from oil and gas exploration was no longer considered an insane gamble.

'It was a long time ago.'

To the rest of the world it was old news. Not for Soren. He had lived the story: the disgraced businessman took his own life after he was caught stealing the pension fund of his employees.

Except he hadn't, his only crime had been trusting his friend and partner, Tor Rasmusson, who had vanished along with the money leaving a trail of financial bread-crumbs that led to Stein Steinsson.

The loss of her husband and the scandal had been too much for his mother, Hanna, who had spiralled into a deep depression then total breakdown.

Seventeen, angry and helpless, Soren had stopped being the straight-A student overnight. He'd got into fights defending his father even though he had been angry as hell with him for leaving them. He had made a point of mixing with the wrong crowd.

Maybe he would have fulfilled the many predictions that he would go off the rails and end up in jail as popular opinion said his father should have, if he hadn't found the stash of tablets his mother was hoarding and the letter she had written ready for the day she would use them.

It had been his wake-up call. He knew then that he needed help, not the sort of help being offered. He didn't need a counsellor, or therapist; he needed a safe place for his mother.

His options were limited.

There was no one, just him, so he swallowed his pride and approached his Sicilian grandfather, the man who had cast off his only daughter when she had ignored the dynastic merger of an arranged marriage and run away with her long-haired Icelandic lover, her Viking, who at the time had been hitchhiking around Europe.

Biagio Vitale was not about to be swayed by a sob story—he did not do sentiment, he did business—and he agreed to offer his daughter a sanctuary and the best professional help money could buy, but in return he wanted Soren body and soul.

He had no heir, and if after eight years Soren had proved himself he would have the option of running the Vitale conglomerate, but in those eight years he would go where Biagio sent him and do as he was told—learn from the bottom up and expect no favours for who he was.

There were no favours but there was a lot of hostility for the rich boy who wanted to be their boss from the hard men who made their living working in hot, sweaty and often dangerous conditions in the oil rigs and steel mills, and from managers who had worked hard to get to the middle, testing the hell out of this kid who had a free ride to the top. Except it wasn't a free ride. In the end he won respect and even made some unlikely friends.

At the end of eight years Soren was in a position to set his own conditions and he never forgot the reason he was where he was.

He knew the truth and one day so would the world. He would clear his father's name.

# CHAPTER TWO

'WELL, IT WAS very thoughtful of you to come. I just wish that Grandpa Henry—'

Soren watched as her sad, shadowed green eyes slid to her grandfather's face. Whatever the truth, her emotion seemed genuine.

'I know he would have appreciated it,' she said, struggling to feel any personal gratitude for his effort.

There was just *something* about this man...aside from the very obvious that made Anna *uneasy*, beyond the discovery that she had a weakness for a pretty face, or in his case *beautiful*. She made the private concession with reluctance mingled with exasperation as her gaze was drawn back to his mouth, a mouth that invited fantasies.

Horrified by the one that sprang fully formed into her head involving the silken touch of his tongue, the slick, warm... She gave a panicky little gasp, pressed a protective hand to her stomach and picked up one of the framed photos. She stared at it blindly for a few sense-calming moments before she made herself look at him with a painted smile that felt in imminent danger of cracking as shock and shame continued to ricochet through her.

She pretended that the biggest problem in her world was the angle of the photos on the shelf and cleared her throat before asking brightly, 'I hope you haven't come too far out of your way?'

To her relief and surprise she sounded sane and not at all like someone who had mentally undressed him the moment she laid eyes on him.

'Not at all.'

Anna pretended not to notice the edge of mockery underlying his response—anything she said was only going to prolong this conversation.

'About the security. You might like to suggest they beef it up.'

Her lips tightened. Did he imagine she hadn't already? Repressing an acid retort, she tipped her head in acknowledgment.

'So what was this journalist after?'

*My God, was he ever going to go?*

Slowly she turned around to face him. 'I have no idea, but look at Grandpa Henry—what sort of person...?' She clamped her lips, squeezing them to a bloodless white as she fought to contain the surge of anger that made her chest heave dramatically against the loose white cotton that Soren discovered was semi-transparent. 'What motivates someone like that?'

Soren arched one of the dark thick brows that framed his startling blue eyes. 'Who knows?' he said lightly. He was not interested in motivation or rehabilitation, he wanted revenge.

'*Anyone* with a conscience,' she snapped and then felt guilty because he hadn't done anything except make her...she began to think about the heat that had...and stopped the thought in its tracks before it reached critical mass.

'A mistake to assume that everyone has one,' Soren

said, looking at the figure in the chair. 'You'd be surprised how many don't.'

A lack of conscience would ironically have won his
own grandfather's approval a lot sooner; a good deal of
his training had involved eradicating this undesirable
trait.

'So, goodbye, then, Mr—'

'Soren.'

'Goodbye,' she said firmly. 'I don't want to be rude…
but I think you should go.'

For a brief unguarded moment astonishment washed
over his face; a second later his sense of irony kicked in
at this role reversal.

*Taste of your own medicine, Soren!*

Though in his own defence he was generally less blunt
when he walked away from a woman.

Anna missed the brief interplay of emotions that
slipped through his guard. She had begun to remove the
items she had packed into the box, more photos to join
those already on the wall and shelves. The music her
grandfather loved, a couple of leather-bound volumes of
his favourite novels… Anything that was familiar made
him feel more secure.

Unaware of the wistful smile that tugged at her lips,
she straightened a framed photo of her parents, the dad
she didn't remember and the beautiful mother who was…
well, who knew where?

Anna's smile deepened as she thought of her absent
parent—beautiful, selfish, but she never pretended to be
anything else and Anna had stopped being angry with
her unmaternal mother a long time ago. She was no longer the little girl dumped quite literally on some often
resentful friend's doorstep because her mum felt the urge

to trek in the Amazon or spend some quality time cleansing her chakras in a Himalayan retreat.

Soren stared at the set of her slender back. He found himself struggling to appreciate the novelty value of being ignored and virtually dismissed by a woman, and, even though he had been about to leave, found himself lingering.

Could she really be what she appeared, which was a concerned, loving granddaughter oblivious to her grandparent's sordid history?

Normally he could rely on his instincts but he found himself resisting them. He was wired to mistrust any blood relation of Tor, but it was more complicated than that. He was strongly sexually drawn to her—were hormones clouding his judgment?

Was her mouth clouding his judgment?

He resented the idea; he resented questioning his own judgment.

For some reason he found himself wanting to make her look at him again. 'So when I come again I will sign in.'

Anna's quiet smile said she knew he wouldn't come again.

'Who are you?'

At the aggressive growl the photo she was holding slipped to the floor. Not that she appeared to register the sound of breaking glass. Soren watched as she closed her eyes, braced her slender shoulders and painted on a smile before turning around to face the hostile suspicion being directed at her by a now fully awake Tor.

'Hello, Grandpa, it's Anna. I came to visit. I brought you some things, some photos from your study and—'

'Who are you?'

'The book we were reading…would you like—?'

There was the vicious expression in Tor's watery pale eyes and he tried to rise from his chair but collapsed weakly back. 'Help, thief…put that down!'

She tensed, her soothing calm paper thin, and she pitched her voice to a coaxing gentle murmur. 'It's me, Grandpa… A-Anna.'

Despite all her effort her voice cracked emotionally. She knew it was the disease not her grandpa speaking, throwing out the wild insults, but it was always heart-breaking to witness.

His mood could change without warning; the episodes of aggression that turned him into a stranger were occurring with more and more frequency.

She flashed Soren a look tinged with desperation. 'Please go,' she said, reacting instantly to her deeply embedded protective instincts, moving to shield her grandfather from this uninvited guest's scrutiny. Heartbreaking enough that this disease had robbed Grandpa Henry of his dignity without there being an audience.

Soren didn't say anything; he had no intention of going anywhere.

'I know what they think but I didn't kill anyone!'

'Grandpa, no one is saying that.' She gasped, horrified at the idea he was lost in this nightmare.

'It wasn't me…he was weak and stupid. What sort of man deserts his family?' he spat out contemptuously.

Every muscle in Soren's body clenched. It was only by a cosmic effort of will that he didn't challenge the man sitting there taunting him. The insidious pity that had been creeping up on him instantly died, because this performance was for him, of that there could be no doubt.

'Who are you?' He turned to Soren. 'Get her out of here, Stein. I have a very important meeting… Where is everyone?' As abruptly as it had emerged the aggression seemed to drain out of him, leaving a tired, shrunken old man sitting there.

'I'm here,' Anna soothed.

'Get her away from me!'

'Please don't be afraid. I'm...' She saw his face change once more, saw the anger, but as always it was the fear she could sense underneath, worse even than the fact that the angry words that fell from his lips had no meaning, that he didn't recognise her—he was *afraid* of her—that cut the deepest.

Blinking back tears, she told herself fiercely that this *wasn't* him, not Grandpa Henry, as she began to slowly back away.

It broke her heart; he was in there somewhere, lost.

'I'm going, it's fine, I'll get Tanya or Will...or—' Her progress came to an abrupt halt as she backed into solid male.

The impulse to lean into the warm, solid strength was hard to resist, but she was used to standing on her own feet.

A rock face would have had more give. Before she could compose herself enough to pull away, hands came to rest lightly on her shoulders. They were large and heavy, not restraining her. She stood there for a moment breathing in the scent of his soap, feeling the warmth of his body, the strength of this stranger's hands.

She was seized by an irrational conviction that if she could absorb some of his strength, she could cope with the fact her grandfather was waving his walking stick at her and yelling what was probably meant to be abuse but was unintelligible.

If hearts really did break hers would be lying on the floor right now in a million pieces.

She was willing back the tears she knew were shining in her eyes as she attempted to pull away. For a moment he didn't react to her murmured *sorry* and a request for him to get a nurse.

When the pressure of his big hands lifted she felt strangely ambivalent about the broken physical contact, which was ridiculous. She had been standing on her own feet for... Well, for ever, really. There had only ever been Grandpa Henry standing between her and being totally alone, and now there was...no one. Straightening her shoulders and tugging herself free of this spiral into pathetic self-pity, she went to move forward but the visitor, still ignoring her request to fetch help, stepped past her.

Soren swore softly under his breath, it went against his every instinct to play the old man's game, but watching her radiate hurt as she fell totally for Tor's act had nudged his dormant protective instincts into inconvenient life. One thing the scene had revealed was that there could be no doubt at this point that for his granddaughter this pretence was real.

While it didn't mean she didn't know, and that she might be deeply involved in the illegal house of cards that was about to crash down on her grandfather was still a question mark, she did believe Tor's act and no one deserved that.

Anna was so distracted by the tactile quality of the authoritative delivery that she didn't even register they were not words, just sounds, not until her grandfather, a smile now lighting his face, repeated them.

'Hun ein vinur...?'

The way her grandfather repeated the gibberish carefully, his eyes seeking reassurance from the tall stranger who stood with his back to her, broke her heart all over again. Instead of acknowledging the hurt, she embraced

her anger, fanning the flame into hot life as she stepped
forward and grabbed the mocking stranger's arm, reg-
istering as she did so the hard tensile strength of the
muscles.

She was ashamed of the flip low in her belly, her self-
disgust lending her extra strength as she grabbed the fabric and yanked hard, making him react.

As he turned to face her she angled her furious glare
upwards—a *long way* upwards. The shock of contact with
the sheer cold, calculating fury living in the blue depths
of his deep-set eyes made her mind blank.

Then it was gone, like a mirage or a trick of the light.

'Don't make fun of him!' she managed to snap out
before her breath snagged hard on the emotional rock in
her chest, making further comment impossible. She just
hated it when she got so mad she wanted to cry.

'I was not *making fun*.' It was no less a ludicrous interpretation, as anyone who knew him would have told
her, than *I was being kind*.

She felt the thread of anger inside her unravelling.
The eyes looking back at her were the bluest thing she
had ever seen in her life, the piercing quality emphasised
by dark iris rings and the framing of ebony eyelashes
that were impossibly long and sooty black against the
equally startling backdrop of a face that was all strong,
perfect angles.

A face dissected by a strong nose, high razor-edged
cheekbones, a square chin with the suggestion of a cleft
and a mouth that was both sensual and cruel.

It was her reaction to his mouth that made her rush
into speech, almost falling over her words in her haste
to not think about the shameful pulse of heat between
her legs.

'I want you to leave, now!'

'Stein!'

Everything inside Soren froze for the second time as he spun around in time to see the warm charming smile he remembered from his youth.

Before he could react the smile was gone and there were tears rolling down Tor's lined cheeks.

In the periphery of his vision Soren was conscious of the small stricken figure who stood there clenched with misery as she witnessed a performance that was clearly directed at him. But then Tor never had cared about inflicting collateral damage.

Even had he fallen for it, Tor's effort was wasted. There was zero chance of pity working its way through Soren's defences. Even if he could rid himself of the conviction that behind the fragility of the shaking hands and the milky pale incomprehension in the pale blue eyes the old man was secretly laughing at him, Soren would *never* have been able to feel pity. That would have been the ultimate betrayal of his father.

'It's me, Grandpa…it's Anna.'

Pitched to a soothing low murmur, the suppressed pain in each shaky syllable held stark, raw grief.

Looking at her, Soren felt some nameless thing break loose in his chest. She looked bone-achingly tired, numb with exhaustion. He could see the quiver of fine muscles under the smooth pallor of her impossibly clear skin— like a road map of her emotions close enough to the surface for him to feel.

He wanted to unhear the pain; it awoke memories of his mother's hurt. Hurt that he had soothed as best his seventeen-year-old self could and she, oblivious to the fact he didn't have a clue how he was going to fulfil his promise of making things right, or what taking responsibility for another person actually entailed, had seemed to take comfort from his words—she'd believed him.

He had never articulated it, not even to himself, but the knowledge that he would never voluntarily take responsibility for another human being again had become part of him during the following months. It had become his emotional fingerprint.

He wasn't going to offer to make this woman feel better, and, if he had, he was pretty sure she would have thrown any offer of comfort back in his face, along with any blunt object that came to hand, he decided, studying her face, not an unpleasurable pastime. This was not a scared woman seeking reassurance.

This was a woman regaining ground she had lost and setting boundaries.

Boundaries that placed him the other side of a very high wall. It was a novel sensation for Soren, who was accustomed to people placating and ingratiating themselves with him.

Her eyes were cool green ice now on his face, which was good because he needed to cool down.

'You've done your duty, and for that thank you, but talking gibberish back to my grandfather is not helpful it…is…*demeaning*…' Her voice shook with anger that still held her rigid. 'He's not a…my grandpa Henry is still in there somewhere!'

*I could tell you some things about your grandpa Henry,* he thought, watching as she moved as if to body-block her grandfather from him.

*So why aren't you telling her, Soren?*

She was going to know soon. The world was about to know it all, he had made sure of that.

'The words make sense in his head,' she explained. 'They just—'

Soren hesitated. The internal battle was brief. It was deeply frustrating to realise that despite his grandfather's years of training he had retained more scruples than he would own to.

'They do make sense.'

'To him, yes, but—'

He ignored her, dismissing her interruption. 'He is speaking Icelandic.'

'My grandfather doesn't speak—' She paused and bit her lip as her grandfather began to speak over her.

Soren was good at multitasking. He could listen to Tor predicting the Icelandic banking meltdown of decades earlier and watch as his protective granddaughter chucked Soren a rot-in-hell look.

The irony was, of course, she was too late to protect her grandfather, at least from the truth, which Soren had already selectively leaked to cause maximum impact... He ignored the scratch of guilt and told himself that that old man didn't deserve such dedication and, while he was willing to admit that his granddaughter seemed genuinely ignorant of his previous life, she seemed more than capable of looking after herself and there were others out there who deserved the truth, others who had lost everything because of Tor.

Anna's teeth clenched as the stranger ignored her and responded to her grandfather, speaking fluent gibberish back.

'I asked you not to—' She stopped as she watched her grandfather's face light up. Eagerness she had forgotten about lit his eyes as he responded with a convincing fluency that was not necessarily significant given her grandfather's confusion.

He didn't seem confused now, he sounded more animated than he had in weeks, and now that she listened she heard a pattern, a repetition in the words that she had never noticed before—because she had not been listening for them.

She was dealing with the first quiver of nagging doubt when she registered that her grandfather was looking at her, his white brows raised in enquiry.

'He is asking if you have done your homework,' Soren translated, recognising that the chances were Tor was never going to drop the act.

*If it was an act?*

He pushed the thought away. 'Maths homework.'

'It's true?' She searched his face. 'You *understand* what he's saying?'

'I do.'

'So all the time we thought he was… Tell him—' Before she could ask the stranger to translate for her the walking stick fell from her grandfather's limp clasp and his eyes closed.

'He's asleep…?'

Soren turned his head from the figure in the chair in time to see her nod in response. Her luminous eyes were fixed on the old man, an entire world of emotion chasing across her expressive features. In the unguarded moment, her face had a piercing vulnerability.

He looked away, feeling he'd intruded on something intensely private.

'He can't sleep at night, it's part of his condition. When he was at home,' she continued, her expression abstracted, her voice so soft now it was almost as if she was talking to herself rather than him, 'I had to lock the doors. The police found him wandering in the park in his pyjamas.'

'You cared for him at home?' He could only imagine what that would entail, but he was sure it would have included putting her own life on hold. He had some experience of having a grandparent take over your life, but his had been a bargain with benefits—it seemed hard to imagine any benefits for this woman.

'For a while.'

'So you were essentially his carer?'

'For a short time.' At least he didn't seem about to acclaim her *selfless* actions, Anna thought, which was a relief. His faint disapproval was preferable to being viewed as either a saint or an object of pity.

'No sleep at night but in the day…he just drops off without warning in the middle of drinking a cup of tea sometimes. He had a bad night and—'

She broke off, her eyes lifting from the slumped sleeping figure to the man standing by the door, his broad shoulders propped against the wall, his eyes fixed on her face. The piercing blue regard made her shift uncomfortably and she bent to pick up the broken glass, wincing as a bubble of blood appeared on her fingertip.

He was pleased to hear her swear crudely. A moment later she flashed him a rueful look and pulled her finger from her mouth and, aware of the sleeping figure, whispered, 'Sorry,' as she rose to her feet, sucking her finger, which immediately drew his attention to her lips with uncomfortable results.

'I've heard worse.'

It was the first genuine grin she'd seen… Oh, my God, he really was sinfully beautiful! She dropped her head and made a meal of extracting a tissue from her pocket. By the time she'd wrapped it around her oozing finger her blush had reduced by a few shades.

'I need to clear up the—'

'Leave that for someone else to clear,' he snapped out in exasperation. 'You should get that attended to.' He caught her hand. 'Let me see,' he said, not looking at her finger but at her face...and Anna was looking back.

She had no idea how long the frozen-in-time heart-racing moment lasted, and it was Soren who broke it, letting her hand fall without a word.

'Heavens, it's just a scratch,' she said. 'I'm fine.' Well, she would be once her heart slowed to near normal. 'I don't understand any of this—is it really possible? All the time we thought...he was confused.'

Confused like the evil old fox he was, or even if he was genuinely ill, either way Soren could think of several million reasons why Tor Rasmusson did not deserve her sympathy or her dedication.

'Oh, poor Grandpa!'

*Poor Grandpa!* It took all his self-control for Soren not to inform this woman just what her *poor* grandpa was capable of, the muscles along his jaw quivering and his nostrils flaring in disgust as his narrowed gaze took in the pathetic figure in the chair.

Anna swallowed and lifted a hand to her head. 'You made him laugh. I haven't heard him laugh for a long time. How can he speak Icelandic? This is all so...' She lowered her voice. 'Can we talk...outside?' She glanced from the sleeping figure to the open door.

Soren followed her towards the door, happy to comply; he hated to be breathing the same air as that man.

Anna's head was spinning. She had no idea how her grandfather spoke the language of a country that up until today she had never known he had even visited. Perhaps, she speculated, it was a long time in the past, like the old music the staff played that soothed him. He still remembered things long gone with amazing clarity sometimes; it was the present that he struggled with.

Anna walked a few feet down the corridor to where a

few easy chairs were set into a square bay window that looked out onto a small landscaped quadrangle.

She didn't sit down but turned towards him. 'Thank you for that.'

'For what?'

'That is the most like himself I've seen him in a long time… I know he speaks French and a little German but *Icelandic*! It never crossed my mind or anyone else that he was actually— I suppose I'd better get a phrase book.' She began dragging a hand through her hair where the natural titian highlights in the deep dark brown caught the sun shining in through the window. 'I know it's a lot to ask but if you're ever nearby…?'

He saw where she was going with this and spared her further embarrassment by cutting in coolly. 'I do not live in this country.'

He watched as she struggled to hide her disappointment; she managed a rueful smile. 'Of course. But now that I know…and that is down to you.' Her smile hit his underused conscience yet again.

Recalling her snarling initial reaction, Anna wasn't surprised by his lack of response to her heartfelt apology. He looked like a man who was in a hurry to escape and who could blame him? She felt that way sometimes. He had come to pay his respects to an old friend of his father, not to be accused of some sort of nameless crime.

She gave an embarrassed grimace; she had wanted him to leave and now she felt a strange reluctance to see him go. 'I was so rude to you. I'm sorry…'

Soren marvelled at how easily she said the words that he struggled with, that his own grandfather had taught him to associate with weakness and failure. Personally he had always found the words empty, but when Anna Randall used them she seemed to mean it.

'I do not melt at harsh words.'

As he pushed away the apology with a flick of his long fingers, the gesture and his deep voice suggestive of impatience, she picked up his faint accent for the first time.

'I still don't understand!' she said, confusion showing in her green eyes. 'I know Grandpa had interests abroad with the charity—he was very hands-on and totally committed.'

For a moment the temptation was there to disillusion her, tell her that the man, the *saint* figure, she was grieving for never existed.

The moment passed, not because he rose above his instincts, but because he knew that she would learn the truth soon enough.

For the moment her ignorance was bliss, if it was true. She had no inkling she would soon be at the centre of a media feeding frenzy when the story broke.

And who knew? Maybe she wasn't the innocent she appeared. Aware that his *wanting* her to be complicit in her grandfather's crime, even though it was patently obvious she thought her grandparent was some sort of saint, was in part an effort to ease his own guilt brought a self-contemptuous sneer to his lips.

Maybe it was time she woke up to the truth. He hesitated. It might be time for her to wake up to the truth, but he found he didn't much want to be the one personally doing the waking.

'Iceland? So you are Icelandic…?' She had heard it was called the land of ice and fire and the description could have fitted this man with his ice-blue eyes that could flare with flame. It was really not a stretch to see him as some sort of sexy Viking.

'On my father's side. I heard from a mutual acquaintance of this situation, and—'

'He remembers you? He called you Stein...?'

'My father, though we are not alike—he died very young.' He paused, shielding his expression as the image that had haunted him down the years floated into his head.

'How many other secrets does he have?' she wondered out loud before raising her gaze to this man who might have some of the answers to the hundred questions in her head. 'Do you still live—?'

'We moved away some years ago,' Soren cut in smoothly. 'My mother is Sicilian by birth.'

Sicilian, well, that explained his vibrant colouring. His ice-blue eyes were the only evidence of his northern genes.

'I still don't understand any of this. My grandfather never mentioned—'

'It is hard sometimes to think that our parents, and I suppose that goes doubly for grandparents, had a life before we came along—like us, they have their own secrets.'

It was only the knowledge that it would make her sound boring that stopped her blurting that she had no secrets.

'I suppose you're right... I wish I knew though.'

*Be careful of what you wish for,* he thought, feeling an unexpected and unwelcome stab of sadness for her soon-to-be-lost innocence.

She looked up, smiling. 'I wish you'd known him... before...seeing him yelling that way...he never raised his voice to me. He was such a decent and honourable man, everyone loved him.'

A nerve jumped in Soren's lean cheek. Not everyone, and soon maybe no one, but he knew without doubt that she would cling to her illusions for as long as she could.

And when they were gone? He left the thought unfinished. That was not his responsibility. There were a lot of people out there, a lot of victims who deserved the truth.

'He was...' Her eyes moved past him. 'It's Dr Greyson.' A smile on her face, she moved past him to meet the group who were walking towards them.

Soren could hear several staff members greeting Anna by name as he turned in the opposite direction and walked away.

# CHAPTER THREE

SOREN LIFTED A hand to his jaw and felt the rough growth of stubble. He had arrived at the London office of the Vitale Group the previous evening direct from the Merlin clinic, drawing a look of reproach from his superbly organised PA, Natalie, who had arrived the day before. She had already sorted every detail of the complex meetings scheduled for the following day…which was, Soren realised as he glanced out of the panoramic plate-glass windows that revealed the wide-awake city below, today.

'You're a distraction.'

'Where's the respect? The—?'

'Obsequious boot-licking…? Wrong PA. Also, I worked for you before you were infallible and a financial genius.'

Soren had grinned and retreated to his office because that was where he'd been heading anyway. He glanced down now, his lip curled in mild distaste as he took in his creased suit. He would definitely be a distraction if he rolled up looking like this, or start rumours of all-night partying.

He grabbed the jacket hooked over the back of his chair, and shook it out. He hadn't been partying, he'd worked through the night, which was not unusual—he liked the lack of distractions his days were filled with.

Except last night there had been distractions, mostly in his own head. Tor had robbed him of the moment he had dreamt of all these years.

Not that he was escaping justice—sure, his diagnosis, faked or real, might make him personally untouchable, but Tor's sins had caught up with him and very soon his reputation would be trashed along with the reputations of all those who had conspired with him.

It felt like coming second in a race, and Soren had never seen the point in that, and being forced to accept it now did not sit well with him.

Unbidden, the face of Anna Randall floated into his head. The green eyes seemed to look at him reproachfully. He swore, she really was too good to be true...but if, as he suspected, she was... He rose in one restless fluid motion, and, jacket slung across his shoulder, dragged a hand through his already ruffled hair.

If she was about to have her eyes opened, she ought, he told himself sourly, to be thanking him.

He doubted she would.

What he needed was a shower and a change of clothes. Would that it were as easy to wash away the totally irrational sense of...no, *not* guilt. Why should he feel guilt? If she got hurt the blame lay at her grandfather's door, not his. If she was innocent, she had nothing to fear. He ejected those green eyes from the space in his head that should be occupied by the new addition to the designer label that was about to be incorporated into the Vitale brand. Since the launch of their designer glasses, they had been steadily buying up their rivals. Pretty soon there would be few that were not owned by Vitale.

He had made it halfway to the door before the phone lying on his desk began to vibrate.

He almost ignored it, the call of the fresh set of

clothes and shave being strong, but found he couldn't and, when he glanced at the identity of his caller, he was glad he hadn't.

Franco was not only his personal lawyer, he was one of the few people who were privy to the true story of his father's suicide. Of course, the scandal had been big at the time, and was out there in the public arena since yesterday's news. But only a handful of people knew the truth, and Franco was one of them.

He trusted the younger man implicitly and his forensic mind had been invaluable in following the trail of destroyed lives and unravelling the multiple identities of Tor and finally tracking him down.

'Franco…?'

'Are you watching this?'

'Watching what?'

'The latest victim of your revenge… How did it go yesterday? Well, looks like she is involved, or at least the police think so—they're interviewing all the charity trustees. You must be feeling very happy right now. Oh, hell, but this is not a pretty sight. I could almost feel sorry for her.'

'Her who…?' He knew he just wanted to be wrong.

'Anna Randall. Looks like you were right and she *is* guilty, but nothing I found suggested… I know her name is on the board of trustees but she has never attended a meeting and—'

Soren, alert now, his voice urgent, his shower forgotten, cut across his friend. 'What channel?'

'Are you kidding? All of them.'

'Right, stay on the line. I might be needing you.' Soren turned to the images on his laptop screen and unmuted the live feed broadcast.

*'These scenes we're watching are of the granddaugh-*

*ter of the disgraced philanthropist Henry Randall, out-*
*side the building owned by her grandfather, who is being*
*escorted to the police station, where she is helping with*
*enquiries. People are asking, Tania, how deep does this*
*scandal go? I understand that the sources you have spo-*
*ken to are denying any government involvement...?'*

Soren pressed 'mute' and watched the images on his
screen of the modern-day witch trial.

What had Franco said? *Happy?*

Anna, a slim, upright figure dwarfed by the two uniformed figures that flanked her protectively—though
not protectively enough to stop her being jostled to the
point where she was swamped enough to disappear from
view completely at intervals. While the rent-a-mob media
crowd—clearly there had been some tip-off—pushed
in, firing their inane aggressive questions as they extended their microphones, waving them into her face as
she walked, her chin high, displaying the sort of dignified
calm under fire that few could have achieved.

Her head didn't go down, she continued to look
straight ahead. It was a masterclass in dignity and as
he watched her face, the pallor pronounced against the
dark chestnut of her hair, he felt his admiration collide
with a surge of emotion that he refused to recognise as
protectiveness.

Soren swore. This was what he had wanted.

But it so wasn't. He wanted revenge, he wanted justice, but this was not justice and Anna Randall was not
his target. Tor should have been standing there, his head
bowed in disgrace, not his granddaughter, and even if she
was not an innocent, if she was involved at some level,
she did not deserve this.

He blanked the screen because, mocked the voice in

his head, *You can't see it so it's not happening—and* you *made it happen.*

Innocent or not. Hell, that woman had guts!

He came to a decision.

'Franco, I need you to do something for me...' Soren detailed his requests, his friend and personal lawyer listened.

'So we're helping her? She isn't the enemy?'

An image of Anna Randall flashed into his head... her dark chestnut hair a cloud around her face. She was a woman who disturbed him on more than one level.

'She's a total pain.'

'All right... I see,' said Franco, who didn't. 'OK, give me... I'll get back to you in...just actually don't hang up.'

A few hours previously Anna's only experience of the press was putting an advert in the local paper to ask if anyone had lost a cat, or could give a good home to the six kittens it had given birth to under her bed.

Her only experience of the police was...well, actually, she didn't have any. Not even a parking ticket. She looked round the anonymous magnolia room, the two chairs on the opposite side of the table, the closed blind on the small high window all adding to the sense of claustrophobia. The only sound was of her knee spasmodically hitting the table; even with both hands pressed to it she couldn't stop the nervous jerking tic.

This was all insane—the police wanted to know how much she knew.

It *should* have been a short conversation—Anna didn't *know* anything—but so far she'd been here two hours. The coffee break suggested she might be here longer. By then, she mused grimly, she might believe she was guilty too.

The first inkling she'd had of the craziness to come was seeing her grandfather's name as she flicked through the news sites before she headed out to treat herself to an outfit for her new job.

*International aid agency at the centre of a scandal...accusations of money laundering and facilitating modern slavery!*

That was when her phone had started ringing. Journalists asking her for a quote, and others asking her leading questions, such as did she feel guilty that her lifestyle had been funded by the most poor and needy in society?

She had made the mistake of responding a couple of times before someone had repeated her response... "'My grandfather is totally innocent. This is a terrible mistake,'" adding, 'Can I quote you on that?'

When the police had rung she had almost let it ring out, which would, she assumed, have meant the policemen waiting in the car outside would have come knocking on her door, though they had come inside anyway to escort her through the nightmare walk of shame.

She shuddered. Every time she closed her eyes she could still see the flashing lights, and the voices, they were playing in her head like a background white noise. They were the things nightmares were made of...other people's nightmares.

'This is so surreal!' she said to the wall, her commentary cut short when a policeman appeared.

'Can I show you the way out, Miss Randall?'

She jumped and almost knocked her chair over as she leapt like a startled deer to her feet. 'I can go?'

*Quick now, Anna, before he changes his mind.*

'You know now this is all some terrible mistake!'

The plain-clothes policeman didn't respond to her comment, just looked at her as though he'd heard it all before and from people who were better liars than she was. Was there such a thing as being so innocent you looked guilty?

'Your lawyer has explained the situation,' he said. 'He and your...*friend* are waiting for you.'

Anna hardly noticed the faint hesitation before he said *friend*—she had friends, but she definitely didn't have a lawyer and actually her best friend, Sara, was suffering from a broken heart and had thrown herself into work and moved to Paris. And Penny was looking after her sister's three children while her sister was convalescing from a fall that had left her in plaster.

There was her mum, who was frequently taken for her better-looking, better-dressed big sister, but her mum was *definitely* not the sort of person to stop what she was doing and come to the rescue. The last time she had made contact she had been in another time zone.

It was a real mystery.

The mystery was solved when she stepped past the policeman into an open lobby that was deserted apart from a uniformed senior policewoman who was deep in conversation with a slim young man in a sharp suit who was making her laugh.

Anna barely glanced at them. Her stare had zeroed in on the tall, dramatically dark fallen-angel figure radiating impatience who stood a little apart and was not engaged in the charm offensive.

He was wearing the same things she had seen him in the previous day, but they were now creased, and the tie was gone. His hair was tousled and his jaw and hollow cheeks covered in a dark stubble, that, along with the glitter in his cerulean eyes, added to the combustible charge in the air around him.

He looked dark, dangerous, disreputable and totally in charge.

*'You!'* She looked around, her hair whiplashing around her face as she searched for the person who was *really* going to rescue her. The odd feeling in the pit of her stomach told her there wasn't going to be anyone else—or something else entirely might be responsible for the *odd* feeling. 'What are you doing here?'

*'Cara...finally!'*

He was beside her in less time than it took Anna to blink, and she couldn't speak now, her vocal cords were frozen, the glitter in his eyes making her head spin as the long fingers of his right hand slid around the nape of her neck, tilting her face up to him.

*He is going to kiss me!*

And then he did, a hard, hungry kiss that sent heat pumping through her body and then, without his mouth lifting from hers, the kiss seamlessly expanded to a slow sensual assault on her senses. His mouth, tongue and lips made the journey along her lower lip, tasting and kissing, while he watched her face as she stood, shocked into compliant stillness.

Until stillness was not enough, and she had leaned into him, kissing him back. The abruptness with which he released her made her rock a little on her heels.

Frustration that she was deeply ashamed of clawed low in her belly as, like an automaton, she reacted to the hand in the small of her back guiding her through the big double doors and out into a small courtyard. Her glazed, shocked glance took in her surroundings: some sort of parking area, high walls on three sides; the double gates on the fourth were open.

It was empty apart from one long low limo with black-out windows. As they emerged so did the driver, who walked around to the boot and pulled out a bicycle.

'What are you doing?' *More to the question what am I doing?* 'You kissed me!' she accused.

'You kissed me back.'

She lifted her chin. 'In your dreams!'

Probably, he thought. 'I didn't know what you were about to say, maybe the first thing that came into your head, which might have contradicted to some degree what we had said, so I was giving the nice policeman an explanation that he can accept, otherwise he might have thought I was kidnapping you.'

She resisted the hand lightly placed in the centre of her back, the hand that was guiding her to the limo.

'I think you are.'

'Rescuing you, yes, you can thank me at a later date.'

'Kidnapping me,' she retorted, ignoring the irony as she literally dug her heels in. 'But thank you, though I don't know how or why you are here doing this.'

'You're limping.'

She clamped her lips over a crude retort; he really did destroy her normally very nice manners. 'New shoes. Now, do you mind? I am more than capable of finding my own way home,' she retorted with dignity, trying to remember if she had put her purse in her bag.

'Just get in the car. Do not—what is the saying?—look a gift horse in the mouth.'

She looked at him, careful not to include his mouth in her flash scrutiny. He was no horse, he was a sleek panther...and no one in their right mind got in a car with a feral big cat.

'I am not getting into a car like that with a man I...

Oh, yes, you've told me your name, but you could be anyone…a journalist after a story?'

'Now you're thinking like a sensible person.'

Her eyes narrowed. 'Are you admitting you are?'

'No, but you should always assume the worst of people. Cynicism is not a fault, it is a survival essential.'

Perplexed by his logic, she shook her head. 'This has been a very confusing day.'

*And she thought it was over?* 'You are far too naive to be a successful criminal.' *Though maybe not to be an accomplice…who cared for her grandfather enough to do anything for him?*

'I'm not a criminal, I'm a librarian!' she wailed in frustration, which turned into indignation when he laughed.

His grin faded as he dragged a hand through his hair. 'Get in the car, Anna.'

She thought of that kiss and shook her head, pausing when she heard a distant rumble that she struggled to identify.

The smartly suited young man reappeared. 'Sounds like someone tipped them off we've taken the back entrance. Thanks,' he added, taking the bike from the driver. 'Best way to get through rush-hour traffic,' he said with a grin to Anna. 'Franco, by the way, and sorry we didn't get you out of there sooner,' he said, mounting the bike and adding, 'I'm off, and you might like to not hang around either, Soren, unless you want to make the evening news bulletins?'

Anna watched him ride away. 'He is…?'

'Your lawyer.'

'He looks expensive.'

'He's a friend and he's right, unless you want to meet up with your friends from the press…?'

He watched the shudder of revulsion ripple through

her before he turned and walked across to the rear door. His sardonic gaze held hers as he pulled it open while the driver, without a word, jumped into the driving seat.

'Your choice.'

Anna stood there torn with indecision. The noise was getting louder, identifiable now as the babble of approaching voices, with a few laughs and curses thrown in.

Choice—there was no choice… She took a deep breath, and, trying not to favour her painful foot, walked up to the limo, not meeting his eyes as she edged past him to settle inside the luxurious leather-lined interior. She shut her eyes as the door closed behind her.

She opened them again when Soren slid in beside her and experienced a moment of panic as she recalled the searing frustration when he had stopped kissing her and the feeling of being totally out of control that had preceded it.

'This is a nightmare, but I'll be home soon.' She soothed herself with the facts and refused to think about the kiss.

'Ah…that might not be such a good idea—'

Her green eyes flew wide in panicked protest. 'But—!'

'The press are staked out outside your flat, unless you fancy running the gauntlet?'

He watched her shudder again and deflate and let his sympathy stir.

'Don't worry, alternative arrangements have been made.'

*And my compliance is taken for granted.* Her eyes narrowed. 'They have?'

He heard the cool in her voice and ignored it; it was less easy to ignore the female scent of her warm skin. 'Yes, it's all in hand, and long-distance walking is not involved.'

She watched as his eyes slid down her slim calves to her narrow ankles and neatly crossed feet.

'What are you staring at?'

Unwilling to admit even to himself that he had lost control of the direction of his gaze, he came back with an exasperated, 'Women and shoes… Why on earth did you put them on if they are crippling you?'

'Oh, I don't know, maybe because the police were waiting for me and I didn't have time to select an outfit that would win your approval.'

At least the cut-off pale blue jeans were comfortable, but she had always felt that the snug fit across her hips only accentuated the boyish narrowness she despised. Normally she would disguise this lack of feminine inches with an oversized shirt or thigh-length tunic, but when the phone had rung she'd been wearing a dip-dye blue sleeveless vest that had shrunk in the wash and revealed slivers of her midriff, a fact she was only just discovering as she now registered a draught around her middle.

She tugged at the hem, but didn't glance down; she knew what she saw would not be confidence-boosting. 'Stop the car!' The decision was so fast she didn't see it coming herself.

'What?'

'I'm not being *arranged* by some random man who says he knows my grandfather.'

He studied her face with an assessing look and folded his hands across his chest. 'Fine, but first things first. Ask away.'

She shook her head. 'What do you mean?'

'You want my credentials, simply ask. I am,' he claimed, spreading his hands in an expansive gesture, 'an open book. Let me start. Well, you already know my name. I am Soren Steinsson Vitale, head of the Vitale

Group, which is, as of last year, the largest media company in Europe. We retain an interest in the engineering company my grandfather started up and in specialist steel manufacturing. Shall we leave it at our interests are diverse? You probably have an electrical item in your kitchen that one of our factories made, and the specialised steel in your—'

'I get the idea—you are rich and were born with a golden spoon in your mouth.'

'Not born—the golden spoon was acquired a little later in life and I earned it. I also speak several languages, and I have my own teeth.' He flashed her a mocking, very white smile. 'But I think perhaps you already know this because you must have put my name into a search engine?'

'Because you're so fascinating?' This seemed like an occasion when the truth was the least humiliating option. 'I might have,' she conceded. 'But after you left, my grandfather had an…episode. People in the later stages of dementia often suffer seizures.'

Without warning the tears welled in her eyes and she brushed them angrily away and then gave the same treatment to the hand that was extended towards her. 'I'm fine,' she snarled.

He concealed his concern with a casual shrug; feeling protective towards an attractive woman was something he did not want to get accustomed to. The women in his life all had one thing in common: self-sufficiency. Maybe two: they all shared his pragmatic attitude to sex. Maybe three: they did not expect him to pretend to feel something he did not.

'He's totally innocent, you know. You *do* know that, don't you? The things they are saying. If you knew him like I do… He's always been there for me. When Mum went on one of her adventures he was there. Social services would have issued a care order after I broke my arm when Mum left me with Maggie, but he stepped...' She paused as her voice thickened with emotion. 'It's all a terrible mistake!'

He looked into her earnest emerald eyes and saw a shadow of the little girl who had been passed around because her mother was a selfish bitch. Maybe Tor had done one good thing in his life but that was never going to compensate for the bad things he had done.

'You'd do anything for him, wouldn't you?' he said, wondering what she had done even if she didn't realise it.

'Of course.' She sounded offended that he could ask. 'Ask your father. He knew... Oh, sorry...'

'Your grandfather changed my father's life.'

Oblivious to the undertones, she smiled. 'After the way those policemen were looking at me, you don't know how good it is to actually talk to someone who knows the truth,' she said, feeling her antagonism lowering. It would have been an exaggeration to say she was relaxed. He was not a man she could ever imagine being relaxed around...any man who kissed as he did. She clenched her jaw and firmly closed down the pathway her thoughts were leading her to.

'The truth usually comes out in the end.'

'That's what I think too!'

He looked into the eyes lifted to his, shining with an idealism that she would inevitably lose in the next few days and weeks—and she'd be better for it, or at least more able to survive in the real world.

While he remained reluctant to give anyone related to Tor the benefit of the doubt, it seemed likely that any involvement on her part had been unknowing...but then ignorance was no defence in a court of law.

# CHAPTER FOUR

'ISN'T THAT YOUR LAWYER?'

Soren nodded as Franco, in the cycle lane, punched the air with triumph as he overtook them, the lane they were in having ground to a slow crawl.

'He is your lawyer,' Soren corrected.

When he had made his request to Franco, his friend hadn't challenged him or asked him why he was doing this, why he was helping Tor's granddaughter, but Soren knew he wanted to.

Anna herself *had* asked him.

Soren was asking himself.

In a rush of unwelcome honesty he likened his own replies to a politician dodging the difficult question and choosing to answer a different one.

Soren was a man who controlled his own destiny. He did not give away that control to regrets or doubts, he set an objective and ruthlessly dismissed anything that interfered with achieving it. Was it a strength or was it a weakness? He didn't know, it was just him—it was the way he dealt with distractions.

Anna Randall sitting beside him would not be dismissed, neither would the sexual vibration between them. He looked at her through the veil of his lashes resenting the fact she could make him feel something he did not want to.

Resenting her and, yes, *wanting* her.

Wanting to punish her for who she was, and wanting to protect her… The conflict simmering inside constantly threatened to boil over at any moment. He felt as if he were walking on eggshells barefoot.

From the moment he had set eyes on her there had been a recognition; he had instantly sensed the fire, the promise of passion that he had wanted to explore.

Tor Randall's granddaughter just wouldn't vacate his head. Innocent or guilty, too attractive for comfort or not, she *was* Tor's granddaughter—that fact alone put her totally off limits.

He faced his uncomfortable facts so why the hell couldn't she? Why could she not see that Tor was as guilty as hell?

What was it going to take to make her see her grandfather for who he was, what he was…?

It frustrated the hell out of him that even after today she seemed to have no real concept of what was coming, no idea of the truth bomb that was about to explode in her face.

Maybe it was something that only those who had lived the experience could appreciate, and he had. He regretted her name would be associated for ever with the breaking scandal, but it was not down to him. He was the catalyst, not the cause.

It was a fact of life that the innocent suffered along with the guilty. She was not his responsibility, and he didn't need the feelings of guilt that were both illogical and uncomfortable. She would have a tough time but she would move on.

*His mother hadn't.*

He pushed away the thought, focusing instead on the steely core he had sensed in Tor's granddaughter, a resilience that his own emotionally vulnerable parent had never had.

Anna would survive but she wouldn't be the same person sitting beside him. What part of herself would she lose?

Why did the idea bother him?

For the first time in many years Soren found he could not distance himself from his emotions. The acknowledgment infuriated him, but rather than give into those emotions he reached the logical conclusion that the best way to make them go away was to address the cause.

He was going to remove her from the path of the oncoming storm and after that it was up to her what she did.

He leaned back into the corner of the car, pushing his head against the cream leather padding.

'Relax,' he advised, thinking she was wound so tight that any false move might shatter her like fragile glass.

It seemed to Anna that this was advice he might well follow himself. No wonder she felt fraught—behind his laid-back facade he was so tense it felt like sitting next to an unexploded bomb!

She glanced at his clenched profile through her lashes... Unbidden, her glance drifted to his mouth.

Fighting the urge to touch her own lips, she blurted, 'I am relaxed.'

It was a lie and his sardonic look suggested she was fooling no one.

'And you're not about to throw yourself from a moving vehicle?'

'I wasn't. I would have waited for it to stop. Oh, all right, not relaxed, but it has not been a relaxing day and, besides, my mother told me never to get into cars with strange men.' The flippant addition was a lie, she hadn't, though it was a story Anna had told so often that she almost believed it.

It was one of her selection of *caring parent* stories. She had built up quite a repertoire of them during her school days so that she could roll her eyes along with school friends and join in as they bemoaned how their parents were such pains who had *no idea*!

What would they have said if they had realised that Anna had nobody telling her what to do, that she didn't want to escape, but longed for the security of some restrictions to complain about?

Even on the other side of the world her mum might have seen the headlines; she'd be worried. Her mum might be selfish, but Anna knew she did care for her in her own way.

'What are you doing?'

He watched as she rifled through the contents of the bag she held on her knee like a shield…*against him*? Unfortunately the shield did not totally conceal the sliver of smooth stomach that his eyes kept drifting to… *Was she that smooth and silky all over?*

'I think I forgot my phone.'

'I would imagine you'd know by this point,' he said drily, handing back a lipstick that had rolled against his leg. He didn't miss the fact she made a conscious effort not to touch his fingers, or that her lips were not coated with any of the 'sweet cinnamon' she tucked back into her bag.

'I should get a message to my mum. She will be worried.'

From what Franco's research had revealed about her mother, Soren seriously doubted it.

Married young, widowed young, Mia Randall had decided that parenthood was not for her, though even before she took off for good she had not allowed having a small child to interfere with her adventurous globetrotting lifestyle.

His friend, not normally one to judge, had offered the opinion that some people should not have children.

Soren did not disagree, but he didn't judge so harshly, perhaps because *he* was one of those innately selfish people that children would be better off without.

This was not information he had as yet shared with his grandfather, who frequently spoke of the great-grandchildren he anticipated. There were occasions when he arranged for Soren to *stumble* over eligible mates, and Soren never called him on it, not because he was afraid of conflict with the old man but because he saved those explosive encounters for things that actually mattered to him.

When it came to marriage they were never going to be on the same page. His grandfather, who was obsessed with his *legacy*, would never understand that Soren lived in the present and did not think about the future or care about his legacy. The past had to this point taken up most of his emotional energy, that and achieving some sort of closure.

'Use mine if you like?' he offered casually.

'I… I don't know her number…or, for that matter, if there's any reception where she is.'

'Which is where?'

Her eyes slid self-consciously from his. 'I'm not totally sure. She was in Brazil the last time she made contact.'

*'Last time…?'*

'It's fine. I'll contact her when I get home… Where are we going?' A glance out of the window told her it was nothing like her north London address. Ambitiously advertised as a penthouse, it was more realistically an attic, a nice attic. The sight of a patch of green through the roof window had swung it for her, along with the fact she could reach two Tube stations in a five-minute walk.

The leafy tree-lined avenue skirting the park they were driving along was several pay grades above where she lived.

'Not far now.'

She glanced sideways, felt her stomach flutter and thought, *Thank God!*

'I still don't… Why are you even here? How did you know that I was there…at the police station?'

'It was hard not to know. I think most news channels carried the story and the pictures of you leaving your flat. There was also a nice little interview with the taxi driver, who spoke quite movingly of your tears.'

She looked horrified by the information. 'Oh, God! I didn't cry.' A few sniffs did not constitute crying.

'It could have been worse, but apparently you reminded him of his daughter. Is the air conditioning too low? You're shivering—shall I turn it up?'

'No, I'm fine.' Dabbing her tongue at the beads of sweat along her upper lip, she managed a cracked laugh. 'Delayed reaction. I've just never been a police suspect before.' She tried to make it sound like a joke and didn't make it.

He fought the urge to comfort her and masked his concern with a show of abruptness. 'It's their job. It wasn't personal.'

'It felt pretty personal.' She paused, realising that the car had slowed and taken a turn under an arch into a private parking facility.

The longing to be in her own space and lock the door behind her was physical in its intensity.

'When will it be safe to go back to my flat?' Anna was inclined to risk it, anyway. It wasn't as if he were going to stop her.

He could always kiss her—that had been pretty effective.

The thought came from nowhere and for several seconds her mind went blank as she relived the wild urgency she had experienced before he had closed it down.

*He* had closed it down!

'I think I should go back to my flat. Surely if I'm so damned infamous…there's nowhere I can hide? There are people in hotels too,' she pointed out. 'Maybe I should run away to Iceland?'

Anna needed her own space. She'd spent the entire day so far putting on a mask for people, trying to prove she was innocent, trying to prove that she was totally cool with breathing the same air as this man.

'Somewhere warmer perhaps?' Soren's gaze ran over the pale contours of her face. Her skin was less creamy warmth and more ghostly pale. Even without the blue smudges emphasised by the shadow of her long lashes there was a bruised quality to her green-eyed gaze.

His scrutiny made her want to cover her face; the impulse made her annoyed with herself all over again.

The car had come to a stop now, but he made no attempt to get out.

'Has no one ever told you it's rude to stare? Or have you never seen a woman without a full face of make-up before?' she grouched.

'Not one that looks like you.'

Their glances held a moment too long, long enough to make her heart thud out of control and put a stomach-quivering question mark in her head, until he continued, his attitude all practicality tinged with something close to boredom that made her feel she was making a big deal out of nothing.

'This isn't a hotel. My mother keeps an apartment here. She rarely uses it.' An expression she struggled to name slid across his face. 'You can stay there until things are settled.'

'You mean until I know if I'm about to be arrested?'

He watched her attempt to make it a joke. Even taking away the quivering lip she clamped down on hard, it would not have convinced a baby, though it did produce a fresh kick of guilt, this time tinged with admiration as the image of her pushing her way through the press pack earlier played in his head on a slow-motion loop.

It took someone with hidden reserves to come out of that sort of thing with dignity, and she had. There must have been some people watching her as she'd looked straight ahead, not reacting to the questions being slung at her like missiles, who had wanted to cheer.

Besides him.

'You've had a bad day, haven't you, *cara*?' His languid delivery almost disguised the concern he resented feeling.

Anna felt her eyes fill with tears and blinked rapidly, trying not to look at the shoulder that was too close and too tempting. 'For God's sake, don't be nice to me,' she demanded through clenched teeth.

Some of the tension left his face as he loosed a laugh. It would seem she required his sympathy even less than he wanted to give it—the more he was around this woman, the more unusual he found her.

*The more attractive he found her.*

'Don't worry, I can never keep it up. Nature will win out in the end.' His white grin held self-mockery.

'You're not a nice person?' Distracted from her misery, she managed a watery smile.

'They call my grandfather Il Demonio. The Devil,' he translated.

Her brows lifted. It seemed dramatic, but there were people calling her grandfather worse at the moment.

'And you're just a chip off the old block,' she joked tiredly, and she *was* tired. She made a conscious effort to allow her rigid spine to flex and felt relief as her shoulder blades burrowed into the support of the backrest. The buzz of tension in her head and the knots in her shoulders were beginning to loosen… It probably wasn't the right time or place and definitely not the right company to lower her defences.

'You're not the first person to make that comparison.'

Stifling another yawn, she shifted in her seat to face him full on, her annoyance showing as she retorted, 'I wasn't and I won't be. I don't care what your reputation is, I judge people from their actions. You visited an old sick friend of your father, and you are here now, helping me. Even though you don't know me and despite the fact being seen with me will probably taint you by association… Will it?' she shot out anxiously.

His lips quirked. 'I will survive.'

'And so far I have not been very grateful. I happen to think you are very kind.' And his actions went way beyond normal *kindness*.

Soren opened the door and stepped out. Guilt seemed to be becoming his factory setting.

To ward off the feelings as he walked around to open her door, he reminded himself that the guilt was not his. *He* was not the villain of this situation. Tor Rasmusson was.

A fact that was hard to cling to when her white-faced gratitude was making him feel as guilty as hell. Frustration made his jaw ache. Obviously he regretted that she, *anyone* innocent, if she was, had been caught up in this, but he wasn't about to regret it.

He wasn't sorry, he told himself, ignoring the contradictory fresh kick of remorse, and there were a whole lot of victims out there who might get some recompense now.

Not apologise, but for a brief moment he toyed with the notion of telling her the truth.

He discarded it almost immediately, even though it would be guaranteed to wipe the idealistic glow from her eyes, which quite frankly would have been a relief.

It was many years since Soren had needed the good opinion of others; his hesitation now was a matter of practicality.

She wasn't ready to accept the truth about her grandfather, although it would be better for her when she did. But he was well aware that the moment he came clean and revealed that he himself was the architect of her grandfather's downfall he would immediately become a monster in her eyes, which was fine by him. He'd been called worse before and often by his own grandfather.

Soren had a very thick skin.

# CHAPTER FIVE

'I'M JUST SO glad that I'm not the only one who knows Grandpa Henry is innocent,' she said as she exited the limo with a degree of poise, if not elegance. She was just congratulating herself on that when she dropped her bag and the contents spilt out and began rolling away across the concrete floor of the garage.

*Maybe he was a monster...maybe he'd spent too long trying to think like a monster. The pursuit of his quarry over all these years had involved inserting himself into Tor's mindset. Had he become the thing he'd been hunting?*

Silencing the inner dialogue, Soren frowned. This wasn't about him; he had nothing to justify. What had he been meant to do? Pat the guy on the back and say, 'All is forgiven, don't do it any more'?

He hadn't been looking for justice for the masses when he'd outed Tor Rasmusson, but they had it anyhow and he had his revenge.

'Can you manage?' he said, unable not to enjoy the view of her tight little bottom.

'Almost,' she said, responding to the impatience in his voice as she chased the last errant item from her bag, which had rolled under a sports car... The extra stretch to reach it caused her top to ride up a little higher, revealing a section of her lower back that no one with testosterone could have missed.

Smooth and pale, her skin had a satiny appearance; he had no way of testing his theory that it would feel like oiled silk without touching it.

He dragged his eyes clear but not before his imagination had supplied a number of scenarios that involved touching, with his hands, his lips... He pushed away the image of her body arching to his touch while he anchored her hips to the... He cleared his throat and reached for the control panel to his right and was relieved when the overhead air conditioning kicked in, flooding the immediate area with an icy blast of air.

She got to her feet. 'The zip is broken.'

'You do know, don't you, that *my* opinion is not the one that matters? It's about proof.'

Anna wasn't sure if her shiver this time was in response to the ice in his voice or the sudden drop in temperature. She closed the zip and tugged it experimentally; it held.

'I don't need proof. I *know...*'

Her calm conviction as she smiled serenely up at him drove him closer to the edges of his self-control. *Nobody* could be that stupid and blind!

'The law relies on facts, not feminine intuition.'

And they had plenty of facts, Soren knew. He had supplied a forensically detailed file that had been forwarded to the police: the list of victims, the varied aliases, and the money. It always followed the money, a lot of it locked away in offshore accounts.

Something in his tone made her glance sharpen on his face. There was nothing to see there beyond the startling perfection, the harmony and strength of angles and planes. Even bone-tired in body and mind she reacted to that beauty…and her feminine intuition was yelling *danger*…

He watched as she gave her head a tiny shake, dragging some rich dark strands of hair from her face and raising her arms to combine them briefly at the nape of her neck, the action lifting her narrow ribcage and emphasising her slim, supple curves.

There was something almost feline about her streamlined body. She made zero effort to be provocative; in fact, as impossible as it seemed to him, she seemed oblivious to the innate sensuality she exuded.

'I'm being realistic, not emotional, all right, I am being emotional but—' She sighed. 'This is all so… Well, at least they can't send him to prison. He's already there. If he wasn't he would be able to clear his own name—' she snapped her fingers '—just like that.' Anna fell into step beside him. 'He can't, so I will.' She wasn't quite sure how yet, but she was pretty sure it would be harder if she were sitting in a prison cell herself.

Soren slowed his pace to accommodate the difference in their stride and the fact she was limping.

'We'll take the lift,' he said in response to her questioning look as they passed the staircase. 'When was the last time you ate?'

It was a masterful change of subject. 'I don't know.'

'Eat, then talk strategy.'

She sighed. 'All right.'

The glass-sided lift whooshed silently to the top of the building. She was in a lift with a man who must be regarded as dangerous by any woman under ninety and she was safe—he was not looking at her, or the multiple reflections of her in the walls, but at his phone. God, it was so depressing!

Not that she wanted to have to fight him off, but just

a little frisson of possibility would have made her feel more like a…woman. *Sure, because there's nothing that makes you feel more like a woman than fighting a man off in a lift.*

*Would you be fighting?*

Soren waited until she had exited the lift before he emerged. The scent of her perfume in the enclosed space had been driving him crazy.

'This way…'

She entered a little ahead of him.

'This is very…' She looked curiously round the loft-style open-plan space; it was like a photo shoot for a glossy magazine. Minimalist and expensively impersonal. She chose the room's selling point. 'Lovely view.' One wall was glass and looked out over the river.

He wasn't looking at the room; he had been looking at her behind and now he was scrutinising her legs. His expression did not suggest admiration.

'First, we sort that foot.'

'It's fine,' she said, trying not to wince as she stamped her foot down to prove her point. While she'd been in the police station adrenaline and panic had blurred any pain, but now her screaming nerve endings were making themselves felt.

'Take it off.' Their eyes clashed and he added drily, 'Your shoe.'

'I won't be able to get it back on.'

He arched a sardonic brow and looked bored. 'And that is a bad thing why?'

She sighed and limped across to one of the immaculate crease-free sofas. Lowering herself onto it, she bent her leg and slowly peeled off the offending shoe, before settling back with a sigh and stretching her throbbing foot out in front of her.

There was a grimace of distaste on her face as she tilted her foot from side to side to see the offending area.

'I think the blister might have burst.' There was no think about it; it was a mess.

'What are you doing?'

'I don't want to get blood on your sofa.' Actually, the rug was white too.

He swore and placed a hand on her shoulder as she struggled to her feet, or at least one of them. At the last minute, overbalancing, she fell back with a grunt.

She slung him an indignant look.

'I have no idea why women put themselves through agony for the sake of fashion.'

*The hypocrisy!* 'Does it never occur to you that the almost-dressed women hanging onto your arm are doing so to stop falling over?'

'How do you know I have women hanging on my arm?'

'A wild guess?' she suggested sourly. Another educated guess was they would all possess endless legs and perfect faces.

'Why buy shoes that don't fit?'

'They were a bargain.'

He looked genuinely bemused by the explanation but then she didn't imagine he did much bargain-hunting.

'Let me see.'

She retracted her leg. 'Why?'

He rolled his eyes. 'So I can post a photo on— Why the hell do you think? So I can see the damage.'

'It's nothing.'

He sighed and looked bored again, or at least bored with a clenched ticcing jaw. 'Spare me the brave-little-soldier attitude and let me see!'

She felt his gaze for a moment before she threw up

her hands. 'All right.' Hands clasped supportively under
her thigh, she lifted her leg and wriggled her toes, a mistake, it hurt, before retracting her foot and throwing out
a childish, 'Happy now?'

The provocation of her pout took him a moment to
move beyond.

His touch was clinical and light around her slender
ankle as he turned her extended foot to view the damage.

What he saw made him swear. 'It's a mess.'

'And I always thought my feet were one of my selling points.'

Her attempt at humour did not go down well.

'You've made it worse walking around on it.'

'I spent most of the time sitting down being grilled.
I didn't really notice until... It's only a blister. I really
don't see what you're making a fuss about.'

He swore again. It was Italian-sounding, and with his
carved features set in a scowl he looked very brooding—
Latin with a side order of Viking thrown in. In short,
very gorgeous.

'What about the other foot?'

'That's not too bad,' she husked, the tenderness in her
foot no longer the problem. It was the tingling imprint of
his light touch that was bothering her...more than a little.
'I don't think the skin is broken on that one.'

'Think or know.'

'Know,' she said firmly.

'Well, that is going to need cleaning and dressing.'

'I'll get it done when I get home.' She had already
decided that she couldn't stay here. She wanted more
than ever to go home, by cover of darkness if that was
what it took.

'You'll probably have gangrene by then. Wait there!'

He delivered the addition as if it had never occurred to

him that anyone would not follow his edicts. She mimed a mocking salute at the retreating back of the man who seemed determined to take over her life.

And she was letting him!

'Oh, God!' she sighed out before sliding back into the showroom-smooth white sofa. Like everything, it looked as though it had never been touched, let alone used.

She swung her legs down to the floor, careful not to jar her foot, and guiltily dusted the pristine fabric before, from her semi-recumbent position, gazing around the very white room, well, multiple shades of white. The effect was actually quite soothing.

Except she was past soothing.

She sat there, her head spinning as the day's events came crowding in, playing like a film on a loop—a horror film.

By the time Soren reappeared she felt as though her head was going to explode with the whirling chaos of disconnected thoughts.

But she clung to the only positive: her grandfather was innocent of what they accused him of. Was she being naive thinking that in the end the truth would always come out?

In the meantime, she had to deal with being one of the central figures in the scandal of the moment, and no one seemed to believe she knew nothing.

As much as she appreciated this offer of a night's respite, she could not see the point of delaying the inevitable and, although she hated the idea of the press intrusion, someone needed to be out there standing up for Grandpa Henry.

She watched as Soren placed a first-aid box on a side table and pulled it across to the sofa.

'It's very kind of you to offer me a place to stay to-night, but I can't hide for ever.'

He didn't respond to her despondent addition, just looked at her through the half-lowered veil of his dark lashes for a moment longer before grabbing a footstool.

'What if you could?' he said, straddling the stool. 'Hide. Not for ever, but for… Come on…'

In response to his imperative gesture, she lifted her foot and extended it warily towards him. 'Could hide?' she queried, closing her mouth over a shocked sigh as his cool fingers grasped her ankle and yanked it onto his knee.

'Until things die down.' His eyes rose from his contemplation of her foot.

She lifted her chin. 'I'm not going to run away. I haven't done anything wrong. Grandpa has not done anything wrong. I want to tell people that.'

*Dio,* he thought, imagining her standing there facing a camera while she defended the old bastard. They would crucify her with the realities.

She shifted a little against the white upholstery as his inscrutable bright eyes brushed her face for a moment longer before he bent over the small foot that lay on his knee.

'Your grandfather is safe—his condition not only makes him effectively immune from prosecution, but immune to public opinion.'

'This is about his reputation, not— Ouch!' she yelled.

'Hold still.' He appeared unsympathetic to her pain, but his touch as he continued to dab the raw area with antiseptic was gentle, and as clinical as his manner. 'I'll put a dry dressing on.' She gave another gasp, this time soft, and when he looked up her teeth were digging into her full lower lip, and she was pale, the dark stain along her cheekbones emphasising that pallor. 'You all right?'

Closing her eyes was Anna's only defence against his penetrative stare and the horrifying possibility he had guessed that her gasp was not connected with her blistered foot but the casual brush of his finger along the sensitive skin of her instep.

'Fine, just get on with it...' She softened her abrupt response with a guilty, 'Thank you.'

The belated polite addition drew his eyes back to her face but Anna, who had kept her eyes scrunched closed, did not see.

'It's going to be painful for a while,' Soren warned, thinking that there was a lot of it about, as he continued to focus his effort on ignoring the pain he was feeling, courtesy of the heavy, hot weight of arousal, the killing pressure in his groin.

'It's fine.' She shook her head and opened her eyes, carefully avoiding his. 'I'm finally getting an opportunity to test out all those relaxation apps.' She needed a lot more than a lavender candle, she reflected, wondering when all the self-control had gone from her life.

*Relax*—that was one thing that Soren couldn't allow himself to do at that moment. He could not afford even temporary hormonal amnesia.

He liked sex.

He liked women.

But, despite his reputation, there was no string of broken hearts, a few bruised egos possibly, but he had no interest in hurting women, and he could smell vulnerable a mile off. Luckily he was attracted to women who were, not just beautiful, but independent, who didn't equate good sex with a meeting of souls.

In Anna Randall's case her vulnerable aura was like

a walk in a warm meadow, the sort that made you want to lie down... *She* smelt like a walk in a warm meadow and he had wanted to lie down with her from the moment he saw her. Actually, lying down was purely optional—any angle would have been fine with him so long as he could sink into her.

Obviously he wasn't going to, and not just because she lit up the big red keep-clear lights in his head. He couldn't allow himself to forget *who* she was—this situation was already complicated enough without him sleeping with his enemy's granddaughter.

Soren took a firm grip of his wayward imagination, deleting the tormenting image of her stretched out on the sofa beneath him with her long hair spread out around them. He continued to deliver a monotone running commentary on what he was doing as he applied a light dressing to the raw area.

'Anna, I said is that too tight?'

His voice sounded to Anna as though it were coming from a long way off. She heard the words but didn't react to them. He had not released her foot; his fingers were moving along the curve of her arch slowly and then back again...over and over... She swallowed hard and clenched her lips over a whimper. The touch had started as soothing and moved into totally uncharted territory.

Who even knew there were so many nerve endings under the skin there? And each one was alive, connecting with other nerve endings; the surface layer of every inch of her skin was tingling. Cheeks flushed hot against her pale skin, her head fell back... This time nothing would stop the almost whimper, a broken sound that she could not immediately associate with herself.

She could hear the sound of the sea, only it wasn't; it was, she realised, her own blood pounding in her ears.

She heard him swear. It was the hook she clung onto to drag her free of the deep drowning sensual thrall she was entangled in.

*Stop drifting.*

'I think…' But she didn't think, she couldn't. His eyes were so deep, drowning blue, bright and fierce, and she was… She swallowed hard and tried to adopt the expression of someone who knew what their name was…what they were doing.

'Anna…' He breathed her name, making it half warning but also strange and exciting. Under the heat in his eyes she sensed a bewilderment as deep as her own and a ferocity that she found unbearably exciting.

Without him breaking eye contact, his fingers moved higher up the curve of her bare calf then higher under the fabric as he reeled her in, pulling until her bottom was on the very edge of the sofa.

Her heart pounded out a heavy beat, until she was barely breathing.

His intense magnetism seemed to be exerting a physical pull. She found herself leaning in; he was leaning in. She recognised the moment they reached a tipping point, but not who made the final move that connected their mouths.

The heat that flared was instantaneous, the combustion seeming to consume the oxygen in the room as the slow, shatteringly sensuous exploration deepened.

The whimper was hers, the groan was his, the rest was lost in a hot blur. Then into the heat haze a noise: the vibration of a phone.

Soren, dark streaks cresting his cheekbones, swore and turned away, rising to his feet and presenting his back to her as he stared at the screen. He swore again, slid it back into his pocket and waited a moment before turning.

'I wouldn't have let you…it…go any…' she blurted, trying not to think about the clash of teeth, the collision of tongues.

His shrug could not have been more languid. 'Sometimes sex is not a bad way to relax after a tough day.'

Her jaw dropped. He made it sound like an option such as a stiff drink or a run in the park—for him it probably was—and it wasn't that she disapproved of his attitude—in fact, on one level, she almost envied him—but she knew that sex for her could never be the casual transaction that it was for him. She knew herself well enough to know that she wanted more, she needed more; there was no way she could separate her emotions from the physical act.

She wanted that intimacy, she wanted to feel that close to another person, but she was also wary of the wanting, for wanting *too* much. She didn't need to see a therapist to work out she was wanting what she had never had.

But her *fear* had always been greater than her *want*.

She hated that in her; she hated that, even though she had grown into a confident, capable young woman, when it came to her love life there was still that little girl who hadn't been special enough, pretty enough for her own mum to stick around.

Did that even make sense? Anna had no idea.

It was as though the craving for love and the deep-seated fear of rejection were constantly battling inside her.

'I think I should be going home,' she said stiffly.

'No, you stay here, I will go, but first… I have an idea.' Something about his casual tone made her think it wasn't. 'You wanted somewhere to hide?'

'You said that—'

A hissing sound of exasperation left his lips. 'I know you want to battle the forces of evil and clear your grandfather's name—'

The way he said it all snide and snarky brought an angry flush to her face.

'He is an innocent man.'

He gave a sigh. 'This is out of your hands, you must see that?' The stubborn set of her chin suggested she wasn't ready to see anything and certainly not sense.

'Just stay here tonight.'

'This is your mother's home—'

He dismissed the objection out of hand. 'The fact is my mother has never been here. I bought the place hoping that… Not one of my best ideas… Look at that view!'

His comment bemused her; the view was worth several million. 'It's beautiful!'

'Not if you're agoraphobic.' It was a classic example of outsourcing the wrong thing. He had just signed the agent's cheques and hired the most expensive interior designer who had put in a bid—not the one who said she needed to meet the person who would be living here before she accepted the job.

So he got expensive white and glass!

'Oh!' Her eyes went from the wide expanse of glass to his face. 'That's spaces and—'

'That's not being able to step through your front door. My father's death impacted her mental health and…but you really don't want to hear this. Now, my proposal.'

'I don't want to hide.'

'Then let's just think of it as a temporary stepping away, a working holiday.'

Despite herself, she was intrigued. 'Working…?'

'My great-grandfather, over his lifetime, accumulated

a rather impressive library, some important manuscripts and various…well, I believe that the word unique has been used to describe it, but the last time anyone with any knowledge of the subject saw it was in the sixties. My grandfather has been talking about cataloguing it for years. Last year he tasked me with it, and I haven't got around to doing anything about it yet.' He studied her face. 'I see I have your attention.'

'That sounds like an incredible opportunity for someone.'

'How about you?'

He was offering her the professional gig of a lifetime. Did he even realise it? 'That isn't possible. My grandfather—'

'Does not even recognise you.'

The brutal truth made her flinch.

'*He* is safe and I am sure he would want to think of you being safe too?' He arched a brow. 'Am I right, he would want the best for you, to protect you?'

'I can protect myself. Where, as a matter of interest, is the library?'

'A rather ancient palazzo in Sicily.'

'Sicily!' she yelped and chuckled. 'I couldn't go to Sicily. My grandfather—'

'Should he need you, it's a very short flight away and Sicily is not the moon. We have running water, fibre connection, and—'

'You live there?'

'Is that a selling point?'

Thinking of the kiss that was never going to happen again, she looked away, regaining her composure before she stuck her chin out and met his gaze head-on with an 'I dare you to disbelieve me' glare. 'It is idle curiosity.'

'I agree it is never a good idea to accept an offer until you know the full job description and conditions—'

'I'm not considering,' she said, a frown forming on her brow when she heard the almost wistful note in her voice. In her defence, it was the sort of job that anyone with expertise would have given a lot for.

Too much to hope he hadn't noticed; Anna doubted anything much escaped him.

'Let's cut to the chase,' he drawled. 'Yours will not involve having sex with me.'

The breath left her chest in one startled gasp; indignant colour flew to her cheeks. 'I never imagined it would!'

There was nothing caressing about his smile, which weirdly echoed the same self-contempt that gleamed in his heavy-lidded eyes. 'You have a very…limited imagination, *cara*.'

Anna decided to stop digging this particular hole, which was already way past her head. 'You can save the big sell. I'm not considering the offer. I can't leave my grandfather and I already have a job offer at one of the most prestigious university libraries in the country.'

'A job offer is not a job,' he corrected smoothly.

'Actually, it is,' she retorted. 'I start next week.'

'I know enough to know that the likelihood of the job offer vanishing is extremely high. You are associated with a scandal that—'

She pressed a hand to her stomach, feeling sick but defiant. 'You're suggesting I'm toxic,' she quivered out.

'I'm saying that your name is trending and not in a good way. Employers are cautious.'

'But not you,' she snapped, trying to sound as though her entire future had just got significantly worse. 'Sorry,' she tacked on with a grimace. 'I have no idea why I'm being so nasty to you. You're trying to help.'

His eyes slid from hers. Considering that many—including her—might deem him the author of the situation she was in, the irony of her gratitude was not lost on him. Each fresh reminder, each non- judgmental glance from her clear green eyes, delivered a fresh scratch of guilt to his armour.

'If you'll let me.'

*She'd let him kiss her. She'd actively contributed to the kiss.*

She pushed the thought away. He clearly considered kissing and what it led to in much the same way she thought of a nice meal and a glass of wine—enjoyable but instantly forgettable.

Which was fine, because Anna had no intention of joining his list of *forgettables* even had the opportunity been on offer.

# CHAPTER SIX

'THIS ISN'T A tentative offer. I've already handed in my notice.' The local library job had only ever been a stopgap after she had fallen victim to the financial belt-tightening and reorganisation at the boarding school where she had been happy, if unchallenged.

She was way overqualified for the job, but she had never needed her grandfather's help financially and she hadn't been about to start, which turned out to be lucky now all his bank accounts, including the ones she had power of attorney over, were frozen.

'Look, I appreciate the offer, but the job is locked in,' she returned, crossing her fingers. Without a job, even if she didn't end up in jail, she could end up owing money.

'Do you have a signed contract?'

'Not yet,' she admitted, adding defiantly, 'I don't think it's a bad thing to give people the benefit of the doubt. Following that logic…are you saying I shouldn't trust you?'

Which, of course, she wouldn't have if she had been six feet with curves and legs that went on for ever and not five four, with legs that matched and the curves of a coat hanger. She might have been worried or flattered or both, but the kiss that had rocked her world had been for him the equivalent of a stress buster after a bad day.

*He hadn't kissed her as if he didn't know she was a woman...*

'Have it your way.'

'I will,' she assured him serenely.

'Anna.'

'This is *my* problem.'

'The problem is you don't think there is one. If there is anything that gets more hits or sells more copy than a monster, it's a victim.'

The cynical suggestion aroused Anna enough to protest indignantly despite being close to comatose with fatigue. 'I am not a victim!'

'I'm not here to debate semantics, but to offer a practical and mutually beneficial solution to your problems.'

Anna rubbed a hand across the tight muscles in her neck and slowly lifted her chin from her chest, where it had dropped, to look at him. On one level she was aware that being able to appreciate the strong, chiselled lines of his amazing face when her life was falling apart said something about her; she didn't push further down that particular road of self-analysis.

'This will die down,' she said, willing him to agree and growing angry when he didn't. 'There will be another scandal.'

'Sure, riding out the storm is an option...but why put yourself through that if you don't have to? And you being here and valuable to any long lens is just going to feed the interest, prolong it.'

She sat down with a bump as her legs suddenly folded.

Her eyes closed, she sensed rather than heard him move away.

'Brandy.'

'I'm already falling over.'

'Because you've not eaten, but don't worry, the food should be here soon.'

'What food?'

'I ordered takeout when we arrived, supper from the Grove.'

'The Grove as in *the* Grove?' The multi-Michelin-starred restaurant had a mile-long waiting list of celebrities who wanted to say they had dined there; also she understood the food was good.

He nodded.

'They don't do takeout...' She stopped—maybe they did if you were Soren Vitale. Without thinking, she picked up the glass and took a swallow of the contents, the glance she threw him carrying the same defiance as the gesture, and then spoilt it by choking.

'I don't like spirits,' she said hoarsely, but the warm feeling was a lot better than the taste.

'Take it slowly.'

The concern that roughed the edges of his dark bitter-chocolate voice brought an unaccountable lump to her throat. Embarrassed by her overreaction, Anna nodded and lowered her lashes to shield herself from his disturbing blue stare.

The alcohol had made her panic recede a fraction, but it had also lowered her emotional barrier. What she needed was her own bed and to cry herself to sleep in the dark.

'This is all so surreal. I keep thinking I'm going to wake up.'

'My advice—'

'I know what your advice is.'

'Being here and available,' he reiterated, 'will just fuel the story.'

'Me not being here would not make the police happy.'

'That will not be a problem. You have a good lawyer.'

She shook her head. 'He's not my lawyer, he's *your* lawyer. You are being so kind to me...' Her voice broke as the emotion totally occluded her throat.

'So you will take the job?'

'I didn't say that,' she protested, thinking this was going way too fast.

'Well, when you do... I'm flying back tomorrow, so if—'

*'Tomorrow?'* She was startled at the suggestion.

He arched a sardonic brow. 'Would that be a problem?'

She laughed. He sounded surprised by the possibility. 'Yes, actually it is, or it would be if I said yes, which,' she added quickly, 'I'm not.'

'In what way a problem?'

Her brow furrowed deeper. God, he didn't lack persistence, she had to say that much for him.

'Do you never give up? All right, you want a problem, how about I have what I'm standing up in?' She held her arms wide to invite his inspection, patting herself down to demonstrate there were no secret compartments.

There were, however, two shallow pockets in her jeans and one had a phone bulge.

'What is it?'

She wriggled her fingers into the offending pocket and pulled them out with her phone. 'It was here all along.'

'So, about tomorrow...?'

She sighed. 'Do you do everything at this speed?'

His dark lashes swept down; when they lifted a moment later the glow in the cerulean depths made her stomach flip.

'Not everything,' he said, utterly expressionless.

It was several slow-moving moments before her

breathless-sounding response dropped into the tense stillness that followed his words.

'I need time to think.' Not about the things happening below waist level—actually, thinking was exactly what she *didn't* need.

'Do you have your passport.'

Her teeth clenched as he continued to act as if her capitulation were inevitable.

'Do you have a tick list or something? Yes, I have my passport. The police wanted it, to check I'm me, I suppose, or maybe they thought I was about to skip the country...' Her green gaze slowly lifted and she shook her head less firmly than she would have liked. 'I have no clothes, not even a toothbrush.'

'Then no problem. I have an account at Harvey Nicks. Tell me what you need and I'll order it.'

'I couldn't do that!' she exclaimed, sounding shocked.

'Why not? I have bought women's clothes before.'

She felt the heat climb to her cheeks. 'I am not one of *your women*,' she retorted.

The dangerous gleam in his eyes made her stomach flip but before it could go anywhere outside her active imagination the intercom buzzed.

Soren said something that sounded Italian under his breath and stalked across to the intercom discreetly set in the wall.

'The food is here.'

'I just need the...?'

'Second door on the left.' He nodded in the direction.

She spent a few minutes in the bathroom, too emotionally whacked to take much pleasure from the luxury fixtures and fittings.

She felt marginally better after washing her hands and face, although one glance told her that her hair was beyond rescue. She put on some lipstick, found it made her look even more ghostly and clashed with the blue shadows under her eyes, and wiped it off again.

Back in the open-plan living area the table by the window had been laid; the dimmed lights emphasised the dramatic night-lit skyline beyond. The overall effect was romantic.

*So long as you don't forget it isn't, Anna.*

He held out a chair and she limped across to take it.

'If I'd known, I would have dressed for dinner.' She scanned the table with some appreciation. It might be a takeaway but not as she knew; the food on the table was served on white porcelain and slate.

'I asked for a light supper.'

'It looks so pretty!' she exclaimed. 'A work of art.'

He looked amused. 'Let us hope it tastes as good.'

He went to fill her glass from the bottle in the cooler and she frowned. 'I probably shouldn't.'

'You should do something you probably shouldn't at least once a day.'

'My mum would approve of that philosophy. This is delicious. I can't figure out what is in this sauce...'

'It's pretty well disguised,' Soren, whose own taste ran to simpler food, commented as he sat back watching her, enjoying her enthusiasm and her unselfconscious appreciation of the food. 'But you don't approve of doing something you shouldn't?'

'Oh, I'm boring. I have no spirit of adventure, Mum says. Poor Mum, she was expecting her daughter to be like her, or at least to be pretty. It came as a nasty shock when I told her I wanted to be a librarian. Her face... I honestly think she'd have been less shocked if I said I wanted to be a sex worker!' She laughed, her gaze lifting a little self-consciously from her plate when he didn't respond.

'Is something wrong?' she asked when she discovered he looked unaccountably stern, angry even. 'I babble when I drink,' she said, putting down the glass she had just picked up.

'I like your voice.'

It seemed an odd thing to say.

'Do you not like the wine?'

'It's gorgeous. Everything is gorgeous,' she said, looking across the table. There were acres of food left over, which seemed a criminal waste. Her grandfather's housekeeper, who had been her female role model growing up, had instilled a frugality in her. 'But I really couldn't eat another scrap.'

'There is pudding in the fridge.'

His teasing offer made her groan and press both hands to her stomach. 'I couldn't...' she admitted regretfully. 'Your driver—has he had any food?'

'Considerate, but I sent Alberto home a while ago.'

'Then how...? Oh, a taxi,' she realised.

'Actually, I'm staying here tonight.'

As his casual bombshell dropped and the ripples of comprehension spread, Anna's glass hit the table with a bump. She barely registered it slopping all over the surface.

'Why?' she exclaimed, then flushed. 'Not that it's any of my business.' This was his house, or his mother's, which amounted to the same thing, *she* was the guest and she was massively overreacting.

'I do not sleepwalk, if that is what is concerning you.'

The taunt seemed unnecessarily cruel to Anna, who might have spent most of her time in the bathroom *avoiding* looking at her reflection, but she had seen enough to know that this was sarcasm. Soren could have his pick, and she was sure that a man like him would be very picky—everything about him came with an *only super-model-level females or above need apply* sticker.

And they, she decided—thinking long legs and inflatable breasts—were welcome to him.

'It isn't!' she said, channelling cold towards his veiled eyelids. 'Sorry if I'm boring you,' she added when he didn't react.

'Also I am a light sleeper.' Though he seriously doubted that the night would bring him any sleep at all. 'So if you have any plans to slip away in the night...'

Anna had forgotten those plans somewhere around her second glass of wine.

'I'll go home tomorrow,' she said in a flat little voice.

'What are you doing?'

Anna stopped stacking plates. 'Clearing the—'

'Go to bed, Anna. You are the guest.'

Escape seemed a better option than arguing or suggesting he didn't know how to stack a dishwasher.

'Last door on the right,' he said in response to her questioning look.

'Right, then, goodnight.'

'Sleep well, Anna,' he called after her.

Anna didn't expect to sleep at all. Maybe it was the room's cool Scandi-blonde vibe or her total exhaustion, but she slept a solid dreamless seven hours and woke wondering where she was.

The blissful amnesia didn't last long. Rolling out of bed, she sat on the edge—she had slept in her bra and panties—and hid her face in her hands for a full indulgent thirty seconds before she remembered she had never got around to contacting her mum.

No one picked up, not exactly a shock, so she left a

text before having a look to see what was going on in the world. Only to discover she was!

She was reeling from the level of her exposure when she noticed the missed calls and the texts.

The university expressed great regret, but they apparently had a duty of care to their students and their reputation to consider so, after due consideration, they had decided to rescind their offer.

It took her a few moments to overcome the waves of nausea before she was able to grab the robe from behind the door. Still tying it, she headed straight to the living area where Soren, wearing a towel wrapped around his middle, was drinking coffee.

Shock nailed her to the spot as she took in his broad shoulders, the deeply tanned, perfect, lean musculature of his torso, his long hair-roughened legs and impressive powerful thighs.

All he needed was a mythical hammer, and he could have been mistaken for the Viking god who wielded it.

'Oh, no!' she groaned. Shock seemed to have temporarily paralysed the self-censoring area of her brain. 'Get some clothes on, please!'

'Good morning, Anna.'

There not being an option of a convenient black hole opening up at her feet, she ignored the sardonic mockery in his voice and the wicked gleam in his heavily lidded eyes.

'Is the job offer still there?'

His grin vanished, replaced by a hard calculating look. 'It is.'

'Good, then I'll take it. Oh, and, yes, you were right: no job. Apparently I am a danger to students!' She gave a shrill little bitter laugh. 'But I need to speak with the clinic first, and the offer of clothes—order a few and I'll pay you back for them.'

His lips twitched. 'I'll take it from your first pay cheque,' he promised.

'But the flight, will there be time…?'

'The new wardrobe will arrive in…ten minutes.'

'You knew I'd change my mind,' she accused.

'I was confident that you would see the advantages of the arrangement,' he corrected smoothly. 'Help yourself to coffee, the croissants are still warm, and I will go to put some clothes on.'

By the time Anna had showered a pile of boxes and bags lay on her bed along with a set of empty designer cases.

She stood there staring at them, shocked at the sheer quantity—this was no one's idea of a capsule wardrobe—while Soren yelled through the closed door.

'Just pick out something for travelling and dump the rest in the cases,' he suggested. 'I need to attend to a few things. Alberto will pick you up and bring you to the airport. Oh, and, Anna, he has instructions not to take you to the clinic even if you beg. The press have the place staked out.'

Did anyone ever say no to him? she wondered, tipping the contents of one of the bags onto the bed. The slither of colourful silk turned out to be several matching bra and panties sets…in the right size.

As the pile of items grew it became clear that there was more than a year's salary worth of designer clothes lying there, including two ball gowns that were not something a librarian wore, and she hadn't got to the line of shoeboxes yet.

# CHAPTER SEVEN

NORMALLY TAKE-OFF WAS a big thing for Anna, and not in a good way. More of a white-knuckle, take-a-deep-breath way. She did close her eyes and take a stranglehold grip of the arm rests of her seat, but there was too much going on in her head to allow for outright gibbering panic.

It wasn't just the novelty of being on a private flight that distracted her.

She was wondering where Soren was, and if the driver had told him she had tried to persuade him to take her to the clinic. As she had pointed out in her attempts to coax him, it was *almost* on the way.

It had seemed worth a try and she hadn't said she *wouldn't* say goodbye to Grandpa. Soren, in his typical overbearing style, had just taken her compliance as a given.

If Soren said anything she'd tell him that she didn't owe him any explanations, she wasn't working for him yet. Actually, it wasn't his reaction that occupied her thoughts, it was her grandfather. She knew he was being well cared for and the likelihood was he really wouldn't notice her absence, but it still felt like running away.

And Anna had never been the sort of person who ran away, *until now*…because, though you could dress it up any way you chose, she *was* running away, taking the easy way out and abandoning her grandfather.

Tears of self-disgust stung closed eyelids as she felt the plane level smoothly off.

'You going to spend the entire journey with your eyes closed?'

The soft, slightly mocking voice made Anna's eyes snap open, wide, wary and probably, she realised with a sinking heart, providing evidence that just the sight of him sitting opposite, his long legs stretched out under the table between them, was enough to send her sensitive stomach muscles into a steep spiralling dive.

She'd heard it said that sexual attraction was something you couldn't rationalise; she now knew it was true. They also said it was something you couldn't control but Anna refused to believe that. She thought of that kiss and really hoped her conviction was never put to the test... She ignored the kick of excitement in her pelvis as she thought about the consequences of failing.

Feeling like someone fighting their way out of a deep hole of their own making, she forced a smile, cleared her throat and, mentally at least, squared her shoulders.

'So, Alberto got you here on time?'

She nodded, noticing him observing her choice of clothes from the wide selection on offer, and worried that the approving warmth in his eyes made her feel good, not to mention *aware*.

For a brief childish moment she was tempted to counteract the feeling by explaining that she hadn't been seeking his approval when she selected the vivid mustard wrap-over pencil skirt with the bright blue cabbage roses on it and the classic navy silk shirt.

'He told you, didn't he? Alberto told you.'

His brows lifted. 'I have not as yet spoken to Alberto.'

'I asked him to take me to the Merlin. I wanted to say goodbye to Grandpa. Don't worry, he refused.'

'Excellent. I won't have to sack him.'

Her eyes widened, the horror morphing into annoyance when she read the gleam in his eyes. 'Very amusing, and actually I think the media storm, or at least the worst of it, might have passed.'

Soren, clean-shaven and looking utterly relaxed, eased his broad shoulders into the leather of the seat.

'You think?' His jacket was gone and his long brown fingers picked at the knot of the discreet grey silk tie that lay pale against the dark blue of his shirt, the deep colour intensifying the shocking cerulean shade of his eyes.

Breaking the hypnotic contact, she pushed her glossy freshly washed hair behind her ears and nodded, explaining.

'I would have worn dark glasses and no one would recognise me in these clothes.'

'Shades… Oh, why didn't you say? That would have made all the difference. Were you thinking of a hoodie too…?'

Her lips twisted in annoyance. 'I don't think this is funny,' she retorted haughtily.

'We are on the same page there. Neither do I.'

Looking at her suddenly made him angry—she worried about her grandfather, who was worthless. The woman didn't seem to realise that a conscience was excess baggage.

Soren thought he had eradicated his years ago—he'd had the best teacher—yet every time he looked at her his conscience ached like a muscle memory.

He focused instead on his anger. There was plenty to

go around: he was angry at himself and angry at her and
the real focus of his fury had been placed out of his reach.

'Perhaps we should concentrate on the things we have
in common.'

She frowned, not trusting this sudden bridge-building.
'What are they?' It had to be a *very* short list.

'A library that needs sorting,' he said, his thoughts a
million miles clear of his professional delivery.

So long as it was his *thought*s there was no problem,
so long as he never lost sight of the inescapable fact that
she was his enemy's granddaughter, and as such off limits, this could work.

Of course, the situation was not helped by knowing
this attraction was mutual. He could have done without
the insight—a beautiful woman wanting you was a big
turn-on.

'Do you have any doubts you're up to the job?'

She blinked, thrown by another of his lightning
changes of mood. 'Is this an interview?' Or a change of
mind? He professional pride injured, her chin went up.
'I'm very good at what I do,' she said, adopting what she
hoped was a coolly professional expression—the cool
wasn't so hard, as he'd made her feel so angry. 'And I'm
actually excited about the challenge.'

His glance was drawn to the soft outline of her mouth.
'Good to know. So it is agreed, going forward, we focus
on what we have in common, not what…sets us apart.'

She nodded and sat there looking at him, trying not
to think about the differences between them: his hardness and her softness, his olive complexion and her pale
skin, his… God, the more she tried not to think, the more
she *was* thinking. Each thought leading her deeper into a
sensual maze, imagining not just the texture of his skin,

but how it would feel to touch, how it would feel against her own. His mouth…

'Am I boring you, Anna?'

She gave a shocked little gasp as his voice jolted her from her fantasies. A wave of shamed guilt washed her pale skin rose and she laughed far too loudly to hide her embarrassment.

'Sorry, I didn't catch…?'

'I was saying that nine to five is not really an option. The heat at the moment makes the middle of the day hard to work in. You have no problem with flexible hours?'

'None at all,' she responded, feeling happier about things she felt totally confident about. Workwise she had no false modesty. She knew her worth: she was good and she planned to be better.

'I am looking forward to enjoying our perfectly professional working relationship. How's the foot?' His eyes slid down her bare legs to her ankles. Her feet were covered by a pair of flat ballet slippers. The leather was butter soft and so comfortable underneath the light padding, she had forgotten about it.

She fought the twin urges to tuck her feet out of sight and stare at his wide sensual mouth.

She lost both battles. 'Much better, thank you. These shoes are really comfortable. About that…they sent far too many clothes.'

'I will speak to someone about that.'

'You have to let me know how much I owe you.'

'I'll let you know.' He paused, his chin resting on his steepled fingers. 'Is there something you want to tell me?'

It was worrying he could read her so well. 'I'm still getting calls from journalists,' she admitted.

'I'd be surprised if you weren't. My advice is to block the numbers and switch your phone off if you need to.'

'I had one caller who said he followed us to your mother's apartment building. He knew that you spent the night…' She paused, waiting tensely for his response, relieved when he appeared thoughtful but relaxed as he digested the information.

'What did you say to him?'

'Nothing. I mean, *literally* nothing.'

He smiled. 'You did the right thing. You have his number?'

She nodded and handed him her phone. 'It's the eleven thirty-one call.'

He nodded and transferred the relevant information to his own phone before returning hers. 'Don't worry, he thinks he has a lever.' The hauteur in his face, the ice in his eyes made Anna *almost* feel sorry for the journalist.

'And he doesn't?'

'No, he doesn't.'

'If he calls again?'

'Say you do not discuss your personal life with the press.'

'Personal…but won't he think that you…me… I…?'

'He already does, but people do not print anything about me unless they are very sure of their facts.' He shrugged. 'I'm not known for sitting back and, erm, *taking* it.'

'My visit to Grandpa would have been a mistake, wouldn't it?'

Her expression prodded his sympathy into life. 'Who knows?'

'I said goodbye via video call.'

'That went well…?' he said, studying her face.

'No… Yes… That is, one of the trustees answered initially and I could hear him in the background and then Grandpa looked directly into the camera. I'm not sure if he could see me but he…he just…*snarled* at me to keep my mouth shut or I'd regret it… He looked…'

The protective urge to comfort her, even if that comfort was based on a false premise, was too strong for him to combat. 'Do not overthink it. He is not himself most of the time.'

Her smile still held an edge of the seeds of suspicion he had seen in her green eyes, the suspicion he knew that she would not admit even to herself.

'That's true. Other times, though, he is sharp as a tack. He doesn't always know who I am when we play chess but he wins…he genuinely wins.'

'And when you return, I imagine he will not know you were away.'

She nodded. 'I suppose you're right. The staff have said they will let me know if there is any…change in his condition. So how long is that likely to be, do you think, before the job is over?'

'Shall we just call this an open-ended arrangement? Unless you want something less irregular…a contract with—'

'No, that works for me.' That was probably what all the women said to Soren before he broke their hearts… Luckily this was a purely business arrangement.

One of the flight attendants passed and Soren spoke to her in Italian. 'I'm having a coffee. Would you like anything?'

'I usually have a brandy before take-off to steady my nerves… It's sort of a…thing for me…' The effect of hanging in the air in a large lump of metal that any enterprising bird could down if it felt so inclined did not even make the same page as flying with this man. 'Is it too late now, do you think?'

His lips quivered. 'I thought you didn't like brandy.'

'I like landing a lot less and it doesn't really matter what it is.'

'Fair enough, anaesthesia it is.' He turned to the attendant and said something rapid in Italian.

'So, you were brought up speaking three languages,' she said enviously.

'Everyone in Iceland speaks English. I learnt Italian later on—'

'Your mother didn't...sorry, I'm being... Thank you.' She smiled in gratitude as the attendant brought her drink.

'My grandfather had some sort of dynastic marriage arranged for my mother, but she met my father. When they married my grandfather disowned her. She never spoke Italian to me or spoke of the Vitale family.'

His matter-of-fact delivery was almost as shocking to Anna as the facts themselves.

'So, my grandfather was your father's friend, not just colleague?'

The muscles around his jaw quivered as he fought to maintain his languid pose, resisting the urge to reveal the truth, reveal that the old man she revered was actually a callous, manipulative, lying bastard.

'He knew all the family.'

'I really don't understand why he never spoke of his time in Iceland.'

He tilted his head in a neutral acknowledgment; he didn't trust himself with any other response.

'There is so much I didn't know, and now it's too late.'

He felt his anger drain away as the tightening in his chest made him wonder if the cabin hadn't suddenly depressurised. The husky note in her voice touched him in a place he hadn't known existed. If she had sobbed and looked sorry for herself he would have been fine, instead—instead he was experiencing one of the emotional responses that his grandfather had taught him to equate with weakness.

'I was young when your grandfather was in my family's life, a teenager. Everyone over twenty seemed old to me, and I was pretty much only interested in my own life and ambitions. Before his death, I barely had a conversation with my father. I didn't have a clue what was going on with him.' He had often wondered if, had he not been so self-obsessed, things might have been different. The lingering guilt was something he had never shared and now…to her… His eyes went to her face, which was predictably softening with empathy.

How the hell this woman survived in the real world when she emoted all over the place was a mystery to him, almost as much of a mystery as why he was opening up to her. The knowledge brought a dark frown to his austerely handsome face.

She watched as his dark lashes came down, filtering out the expression she had imagined she'd glimpsed in his cerulean eyes, something close to shock.

'That doesn't make you an unusual teenager.' He might have been an average teenager, but he was not an average man, and it was not just that he was so incredibly off-the-scale good-looking, it was the currents below the surface of calm, his complexity reflected in the way his eyes could change from ice-cold frigidity to volcanic smouldering emotion.

Anna wasn't sure which end of the spectrum was easier to deal with. The entire unpredictability factor made him exhausting to be around…and then there was the added complication that she knew what it felt like to be kissed by him.

Soren watched her take a massive gulp of brandy

and choke a little as it hit the back of her throat, and he thought about tangling his fingers in her hair, dragging her face up to his and kissing her.

One of the more sensible pieces of advice his grandfather had given him was *Never sleep with the help,* and he ought to know. It was a badly kept secret that a housemaid Biagio had impregnated had a pension for life and a nice house in Palermo.

The only thing she'd had to do was sign away her unborn child's rights to the Vitale estate. The baby had been stillborn, but to his grandfather's dismay the contract his legal team had written was airtight.

'Have you told any friends where you're headed?' By this point he felt quite philosophical about the answer.

'No,' she said, relaxing as the brandy—or it might have been whisky; it seemed to her they both tasted similar—ironed out the kinks in her spine. She was actually feeling much more mellow. 'I told Sara and Penny that I have a live-in job, not where. They wouldn't talk to journalists anyway.' She ignored his doubtful look and gave her head a sharp positive shake.

She totally trusted her friends. She knew Penny from university, and she and Sara went back to primary school when Sara, a writer these days, had honed her early skills at fiction using the stories Anna told about her mother with some interesting additions of her own.

'Boyfriend?' He threw the question in casually.

Anna, who wasn't looking at him, shook her head. 'Not for a while.' Her brow puckered as she tried to remember the disastrous double date that had to have been a good six months ago now. She liked the safety of double dates. 'Tim, no, *Tom* dumped me. Oh, it's fine,' she added cheerfully. 'He wasn't really my type. Penny has this theory that I only date men I don't really *like* because I don't mind being dumped by them. I think *one* date doesn't really count as *dating*...' She stopped and looked from his face to the glass in her hand. She put the glass down carefully, no longer looking at him at all. 'Can I have some of that water?' she said, nodding at the jug that stood on the table between them.

The ice chinked against the glass as he filled it for her.

'Relax.' He delivered a tight smile, assuming that when she said dumping she was actually the one doing it; the likelihood of a man dumping Anna seemed far-fetched to him. 'I'm not judging. Well, actually, I'm in no position to judge.'

Her sex life was not his business.

Yet you feel such a keen interest in it, mocked the voice in his head.

His hooded gaze drifted over her face, sliding to the cushiony softness of her mouth. He was consumed by a primal urge to part those lips and plunge into the soft sweetness, make her forget every man who had ever tasted her before.

Disconcerted by his unblinking regard, Anna looked at him blankly, thoughts zipping through her head and never quite connecting. She took a deep gulp of ice water and things slotted into place: for *date* he had heard one-night stands.

She opened her mouth and then closed it again. If this had happened with any other man she would have burst out laughing, but she seemed to have had a sense-of-humour bypass.

The irony was, of course, delicious, but he was never going to be in a position to appreciate it, and it was in-finitely less embarrassing if he carried on believing she had an impressive back catalogue of lovers whose names she had forgotten, when the truth, the increasingly *embarrassing* truth, was that she was a virgin.

Not a lifestyle choice, just circumstances, caution and a low sex drive and possibly there was a grain of truth in Sara's theory—her friend had a library of self-help books and an encyclopaedic knowledge of them.

Her favourite quote for Anna was: *You have to believe you deserve to be loved.*

Sara *meant* well, but there were times when Anna dreamed of donating her friend's library to a charity shop. Though sometimes she thought there might be something in her friend's more recent theory, which was Anna wouldn't commit because she was afraid of being rejected—her mum leaving her had made her afraid to care enough to have someone walk away.

For Anna it was much simpler: she didn't see the point in sex if it had no meaning for her. Sure, she was curious, but she had a suspicion, like most things that were given a big build-up, it was probably going to be a letdown when it eventually happened.

Her eyes settled on Soren's hands, his long brown tapering fingers—maybe not so disappointing if the first time was with someone who knew his way around—

'I'm going to sit up front with the pilot, a friend... And you couldn't be in safer hands—he's ex-navy.'

She gave a nervy jump and felt the shamed colour score her cheeks as he got to his feet. Incapable of responding, she just nodded.

It wasn't until he had vanished that she realised she hadn't asked the practical things like what happened when they landed.

# CHAPTER EIGHT

ANNA GAVE A sigh of relief as her first ballet slipper hit the tarmac. She didn't go overboard with the relaxation—this was not the end of anything, it was the beginning of a step into the unknown—but before she could get worried about the unknown the heat hit her.

By the time she was ushered into the terminal building her shirt was sticking to her back, but the air conditioning inside was marvellous. The crew member who had escorted her handed her over to an airport official, who progressed her through the formalities in painless moments.

She had refused the offer of refreshments when the suited figures of what she assumed was Soren's VIP welcome committee surrounding the man himself melted away before he reached her. 'Sorry, I had some things to do. You were looked after?'

'Very well, thank you, and there's no need to be sorry. I didn't expect you to come and hold my hand for landing,' she said spikily, thinking, *It would have been a nice gesture, though, considering you knew I was petrified.*

Catching the disgruntled direction of her thoughts, she performed a self-correcting U-turn, reminding herself that she was here as an employee, not a guest. She would have to put some appropriate barriers in place if

KIM LAWRENCE 105

this was going to work, though the unusual way that this
situation had come about made it harder than it would
have been otherwise.

'The luggage has been unloaded.'

He dragged a hand through his hair. His jacket and tie
were back in place, but the lightly hair-roughened section of brown wrist banded by a wafer-thin expensive
watch exerted a stomach-tightening fascination on Anna.

He lowered his arm and she turned away, killing dead
her theory that the exhausting electrical atmosphere on
the plane might vanish or at least lessen once she had escaped the confined space.

It hadn't.

*So live with it, Anna.* The only other option was to
make a total fool of herself. Even had there been any possibility that he would look at someone like her...though
she had noticed that she forgot in his company that she
looked like a coat hanger. He didn't look at her as if she
were a coat hanger, he looked at her like... She felt the
hot shudder low down deep inside and shocked herself
back to the present.

She was standing here in a public place having a hot
fantasy about who she—

'I'd like to miss the traffic.'

'What? Yes, of course, sorry...flying is so tiring.' She
gave a little yawn.

'Well, we could stay overnight here in Palermo, if
you like, travel in the morning. We have a house here.
The staff—'

'No, that's very...considerate, but I'm fine.'

'Good. I'd planned on getting there before dark.'

'You're driving?'

'You have a problem with that?'

'No, of course, I just thought you had a driver.'

'Alberto has gone on ahead.'

Alberto would reach the palazzo several hours ahead of them, refreshed after a helicopter transfer, which had been Soren's own planned mode of travelling. But seeing how she dealt, or didn't, with flying, he could not imagine that Anna would have coped any better with a helicopter transfer that many would consider breathtaking.

'He drives, certainly, but he's not *my* driver. He multitasks, but he is a security expert.' Security was so much part of Soren's life that he took it for granted, and he forgot sometimes that his life was different from others'. Seeing Anna's eyes widen reminded him that his normal was not normal.

'I like to keep things low-key and, relatively speaking, discreet.' Unlike his grandfather, who travelled with a small personal army, in Soren's opinion more to draw attention than avoid it. 'I also enjoy driving.'

'I hate it. It took me four times to pass my test.'

'Did it not occur to you that someone was sending you a message?'

'I happen,' she retorted with dignity, 'to be a very competent driver. You miss so much when you're behind the wheel and I got full marks in my theory test.'

'Well, that's a clincher. Also, you'll be pleased that this is a very scenic island. Not everyone likes our roads but there are plenty of things for you to see while I drive... Did I mention what a lovely thing it is to drive in silence...?'

She directed a narrow-eyed glare up at his too handsome face and saw the lazy glint of humour shining in his eyes. Finding herself wanting to respond to the gleam, she fought off a smile and hitched her bag on her shoulder.

'Lead the way.'

She'd just said *'Lead the way'* to a man, probably for

the first time in her adult life… She knew some women were drawn to men who liked to lead. She was not one of them.

Soren was already striding off, making no allowances for the difference in their leg length.

There was a lot of traffic to negotiate so, despite her determination to keep up a steady flow of chatter just to annoy him, Anna was silent as he negotiated the maze of streets that she assumed were shortcuts.

A few miles after leaving the fascinating architectural mix that was the city, they reached the countryside and she made her first tentative comment. She really didn't want to distract him from the tortuous, steeply rising road they were now negotiating.

'Is Sicily all mountains?'

He flashed her a sideways grin. 'You are not the first person to observe this, and, yes, pretty much mountains and trees, but we have some good beaches, some historical gems and one pretty spectacular volcano. You might,' he teased, 'have heard of it.'

'So I understand.' She closed her eyes as they hit a blind bend.

'I thought you liked the scenery?'

She opened her eyes and directed a resentful look at his perfect profile. 'I also like to live.'

'Relax.'

In truth she was almost glad of the hairpin bends— at least they provided a distraction from the company. 'How far is—?'

'Just over two hours to the nearest town on the coast. We're inland, in the mountains. Try and get some rest and stop braking.'

'I'm not,' she began, then looked at her foot that was flooring a non-existent brake.

'You have quite excellent reflexes.'

She clamped her lips. 'I suppose you think you're amusing,' she said, lifting her floored foot and realising at the same moment that the road had become a lot less white knuckle. They had reached a flat, fertile plain, with the glitter of azure water ebbing against it, white flecks just visible against the purpling evening sky.

'It's breathtaking.'

'Yes.'

She knew he was not looking at the view, and her sensitive stomach flipped as she looked away quickly.

'I'd feel happier if you looked at the road occasionally and kept both hands on the wheel.' Being enclosed in the same space as Soren felt like a damned hormonal war of attrition.

'You sound nervous… I have driven this route once or twice, you know.'

Anna's heart was in gymnastic mode again as she framed a tight nervous smile aimed somewhere over his shoulder.

'This time of night the mosquitos are hell. Do you mind rolling up your window?'

'Like the Highlands. I bagged a Munro and a billion bites last year.'

'You climb?'

'I hike…gentle hills with well-marked trails.'

'So where do you take your risks…or don't you…?'

They were climbing again, the views either side now cut off by trees. 'I don't see the fun in jumping without a parachute.' She took advantage of his focus on the road ahead to study his face in profile. The angle emphasised the sybaritic slant of his cheekbones. It was easy to see him as an adrenaline junkie. 'And while we're on the subject, do you mind slowing down?'

He flashed her a white grin that made her think of the wolf. 'A man has to remind himself he is alive sometimes.'

Despite the grin and the contention, he did slow a little, but it soon became obvious this was not because of her plea but was because they were approaching a massive set of ornate wrought-iron gates, which swung open as they approached. Presumably their presence had been observed by the strategically placed cameras Anna noted.

'Yes, Big Brother is watching,' Soren said drily.

As the four-wheel drive crunched on the gravel the gates closed behind them with a clanging finality. In the fading light the road cut into the tall pine trees that stretched out as far as she could see, looking like a dark river lit by regularly spaced illuminated bollards along the winding length.

'Light at the end of the tunnel.' He brought the car to a halt and turned the engine off even though they were several hundred yards away from the forecourt.

'Oh, my!' Anna had reasoned that to boast a library of any size the palazzo was not going to be a farmhouse but the sheer scale was a shock.

'Baroque, neoclassical and Sicilian rococo,' he listed, anticipating her reaction. 'The place took so long to build the fashions kept changing.'

'It's just so vast! And the colour...?'

'Pompeiian red. It makes an impression, hence the white pillars, all a bit...phallic.'

'I think *that* might be in the eye of the beholder.'

His lips quivered. 'As for the size, back in the day the entire extended family would have lived here. Now... well, I am the family.'

Until he had children, she thought, her heart sinking a little as she pictured him with his arms around an adoring tall, beautiful blonde, a gaggle of assorted gorgeous children around them.

'I remember the first time I saw it.'

She shook her head and banished the blonde. 'I forget you were not brought up here.' His blue eyes were the only thing that marked him out as not being totally Latin. How old were you when you…?'

'I was seventeen.'

Her heart ached for him. He'd only been a boy when his family had been hit by tragedy. 'And you'd never met your grandfather?'

He shook his head.

'It's sad it happened that way, but at least your family were reconciled.'

He gave a strange laugh. '*Reconciled?* I suppose that is one word for it. I came to ask for a place for my mother to stay…he set the dogs on me!'

Anna's eyes widened. 'He didn't know who you were?'

'Of course, he knew who I was. Biagio was testing me. He just wanted to see if I'd come back. He said I wouldn't be worth keeping if it was that easy to get rid of me.'

'That's terrible!' she gasped. 'You came back?'

'I had no other option. I was in no position to take care of my mother, we were broke, therefore no choice, and no grown-ups to come and rescue us, and she was… She is fragile and my father's death and scandal, it all affected her badly.'

'Scandal?'

He nodded. 'My father's partner emptied the pension fund and absconded, leaving my father to carry the can.'

'That's why you're helping me—because your father was falsely accused too!'

'It has taken me some time, but I am about to clear his name.'

'That's marvellous. Your mother must be so proud.'

Soren suspected that at the moment she would not be at all proud of him. 'My mother does not do hate… She is into forgiveness. Whereas I *do* do hate. I hated this place with a… I hated it and Biagio.'

'And now?'

She watched him staring at the magnificent building. He was very easy to watch; even his frown was beautiful.

'More of a love-hate thing these days. There came a point, I don't know when, that I found I was happy to be returning. Now I spend more time here than is strictly necessary. People make a place and some good people live and work here, and Biagio has removed himself, which is a plus.'

'So your grandfather is proud of the estate?'

'He has never spent much time here. For him it is a status symbol, no more. The only thing my grandfather loves is money, prestige and power.'

'He sounds terrible!' she gasped, then, when he looked at her, made a self-conscious apology.

'He is what he is…' he observed phlegmatically. 'Thanks to him I have learnt a lot, and most families are dysfunctional.'

Anna thought about her mother and nodded, feeling unexpectedly in accord with him on the subject.

'Actually, my mother rejected me.' She blinked. She had never said that out loud before, never lowered her defences enough to let anyone see the old hurt.

Perhaps, she mused, there was something in the air in this magical place besides the smell of cypress and wild thyme.

She saw his expression and panic slid through her. 'Sorry, too much sharing,' she said, sounding nervous and not quite meeting his eyes, not wanting him to know how vulnerable she felt.

'Probably better than a kid who grows up thinking the only thing they have going for them is a pretty face.'

She looked at him, startled. She had never thought of it that way before.

'Sometimes it's the way you look at things. My grand-father's methods may have been tough, but I learnt the business from the ground up. I never ask anyone to do anything I have not done myself. I have him to thank for that.'

'Where does your grandfather live now?' she said, feeling pleased she was not going to meet the man, who sounded like a total monster to her.

'Whichever marina the beautiful people are occupy-ing—he has taken up residence on his superyacht. He calls it his retirement.'

'And your mother, will she be here?'

'She has a cottage in the grounds. She *might* be here for the ball.'

'Ball?'

'There is the charity ball every year, at the end of the olive harvest, mid-October.'

'So late?' She was surprised.

'It's still twenty-three degrees here then, and the ol-ives are still on the trees. Historically it was a tradition for all the local families to come together—the farms brought their harvest to the palazzo to be milled and the profit was split fifty-fifty. The ball was a celebration of the harvest, a community thing.'

'And now?' She turned away from the illuminated building.

Cynicism crept into his face. 'Oh, now it is wall-to-wall designer, famous faces. It's become a PR event, a marketing opportunity.' His expressive mouth conveyed the depth of his cynicism. 'You'll see for yourself.'

'I'm staff.' And October was a long way off.

He dragged his eyes off her face, her skin washed to a silver glow by the moon, and directed his stare at the ancient building. 'Oh, we might let you out of your attic if you're good,' he said, thinking he would very much like to see Anna *bad*.

'Oh, Grandpa would love this...or he would have,' she tacked on sadly.

Her words killed the intimacy and brought reality crashing back. This was Tor's granddaughter, which put her out of reach. While he was rebuilding the walls that he'd lowered, beside him Anna gazed raptly and oblivious at the palazzo.

He started up the engine.

He felt her questioning look but didn't react. Pulling up on the forecourt a few moments later, kicking up gravel as he hit the brakes, he was out of the car before she had unfastened her seat belt and opening the door for her.

She looked confused; he knew he'd see hurt in her eyes if he looked, so he didn't. 'I've still got work to do,' he said shortly. 'It's late so I'll get Domenica to show you to your room. You all right having your supper there?'

Confused by his sudden change of attitude, she followed him up the flight of steps and through the porticoed entrance. Around them she could hear the night creatures, the rustle and cries in the darkness. It was a lonely sound.

They stepped into an overwhelming space lit by a massive chandelier, and she blinked. Faces stared back from the ancestral portraits that lined the walls. The fine stucco panels on the ceiling were decorated with pastoral scenes; the detail, even from this distance, seemed remarkably accomplished.

'Here is Domenica now.'

On cue a woman had silently materialised, wearing a pale silk blouse and conservatively plain pencil skirt; her dark hair was streaked with silver, but her face was unlined. She was very attractive.

'I hope you both had a good journey.'

Soren gave a grunt that could have meant anything, or he might have been clearing his throat. Her confusion tipped into anger.

Was this because he'd let her see that there was a chink in his armour? Was he regretting allowing her to glimpse his vulnerabilities? Or maybe she was the fool seeing a wounded hero, when all he was was a top-of-the-food-chain male animal who used women.

'This is Domenica, who is a great deal more than a housekeeper.'

Now, there was a choice of words to incite speculation, and of course it did, though Anna struggled to hide her thought processes behind a smile.

'Our journey was…long,' Soren said, thinking, *Too long.*

He had only intended to give Anna the basic facts about the palazzo; instead he had found himself opening up in a way that was utterly alien to him. It made him uncomfortable to think about the things he had said to her, inviting her and her small feet to wander around in his head.

The decision to spare her the helicopter transfer had come back to bite him big time… The orally focused thought inevitably drew his eyes to her soft mouth.

The thought of loosening the tight seam of her lips

took immediate residence in his mind— He cleared his throat and reclaimed his control.

It was past time to kill off the self-indulgent fantasies. He should not need to remind himself that sleeping with the enemy, or any relation to the enemy, even when that relation excited him to a painful degree, was fraught with complications that were too high a price to pay for a few moments…maybe many…of pleasure.

Anna stood back and wondered if their switch to fluid flowing Italian was intended to make her feel excluded, or was she being oversensitive?

Either way, she did.

The conversation went on above her head as Anna allowed her gaze to flutter around the massive space— everything about it was intended to awe, and of course it did. It remained to be seen what the parameters of this woman's role were, but she did seem to have a very easy relationship with Soren, though intimate might have been a suggestion too far.

'Right, I will leave you in capable hands. Tomorrow— well, it might take you a while to get your bearings.'

'I only need to get my bearing of the library. That's what I'm here for,' she said, pleased to see a flash of something close to surprise in his eyes. He wanted things on a business footing and that, she told herself, was fine by her.

She didn't look back as she mounted the staircase behind the older woman, even though his footsteps had stopped and she could feel the imaginary imprint of his eyes between her shoulder blades like a laser-guided gun sight.

The woman gave a running commentary on the history of the building as they walked along seemingly endless corridors. Anna's brain retained a few descriptions, such as Sicilian Baroque, but for the most part the information slid over her head.

A few of the many doors they passed were open; she would have lingered at some, but the woman's pace was as relentless as her delivery of detail.

Anna was relieved when she finally came to a halt.

The attic that Soren had taunted her with was a suite of rooms that were beyond luxurious, and, despite the ancient fabric, the plumbing was five-star state-of-the-art decadence.

She salivated at the idea of testing out the massive marble tub or, for that matter, the shower that was twice the size of her bathroom at home.

When the subject of supper was introduced, Anna shook her head and patted the crewel-work cover of the four-poster they were standing beside. The bed had been turned back and she recognised one of her new nightdresses arranged artistically on the silk cover.

She resisted the temptation to say *What? No chocolate mint on the pillow?* and smiled. 'Actually, I'm not hungry. The tea—' she nodded to the table beside the fireplace filled with an urn of fragrant flowers, where a tea tray with a snowy cloth was set '—will do me just fine.'

The woman gave a gracious nod. 'Well, if you are sure. There are cold drinks in the fridge, but should you change your mind or want anything at all, just dial zero.' She indicated the old-fashioned phone set on a bedside table.

After a short solo exploration Anna found all her personal items along with her new wardrobe, which must have travelled ahead, laid out neatly in the cavernous drawers and wardrobes of the separate dressing area.

She finally kicked off her shoes and, with one of the

silver-backed brushes from the dressing table in her hand, wandered into the football-pitch-sized bathroom—a slight exaggeration, but not much!

Taking the lids off some of the row of crystal glass-topped bottles, she inhaled the various fragrances before selecting one. Sitting on the edge of the tub, she switched on both taps and poured some of the oil into the gushing water. It immediately foamed and filled the space with the exotic fragrance.

She let her clothes drop where she stood and stepped into the scented water, willing her mind to go blank as the warm water did its magic on the various tense knots in her body.

She might even have fallen asleep, if the water hadn't cooled and a low distant rumble hadn't made her lift her head.

Wrapping a sarong around her and towelling her wet hair, she padded back into the bedroom in time to see a flash of light at the stone mullioned window; the accompanying rumble came some time after.

The storm was a long way off.

She pulled on the neatly arranged slip that lay on the bed—having someone pick out her nightdress for her was a first—and climbed into the bed feeling like the princess in one of her favourite childhood fairy tales. She had once taken a pea from her dinner plate hoping to be able to feel it, but she had failed the royal test miserably.

# CHAPTER NINE

SHE HADN'T EXPECTED to sleep but, under acres of goose down and silk, exhaustion claimed her almost immediately. Her awakening was as abrupt as her sleep was deep and dreamless. Sitting bolt upright in bed in the pitch black for several seconds, she did not even know her name, let alone where she was, and then the total blackout was briefly broken by a flash of white light that seeped around the heavy drapes outlining the two windows on the opposite wall.

A second later the crash came, no longer a distant rumble; it sounded as though it was directly overhead. Reaching out in the darkness, she fumbled for the lamp, a few more fumbles and she found the cord switch—nothing happened.

She took a deep breath and waited for the angry rumble to pass. Anna was not terrified of storms, but they were not her favourite thing. She used the next flash of lightning to locate her phone and switched on the torch.

Her relief was tinged by caution when she saw that the charge was low. She slid aside the covers; a quick tour of the room's light switches confirmed her initial suspicion that there was a power outage.

She picked up the old-fashioned internal phone and noted that it did indeed rely on the power supply and the charge on her phone showed her only light source was about to run out.

The idea of cowering under the covers for the rest of the night while what sounded like Armageddon raged outside her window did not hold much appeal.

Switching off her torch to conserve what power she had, Anna was about to lie down when she remembered the burnt-down candle beside the bath that had made her wonder who before her had used the bathroom, and had a couple shared the massive bath.

She made it to the bathroom just as the power on her phone faded out.

'Do not panic, Anna.'

Her words were drowned out by an extra-loud thunder crash. Arms outstretched, she visualised the room in the dark, managing to find the cool marble edge of the bath.

She considered one bruised shin after a misstep was a price well worth the prize when she located the candle and the silver matchbox beside it.

The one match inside made her heart drop a little but, with an expression of fierce concentration on her face, she took a deep breath and struck the match. Still holding her breath, she applied it to the candle wick.

A moment later the small flame caught, and the room was gently illuminated. Her initial triumph was short-lived when she saw how little of the candle remained. Her light supply was still limited so it looked as if sleep was her only option. The depressing thought triggered a light-bulb moment—which seemed pretty appropriate in the circumstances.

She was sure that she remembered the row of stone niches just before they reached the door to her suite, each one filled with an ornate candelabra complete with candles.

It had been really close and she was sure it would be easy to locate, she just had to literally follow her nose.

It became apparent very soon that her confidence was misplaced, the following-her-nose thing had not worked out so well and, as the candle she was carrying was burning low, the sensible, actually the *only* course of action left open to her was to retrace her steps.

As she reached a second junction that she had not previously noticed she didn't even bother debating which one to take; it didn't matter. She was totally lost in this damned maze of a castle wearing nothing but her nightdress—however this situation ended, it was not going to be ego-enhancing and it was going to be in the dark.

If she found her way to her bedroom, it would be sheer luck, and hers, and the candle, seemed to be running out.

She was debating what would happen if she just screamed out for help when the corridor was lit by a lightning flash that came through an open door to her left. As the thunder rumbled she stepped towards it, pushing the heavy metal-banded door, which swung in silently to reveal a room that was so massive her flickering candle barely penetrated the blackness. As she was about to step out there was another lightning flash that shone in through a row of high windows that almost reached the black-and-white-checked floor of a room with a dizzyingly high vaulted ceiling.

Before the lights faded she saw the echoing space was totally empty apart from a grand piano in one corner and, of more significance, the candles sitting on the stone sills along one wall—not one or two, but dozens.

She stumbled a little in her haste as she crossed the room and, by some sort of miracle and with the help of her tiny guiding flame, which was getting fainter by the second, found them at the first attempt. Her hand shaking, she held her breath as she lit the first one, which revealed a jar of long tapers, so, putting down her guttering candle, she picked one up and began to light the others, leaving a trail of flickering flames in her wake as she moved down the room.

After the next lightning flash, the room was not as dark and she stepped back in awe, her head falling back to view the awesome splendour of the frescoes painted on the intricate barrelled ceiling.

Anna did a slow full three-sixty spin. She was standing in the middle of a ballroom straight from a fairy tale. Windows down one wall, a massive fireplace on the opposite one. The rows of chandeliers suspended from the intricate ceiling caught the candlelight and revealed the steps she had avoided bumping into at the far end that led to the raised dais that housed the grand piano. There was enough room for a full orchestra to join it.

Utterly enchanted, she forgot that she was lost, forgot that she was barefoot and dressed in a nightdress, and she climbed up on the dais and lifted the lid of the piano, pressing a key... Hearing the sound bounce back at her, she really wished she could play, but despite her lack of skill she could hear the music in her head.

The gym was at basement level and the music playing in his ears had drowned out everything else as he pounded his way up a virtual hill, pushing his body to the physical limit and then beyond, working towards some sort of relief from the hunger that was gnawing at him. It was not complicated, it was sex, hormones—his need to reassure himself of the fact was annoying.

He had decided that the simplest way to cope with the disruptive influence on his peace of mind that was Anna

Randall was to remove himself from the situation. Less a retreat and more a strategic withdrawal.

Immersed in his private physical combat seeking the level of exhaustion that would give him some relief, he didn't reach relief but at least a workable explanation for the situation. He did not deal with celibacy well and Anna Randall had arrived right in the middle of a dry spell. His first inkling that there was a storm raging anywhere but in his head was when the lights went out.

Cursing at the interruption, he removed his ear plugs and waited, with the sweat cooling on his overheated body, for the emergency generator to kick in. It didn't.

Locating his phone and then a towel, he headed for the shower, catching his breath as he stepped into the unheated stream of water, which, while not his choice, was probably not such a bad thing. It took the edge off the frustration that had robbed him of sleep, but it didn't make the face, the voice and the body that had robbed him of peace of mind vanish.

Retrieving his shorts but leaving the sweat-stained vest on the floor, he hooked the towel over his shoulders to catch the drips from his saturated hair and gave the lights one more try before he walked past the glass-fronted lift and made his way up to the ground floor using the spiral flights of stone steps, their surface worn by the generations of feet that had used them before him.

At the top of the stairs he gestured to the dogs who were silently shadowing him and after throwing him a canine look of reproach—they had been hoping to sleep on his bed—they peeled away, heading towards the kitchens and their beds.

The storm was still raging; he could feel the static of electricity in the heavy air. Even though the rain had not begun to fall yet, he accepted it would be suicidal to venture out to check out the backup generator, which was housed—rather impractically, he had always thought—in a building that was hidden by a bank of tall cypresses. One had fallen last year and just missed the roof.

He wondered as he made his way to the back staircase that led to his private apartments what other damage might have been sustained to the buildings. Having been born in a land that was exposed more than most to raw nature, he felt a certain affinity with the extremes of nature the mountains here offered.

He was halfway along the corridor when above the rain, which had just begun to fall and was lashing against the windows, he heard the tinkling sound of a piano chord.

The incongruous sound froze him in his tracks.

He knew where the only piano in the place was located, but why anyone would be in the ballroom at this time of night eluded him.

Perhaps, he mused, one of the ghosts he had heard so much about but never seen was out and about. It was not white apparitions rattling their chains that had troubled Soren's sleep. He had hoped his own ghosts would be laid to rest after he had exposed Tor; he should have known that life was never that clear-cut.

There was no music coming from the ballroom, but light was leaking into the darkness through the half-open doors.

Soren slid his phone into the pocket of his shorts and stepped inside his trainers, making no sound on the floor.

The sight that met him stopped him in his tracks; his chest lifted as he breathed in sharply. The light he had seen came from the candles all along one wall…a remnant of a photo shoot his grandfather had given permission for the previous month.

To Soren's annoyance and the staff's great inconvenience the place had been invaded by a famous photographer he'd thought was long dead, an incredible number of people who it seemed were required for a fashion shoot, and the models themselves, beautiful women who posed in very little clothes that cost an impossible amount of money. The candles were meant to lend atmosphere but had apparently not been moody enough.

They had been extinguished and left.

They were burning now and so was he.

The flames flared and the vaulted ceiling reflected back the light, leaving the checked pattern of the floor flickering on the walls.

He barely registered these details. He had hardly breathed since he had walked into the room, not once his eyes had focused on the supple figure who, arms crossed over her chest like some sort of sacrifice, was swirling around the floor in circular patterns. Her eyes were closed, her slim, vulnerable neck extended, her hair a silk cloud down her back as she moved to the music in her head.

Wind found its way through the invisible cracks in the ancient stone window frames, making the candles flame and dance and causing the silk slip that ended mid-calf to flutter, drawing even tighter against her body and clinging like a second skin to the lovely line of her legs and the tight roundness of her behind. She suddenly spread her arms wide, causing one thin strap to slip down the smooth curve of her shoulder, the action revealing her high pert breasts, the nipples pushing through the thin fabric.

Fire slid in a steady pumping stream through his body. Something moved in his chest—it felt like fingers closing around his beating heart. He couldn't breathe.

If he took another step, if he crossed that line, Soren

knew there would be no going back. She was who she was, that could never change, and she didn't know who he was.

He *knew* everything inside him told him that if he took that fatal step there would be consequences to pay, but from the first moment he had set eyes on her he had wanted her…wanted her in a way that had nothing to do with logic or sanity. He ached for her in his bones.

It was as if she had set fire to some primal instinct in him, Soren thought as he watched her twirl. He had never seen anything as beautiful and desirable as the dancing figure. Her beauty touched him and the desire overwhelmed him absolutely, wiping his mind clear of any thought other than possession. There was no space left for reasoned thought; its absence left just instinct and blind, relentless hunger.

Enemy, lover, the words had no meaning; nothing had meaning but the need pounding through him.

He might well regret this tomorrow, but he could not think beyond the here and now, and the need to possess her had his heart pumping a steady stream of logic-defying lust through his body.

'May I have this dance?'

Anna, who had heard nothing but the sound of the music in her head, gasped and fell off the balls of her feet with a bump.

'Soren!' She had just been imagining she was in his arms and now he was here, unless she'd gone mad, which was a distinct possibility. The clash of dream with reality in the form of flesh and blood… She lost the thread of her thoughts as her eyes did a head-to-toe-and-back-again survey.

In a suit he could stop traffic. It turned out that not

wearing a suit, in fact wearing very little, he could stop the world on its axis!

The earth-stopping little consisted of a pair of shorts that hung on his narrow hips and revealed every inch of his muscle-ridged flat belly. He had the sort of lean, muscular, not-an-ounce-of-spare-flesh body that a professional swimmer spent a lifetime trying to achieve.

She could see his wide shoulders cleaving through the water and his long muscular legs... Actually, she could see them tangled in her own, which only added to the reality-meets-fantasy vertigo she was suffering.

'I was looking for a candle,' she heard herself say.

'You found a few,' he said, his eyes leaving her face but only for a split second. 'Dance?'

*Was he making fun of her?*

'There's no music.'

'I can hear it,' he replied, taking her waist and the situation into his own capable hands.

His hand on her waist brought home belatedly her state of undress, which was equal to his... She panicked, then stopped as, holding her eyes, he caught hold of her right hand, placed it against his chest and stepped into her.

Before she could protest—she liked to think she would have—he began to move. At that moment even the theoretical possibility of resistance vanished.

He was tall, she wasn't, this shouldn't have worked but it did—the differences were part of the formula that made it work. He was hard, she wasn't; even with her sharp angles and lack of curves she had never felt softer and more female in her life, as they continued to circle the floor, both hearing the same song.

As if in a dream Anna felt she was floating...it might even be an actual dream...

Jolted free of the lovely place she had inhabited by an

extra-loud rumble of window-rattling thunder, she gasped and instinctively burrowed closer as his arms moved to encircle her. When she tried to pull away, he held her firm, one hand now splayed across the curve of her taut behind. The other moved to the back of her head and a finger at the angle of her jaw tilted her face up to his.

He looked so beautiful so predatory that she ached.

'You're a very good dancer,' she said, making herself think about all the women he'd practised with—and she wasn't thinking dancing—just to cool down the fire inside her. Masochistic, yes, and it didn't even work. The fire carried on burning… He was just so beautiful.

One hand was trapped between them, the other she raised and laid on his shoulder, before allowing her fingers to slide down, feeling the quiver of surface muscles as she spread her fingers down his back.

He swore… They were no longer dancing, they were standing stock-still in the middle of the room, both barely breathing, staring at each other.

The thickness in the atmosphere had nothing to do with climatic conditions.

*Bad idea, Soren!*

He tried to listen to the voice yelling in his head, he made a genuine effort, but passion, lust, her passion-glazed eyes and parted lips drowned out the voice of reason.

He held her eyes and jerked her in hard, smiling a skin-prickling predatory smile when she whimpered as his erection ground into her belly.

'I have a serious problem with your mouth.'

The electric touch of his finger on her lips made her quiver. 'It's too big, I know,' she pushed out breathily.

'It's perfect. It just makes me so hungry…and you make me…' The rest of his words were lost inside her mouth as his tongue slid between the seal of her lips, deepening the combative clash of tongues and teeth.

Outside the thunder crashed and a pane of glass cracked, causing the nearest candles to gutter and die in plumes of dark smoke. Neither of the figures engrossed in each other noticed; the touches and sighs, the deep, drowning, hungry kisses grew wilder and fiercer until Soren, breathing hard, put her from him.

'My room,' he said thickly, before he kissed her hard.

Anna wound her arms vine-like around him, revelling in the hard, hot heat of his body. Her face level with his bare chest, she pressed open-mouthed kisses against his golden skin, tasting the salt, loving the texture.

He dug his fingers into her hair, yanking her back to look into her face; a moment later he was sweeping her off her feet and into his arms.

Anna wound her hands around his neck as he carried her from the candlelit room. The dark closed in but he seemed to know where he was going; he *definitely* knew what he was doing.

Occasional lightning flashes illuminated their route, throwing out eerie monochrome flickering images on the walls as they progressed up a flight of spiral stairs.

A door kicked open hit the wall and made something in the room fall and smash; the noise barely penetrated her sex-soaked brain. They fell together onto a bed and as he shifted himself off her for a moment, she breathed for what felt like the first time in minutes as she sank into the mattress and gazed up at the man kneeling over her, who looked like the living embodiment of the storm that raged outside, primal and wickedly exciting.

Her brain was mush; she *ached* for him. Reacting to the throb of need between her legs, she reached up her hands, fastening them to his hips, and she pulled him down, arching to meet his body, hungry for the contact.

The eyes looking up at him were green pools of confusion and need that Soren could readily identify with. She was vibrating with tremors that shook her entire body. He had never known a woman who was this responsive; he'd known the passion was there but the intensity of it still surprised and excited him. She was a temptation that he could not resist.

The sliver of silk she wore was the only thing between his bare chest and her skin, and then it wasn't... Anna wasn't even aware of him peeling it off, until she experienced the first breath-catching skin-to-skin contact.

She gasped at the heat of his skin, and then as he pulled back to look at her she felt the first stab of self-awareness and awkwardness as they lay side by side facing one another.

He was so perfect and she... Thinking of the women she had seen pictured with him, women that were everything she was not, she lifted an arm to cover herself. 'I'm—'

A finger pressed to her parted lips, he cut off her words. 'You have the most perfect, sensual body, elegant...sleek, exquisite. I want to see you, *cara*.' His throaty whisper against her neck made her shiver and drop her hand.

He took the action to be an invitation and his hand dropped from her flushed face to her small, smooth breasts; the peaks hardened and pinched tight under his scrutiny and his husky, fervent, 'Perfect.'

Anna felt excited and empowered and unbearably aroused as his blue eyes moved hungrily over her body, the scrutiny accompanied by a low growl, half appreciation, half pain.

The carnal intent on his face made her pull back, but not because she didn't like it, not that it didn't excite her.

'No, Soren, I have to tell you this…'

Something in her voice, the urgency, penetrated the fog of lust in his head. Breathing hard, he rolled away from her and lay on his back, one arm curved above his head, his flat belly sucked in as his chest heaved. The eyes that stared back at him were wary, filled with need, glittering like twin emeralds. Looking at her, he felt something beyond lust, something he denied a name, something it would be safer to detour around, but it didn't go away.

'Look, I'm not sure if this makes a difference to you but the one-night-stand thing…'

'I'm not interested in your sexual history.' He was only interested in making her forget it and every other man she had slept with. He did not doubt for a second his ability to do so.

'That's the point. I don't have any.'

He'd been staring up at the ceiling but at this he turned his head her way, the flush along his cheekbones making them look like razors. All his features were more sharply defined. The deep febrile glitter in his darkened eyes made her shiver low in her belly and wish she hadn't told him and risked this not going any further.

If he rejected her now, she'd die.

'What are you trying to say?'

'I am saying I'm…well, I suppose…a virgin.'

# CHAPTER TEN

HE LOOKED AT her as though she were talking a foreign language. The muscles along his jaw quivered. 'Is that a joke?'

'A person has to have a first time.'

*Not with me, they don't,* he thought, but somehow the words never made it to his lips, because he was looking at her mouth and it was hard to speak when he did. He just wanted to taste her.

'And I was a late developer,' she added, glancing down and giving a little grimace.

It seemed to her that his anger came from nowhere.

'Do not do that!' he growled, taking her face between his hands and throwing one heavy hair-roughened thigh across her hips.

'What? I...' Her wide green eyes reflected her bewilderment.

'*Believe* you're beautiful.' He took her hand and placed it against her own breast. 'Just feel how beautiful you are.' His fallen-angel grin gleamed white as he stared down into her shocked face. 'Say it!'

'I'm beautiful,' she whispered and felt every inch of her skin prickle with heat. 'Oh, God!' she groaned as she reclaimed her hand and held it above her head, hiding her eyes.

But he took her left hand instead. 'That's better. I want to see you.' He kissed his way up the curve of her neck.

'It's all right, you know,' she whispered against his cheek, before licking a wet trail across the sensual curve of his upper lip and kissing the corner of his mouth. All the while she tasted him her hands were moving in circular sweeping motions over the hard muscles of his shoulders and back. 'I just want to live in the moment. I want this, you, now, Soren.'

Her throaty plea broke whatever bonds remained, desire overrode everything, sanity vaporised in the heat that flared white hot between them as he rolled her under him and began to kiss her, the air around them shimmering with the heat the entwined pair were producing.

She gasped and moaned as he touched her everywhere, wakening nerve pathways, pleasure pathways she had never known existed. She clutched at him, revelling at his hardness and strength, responding to instinct as she arched into him, not wanting to be closer, wanting to be part of him.

He levered himself away for a moment, but it was only to divest himself of his shorts. Her insides liquefied as she watched him through the shades of her lashes, her cheeks flushed with passion, her small breasts rising and falling in tune to her shallow, fast inspirations.

Her scrutiny seemed to arouse him even further, if that were possible. She had to satisfy her carnal curiosity. Rolling a little to one side, she reached out, and, tongue caught between her teeth, she ran her fingers down the silky hard length of him, before her hand tightened around him, drawing a deep fractured groan from his lips.

She gave a small whimper of protest as he took her hand. 'Not now, I can't...' His face was a primal mask of need as he pinned both her wrists above her head with one big hand and, arching over her, kissed his way down her quivering body.

Her thighs parted to aid his carnal exploration of her most intimate core, the intensity of the sensations sweeping through her so intense that the pleasure bordered pain.

As he touched the aching area where her pain was centred she pushed against him in the grip of a hunger beyond anything she had ever imagined.

She grabbed his head and pulled him down, not sure what she was babbling against his neck, but he seemed to understand her incoherent pleas as he ran a soothing hand down her face before kissing her, a deep, drowning, painfully slow kiss that relaxed the taut muscles in her body.

On some level she was aware of him reaching for a condom, but then he settled between her legs and her awareness contracted, focused on his dark beautiful face, until nothing else existed.

'Put your legs around me, *cara*.'

She responded to the growled instruction without taking her eyes off him. The stripped-back raw expression on his face was utterly riveting. He bent in, his lips teasing and taunting her mouth, dipping in and out of the honeyed wet interior with his tongue.

Her ankles tightened around his waist to increase the tortured pressure at the juncture of her legs, growing slick as the pressure increased.

Her body arched as he entered her, her eyes squeezing tight shut as, with a series of sharp pants, her sweat-slick body adjusted to accept him. All her being was focused inwards on each new sensation as pleasure pathways awoke, as she moved with him as he touched places deep and then deeper inside her, part of her.

Then, just at the point when she really thought she was losing her mind in the delirium of pleasure, he whispered in her ear, urging her to let go, to trust him.

She did.

She didn't fall back to earth, she floated back...

It was the sun shining directly in her face that woke Anna. She lifted a hand to shield her eyes and stretched languidly. She grimaced—she felt stiff—and her eyes flew wide. Lying there on her back, staring at the ceiling, she reached out and patted the bed either side. One side carried a slight dint, cold as if whoever had made it was long gone, the other revealed a nightdress.

Clutching the nightdress to her chest, she sat up and looked around the room she had not seen in the light. It was empty. The night's events slid through her head, from the dancing by candlelight to the making love for the second time, just as intense but slower and even more mind-blowing than the first time.

She'd been wrong: the reality had turned out to be not a let-down at all; the reality had turned out to be incredible! She looked around the room again and a flicker of uncertainty found its way to her face.

She was no expert on morning-after etiquette, but waking up alone did not feel like the perfect way to start the day after the night before.

Pushing aside the rumpled bed covers, she pulled the discarded nightdress over her head and, wriggling her way into it, got out of the bed.

She looked around, not sure what to do, apart from the necessary, which required a bathroom. The first door she opened was a large walk-in wardrobe with pretty mono-chrome contents; the next was the bathroom. It was just as luxurious as her own but with a much bigger shower and less choice on the perfume and potions front.

She emerged five minutes later feeling more comfortable. She'd tamed her tangled hair with a silver-backed brush and given her hands and face a perfunctory wash but had resisted the temptation of the shower, and was glad she had when the door opened and Soren appeared.

Her heart skipped a beat as she stood there leeching composure, then she noticed he was not alone.

Her eyes flew from his face to the two powerful-looking dogs, pale gold in colour. They had dark masked faces, almond-shaped intelligent eyes; their muscular, powerful bodies seemed to quiver with energy.

'This is Ragnar and Rok.'

'Clever,' she said, sending him a shy smile. He was wearing a shirt open at the neck, the sleeves rolled up and jeans that were dusty at the knees.

'Boys, this is Anna.'

'Are they safe?'

His eyes glimmered, the high-voltage smile appearing and causing the expected damage to her nervous system. 'Not a word that I would use, but they are extremely well behaved, and you are totally safe, always supposing they don't think you are attacking me.'

'I'll keep that in mind,' she said, moving towards where they both sat like sentinels. 'What breed are they?' she asked, holding out her hand.

'Malinois... Belgian Shepherds, intelligent and smart. They get bored easily and need a lot of stimulation.'

A bit like their master, she thought, wondering how long it would be before Soren was bored with her...maybe he already was?

Tickling one of the animals behind his ear, she pushed

the question away, telling herself that *she* might be the one who got bored first.

*You keep telling yourself that, Anna,* mocked the voice in her head.

'Good boys,' she said, smiling as they each licked her hand after sniffing her.

Watching with a half-smile, Soren laid a tea tray on a small table. He clicked his fingers and the dogs padded away and lay down, heads on paws beside the bed.

'You were sleeping. I didn't want to disturb you. I had an early morning call. The standby generator, the roof was taken down by a fallen tree, some emergency repairs were required.' He relayed the situation in a verbal shorthand that gave her the relevant details quickly. 'It's up and running now. Apparently the mains electricity won't be online until later.' He held her eyes. 'That was quite a storm last night.'

'I won't forget it.'

The way his eyes darkened made her sensitive stomach muscles quiver. He dragged a hand through his dark hair. 'I need a shower. Help yourself to tea or coffee. I won't be long.'

'I need a shower too,' she called after him.

He stopped, framed in the doorway, his eyes gleaming wickedly. 'What are you waiting for, then? An invitation?'

She released the tense little breath she'd been holding and, feeling bold and channelling her inner sensual siren, she strode past the dogs and into the bathroom after him.

He was already unbuttoning the shirt. Unable to take her eyes off him, she watched him, the knot of anticipation in the pit of her stomach tightening painfully.

Soren lifted his head and looked at her. 'You like to watch?' he purred, dark challenge in his eyes.

'I like watching you,' she whispered as the shirt hit the floor. His hands were on the belt at his narrow waist now as he walked towards her, stopping within a couple of inches of her unzipped, and let the jeans slide down his legs. Stepping out of them, he stood there in just his boxers, which did nothing to hide the extremity of his arousal.

She felt the pulse of need in the slick heat between her legs and felt her self-control slipping like sand grains through her fingers. She didn't try to catch them, welcoming the liberation of giving up control.

She shivered as his eyes locked on hers. She hardly recognised the instincts that had taken control of her, but amid the glorious confusion in her head she knew she'd be safe with Soren, in a very dangerous way.

As he kicked himself free of the boxers she couldn't stop her eyes dropping. Her inner temperature jumped several mind-numbing degrees as a raw longing slid through her shaking body…

*God, yes, she was shaking…*

God, he was so beautiful.

'Now you, I think.' Leaning over her, making her more conscious than ever of his physical dominance, he took the hem of her nightdress and peeled it over her head in one practised motion.

'Pretty,' he said, throwing it over his shoulder. 'But this…oh, yes…this is very much more…more everything.'

He leaned against a pad on the wall and the shower kicked in; taking her hand, he pulled her with him inside. They stood there face to face, the pulses of water hitting them from all sides drenching them in seconds. None were as powerful as the sensations ripping her apart inside or as sharp as the spiralling excitement that held her in a vice-like grip.

'Here, let me.'

She saw the bar of soap in his hands, watched him work it to a lather and cover one breast, his fingers gliding over her wet skin as he stroked and massaged, leaning in, one hand braced on the glass wall above her head, so that she kept receiving a tantalising nudge of his erection. She tried to push into him but he held her off.

Then he turned her around. Anna, in a delirium of pleasure, laid her hands flat on the glass wall to stop herself falling as he began to run his shapely hands down her body, massaging and stroking down the length of her back and then her bottom, and—

She gave a broken cry as his hand slid between her legs parting the sensitive folds of flesh. Just when she thought she would die from the pleasure of it he turned her around to face him.

Their eyes connected, his navy with passion, and the moment stretched until it snapped and he caught her by the waist, lifting her up as he slid hard into her. Anna wrapped her legs around his waist and let him take her to some place inside herself, some place deep and hot she'd never even dreamt existed.

As she stepped out of the shower her legs felt so weak he had to support her. Picking up one of a stack of towels, he tenderly dried her off.

'I didn't do anything for you,' she whispered.

His laugh was deep and warm. 'You do everything for me, *cara*, but, if it makes you feel any better, next time it's your turn.'

'So there will be a next time?'

Her smile faded as she watched an odd expression drift across his face, robbing his eyes of warmth.

'Perhaps we should…slow things down a bit?'

Her smile froze as the hand she had lifted to his face fell away. 'Slow…?' she repeated. The word still didn't make sense.

'Get to know one another.'

Anger, hurt and self-disgust rushed into her head, making it spin.

He had set out to use her and she had let him.

Last night for him had been just sex and that was all he wanted, and it turned out the sex wasn't even interesting enough by his high standards to want more. She was just a boring little virgin.

'Anna, this is not—'

'Personal… Oh, I know.' She took a deep breath, pinned on a brilliant smile as her deep hidden fears rose up to mock her: she was not a lovable person. Only they weren't irrational fears after all. It was true.

'This is not about you, it's me…' he said between clenched teeth. 'There are things—'

'Wow, that is *so* original,' she drawled with mock admiration as she cinched the towel so tight across her breast that it hurt. 'You know, I would admire you more if you were simply straight with me… No, it's fine,' she tacked on, mirroring his step forward with two hasty ones back. If he touched her she would forget her pride, what there was of it, and make a fool of herself. 'And you're right—let's keep this professional. You're paying my wages. We shouldn't be sleeping together.' She could come out of this with her pride intact, if not her heart.

'This has nothing to do with work.' He hated seeing her hurt, hated being responsible for it, because he had been too impatient to wait.

*Wait for what, Soren? It's not as if you wanted a deep and meaningful relationship—you wanted sex, you got it.*

She arched a brow. 'No...?'

What could he say to her—that he'd set out to use her? That he'd let his own need outweigh every consideration, her inexperience? He'd been so blinded by lust that he'd almost forgotten to use protection and she was so inexperienced she'd not even registered the fact. At least he didn't have that on his conscience—if he hadn't looked after her, he would never have forgiven himself.

He wasn't going to tell her any of that, or that he'd believed the worst of her. That in itself seemed ludicrous at this point.

The only lies had been his and... *Dio*, he really had laid the foundations of this mess, and as for truth setting him free?

Not on this occasion.

Last night had been the moment for truth or restraint and he had taken the third path, and now the truth would cause more damage than silence... If he told her now he would be the monster, not Henry.

Why should he care what she thought?

But he did!

The irony of this situation was not lost on Soren. For the first time in his life he was thinking of something *beyond* casual sex; he was in virgin territory, quite literally, and he was pushing the woman he wanted more from away.

How much more he didn't know—he was the one who felt like a virgin.

It was a situation of his own making; he had known there would be consequences, and there were. Consequences to sleeping with her without telling her the truth. She had slept with the person she thought he was; the reality was something different. Last night he just hadn't been able to resist her; the way she made him feel by-passed all logic.

Her beautiful face was closed off and hard. 'Right, I'm late for work. I don't want to make the boss mad. Late on my first day not a good look.'

The dogs, alert to the human emotion in the air, began to whimper.

Soren held up a hand and they both slid down onto their haunches, ears pricked but silent, their almond-shaped eyes moving from one human to the other as they lay there panting.

'Anna!'

She flung off his hand. 'Which way is my damned room?' She sniffed.

He moved in front of the door and stood there like a sentinel. 'Last night...you were the best sex I have ever had in my life!' he pushed out in a driven voice.

She stopped dead, her anger peeling away to leave just the hurt exposed, which from Soren's point of view was worse.

'Why would you even say that?'

'Because it's true and I don't want you to walk out that door. You are *exactly* what you seem to be... I am not. There are things you don't know about me yet, things that might make you feel differently.'

'Then tell me.' What? she wondered. What could be so bad?

'It's complicated and I'm not sure you're ready to hear what I need to say, and until you are...can we get to know one another? Do the normal things that people do...?'

'A date, you mean?' She turned over this choice of words in her head. Best sex, while flattering, was not exactly an avowal of love, but you couldn't fall in love in days; she had never believed that. She believed love was something that grew out of respect and shared values, laughter?

His brows lifted and an odd laugh emerged from his lips. 'I hadn't thought of that, but why not? Sure, a date.'

'*Best sex?* Really?' She thrust out one hip to a provocative angle and moistened her lips. 'Sorry,' she said in response to his deep groan of pain. 'But I've been going slow all my life and I have a lot of catching up to do.'

'Sometimes, Anna, the only way to move forward is to go backwards.' Even to him that sounded like running away, and would that be such a bad thing?

Maybe it was the honourable thing, because he knew, even if she didn't at this point, that Anna was in danger of falling in love with him. With the realisation came the understanding that, even if he hadn't known it, a woman's love was something he had been avoiding all his life.

*Backwards...?* Anna could not think of any situation where what he said was true, but she let it pass. He had trusted her with his secret, or at least allowed her to know it existed, and that had to mean something, didn't it?

*No one falls in love in days, Anna.* She repeated the words in her head until the flurry of panic passed.

'Well, don't ask me to forget last night happened because I couldn't if I wanted to and I don't!'

'You don't regret it?'

'Of course not.' She thought about asking him if he did but she wasn't sure she'd like the answer.

# CHAPTER ELEVEN

So HE'D LASTED an entire day.

He had fought the fevered mind-numbing hunger and won. Of course, he had removed himself from temptation's way, actually put several hundred miles between himself and the source of his ultimate desire, but all was fair in lust and... He inhaled sharply as that source came into view.

*It was definitely too soon to declare victory!*

Thanks to the incline of the undulating path she was walking down he knew Anna wouldn't be able to see him for another few moments, which meant that Soren did not have to filter his stare.

His hungry blue eyes burned with a flame as hot as the fire inside him as he watched the slim figure approach. She moved with a natural grace that made him think of a ballet dancer; her hair was loose the way he liked, the sunlight picking out the darker titian threads in the waves that fell on her bare shoulders.

The simple square-necked dress she was wearing was sleeveless and cinched in at the waist by a narrow silver belt before falling into a bias-cut skirt, the fluid fabric suggesting the outline of her shapely thighs as she moved.

'Hello.' She tried not to eat him up with her eyes, but she was pretty sure she was not succeeding. Her

room was littered with outfits discarded during her hunt
for something that fell into Soren's interpretation of
*casual*, which had been his one-word response to her
texted question.

His casual, it turned out, was an open-necked pale
blue shirt, sleeves rolled up to the elbow, and a pair of
black jeans that made it hard for her to lift her eyes and
her mind from the hot place they had sunk to.

She watched him pull out designer shades and thought
that was an excellent idea as she rummaged for a pair of
her own and hid behind the oversized dark lenses, aware
as she did so of him uncoiling his long lean frame from
the gleaming sports car.

'You look lovely.'

*Glow* was an acceptable response to the compliment,
but the furnace that lit inside her was not.

She wafted a hand across her face and murmured an
explanatory, 'So hot.' Before tacking on an unwise, fer-
vent-sounding, 'So do you—look lovely, I mean,' as she
slid into the low-slung car, grateful that she'd chosen
to wear flats. She'd have definitely fallen off her heels.

The car purred silently into life. She was glad the roof
was down—the breeze and the scent of pine diluted his
unique male fragrance that made her awareness of him
ten times worse.

'Where are we headed?'

'The coast, to a little place that not many tourists have
discovered yet. Do you like seafood?'

'I do.' If the conversations stayed this simple, she
could cope.

'Then it was a good choice.'

'I can make up time by working this evening, unless

this is a working lunch?' Sometimes you had to ask if you wanted to know.

Their eyes met briefly before he refocused on the road ahead. 'It isn't.'

'So it's a…?'

His lips twitched. 'It's a date… You are very persistent, *cara*, you know that?'

'It's lunch time and your text was…' Brief and to the point, signed off with his initial. It had not involved any avowals of love—*in your dreams, Anna*—or even lust… She would have settled for *I'm missing you* or even *I'm looking forward to seeing you*.

If it hadn't been for the distractions offered by the library, he would have invaded her thoughts to the exclusion of everything else—even in the library she had found herself wanting to share a new and exciting discovery with him.

'You can have dates at lunchtime.' The timing was not an accident or even convenient, but candlelight and Anna might prove too potent a temptation for his willpower.

A man needed to know his own limitations and since Anna had appeared in his life Soren had been redrawing his. Possibly payback for being smug about his iron self-control?

'You want the roof up?' he asked, aware in the periphery of his vision of her struggle with her glossy hair while he wanted to feel it against his skin as she sat astride…

'No, this is lovely. Sicily is very beautiful…oh!' She bounced a little in her seat, hand still clamped to her hair. 'I can see the sea!'

'Next you'll be asking me are we nearly there… Not long now. Another fifteen minutes.'

The small village consisted of a long straggle of pink-sugar-coloured houses along the shore of what appeared to be a working fishing harbour. Driving past nets strung along the sand, Soren pulled up beside a few other cars parked alongside a whitewashed building built into the stone wall of the harbour.

'This is a beautiful spot.'

'I hoped you'd like it.'

As they were escorted by a suited figure through the rustically decorated interior where most tables were occupied, she knew all eyes were on them, or at least on Soren, but she pretended not to notice. Soren didn't need to pretend; he was, she realised, genuinely oblivious.

Seated at the gingham-clothed table on the wooden deck constructed over the water, Anna looked around from under the shade of a parasol that fluttered gently in the breeze.

'Oh, they don't seem very busy,' she remarked, surprised at the empty tables and wondering why anyone would choose to eat inside.

'No, they don't,' Soren, who had booked out the entire outdoor seating area, agreed. 'Oops!' he added as her elbow caught a glass.

The butterfly touch of his fingers on her wrist brought their eyes, no longer protected by tinted glass, on a collision course.

Anna heard him swear. She couldn't have said anything to de-escalate the tension even if her throat hadn't already closed. Her brain might have frozen, but her senses had not!

A waiter appeared, oblivious to the atmosphere, though his expression did alter slightly as he met Soren's eyes.

Soren began to translate the menu and, though normally she would have enjoyed asking questions and making her own choice, she was seized by the sudden strong urge that this just be over with; it was a bad idea.

*It was agony!*

'Choose for me,' she said, thinking, *Words I never thought I'd hear myself say.*

He dragged his eyes away from the sensual promise of her plump lips. 'That doesn't sound like you.'

She looked straight at him. 'I don't feel like me.'

In his mind he saw himself swiping the crockery from the table and taking her right there and then as he laid down the menu, gave the order and said, 'They do the best prawns here.'

The food was delicious, and the wine, which Soren, as designated driver, didn't touch, helped take a few of the kinks from her spine and the panic out of her eyes. It also inevitably made her quite talkative.

She looked at her empty pudding bowl and up at him, realisation settling and bringing a worried frown to her forehead. 'I've probably been boring you, but the library really is…amazing.'

Boring, no, driving him insane, yes, the way her beautiful little face lit up with animation when she spoke of the books she loved… He could have watched that for ever and as for her voice… *For ever?*

When did that happen?

He dragged a hand across his jaw as his blue stare skidded away from hers. 'Do you want coffee or shall we…?'

His abruptness and his obvious desire to get the hell out made her wonder…*was their first date going to be their last?*

Of course, if the stars had been out and the drive had been moonlit on their way back, the sexual electricity zigzagging back and forth in the car would have had an inevitable ending. But there were no stars or moon and Soren had turned his mobile on speaker and their return journey involved a three-way conversation in a foreign language to which she was a miserable listener-in.

If he had wanted to kill the mood, he could not have arranged things better.

Anna got the call from the Merlin just as they got back.

She glanced at Soren.

'It's the Merlin. Grandpa had some blood tests yesterday. I have to take it.'

He watched as she walked up the path, the receiver pressed to her ear. He could see the worried stiffness in her spine and found himself wanting to lighten the burden she was carrying.

*What happened to simply wanting to take her to bed?*

Anna spent the evening in the library, heading there like a homing pigeon seeking the solace of the books. It was several hours before she became so engrossed she stopped waiting for Soren to come and invite her to share dinner with him.

The next day she decided not to wait. If he wanted her, he would have to do the looking; she was not hanging around for him. Feeling rebellious and miserable, she took a coffee and croissant into the library and had barely sipped the scalding liquid when Soren appeared.

She fought to retain the coolness she had decided to treat him with and lost. After all, he hadn't actually done anything to justify her resentment except not touch her.

Remembering how his touch had made her feel things, had sent her deep into herself to a place she hadn't known existed, caused her to choke on her hot coffee.

'You weren't at breakfast.'

'You noticed.' She closed her eyes and winced, opening them and offering a twisted smile and—'Sorry.'

'I was wondering about your grandfather's blood tests…?'

She was touched by his concern; her forced smile became genuine. 'They were OK, actually, and the clinic have taken on extra security, which makes me feel easier, but I worry.'

'Why?' Her worries were his… The admission hovered somewhere unacknowledged in the back of his mind.

'Well, security doesn't come cheap, but they haven't even suggested Grandpa leave and I thought they might,' she admitted.

'Why would they? He's fetching them a lot of publicity and there's no such thing as bad publicity.'

'They have been very understanding.'

They had been very astute; he had funded the security, but they had held out for an addition to their physiotherapy team.

'I just can't understand who would be low enough to do this to Grandpa, what sort of low life…'

Soren cleared his throat. 'You're very close.'

'Grandpa was always there. If it wasn't for him social services would have put me in care, and he never made it seem like it was a bother, though I'm sure it must have been. He came to all my parents' evenings, flying in specially from business sometimes. I can't imagine what my life would be without him.'

'And now you are there for him. You might,' he began softly, 'need to be prepared to hear some bad things about him.'

'Oh, I've heard what they are saying…and I can't wait for the day when they are going to have to apologise.'

'You are so convinced your grandfather is innocent?'

She stiffened and glared at him, her tension levels in the red zone in seconds. 'Of course he is innocent!'

Her defensive stance made him wonder if maybe she wasn't having doubts of her own, doubts she was not ready to own—yet.

He watched as she got out a pair of white gloves. She made him think of a bright light in the middle of the dusty book-lined room.

'Looks as if you have made a lot of progress in my absence.' It looked exactly the same as when he'd last been here to Soren, but his housekeeper, deeply impressed by Anna's work ethic, had assured him that she had spent every waking moment in here during his day's absence.

'This is much more than…' she sighed, turning a full three-sixty as she took in the crammed shelves '…than I ever imagined.'

He watched her move around the room with every appearance of having forgotten his existence, reverently opening pages of volumes thrown casually on the table and pulling others that caught her eye on a shelf, exclaiming as she made each fresh discovery.

Finally she paused and faced him.

'You do realise how rare some of these are? I have never seen so many first editions,' she added excitedly. 'There are volumes here that were assumed lost…'

'So, valuable, then?'

'There is a small fortune…no, actually, a very large one on these shelves and the condition of some…' She shook her head reproachfully. 'It's disgraceful.'

'Sorry,' he said meekly, drawing a reluctant grin from her.

'I got a bit carried away but, in all seriousness, this is

a very special collection. You might want to have someone more experienced than me.'

'I wouldn't change your experience for the world.'

The message in his eyes sent a throb through her body, and her interest in the rare books declined.

She brought her lashes down in a silky veil. 'That's good to know,' she said softly.

'I'll leave you to get reacquainted with your books, but if you feel like cooling down before dinner…the outdoor pool…? I'll be there around five.' Leaving the offer open, he left.

At five thirty-one—Anna didn't want to appear too eager—she arrived at the pool fed by a mountain spring, built into natural rock and boasting breathtaking views of the mountains, which some mornings, Soren had told her, were reflected in the still green surface.

Anna was eager, and she was determined; she had had enough. She could not last another day, another hour, another minute like this! Her jaw tightened. Him holding her at arm's length was a challenge she had decided to accept.

The surface was not still as she approached, though the economic strokes as Soren powered his way up and down barely made a ripple.

She stood at the side, watching this display of power and grace as he cleaved through the water.

She sensed the moment he registered her presence.

He paused and began to tread water. Pushing his wet hair back from his face, he grinned through the drips.

'You coming in?'

'How do you know I can swim?'

If he didn't touch her she'd die—or she'd kill him for doing this to her.

'Can you?'

'Not as well as you. Is it cold?'

'Fed by a mountain spring is the clue.'

Anna took a deep breath and, very aware that he was watching her, she loosened the tie around the silk kaftan that had come in one of her packages along with two swimsuits and a bikini. She had finally opted for the plain black swimsuit. Cut high on the leg revealing what felt now like acres of bottom, it had a deceptively modest V-neckline at the front but the back was cut almost to her waist. The stark simplicity was relieved by a thin chain belt.

She draped the kaftan across one of the chairs set around a table, walked to the edge of the pool and performed a creditable dive.

The cold hit her heated skin and made her gasp. She kicked hard and with a sinuous little wriggle came up for air a few feet away from Soren.

'You're a water baby. Race?'

She shook her head. 'I'm not in your class,' she shouted back.

Soren had clearly adjusted his pace because there was no way she could have kept up otherwise as they swam several lengths side by side in silence.

It was Anna who stopped, breathless, and flipped onto her back, arms spread, using the occasional kick to keep herself afloat as her hair hovered around her like fronds of seaweed and she turned her face to the last rays of sun hitting the water. The rest of the pool was already in shade. 'I'm out of condition.'

'You look like a mermaid,' he said, coming up beside her. 'And your eyes are the same green as the water.'

She gave a lazy kick and flipped over onto her stomach. 'Race you back!' she yelled, already several feet ahead as she struck out.

'You cheated.'

'You won.'

Grinning, he heaved himself in one lithe motion onto the side and, bending down, held out his hand. After a moment she took it and allowed him to haul her out.

She landed lightly but almost overbalanced and fell into him. She stood there and stared at him through her wet eyelashes, sleek and so perfect it made her ache just to look at him. 'Sorry.'

He experienced a bolt of pure blinding lust that literally immobilised him. 'You all right?'

She shook her head. She hadn't come here looking for love, but it had found her. 'I stubbed my toe.'

'You're shivering.'

'I forgot to bring a towel.'

'Share mine,' he offered, bending to pick up his discarded towel from the floor. 'Come sit over there in the sun. You'll soon warm up.'

Wrapped in his towel, she followed him across the paved area to the carved oak chairs with cream cushions set around a table. The parasol was down and the table was in full sunlight.

'I could get some drinks sent down if you like.'

'No, thanks.' She handed back the towel and their fingers touched, not accidentally, on her part at least, and stayed that way...

'No!' she snapped suddenly pulling her hand away. 'I don't want to hold your hand. I want to—' She stopped and bit her lip. When she looked up he was watching her with eyes that had darkened to navy.

'What do you want to do to me, Anna?'

She shook her head, sending a shower of icy droplets

around the immediate area. They sizzled and died in seconds on his hot skin as he leaned in close so their faces were touching, his nose against hers.

'So whisper if you can't say it out loud.'

Frantic with longing, Anna closed her eyes and did.

He lifted his head and looked into her eyes. 'There are all kinds of slow.'

Her insides fluttered and grew hot. 'There are?'

'Absolutely.'

She nodded and fell into him with a sigh of relief as his lips clamped down hard on hers. 'I can't keep my hands off you,' he groaned out. 'You can say whatever you want to me, you know. Would it help if I told you what I want to say to you, what I want to do to you, have you do to me…?'

Frantic with passion from the seductive voice in her ear, she nodded and whispered, 'Please.'

'Someone might come,' she said a while later as she fought her way into her swimsuit.

Soren watched her contortions with a lazy smile. 'No, I swim naked normally, so people keep away. Did I buy that swimsuit?'

'Yes.'

'It was worth every penny.'

'Does no one else use the pool?'

'Most people prefer the indoor heated…my mum swims in the sea usually, but she comes here sometimes. I think she misses the hot springs at home. I'll take you there some time. It's quite an experience.'

She didn't take the offer seriously, but it was a nice thought. Two days—if it hadn't been for the library she might have gone mad, but it had given her time to think, maybe too much time, and she didn't know an awful lot she hadn't before, but she did know that whatever this was…whatever she felt, or didn't, she wanted to extract every last moment of pleasure and build as many memories as she could.

Which probably translated as she was his for the taking… Did he want to take her?

'This must be quite a change from Iceland for her.'

'Mum is Sicilian. It's Dad she misses.'

'Sorry.'

'I found him.'

She dropped down beside him at the table and touched his bare arm. 'You're cold.'

'He took his own life.'

'Oh, Soren…'

'I was mad with him for so long for leaving us. It's not true that it's an easy way out. It's not…easy at all. It's ugly.' Anna listened in horror, afraid to move or say anything in case he stopped.

She watched as the glazed look in his eyes suddenly cleared; he blinked and looked at her as if he was shocked to see her sitting there.

'If you want to talk.'

He looked at her hand on his arm and laughed. 'I have spent the last twelve years trying not to think about it. Talk? That's the last thing I want to do.'

She thought of the pain and memories he had hidden away and her heart ached for the boy he had been and the self-contained man he was now. She had let down her barriers and allowed him in, but she could not see him ever letting her in.

'Well, if you ever do…you know where I am.'

'So how long will the library keep you here?'

'The library is not a month's work, it is more a lifetime's work, but I'll be here as long as…' She shook her head. 'Although, I have to go home soon. My grandfather's condition is not going to improve. He is very sick. He needs me.'

'You can't go!' He intercepted her startled look and made a corrective tone adjustment. 'Yet. You can't go yet. You've barely started.'

'I'm loving it,' she said, her wistful expression fading as somewhere in the back of her head a voice added, *I'm loving you.* 'But I have to go at some point.'

# CHAPTER TWELVE

SOREN HAD DECIDED to walk rather than drive. The track through the forest was only just over a mile and it was clear most of the way.

When he arrived at his mother's cottage she was in the garden, straw hat on her head, watering the herbs she cultivated.

His suggestion he install an irrigation system for her to cut down on labour had been politely refused. There was pleasure in the work, she said. Why would she want to cut it down?

She smiled when she saw him and then as he got closer and she could see his expression her frown appeared.

'What's wrong?'

'Not wrong, right... I found Tor Rasmusson. I didn't want you to find out from someone else.'

She nodded. 'I never doubted you would.' She searched his face. 'It does not appear to have made you very happy...but then revenge rarely does.'

'I cannot forgive and forget as you do. I am not that person.'

'I don't forget,' his mother corrected gently. 'There is more, isn't there? Come sit in the shade and tell me.'

Soren gave his mother a potted version of the story.

The only time she looked surprised was when he told her that he had brought Tor's granddaughter here.

He outlined his reasons—well, not all of them.

'I think that was very kind of you, Soren.'

'I am not *kind*.'

'It's not a shameful thing, you know,' she said sadly, 'to care about someone else. You're fond of this woman, aren't you?'

'She is Tor's granddaughter.'

'You are depriving yourself of so much pleasure in life.'

Saving himself from so much pain, he thought, wondering how she could still believe this when losing the man she loved had nearly killed her.

'I am using her.'

'Oh, Soren!'

'It's true. I wanted to see if I could trip her up... I wanted her to be guilty.'

His mother said nothing as Soren stared broodingly into the distance.

'She is his granddaughter. How can I ever forget that?'

'How will you know unless you try?'

Soren stared at his mother. 'And you wouldn't have a problem with that?'

'Life is short, Soren, too short to let a chance of happiness slip away without even trying.'

'What would be the point? When she finds out that I outed Tor, who she thinks is some sort of saint, she will never forgive me.'

'Oh, Soren... I hate to repeat myself, but how will you know until you try?'

For the first time Anna was not eating dinner alone and she had dressed for the occasion: a turquoise chiffon slip dress that swirled when she moved. Her foot had healed enough for her to slip on some heels, and she had pinned her hair into a loose pile on the top of her head before freeing a few tendrils.

The conversation, thanks to the presence of waiting staff, was pretty stilted.

Then finally they were alone.

Soren seemed tense, she assumed something to do with the business that had taken him away.

'I have been thinking about what you said about going home and I want to propose a compromise. You could commute.'

She stared at him. 'Between Sicily and London?'

'I do…'

'That is not practical and you know it. I'll help you find someone to replace me. There are actually a lot of people who are better qualified than I am.'

'It's not your qualifications, it's your…enthusiasm.'

Anna paused with her fork in mid-air, about to put a mouth-watering spicy prawn into her mouth.

He planted his elbows on the table and mirrored her actions. 'I actually would like to be closer to your… enthusiasm.'

Her eyes darkened and danced. 'In that case, shall we take our puddings to my room?' This might not last for long but she was going to extract every single moment of pleasure that she could.

'You want a pudding and me…' He waved a hand across the table. 'After what you just put away.'

'It's my metabolism. I can eat what I like and never put on an ounce. I know, I've tried. Anyway,' she added, getting to her feet and shaking out the napkin that had been lying across her knees, 'I can always take more pudding.'

A lot later that night she realised that she could always take more Soren. Her appetite for him seemed to be utterly insatiable.

'Are you asleep?'

She lifted her head off his warm chest; in the darkness her eyes were luminous. 'Nearly.' She yawned.

'Sorry.' He started stroking her head again. 'Go to sleep.'

She sighed and sat up, the covers sliding to her waist. She marvelled at how unselfconscious she felt, knowing he was looking at her, liking that he was looking at her. The knowledge made her nipples, still tender and aching from his recent ministrations, harden.

'What is it?'

'Nothing…'

He rolled away and she stroked his smooth back, enjoying the way the muscles contracted under her fingertips.

From nowhere, it seemed, he asked, 'Do you remember your father?'

'No, I was a baby when he drowned.'

'So you have no memories of him? How I envy you!' he pushed out in a growl of pain that shocked her.

She pulled herself against his back and laid a hand on his chest. Where his heart had been thudding slow and strong moments before, it was now pumping frantically, seeming to be trying to batter its way out of his chest.

'You must miss him…?'

There was a long silence. 'I remember him…' he said, his mind sliding back to that day. The window he'd come in to latch still banging as the storm outside picked up, the smell of the place, hay—he still couldn't stand the smell of hay. 'I knew he was dead, but I couldn't, I *wouldn't* let myself believe it.'

She bit her lip to stop herself crying out, afraid that if she did or said anything he would close up again like earlier; he would freeze her out the same way he froze the world out.

Her tender heart ached for his pain.

'I tried to wake him up and then I just... I hate that he'd been alone and I didn't want to leave him alone...' She slid her hand into his, interlacing their fingers before she carried his hand to her lips.

'A neighbour came and found me...called the... I hated my father then for what he'd done, for leaving us, and later I found out why and discovered there was someone else who was to blame.'

'I hope that person rots in hell,' she declared fiercely.

'My mother does not believe in revenge—she believes in love.'

Love was feeling another person's pain as if it were your own, it was wanting... Her thoughts froze. This was love; what she was feeling was love. She'd fallen in love with the real man, not the man the world saw, but the man she could feel shaking, the man who had protected her from a sense of honour that he would have denied.

'I should not be dumping my rubbish on you!' he suddenly said, rearing up in the bed, the anger in his voice aimed at himself.

'That's what...friends are for,' she said, glad that in the dark he couldn't see her brushing the tears from her cheeks. She couldn't have love, she'd take what she could get, but her heart was his whether he wanted it or not. She had no choice.

Her heart ached for him.

Her heart ached for herself.

She loved him.

She pretended to be asleep when he slipped from her bed in the early hours.

This morning as they sat across the breakfast table the awkwardness in him was obvious. What was also obvious was that he was regretting revealing the part of himself he had last night.

'Please don't shut me out,' she said quietly.

'I need a therapist. I will visit one. I need a woman in my bed. I will take one.' The brutal words were intended to hurt but he got little pleasure from the pain in her eyes.

'Fine,' she said, thinning her lips to hide the tremor and folding her napkin with careful precision. 'I'll go to work.'

She did but halfway through the morning she took off her white gloves and headed for the door. He was trying to push her away, but she didn't have to let him.

Without really knowing why, she made for the swimming pool, and he was there, eating up length after length with a metronomic precision that she found riveting.

She knew that he was aware of her presence, but he didn't immediately stop; she was prepared to wait.

Finally, when he levered himself out of the pool and stood there, the water streaming off his sleekly muscled, powerful body, the sight of him almost broke her resolve. He really was the most beautiful thing she had ever seen in her life.

'I want to talk to you.'

'We are talking,' he said as he began to scrub at his dark hair with a towel.

'This is business. We need a business setting.'

He stopped rubbing his hair and let the towel hang loose around his neck as he moved forward. She would have mirrored the move only a step backwards would have put her in the water, so instead she stuck out her chin and stood her ground.

'What business?'

'I need... I *want* to go and see my grandpa. According to the clinic, things have cooled down.'

He arched a sardonic brow. 'You are asking my permission?'

Her jaw clenched. He really could be an arrogant bastard when he wanted to be. 'No, I am damn well *not* asking your permission. I am asking if you want me to come back.'

He looked as shocked as she'd ever seen him; his eyes slid from hers in a very telling way. 'It's complicated.'

'It's not that complicated,' she said.

He laughed without humour. 'You have no idea how complicated this is.'

He moved away as if to dive back in and she felt her temper flare. 'You know, Soren, while you're swimming up and down you might like to reflect that you're not the only person who has suffered some trauma. Your dad left you because he was ill—mental illness is as much an illness as any physical ailment. My mum left me because she thought I was boring—that's not such a nice thing for a little girl to know.

'You know, I used to think that she might have stayed if I was prettier. She likes pretty things. I was a major disappointment. I didn't even fill out.' She glanced down at her non-existent bust.

His heart raged at the thought of this callous bitch. 'Your mother is a selfish narcissist!' His eyes flared, sparking blue contempt and fury, his heart aching for the little girl she had been.

'I'm not going to disagree with that analysis, but it took me twenty-four years to reach the same conclusion...

She paused while he swore with an inventive fluidity in several languages.

'Oh, I know it's not in the same league as what happened to you.' Compassion softened her eyes as she continued but the passion had drained away, leaving her feeling pretty damned vulnerable. 'But the point is...' She stopped and drew a deep breath, and realised that actually she had no idea what the point was.

'Well, you can tell me all about your complications in, what shall we say...twenty minutes?' Without waiting for a response, she stalked off, head high.

Anna walked back through the garden. It covered acres and an army of gardeners kept it immaculate. She had explored a fraction of it, and it was now entirely possible she might never get to explore the rest.

Of the areas she had explored there was one that had already drawn her back. She headed that way now because what it lacked in formal planting, classical design or manicured green expanses it made up for in soothing charm.

She had started the familiar circuit when Ragnar and Rok appeared, as they had begun to do. They fell into step at her side even after she had opened her hands to reveal she had no treats.

Maybe it was the canine-greenery combination, but she felt the calm working its magic as she walked through the dappled shadow of the soothing glades where the organic planting blended seamlessly into the encroaching wild countryside it bordered.

She left more composed but still not sure if she really wanted to do this, if she wanted to push things this far, when she knew it might not work out the way she hoped.

It was in this ambivalent frame of mind she arrived at the area of the palazzo that was a home office, but not in the conventional sense. There were several satellite spaces, a conference room, a gym, and Soren's private domain, a large room with an outer office.

There was one person in the outer office, one of the assistants who seemed to operate on a rota basis, working, as far as she understood, between Palermo or Rome and here. She knew this woman's face but not her name.

The woman had no problem identifying her, but then the fact she had divided her time here so far between the library and Soren's bed probably made her stand out.

There were few mistress-slash-librarians around.

She might even be unique.

The woman slung a laptop case over her shoulder. 'My transfer is waiting, he isn't here yet, but go through,' she said, with a wary eye on the dogs, who hadn't waited for an invitation and when Anna entered had already settled themselves on the leather chesterfield.

Anna didn't sit down. She walked down the room, gazing but not seeing any titles in the book-lined walls to distract her.

She had issued what amounted to an ultimatum and she was regretting it. The timing, she decided, was wrong; she should have waited.

*For what? For him to realise he's wildly in love with you? The only place that's going to happen is in your dreams.*

She shook her head to clear the mocking voices. That they were not going to end up together was pretty much a given, but if anything she said or did helped push Soren in a direction that led to healing the wounds he carried from his past, that could only be a good thing.

The strident ringing of the landline on Soren's desk made her start, then as the ringing stopped and the message machine kicked in Anna began to move automatically towards the door.

Though it would be hard to eavesdrop when the one-sided conversations seemed to be in Italian, she had started to recognise the odd word and phrase.

She was actually at the door when she heard a familiar name, at the same moment the person speaking switched seamlessly to English, the way she had heard Soren do on many occasions.

She recognised the voice, identifying him as the young lawyer she had last seen cycling away. She turned and stood beside the desk, unashamedly listening to the lawyer give a detailed report.

By the time he was finished she was deathly pale and shaking; inside she felt frozen.

When Soren walked into the room, he knew there was something wrong, something badly wrong—he could literally feel the waves of tension rolling off her hunched body.

His intention was to tell her the truth, finally, but the second he walked in he knew that this wasn't the moment.

'What is wrong?' Only one thing he could think of would make her look like that. 'Is it your grandfather?' He had lifted his hands to frame her face when she placed both her own hands on his chest and pushed viciously hard.

'Do not touch me, you bastard!' she growled, putting all the venom and hurt she was feeling into the one word.

'Anna, what…?'

'My grandfather? Yes, it *is* my grandfather. I hate to disappoint you, but he's alive.'

It was at that point he saw the light flashing on the phone on the desk and he closed his eyes.

'I don't know what you heard.'

'I've heard that you planted the lies about my grandpa!' she bellowed incredulously. 'And now you've decided to blame him for your father's suicide, which of course is brilliantly convenient when he can't defend himself.' She looked up at him with an expression of supreme disgust on her face. 'You're twisted, you know that? Not content with punishing an innocent, sick old man, you thought you'd really stick the knife in by—'

'I was trying to protect you.'

'Oh, God, yes, I feel *so* protected.'

He winced at the acrid bitterness in her voice.

'If protected means lied to and used and... Was it your plan all along to make me fall in love with you?'

'I never wanted to hurt you, Anna. I tried to keep my distance, but you are so... I was wrong about you.'

'Oh, God, yes, I'm gorgeous,' she drawled sarcastically. 'And if you were wrong about me, why can't you be wrong about my grandpa?' She lifted a shaking hand to her head. Her choice was brutal—either her grandfather was a monster or the man she loved was.

'This isn't what it looks like...'

Her breaking-glass laugh cut across him. 'And I was *grateful*!' She pressed a hand to her mouth. 'I feel sick...' She swallowed and revived enough to fling out with spitting fury, 'I also feel so stupid, but, you know, some day soon I'll start feeling less stupid, but you...you...you'll always be a total, complete bastard!

The muscles around his jaw quivered but he said nothing. Anything he said would have been the equivalent of throwing oil on a fire, he knew that.

'I thought you were trying to protect me... God, an old man who has never done anyone any harm and you set out to—'

'Enough, Anna. I understand you're upset, but this is no conspiracy. I'm sorry, but your grandfather is guilty of everything he is accused of and more. He has a dozen aliases. When he was in Iceland he used the identity of a dead boy. He was my father's partner. He embezzled from the firm and left my father to carry the can.'

'You're rich…you planted the evidence!' she yelled wildly.

He caught one of her flailing arms and lowered his voice to a soothing tone intended to reassure the dogs, who were looking unsettled by the commotion, as well as Anna. 'Calm down, you're going to hurt yourself.' He pursed his lip in a whistle and both animals settled down on their haunches.

Anna, who was pausing to gulp for air, didn't register the canine-human interchange as she pulled her hand free. She *had* been calm, she had been ice calm and then he had walked in and she had gone up in flames. She stood there shaking with the aftershocks of a mind-numbing rage she had never experienced the like of before.

She scanned his face.

'You're not even denying it?'

He found her subdued tone even more disturbing than her furious shrieking.

Anna swallowed a sob, hating that there was a tiny part of her that had wanted there to be an explanation, even though she knew in her heart that it wasn't possible.

'The truth is your grandfather is a crook. He has ruined countless lives, including those of my parents. Perhaps the only good thing he has done in his life is take care of you.'

Her breath coming in short, sharp pants, Anna shook her head and covered her ears. 'You're trying to turn me against him. Well, it won't work,' she gritted. 'I *know* my grandfather.'

He picked up on the expression that flickered at the backs of her green eyes. 'But you're wondering, aren't you? That's why you're so angry. You have your doubts.'

Unable to quite meet his eyes, she looked past his shoulder. 'I have no doubts at all. Now, if you'll excuse me, I have some packing to do.'

'Come back, Anna. Go home, check out your grandfather, check out the facts and come back. We can talk...'

She looked at him as though he were insane. 'Talk... the only thing you ever wanted from me was sex and that particular well is dry!'

His jaw clenched. 'I don't seem to recall you complaining.'

'Oh, you were great. I can't wait to sell the story of my nights in the billionaire's bed to the tabloids, then I'll use the money to sue you,' she said, feeling quite pleased with her inspired fictional revenge.

'You wouldn't do that.'

'But you're not quite sure, are you?' she taunted.

'Anna.'

Not breaking her stride, she made her feelings clear with the use of a universally understood hand signal.

# CHAPTER THIRTEEN

'I'M TOO LATE...?'

'I'm sorry.'

The matron curved an arm around Anna's shoulders and pulled her into the office, pushing the weeping young woman down into a chair.

'He slipped away quietly. There was no pain.'

'He was alone!' Anna sobbed, the tears spilling unchecked down her cheeks.

The older woman, her eyes soft with compassion, squeezed Anna's shoulder. 'I was holding his hand. He was not alone. No one here is ever alone. Would you like a few minutes to gather your thoughts?'

Mutely Anna nodded.

'I'll be back shortly with a nice cup of tea.'

'Do you know if anyone called my mother?'

'We tried to contact her when we were trying to call you, but there was no reply.'

Anna nodded and the door closed. She pulled out her phone, wiping her face on her sleeve, and dialled her mother's number. By some miracle it was picked up immediately.

'Mum, it's Anna.'

'Anna? Oh, Anna, darling, how lovely to hear from you. You naughty girl...you are such a stranger.'

'Mum, I have some bad news.' She took a deep breath. 'Are you alone?'

'No, Gregor is here and—'

Anna, eyes closed, teeth clenched, cut across her. 'Mum, Grandpa is dead. And I wasn't here.' Her voice shook and wavered. 'I was on a flight and I wasn't here!' she wailed.

'Anna, you know what crying does to your eyes. And not really a shock, darling—he wasn't young, was he?'

Anna gave a laugh of sheer disbelief and wiped the mist from her face again. 'And, Mum, I don't know whether you have read anything, but before he died there have been some horrible stories, the police are involved and—'

'Oh, he finally got caught, did he? I always told him he would be.'

The response took her breath away. 'Mum...you're saying it was true? You knew?'

'And you didn't? I assumed you would have realised by now—your grandfather, my dear, was a master con man. Your dad, of course, was very disapproving, but I always thought it was a bit of a hoot until the Iceland thing happened and that man killed himself. For a while Henry did behave himself, but old habits die hard and before long he was at his old games again. But, you have to admit, he was never mean to us, was he? I wonder what's in the will.'

Her mother's voice faded into the distance as her hand lowered and she cut her off.

She sat there, a blank look on her pale tear-stained face, staring ahead. Soren had been right about everything and he'd been searching for justice for his father... It all made perfect sense now. *He'd used her...* She had never been any more to him than a means to an end.

He had made her love him and he had never cared for her; she had been a useful idiot, that was all!

By the time the matron returned she was quietly composed, at least on the surface. Inside, her heart was a solid block of ice, it might never thaw, but she would never *ever* forgive Soren.

It was meant to rain at funerals but the day they laid her grandfather to rest the sun was shining. It felt wrong, but then a funeral could not feel anything but wrong.

'Right,' said Sara. She and Penny had been there to support Anna but, other than a couple of staff members from the Merlin Clinic and a couple who Anna suspected had come to the wrong funeral, but ended up staying to swell the sparse number, that was it.

Most of the charity trustees were either in jail or on bail or, in one case, in the middle of being extradited. And all of his friends had long vanished into the woodwork. Her mum, who it turned out had always known about her grandfather's nefarious activities, was spending the month in a retreat to equalise her out-of-balance chakras.

Penny and Sara had given her some time at the graveside alone before they decided to drag her away.

'So how about we have a little wake down the pub?' Penny said.

'I don't think—' Anna began.

'She'd love to,' Sara said over her head.

'I am here, you know.'

'*Here* being the most depressing place in the world, so let's go to the pub.'

Anna allowed herself to be dragged along, though she didn't drink the shots and her friends pretended not to notice.

'So who was the tall guy on the hill?' Sara asked during a lull in the rather forced conversation.

'What...?' She caught Sara's hand mid-shot. 'Focus, Sara. What guy on the hill?'

'The one who came late and didn't like to intrude. You know...your average six-four, godlike, stepped-off-Mount-Olympus figure in a really expensive suit.'

Anna's heart started to thud in her chest. 'Did he have blue eyes?'

'The man was like two hundred metres away. I didn't get the eye colour, just the general aura of yumminess.' She frowned a little blearily. 'Why? Is he someone I should know? Was it the guy off the telly who advertises...? What's-his-name...' She stopped, her eyes widening. 'You... A man... Wow, does that mean you finally—?'

'Hush, Sara, it's a funeral. Lower the volume.'

'A wake—the wakes in my family are seriously loud. If you don't get wasted, you're not invited again.'

Over her head Penny rolled her eyes. 'Well, I don't have your stamina so sorry, folks, I need my bed.'

'I'll walk with you,' Anna offered, and Penny mouthed her thanks over Sara's curly head.

It was slow progress, hampered by the fact that Sara had moved from loud drunk to sleepy drunk.

'She is such a lightweight,' Penny said affectionately as they both watched Sara's zigzag approach to the hotel steps. 'But you've got to love her, and she has been so worried about you.'

'I'm fine. Don't worry.' The two women embraced.

'Well, you know where I am if you need me,' Penny tossed over her shoulder as she hurried on her five-inch heels to catch up with her roommate.

In no particular hurry to get back to her flat, Anna walked through the park.

She knew she ought to be feeling something, but she just felt empty and a little ashamed when she realised how desperate she had acted at the mention of a random tall guy.

She fished the key out of her bag and stood at the door of her flat. It was not a big space, but as all the stuff from her grandfather's house that hadn't already been sold—for which read worthless tat—was stacked in cardboard boxes in her living room, the small space was even smaller.

As she put the key in the lock, a noise to her right made her spin round—a woman had been mugged two streets down only last week.

'I have a…' She paused, key in fist, and almost slid down the wall that her visitor had just slid up with a sinuous grace that made her stomach flip in a way she remembered very well.

'What are you doing here?' she asked, tipping her head back as he reached his full impressive height.

They were both dressed in funereal black but there the similarity stopped. Despite the fact he had presumably been sitting on the floor, there was not a crease or a speck of dust on him.

Her suit was creased and some of the crisps that Sara had sprayed on her when she'd laughed had stuck to her jacket, she hadn't looked at her updo since eight a.m., so she was assuming it could use some work, and her lipstick was long gone.

He wasn't wearing lipstick…his mouth… She swallowed and suddenly wanted to throw herself at him.

She controlled the impulse.

'I said what are you doing here?'

Now she noticed he didn't look so hot—not creases, but there were very dark shadows under his eyes and he'd lost weight, which had sharpened his features. Haggard was going too far but he did not look the picture of health.

'What are you doing here?' she repeated again.

'I came for you.'

Her brain said caution, her heart said… She was not going to be misled by her heart any more.

'You'd better come in, but I'm warning you it's a mess.'

'Fine.' He stepped over a packing case before she thought to warn him about it.

Outside he looked bad, inside he looked awful, in a gorgeous way, of course. 'You look terrible. When did you last sleep?'

'I came to apologise.'

'What for? You were right. My grandpa was an evil monster.' An evil monster that she had just put into the ground.

He watched her beautiful lips quiver and brutally quashed the urge to put his arms around her. It was a privilege he had lost, but one he had every intention of winning back. 'You got to see him before he…died?'

'I went straight to the clinic after I got off the flight,' she recalled. 'They'd been trying to contact me all day. He'd already slipped into a coma. Were you there…at the funeral?'

'You saw me?'

'No, my friend, Sara, she described you. So, Soren,' she said, feeling quite proud of how civilised she was being, 'what does bring you here?'

'I have already said. I came for you.'

She shook her head, unable to stop her traitorous heartbeat quickening. 'Me as in…?'

'Just you.'

'Are you mad?'

'If it will win me any brownie points, definitely, I'm certifiable. But if not, I'm not mad, just desperate and willing to... *Dio*, Anna, I am so, so sorry,' he groaned. 'What happened was all my fault. You were right in everything you said about me except one. I never wanted to hurt you. I only ever wanted to protect you.'

'But you were right. My grandpa was a crook. He was responsible for your father's death and others too,' she admitted heavily. 'I think I must have known at some level, I *should* have known, but he was always so good to me.'

'No one is all black. There are shades of grey.'

Not according to the police, who, once they had established to their satisfaction that she was not involved, had been willing to show her the proof of her grandfather's guilt.

His death had meant, they had explained, that she was not obliged to back any financial recompense to those he had cheated. Legally she could keep the house, which, it transpired, her grandfather had transferred to her name.

Anna hadn't wanted any of it. It was all sold, the proceeds going to his victims, except for the stuff in the boxes that no one wanted.

'I said some terrible things to you and I don't expect you to forgive me,' she said.

'There is nothing to forgive. I should not have let you find out that way—I was a coward,' he declared, drawing a startled look from Anna. 'I knew what you would think if I told you, and I could not bear the idea of you seeing I was no hero. The guilt every time you said thank you and—'

'Soren...you said you *came* for me. What did you mean?'

'Just that, I came for you, to take you back with me. I

know I have a lot to prove, but you belong with me. It is true when I first met you I thought, I *wanted* you to be guilty too…but in my heart and my body I knew you were innocent. I just wouldn't let myself believe… I couldn't trust my instincts.

'I was a coward, Anna. I have been so stuck in the past, convinced that revenge would free me from the nightmares, but it didn't, Anna, my sweet, beautiful Anna, you did. I have been afraid of committing to a future… You are my future and I didn't recognise it until it was too late… It's not too late and I won't leave without you… You're crying?'

'Of course, I'm crying.' She sniffed. 'I've been so lonely, loving you, thinking you hated me, thinking of those terrible things I said to you…and you made me feel beautiful—'

'Enough!' He cut her off with an imperative slashing motion of his hand. 'You love me?'

She nodded.

His fierce grin flashed white and he grabbed her, hauling her into him. 'Then the rest it is—'

'Kiss me, Soren,' she said, her eyes on his face. 'Just, please, kiss me. I've been so lonely.'

'You will never be lonely again, *cara*,' he promised.

It was two weeks since his grandfather had told Soren he would disinherit him if he married her and two weeks since Soren had told him to go to hell.

Biagio had been bluffing and he had realised that Soren was not—he was now the guest of honour at their engagement party. In fact, his attitude had undergone a total change to the extent he had personally taken control of the guest list for tonight, which was why the intimate dinner was now a ball for five hundred.

Soren had wanted to confront him, but Anna had persuaded him to let his grandfather get on with it if it kept him happy.

She was trying to decide on her earrings—the diamond drops were nice, but Soren said the emeralds matched her eyes—when there was a tap on the door.

Anna adjusted her robe and yelled out, 'Come in.'

'It's only me, Anna.' Hanna Steinsson came in. 'I hope you don't mind. Soren said you wouldn't.'

'Of course not. What a pretty dress. You look lovely.' Her future mother-in-law was looking very youthful in a pale lavender crepe ankle-length bias-cut dress.

'Thank you. There are a lot of people here already.' Her eyes went to the red dress. 'You will look stunning. What a shame your mother can't be here.'

Anna smiled. In the short time she had known her she felt closer to Soren's mother than she did her own.

'I can't decide what earrings to wear—what do you think?'

'Well, actually, I was thinking, I was hoping… When Soren said you would be wearing red, and with your colouring…' She put a padded velvet box on the dressing table. 'Open it. I would like you to have them. They were my own mother-in-law's once.'

Anna opened her box and gasped. Inside lay a string of fire opals and a pair of chandelier earrings.

'They are beautiful and far too much. No…' She shook her head. 'I really couldn't take them.'

'It will make me happy if you do.'

Tears sprang to Anna's eyes. 'You are so kind. I was sure you'd hate me because of who I am.'

The older woman bent and kissed her cheek. 'Anna, my dear, you are the woman my son loves and that is who you will always be to me. I just wanted to say how happy I am for you both now, because I know you will not be offended if I slip away early... I struggle with the crowds, you know.'

Anna sprang to her feet and hugged her. 'I think I wouldn't mind coming with you.'

Hanna shook her head. 'No, my dear, you have a good time—this is your night and I know that Soren wants to show you off.'

When Soren came in a little while later the dress was still on the hanger but she had finished her make-up and was wearing the opals.

'Mum will be happy to see you wearing those.'

'She is lovely, Soren.'

'I knew it was a mistake to let him invite half the damned world tonight. Biagio is down there now inviting everyone to our wedding, telling them to keep Christmas week free.'

'Ignore him,' Anna soothed as she shook out the red dress and laid it on the bed. Without the confidence she had gained from being loved by Soren she would never have had the poise, the sheer nerve, to appear in public in something that was so...revealing, so in-your-face sexy.

'Are you going to be able to dance in those shoes?' he asked, looking at the spindly heels she had selected.

'I can always take them off.'

He grinned. 'So long as you put them back on when we're in bed.'

Anna struggled to pretend outrage.

'So how are thing going down there?' she asked warily. She had strayed into the organised chaos early when it became obvious that organised was debatable. She had not put up too much resistance when Soren had got all masterful and removed her from it.

He sat down on the bed. 'Do you really want to know…?'

'Ooh, that bad?' She shook her head. 'Definitely not. I shall just waft in there looking sexy and beautiful.'

'You always look sexy and beautiful.'

'You are a dutiful fiancé and I will reward you.'

'I am relying on it.'

'But tonight I'm making a big push-the-boat-out glam-up effort.'

'Fair enough, it will be much appreciated. One thing I should warn you about… Biagio has brought his… *friends…*'

Her face dropped. 'No, seriously…both of them?' His grandfather, who was suffering from what Soren called a displaced alpha male syndrome and Anna called a second childhood, had two twenty-somethings in residence with him on his yacht.

'It's window dressing. He's not actually *doing* anything with them—he's eighty, for God's sake!'

'They've not come in bikinis, have they?'

'They are wearing clothes…sort of.'

'I can't wait,' she responded, straight-faced.

'Let's face it, it's not as if anyone is going to be looking at them, is it? Not with my lovely fiancée there,' he purred, dragging her down onto his knee and sliding his hand inside her silk robe to massage her breast. He stopped when she winced. 'Is something wrong? Did I hurt you?'

'No…nothing is wrong, Soren,' she said, laying her hand against his cheek. 'I'm just a bit tender…'

Sudden comprehension lit his face, his expression changed and wonder slid into his eyes. 'That is why you didn't drink any champagne last week.'

She'd thought nobody had noticed she was drinking sparkling water. 'I wasn't sure then, but I am now… It's

early days,' she warned. 'I don't want to go public yet...
but I do think maybe we might not want to wait for a
Christmas wedding. Maybe a nice small village wedding next month with our friends?'

Soren laid a protective hand on her flat belly and
kissed her lips deeply.

'It will be our private secret for as long as you wish.'

'You do know that the plus side to this is I might actually get boobs? Mum will approve.'

At the mention of her mother his expression darkened.
He made an effort for Anna's sake, but he would never
be able to relax in the company of a woman who had not
appreciated the gift she had been given. As always, he
experienced a rage when he thought of her, made worse
because he knew it was powerless, but he accepted it for
Anna. The self-absorbed woman did not have the emotional intelligence to ever comprehend what she had done
to her daughter.

'Don't worry, I won't be telling her, but your mum, if
you don't mind...?' She was pleased to see the look of
delight she had hoped for on Soren's face. She would have
made a point of cultivating a relationship with Soren's
mother in any case, but she took a lot of pleasure from
the relationship.

'She will love being a grandmother.'

Anna swung her head, holding her rich hair back from
her face to look at the man beside her. 'Scary or what?'

'I imagine all prospective parents feel that way—one
perfect new life to mould. It is quite a responsibility. But
you will be a perfect mother.'

Anna grinned, but tears prickled her eyes. So much
could go wrong that she didn't want to take anything for
granted, but she knew that a baby, Soren's baby, would

make her life too perfect to be true. 'The next eighteen years or so will tell.'

'And now,' Soren said, breaking the mood as he leapt to his feet and clapped his hands, 'it is my responsibility to get you into that dress and onto that staircase.'

'Couldn't I just slip in a side door?'

He produced one his best autocratic alpha looks. 'My wife-to-be, the mother of my child, does not slip in through side doors. I want the world to see what a lucky man I am.'

'Lucky, yes, you are, but world…quite a lot of people would be more accurate.'

He stood there looking at her. 'Are you ever going to get dressed? You are so last minute.'

'I have my face on, my hair is done, there is a reason for the fact my dress is on the bed and not on me,' she said, unfastening her gown to reveal the strapless bra and French knickers she wore underneath before reaching for the sliver of red silk. 'I get ready early and you undress me, which makes me late and flustered.'

His eyes darkened dangerously. 'Is that a challenge?'

She whisked away laughing and slipped into the bathroom, locking the door behind her just to be on the safe side—when it came to Soren a lock was a useful supplement to her non-existent willpower.

'Wait downstairs!'

Soren looked at the locked door, an expression of frustration on his face. 'Don't you trust me?' he complained.

The response did not try to spare him. 'No… I look very hot—you wouldn't be able to keep your hands off me.' She looked in the mirror as she spoke. She was only half joking; she barely recognised the person staring back at her. The dress was *just* right. It managed to make her look as if she had a bust, which was a minor miracle, and it made her long and...*sinuous and sexy*.

At the top of the staircase Anna paused and thought, head back, chest up, girl, and began her descent, hoping like hell she didn't fall off her heels.

It was the hush followed by murmurs and a collective gasp that made Soren turn his head. He was frowning, having just managed to fight off the clinging attentions of one of his grandfather's bikini bimbos.

Soren stilled, the tightness in his chest making it hard to breathe as he watched his lovely future wife float down the staircase. He roused himself from his stupor and walked out to greet her, bowing formally at the waist as he took her hand.

Their eyes connected.

'*Tesoro mio*, you do indeed look...*very hot.*'

He pulled her into him, moving from just friends to lovers with a smooth adjustment, then smiled and thought, *Better...much better*.

Together they circled the empty floor to the strains of the orchestra, but actually they didn't need the music. They were moving to a very different tune, a tune they both remembered well.

# EPILOGUE

ANNA FROWNED. 'The priest is here. Everyone's in the chapel. They're waiting.'

Sara, who was admiring her godmother's hat in the mirror, turned around. 'Well, it's not like they can start without them, is it? No babies…no doting dad, no christening—not rocket science.'

'I know you're right, but I simply don't know where they can be.'

'Oh, I don't know. In one of the twenty million rooms in this place…? Me, I would happily live in any of your bathrooms. The interior designer had a serious fetish, not that I'm complaining. I get so turned on by plumbing.'

'I'll go check the… I'll go check.' She stopped. Sara wasn't listening to her; she was staring with a soppy smile at the ring on her left hand. Since her engagement to Franco she'd been doing that a lot.

Anna glanced in the mirror to check herself out. The babies were only three months and most of her baby tummy was gone, mainly because she was never still. Twins did not allow for much down time. She didn't know how she would have coped during the early weeks when the babies wouldn't sleep and she was shattered without Soren, who had turned out to be a very hands-on dad.

When he'd announced he was taking paternity leave

his grandfather had been outraged, but since the babies had arrived he had calmed down. His boast was that only a *real* man, a Vitale, could father two babies...even if one was a girl.

Evangeline had been born first, her bright blue eyes so like her father's wide open; Arturo had come a half-hour later. Smaller by a few ounces, he'd spent his first few nights in special care.

He had caught up now to his sister and had a fine pair of lungs, eyes as green as her own and, according to his father, a temper just like hers too. Anna still found herself waking him to check he was breathing.

He'd been breathing all right last night. She hadn't had a wink of sleep and, after they had both been dressed, Soren had offered to have them so that she could get ready in peace.

Now she was ready and the guests were all in the chapel but the babies and their father had vanished... where...? A slow smile spread over her face as she began to retrace her steps, suddenly sure where she would find them.

Her instincts proved dead on.

She walked into the ballroom, empty but for the candles burning in the windows and the solitary figure, a baby in each arm, who was circling the floor.

She walked across to join him.

'You vanished,' she whispered, looking down into the face of each sleeping baby. 'They are so cute when they are asleep. Why didn't you tell me where you were going?'

'I knew you'd figure it out, and you did.' His logic was inarguable.

'You're impossible,' she complained without any conviction.

He flashed his devil-on-steroids smile and her knees went weak. 'People are waiting.'

He shrugged. 'I wanted to show the babies where I fell in love with their mother.'

'Did you?'

'I think I fell in love with you the first time I saw you, but I was too scared to admit it even to myself, but that night, it was special.'

Throat thick with tears of emotion, Anna nodded and slid her arms around him to complete the circle.

'I think our children are very musical.' He gazed down with paternal pride at the infants in his arms.

'Isn't it a bit early to tell?' she ventured with a smile.

'They recognised *our* song straight away. They obviously get it from me.'

Her lips quivered. Her husband had many talents, but musical…? 'You're tone deaf, Soren.'

'I don't hear the music with my ears,' he retorted. 'I hear it with my heart, where you are, *tesoro mia*.'

To hell with her make-up. Anna let her tears flow… tears of joy. 'Keep me there, Soren,' she whispered.

She knew he would.

* * * *

# COMING SOON!

We really hope you enjoyed reading this book.
If you're looking for more romance, be sure to
head to the shops when new books are
available on

## Thursday 28th April

To see which titles are coming soon, please visit
**millsandboon.co.uk/nextmonth**

MILLS & BOON

# MILLS & BOON®

## Coming next month

### CROWNING HIS LOST PRINCESS
Caitlin Crews

"I don't understand this...sitting around in pretty rooms and *talking*," Delaney seethed at him, her blue eyes shooting sparks when they met his. "I like to be outside. I like dirt under my feet. I like a day that ends with me having to scrub soil out from beneath my fingernails."

She glared at the walls as if they had betrayed her.

Then at him, as if he was doing so even now.

For a moment he almost felt as if he had—but that was ridiculous.

"When you are recognized as the true Crown Princess of Ile d'Montagne, the whole island will be your garden," he told her. Trying to soothe her. He wanted to lift a hand to his own chest and massage the brand that wasn't there, but *soothing* was for others, not him. He ignored the too-hot sensation. "You can work in the dirt of your ancestors to your heart's content."

Delaney shot a look at him, pure blue fire. "Even if I did agree to do such a crazy thing, you still wouldn't get what you want. It doesn't matter what blood is in my veins. I am a farm girl, born and bred. I will never look the part of the Princess you imagine. Never."

She sounded almost as final as he had, but Cayetano allowed himself a smile, because that wasn't a flat refusal. It sounded more like a *maybe* to him.

He could work with *maybe*.

In point of fact, he couldn't wait.

He rose then. And he made his way toward her, watching the way her eyes widened. The way her lips parted. There was an unmistakable flush on her cheeks as he drew near, and he could see her pulse beat at her neck.

Cayetano was the warlord of these mountains and would soon enough be the King of this island. And he had been prepared to ignore the fire in him, the fever. The ways he wanted her that had intruded into his work, his sleep. But here and now, he granted himself permission to want this woman. *His* woman. Because he could see that she wanted him.

With that and her *maybe,* he knew he'd already won.

"Let me worry about how you look," he said as he came to a stop before her, enjoying the way she had to look up to hold his gaze. It made her seem softer. He could see the hectic need all over her, matching his own. "There is something far more interesting for you to concentrate on."

Delaney made a noise of frustration. "The barbaric nature of ancient laws and customs?"

"Or this."

And then Cayetano followed the urge that had been with him since he'd seen her standing in a dirt-filled yard with a battered kerchief on her head and kissed her.

He expected her to be sweet. He expected to enjoy himself.

He expected to want her all the more, to tempt his own feverish need with a little taste of her.

But he was totally unprepared for the punch of it. Of a simple kiss—a kiss to show her there was more here than righting old wrongs and reclaiming lost thrones. A kiss to share a little bit of the fire that had been burning in him since he'd first laid eyes on her.

It was a blaze and it took him over.

It was a dark, drugging heat.

It was a mad blaze of passion.

It was a delirium—and he wanted more.

*Continue reading*
CROWNING HIS LOST PRINCESS
Caitlin Crews

*Available next month*
www.millsandboon.co.uk

# MILLS & BOON

## THE HEART OF ROMANCE

## A ROMANCE FOR EVERY READER

### MODERN

Prepare to be swept off your feet by sophisticated, sexy and seductive heroes, in some of the world's most glamourous and romantic locations, where power and passion collide.

### HISTORICAL

Escape with historical heroes from time gone by. Whether your passion is for wicked Regency Rakes, muscled Vikings or rugged Highlanders, awaken the romance of the past.

### MEDICAL

Set your pulse racing with dedicated, delectable doctors in the high-pressure world of medicine, where emotions run high and passion, comfort and love are the best medicine.

### True Love

Celebrate true love with tender stories of heartfelt romance, from the rush of falling in love to the joy a new baby can bring, and a focus on the emotional heart of a relationship.

### Desire

Indulge in secrets and scandal, intense drama and plenty of sizzling hot action with powerful and passionate heroes who have it all: wealth, status, good looks…everything but the right woman.

### HEROES

Experience all the excitement of a gripping thriller, with an intense romance at its heart. Resourceful, true-to-life women and strong, fearless men face danger and desire - a killer combination!

To see which titles are coming soon, please visit

millsandboon.co.uk/nextmonth

# LET'S TALK
## *Romance*

For exclusive extracts, competitions
and special offers, find us online:

- **f** facebook.com/millsandboon
- 🐦 @MillsandBoon
- 📷 @MillsandBoonUK

**Get in touch on 01413 063232**

---

For all the latest titles coming soon, visit
**millsandboon.co.uk/nextmonth**

---